GW00326439

The Shot

PHILIP KERR

First published in Great Britain in 1999 by
Orion
An imprint of Orion Books Ltd
Orion House, 5 Upper St Martin's Lane, London WC2H 9EA

A CIP catalogue record for this book is available from the British Library

Typeset in Great Britain by
Deltatype Ltd, Birkenhead, Merseyside
Printed and bound by
Clays Ltd, St Ives plc

Grateful acknowledgement is made for permission
to quote from *The Threepenny Opera*
© 1928 Universal Edition
© 1955 Weill-Brecht-Harms Co., Inc
Renewal Rights Assigned to The Kurt Weill Foundation for Music,
Bertolt Brecht and Edward and Josephine Davis,
as Executors of the Estate of Marc Blitzstein
Reproduced by permission of Alfred A. Kalmus Ltd

For Robert Bookman

'Y' know when that shark bites, with his teeth, babe,
scarlet billows start to spring; Fancy gloves, though,
wears old man Heath, babe, so there's never, never
a trace of red.'

Mack the Knife
The Threepenny Opera by Kurt Weill

PART ONE

1

In the Kingdom of the White Caesars

Helmut Gregor feared the sound of his real name as another man might fear the name of his worst enemy. But thanks to the generous support of his family and the agricultural business that continued to thrive in Günzberg, Bavaria, he managed to live very comfortably in Buenos Aires.

An old but attractive capital – it is a well-named city of good airs – Buenos Aires has many fine boulevards and an excellent opera house, and on a cool July afternoon in 1960, the middle-aged German doctor could still think himself in his beloved Vienna, before the war – before the defeat of Germany had necessitated such a protracted period of exile. For almost ten years he had resided in a quiet country house in the predominantly English suburb of Temperley. At least he had until now. After what had happened to Adolf Eichmann, Helmut Gregor considered it safer to move into the city centre. And until he could find a suitable apartment in the *microcentro*, he was currently staying at the elegant and modern City Hotel.

Other old comrades, alarmed by the audacity of the kidnapping – Eichmann had been snatched from his own house in San Fernando by Israeli intelligence agents and spirited away to Jerusalem – had fled across the Rio de la Plata to Uruguay and the city of Montevideo. The cooler Helmut Gregor, noting the world's condemnation of Israel's violation of international law and the possibility that the Israeli embassy in Argentina might be forced to close down – not to mention the rather satisfying wave of anti-Semitic violence that had recently occurred in Buenos Aires as a result of the illegal Israeli action – had reasoned that in all probability Buenos Aires was now the safest city in all of South America. For him and others like him, at any rate.

There seemed little chance of the same thing happening to Helmut Gregor as had happened to Eichmann. Especially now that sympathetic friends in the right-wing Argentinian government had arranged for him to have twenty-four-hour police protection. It was Gregor's opinion that by living in the middle of nowhere and lacking the kind of money that would have bought some protection, Adolf Eichmann had made it easy for his Israeli enemies. Even so, he had to admit that the Jews had carried off the operation with considerable flair. But he did not think they would, or could, snatch him from the biggest hotel in Buenos Aires.

Not that he stayed skulking indoors all day. Far from it. Like Vienna, Buenos Aires is a city made for walking, and like the ancient capital of Austria it boasts some excellent coffee houses. So every afternoon, at around three o'clock, and accompanied by the melancholic, swarthy-featured policeman who was his afternoon bodyguard – but for the man's piercing blue eyes, Gregor would have said he looked more gypsy than Spanish – the German doctor would take a brisk walk to the Confiteria Ideal.

With its elaborate brass fittings, marble columns, and, in the late afternoons, an organist who played a medley of waltzes and tangos, the Ideal café, just off Corrientes, seemed a perfect evocation of old Austrian *Gemütlichkeit*. After drinking his usual *cortado doble* and eating a slice of delicious chocolate cake, and having closed the cold dark eyes that had seen his own hands inflict a whole *Malabolgia* of horrors, it was quite possible for the doctor to imagine himself back in Vienna's Central Café on Herrengasse, anticipating a night at the Staatsoper or the Burgtheater. For a while anyway, until it was time to go.

As he and his bodyguard collected their coats and left the Ideal at the usual time of a quarter to five, it would have been quite impossible for Helmut Gregor to have imagined himself in any way worse off than Adolf Eichmann. And yet he was. It would be another twenty-three months before Eichmann would meet the hangman in Ramleh Prison. But judgement was rather closer to hand for the doctor. Even as he was leaving the Ideal, one of the waiters, himself a Jew – of whom there are a great many in Buenos Aires – had ignored the doctor's generous tip and was calling the Continental Hotel.

'Sylvia? It's me. Moloch is on his way.'

Sylvia replaced the hotel room's telephone receiver and nodded at the tall American who was lying on the big bed. He threw aside the new Ian Fleming he had been reading, stubbed out his cigarette, and, having climbed up on top of the large mahogany wardrobe, adopted a prone position. Sylvia did not think this behaviour eccentric. Rather, she admired him for the efficient professional way he approached his task. Admired him, but feared him too.

The Continental Hotel, on Roque Saenz Pena, was a classic Italian-style building, but it reminded the American most of the Flatiron building in New York. The room was on the fifth-floor corner and through the open, double-height window he could see right up the street to the corner of Suipacha, a distance of over one hundred and fifty yards. The wardrobe creaked a little as he leaned toward the Winchester rifle that was already carefully positioned there between a couple of pillows. He always disliked poking a rifle out of an open window, preferring the comparative anonymity of a makeshift marksman's platform constructed inside the shooting position. Moving the wardrobe away from the wall by six or seven feet had created the perfect urban hide, rendering him virtually undetectable from the street or the office building opposite. Now all he had to worry about was the unsuppressed noise of the .30-calibre rifle when he squeezed the trigger.

But even that, he hoped, had been taken care of: Sylvia was already signalling to a car parked on the other side of the street. The black De Soto, a popular car in Buenos Aires, was old and battered, with a tendency to backfire, and, seconds later, there came a report, as loud as any rifle shot, that scattered the seagulls and pigeons on the ledge outside the window like a handful of giant-sized confetti.

Not much of a ruse, thought the American, but it was better than nothing. And anyway, BA wasn't like his hometown of Miami where the locals weren't much used to the sound of firecrackers, or gunfire. Here there were plenty of public holidays, always celebrated at maximum volume, with cherry bombs and starting pistols, not to mention the odd revolution. It was only five years since the Argentinian air force had strafed the main square of the city during the military coup that had overthrown Peron. Loud bangs and explosions were a way of life in Buenos Aires. And sometimes death.

Sylvia collected a pair of field binoculars and stood with her back against the wardrobe, immediately underneath the barrel of the rifle. More powerful than the 8X Unertl scope mounted on the American's rifle, the binoculars were to help her ensure that among the many pedestrians who passed along the length of Roque Saenz Pena, the target was properly spotted and a kill detected.

Sylvia glanced at her watch as, in the street outside, the De Soto backfired once again. Even with some cotton wool in her ears to stop her being deafened when the American finally pulled the trigger, the echo-chamber effect of the backfire between the tall buildings of Cangallo and Roque sounded more like a bomb going off.

Having achieved a solid body position, the American took hold of the rifle butt with his non-shooting hand and pressed it firmly against his shoulder. Next, he clasped the grip, slid his forefinger through the trigger guard, and positioned his cheek against the smooth wooden stock. Only then did he check the eye relief through the scope. The sight was already zeroed, following an uncomfortable three-hundred-and-fifty-mile round trip the previous weekend, to the valley of the Azul River, where the American had shot several wild goats. But even with a correctly boresighted rifle, this promised to be a much more difficult target to hit than a goat. There was a considerable amount of traffic along Roque Saenz Pena and across Cangallo, to say nothing of the confusing effect of the ancient seaport's many crosswinds.

As if to confirm the difficulty of sniping in an urban environment, a *colectivo* – one of the red Mercedes buses that served the city – obscured his practice view through the scope just as he had been positioning the cross-hairs of the reticle on an old *porteño*'s wide-brimmed hat.

6

'Moloch should be coming into view any second now,' Sylvia said loudly, because, like her, the American was also wearing ear protection.

The American said nothing, already concentrating on his breathing cycle: he had been trained to exhale normally, and then hold his breath for just a fraction of a second before squeezing the trigger. He had no doubt that Sylvia would correctly identify the target when he hove into view. Like the rest of the local Shin Bet team in Buenos Aires, she knew Moloch's face almost as well as she had come to know Eichmann's. And if the American did have a concern about her, it was that to confirm he had hit or missed his target he was relying on someone who had never before seen someone shot dead in cold blood.

Any rifle's recoil prevented the shooter from seeing if he had hit his man. Especially when the target was standing more than a hundred yards away and in a crowd of people. At that kind of distance a shooter needed a spotter like a pitcher needs an umpire behind home plate, to call balls and strikes on the batter. The least amount of squeamish hesitation on her part and they risked losing the opportunity for a second shot. Observing bullet impacts was easy; detecting a miss – even the best marksman could miss – and describing where the bullet went was the hard part.

The American held no opinion of his professional skills except to say that he was able to command a high fee for his services. It wasn't the kind of business where you could claim to be the best. Or indeed where others could legitimately claim that distinction for you. Moreover, he disliked that kind of reputation as much as he eschewed inflated claims of his own excellence. For him discretion and reliability were the two defining features of his way of life and the fewer people there were who knew about what he did and how well he did it, the better. The most important part of the job was getting away with it, and that necessitated the kind of quiet, unassuming, unsigned behaviour that was characteristic of only the most self-effacing of people. In none of this, however, did he consider himself to be at all atypical of anyone in that particular line of work. He knew there were other marksmen out there – Sarti, Nicoli, David, Nicoletti, to name but a few – but other than their names he knew very little about them, which told him that they aimed to be as anonymous as he was himself. His name was Tom Jefferson.

There was one thing he knew was quite unusual about his own situation, however, and this was that he was married, and to a girl who knew exactly what he did for a living. Who knew what he did, and approved of it.

Mary had accompanied Tom on the trip to Lake Tahoe to pick up the contract. That had been the plan anyway; things happened a little differently when finally they arrived in Lake Tahoe.

They flew Bonanza Air from Miami to Reno, from where they drove to the Cal-Neva Lodge on the North Shore's Crystal Bay, at the invitation of a man named Irving Davidson. Mary, a second-generation Chinese, had never been to Tahoe, but she had seen the Cal-Neva's advertisements in the magazines, ('Heaven in the High Sierras') and she had read about how the resort was part-owned by Frank Sinatra and Peter Lawford, and how Marilyn Monroe was a frequent visitor there, as were members of the Kennedy family. Mary, as interested in the Kennedys as she was a fan of Monroe's, was keen to stay in such a glamorous spot.

And she took to the place as soon as she saw it. Or rather as soon as she saw Joe DiMaggio and Jimmy Durante having a drink in the Indian Room. But there was something about the Cal-Neva Tom didn't like. An atmosphere. Something indefinably corrupt. Perhaps it was because the operating philosophy of the place seemed to be that money could buy you everything. Or perhaps it was because the resort had been built by a wealthy San Francisco businessman with the express purpose of circumventing Californian law. Located on the state line dividing California and Nevada, the resort comprised a central rustic lodge with an enormous fireplace, a cluster of luxury chalets, and a casino which, because of the laws banning gambling in California, was located on the Nevada side of the border. The state line ran right through the middle of the swimming pool enabling bathers to swim from one state into another. Tom was glad that, as things turned out, he only had to spend one night in the place.

Soon after their arrival it became clear that their host and potential client would be unable to join them. Telephoning the discreet chalet where Tom and Mary were relaxing together in the large hot tub, Irving Davidson explained the situation.

'Tom? May I call you Tom? I'm afraid that some business is going to detain me here in Las Vegas for a while. Look, I'm very sorry about this, but I'm not going to be able to come up there and join you. That being the case, for which once again you have my apologies Tom, I was wondering if I could prevail upon your time and patience a little further. I was wondering if you would mind driving down here to meet me and my associates here in Vegas. It's about four hundred and fifty miles down Highway ninety-five. You could leave just after breakfast, and be here late afternoon. It's a nice drive. Especially if you're in a nice car. Living in Miami, I bet you drive a convertible, Tom. Am I right?'

'Chevy Bel Air,' confirmed Tom.

'That's a nice car,' said Davidson. 'Well, there's a Dual Ghia at your disposal while you're in Nevada, Tom. That's a really beautiful car. But here's the kick: it belongs to Frank Sinatra. How does that sound? And when you arrive in Vegas you can stay in the suite Frank has here at the Sands. Everything is fixed. What do you say, Tom?'

Tom, who had never much cared for Sinatra's music, was silent for a moment. He sensed that the suite was for him alone. 'What about my wife?' he asked.

'Let her enjoy herself where she is. Listen, she's got everything she needs right there. A drive through the desert with the hood down, she doesn't need. Her hair doesn't need it. Her complexion doesn't need it. There's a pretty good beauty salon in the Lodge. I've booked her a whole morning in there. And I've arranged for her to have five hundred dollars' worth of chips to play with in the casino. She needs anything else, all she's got to do is pick up the phone and Skinny'll fix it for her. That's Skinny D'Amato. The general manager? He knows all about how you and Mary are my special guests. I believe that some celebrity guests are coming in tomorrow. Eddie Fisher and Dean Martin. I can have Skinny introduce her if she wants. So what do you say, Tom?'

'Okay, Mister Davidson. It's your party.'

Early the next morning, Tom left Mary very excited about the possibility of meeting Dean Martin and drove Sinatra's expensive

9

convertible to Vegas, as requested. On the way down he listened to a country music radio station and, by the time he arrived, he thought he must have heard Hank Locklin sing 'Please Help Me I'm Falling' as many as a dozen times. Tom preferred Jim Reeves. Not just his most recent record, 'He'll Have to Go', but also because he sometimes fancied he looked a little like a younger, slimmer version of the singer.

It was around five when he turned off 95 on to Las Vegas Boulevard, and saw the Strip, which was always a picture to warm the heart of any magazine pictures editor. He checked into the Sands and went up to a suite that was the size of the Fuller dome. On the Formica free-form coffee table was an enormous basket of fruit, a bottle of Bourbon, and a card inviting Tom along to Davidson's own suite for drinks at ten o'clock. So he lay down on the bed and dozed a little, then took a bath, ate a banana, put on a clean shirt, and walked around the Strip for a while.

Tom did not gamble. He did not even play the slots. Tom had little time for the old Vegas saying that the more you bet, the less you lose when you win. But he did like to look at bare-breasted girls, of which the Strip had a plentiful supply. The Lido show at the Stardust's chic Café Continental was good, and so were the Ice-cubettes at the Thunderbird's Ecstasy On Ice review. He liked to see breasts, lots of them too, but most of all he liked to see a woman's ass, and for that you had to go to Harold Minsky's harem headquarters at The Dunes, where there was more bare flesh on display than any other show in Vegas. A winning pile of chips on a craps table was nothing to look at compared with a good piece of ass in a spangled G-string. When he'd seen enough, he went back to the hotel, took another shower and then knocked at Davidson's door.

It was Davidson himself who answered.

'Tom, come on in.' He was a smooth, sharply dressed little George Raft of a guy who was possessed of a politician's easy manner. 'Here, let me introduce you to everyone.'

Three men stood up from an ersatz leopard-skin couch that curved around the Lucullan suite's rough stone walls. The drapes were pulled over the silver-screen-sized window, as if privacy was of paramount importance.

'Morris Dalitz, Lewis Rosenstiel, and Efraim Ilani. Gentlemen, this is Tom Jefferson.'

Even before he'd greeted everyone, Tom had guessed he was the only gentile in the room.

'Pleased to meet you, Tom,' said Morris Dalitz.

His was the only name Tom recognised. A big man, with a fleshy, big-nosed face like a coarser version of Adlai Stevenson, the guy crossing the thick pile rug to shake Tom's hand was Moe Dalitz, the godfather of Las Vegas. Or so the Kefauver Committee had said a few years back. All Tom could say about Rosenstiel, catching sight of the man's fancy diamond cufflinks as he, too, shook Tom by the hand, was that he looked rich. Which was the only way to look in Vegas. The third guy, Ilani, wearing a plain white short-sleeved shirt and open-toed sandals, and who looked as poor as Rosenstiel looked rich, just lit a cigarette and nodded.

For the first few minutes it was Davidson who did most of the smooth talking. That seemed to be what he was good at.

'Get you a drink, Tom? We're all having Martinis.'

Tom saw that everyone didn't include Ilani, who was drinking iced water.

'Thanks, I'll just have a Coke.'

'Keep a clear head for business, huh? I like that. It's the only way to survive in this town.' Davidson fixed the drink himself off a drinks trolley that was shaped like an airplane wing, and handed it over with the kind of big-shot swagger that made Tom think he didn't often mix the drinks. 'Suite okay?'

'When I've been all the way round it, I'll tell you.'

Davidson smiled. 'And the drive down from Lake Tahoe?'

'The landing and takeoff were okay.'

'That's a nice car, the Dual Ghia.'

'Yeah, it's a swell car,' agreed Tom. 'Real smooth. Like the owner, I guess.'

'Is that an American car?' asked Rosenstiel.

'It's a fucking Chrysler,' Moe Dalitz told him.

'Yeah? Sounds more Italian,' said Rosenstiel.

'Sinatra's got one,' said Davidson. 'Peter Lawford, too. Tom drove Peter's car down here for us.'

Tom smiled quietly, wondering which of the two stars the car really belonged to, if either. Not that it mattered any to him.

'Hey,' he said, sitting down on the sofa and sipping some of his Coke, 'for all I care about such things, Elizabeth Taylor could have driven naked across America in the car and not wiped the seat when she was through with it. I'm here, so let's talk business.'

'Sure, sure,' Davidson said smoothly. 'We're all businessmen. The four of us you see here now represent a variety of business backgrounds, Tom. But Morris, Lewis, and myself are meeting you in our capacity as members of the American Jewish League Against Communism. And in our desire to help Mister Ilani. This particular matter does not involve any communists, you understand, but fascists.'

'Makes a pleasant change,' chuckled Dalitz.

'Mister Ilani is concerned with the pursuit and punishment of Nazi war criminals. I take it you've heard of Adolf Eichmann, Tom.'

'I read the newspapers.'

'Since Prime Minister Ben-Gurion told the Israeli parliament that Eichmann was in his country's custody, Israel's been in pretty bad odour with the international community. To say nothing of the very severe diplomatic difficulties that now exist between Israel and Argentina. The whole affair has left Mister Ilani here with some unfinished business back in Buenos Aires. Someone he'd like to have seen in Israel, standing trial alongside that bastard Eichmann. Only Mister Ilani and his people can't go back, for obvious reasons.'

Tom sneaked a glance at Ilani. With his pale skin, hairy body, and heavy glasses, Ilani looked more like the chairman of the local chamber of commerce than someone who worked for Shin Bet or Mossad.

'At least not right now. Not for a while, maybe. So, the next best alternative would be to have this second man, himself an important war criminal, brought immediately to book and subjected to an extreme penalty without the visible benefits of legal process, as the people of Israel would of course prefer.'

'In other words,' added Moe Dalitz, 'we want this Nazi bastard hit.'

Tom nodded slowly. And addressed his next remark Ilani's way.

'I used to have an English friend,' he said. 'A British army officer, stationed in Jerusalem. This was twelve years ago. Nineteen forty-eight. Anyway, this friend got himself killed. Shot in the head with a six-point-five-millimetre Mannlicher Carcano rifle at eight hundred yards.' Tom pursed his lips and raised his eyebrows. 'Centre forehead at eight hundred yards,' he repeated. 'Helluva shot.'

'Are you saying you don't want this contract, Mister Jefferson?' This was Ilani speaking. To Tom's ears his accent sounded more Spanish than Hebrew. 'You have something against the State of Israel, yes?'

'I don't give a fuck one way or the other about the State of Israel. What I'm saying, Mister Ilani, is that you have some pretty fine marksmen back in Israel. I can't see why you need my services.'

'In view of the delicate state of relations between Israel and Argentina,' explained Davidson, 'it would be best if a professional was brought in to handle the contract. Someone who isn't Jewish. Our information is correct, isn't it, Tom? You're not Jewish, are you?'

'Me? Hell no. I'm a Roman Catholic. At least that's what it says on my army record. It's been a while since I went through the church doors, mind you. God and me haven't talked in a long while. You might say it's an occupational hazard.'

'I've read that,' said Ilani. 'Your army record. US Marine Corps. You speak several languages, including Spanish. Served Guadalcanal, Okinawa. Ended World War Two with the rank of Gunnery Sergeant, and with twenty-three kills. Attached to UN nineteen forty-seven to -nine, and a member of US Armed Forces in Korea when North Korean troops crossed the thirty-eighth parallel. Captured Pork Chop Hill January nineteen fifty-three. Repatriated August. Honourable discharge. Several decorations et cetera, et cetera. It's very impressive.'

'You're pretty cute yourself, Mister Ilani,' Tom said with a smile. 'All that information without so much as a note in front of you. A regular Charles Van Doren, that's what you are, sir. I'll bet you could answer twenty-one about anybody in this damn room.'

Moe Dalitz, who had got up to fix himself another drink, snorted loudly. 'As long as the man doing the asking isn't Bobby Kennedy, I really don't mind how many fucking questions it is.'

Rosenstiel laughed uproariously and lit a large cigar. 'Maybe we should ask Tom to fix Bobby too,' he said. 'Two rats for the price of one.'

Tom lit a Chesterfield and let them carry on with this line of conversation for a minute or so before drawing them back to the contract that was on the table.

'You said this man who lives in Buenos Aires is a Nazi war criminal. What's his name and what did he do?'

'Doctor Helmut Gregor,' answered Ilani. He unzipped a cheap plastic briefcase and took out a file that he handed over to Tom. 'That's the name he lives under now. You'll find everything you need to know about him in this dossier. I'm afraid I'm not at liberty to tell you his real name. But to be quite frank with you, few people have ever heard of this man. It is enough to say that he tortured and killed thousands of people, but mostly children.'

'Even we don't know his real name, Tom,' said Davidson.

'Won't the Argentinian government guess that Israel is behind this operation?' asked Tom.

Ilani shrugged.

'Since the Argentinian government denies that this man is in their country at all,' he said, 'it is unlikely that they will wish to draw attention to the fact of his having been there by complaining about his assassination. In all probability they'll sweep the whole matter under the rug. This is to your advantage, Mister Jefferson. You should be able to leave the country without too much trouble. Of course, supposing you take the contract, you will be assisted by a local team of Argentinian Jews. They've been keeping Gregor under surveillance since the arrest of Eichmann. They will supply you with everything you need on the ground. A suitable rifle, transport, hotel accommodation. With the help of the American Jewish League Against Communism I will supply you with a US passport and a suitable cover story.'

'What about a visa?'

'Visitors of US nationality are admitted on a passport without any consular visa.'

'You'll be travelling as Bill Casper, a Coca-Cola sales director, from Atlanta,' explained Davidson. 'It so happens that I'm a registered lobbyist for Coca-Cola among others. I've escorted teams of soft-drinks executives, including the real Mister Casper, on missions all

14

over the world. Incidentally, the real Bill Casper is currently vacationing in Brazil. Enjoying the spas of southern Minas Gerais. When you get to BA you can hand out some Coke, make the hit, and then fly home.' He shrugged as if to say that was all there was to it.

Tom nodded, holding off a smile as he held two of these images in his head: drink Coca-Cola, and make the hit. Simple. Maybe some Madison Avenue type could get an ad campaign out of that. The hit that refreshes. Only Ilani was shrewd enough to spell out the reality of what was being proposed.

'Of course it won't be that easy,' he said. 'Otherwise . . .'

Tom gave in to the smile, relieved that there was at least someone who recognised the existence of a few potential problems.

'Otherwise,' said Tom, 'you wouldn't be prepared to pay me twenty-five thousand dollars.'

'Damn right,' said Rosenstiel.

Tom wondered if it was Rosenstiel who was putting up the money for the contract. It was no longer just the diamond cufflinks that made Tom think he was loaded. By now he'd added on the Duoppioni label inside the coat of Rosenstiel's silk suit, the Italian tasselled loafers, the Rolex watch, and the Dunhill gold lighter.

'Since Eichmann's arrest, Gregor is well guarded,' said Ilani. 'He has some powerful friends in the military government. Officials he has bribed with large sums of money.'

'While we're on that subject,' said Tom, 'my terms and conditions include fifty per cent of the consideration, in advance, in cash.'

'No problem,' said Moe Dalitz.

'Then we have a deal,' said Tom. He had been wrong about Rosenstiel. It was the casino that was going to put up the money for the contract. That was okay. They'd probably let him win at roulette, or something. Just as long as they didn't expect him to take his money from a slot machine.

He handed Davidson a sheet of paper.

'My bank is Maduro and Curiel's in Curaçao,' he said. 'That's the cable address and my account number. When the service has been rendered, I'll telephone to let you know so you can deposit the balance of my fee.'

'There is one more thing,' said Ilani. 'We'd prefer it if you could go to Argentina immediately on your return to Miami.' He handed Tom a ticket. 'There's a Braniff flight from Miami to Buenos Aires this Friday. We'd like you to be on it. It's just possible Gregor may yet disappear altogether.'

'I understand,' said Tom. 'I can be on that flight. But can you do the passport by then?'

'You'll have it by tomorrow morning,' Ilani confirmed.

'Then there's just the deposit.'

'Sure, sure,' said Dalitz. 'Ever play keno, Tom?'

'I'm more of a golfer than a gambler.'

'Keno was the national lottery in ancient China. Funds acquired from the game were used to build the Great Wall of China. Which ought to tell you that the house percentage is bigger than on any other casino game. Maybe in Disneyland they win money at keno, but anywhere else it's the original hard way bet. Damned if I know why but it's about the most popular game in the joint. Vegas loves a winner, Tom. And tonight, my friend, you're it.'

Moe Dalitz handed Tom a keno form. It was divided horizontally into two rectangles. The upper half was numbered 1 through 40, and the lower half 41 through 80. Fifteen numbers had already been marked with a thick black crayon and, in the right-hand corner of the form, was the price of the ticket: $100.

'Hand this is in at the keno lounge desk,' Dalitz told him. 'Pay for the bet. The lady will give you back a ticket with the number of the game you're playing. Then watch the keno board. After twenty numbers have appeared turn in your ticket and collect your money. Only don't hang around before the next game, otherwise you'll forfeit your winnings. All thirteen grand of it.'

Grinning affably, Dalitz toasted Tom, and said: 'Congratulations. You're leaving Vegas with a small fortune. To do that most people usually have to arrive in Vegas with a large one.'

It was the first time Tom ever played keno. And in view of the ease with which the fix had gone in, he thought it would be the last time, too. The whole experience confirmed Tom's belief that luck was something only suckers believed in. Like God. And Justice. Perhaps there were those who might have seen some kind of Nemesis in what

16

was about to befall Helmut Gregor. Tom was not one of these, however. He had no illusions with regard to what he was doing. However heinous the man's crimes, this was plain murder. And plain murder was what Tom was good at. The way some guys were good at pitching a baseball, or playing a saxophone. Not much of a talent, maybe, but enough to make a good living. Tom would have put a bullet through Walt Disney's head if someone had come up with the twenty-five grand.

For considerably more than that – a cool two hundred and fifty thousand dollars, to be precise – a consortium of embittered Cubans, angry at Eisenhower's lack of support for their now-exiled President, Fulgencia Batista, had contracted Tom to assassinate Ike during his state visit to Brazil, back in March. Had the Cubans managed to stay out of gaol – all of them were now imprisoned in the notorious Isle of Pines – and come up with even half of the money, it might have been the easiest of jobs: on the newsreels he'd seen Ike riding the length of Rio's mile-long Avenida Rio Branco sitting right up on the back of the open-top limousine so that the crowd with its tickertape welcome could get a better view of him. It had been a rare opportunity. The car had been travelling at just eight miles an hour. Usually, American presidents were not so easy to kill.

'Moloch. There he is,' Sylvia reported. The biographical charm bracelet she wore on her wrist clinked noisily as she rocked up and down excitedly.

Her scent was in his nostrils. Something nice. Better than the stink of gunpowder that was to come.

'I see him.'

Tom's voice was calm, even appreciative, as if he was observing a rare bird, or a girl undressing in front of an open window. The man who had just rounded the corner looked respectable enough and like someone Tom had once known. Tall and dark-haired, Gregor cut a well-dressed, handsome figure and seemed hardly German at all. More like a typical *porteño* male: dressed with the care of a Frenchman, and possessed with the attitude of an Englishman. Josef Goebbels in a grey suit, with two good feet and an extra six inches.

Tom could easily see how, for over ten years, the German had managed to fit right in.

He took aim, which was another kind of concentration, choosing the exact spot he wished to hit. It was an old sniper's trick: pick a point of impact that was the same size as your bullet. When shooting at the side of a man's head, Tom favoured the tip of the ear. Shooting from the front, as in this case, he always aimed at the philtrum, the little groove in the target's upper lip. Either way you were certain to hit the brain stem. And at less than a hundred and fifty yards, teeth and bones were hardly likely to deflect a .30-calibre bullet. Tom could shoot groups of one inch at a range of one hundred yards. For a precise shot to the central nervous system, that was really his maximum range. So, keeping the scope's reticle steady on the man walking toward him, and his aiming spot, he waited for Sylvia to report that the target was clear of other pedestrians and traffic. It was like watching a silent movie, except that the picture he could see was in colour.

For almost thirty seconds a horse-drawn carriage obscured his view of the target. Then, the driver, wearing a tweed cap and blue suit, cracked his whip and the single horse broke into a trot and turned the corner of Cangallo, leaving Tom with what Sylvia confirmed excitedly was now a good clear shot.

Slowly he started to gather the trigger under the tip of his forefinger, taking just the slack out of it, until he felt the heavier resistance of the sear, and, gathering his breath once more, pulling back only to the point of release. He was only a second away from firing when Gregor turned his head and glanced behind him as if to be reassured that his police bodyguard was still in tow. Seeing that he was, Gregor looked to his front again, smiling now, and then slowed as he approached the street corner, ready to cross over Cangallo. He did not seem to have a care in the world. Or a conscience.

'You're clear to fire,' repeated Sylvia. 'There's nothing coming either—'

A split second before she heard the gunshot above her, she saw the German reach up for his mouth as though he had felt the sharp pain of a sudden toothache, and his head was momentarily surrounded with what looked like a circle of crimson light as the back of his skull blew off. Both the bodyguard and a pedestrian walking to the rear of Helmut Gregor were splattered with blood and brain coming toward them. Even to Sylvia's untrained eye it was plain to see that Gregor had suffered a fatal head shot. But swallowing her horror she followed his poleaxed body down on to the sidewalk, and continued to report the silent scene visible through the binoculars. Her first thought was that it seemed incredible that Gregor could have been killed from such a distance.

'It looks as though you blew the nose right off his face,' she said.

Tom bolted the rifle and relocated his target now lying in the gutter. This time he aimed at the throat, just below the lower jaw.

'And I think also the back of his skull,' she added. 'He must be dead. No, wait. I think his leg moved a little.'

Tom thought it was probably just a spasm, but he squeezed off a second shot anyway, to make quite sure.

'Jesus,' exclaimed Sylvia, hardly expecting that Tom would have bothered to fire again. Still watching through the binoculars, she caught sight of Gregor's jaw fly off like a piece of broken pottery. Shaking her head, she threw the binoculars on to the bed, and added that the man was now dead for sure. Then she took a deep breath and sat down heavily on the floor, with her back against the bed, and dropped her head between her knees, almost as if she herself had been shot.

The cruelty of what she had seen appalled her. The cold-bloodedness of it, too. She had only a vague idea of the dead man's crimes: that he had done things of unspeakable cruelty. She hoped so. She took no pleasure at all in having participated in this man's death, however wicked he might have been. Her only source of consolation was that for Helmut Gregor, the invisible hand that had killed with such detached precision had struck him like the fist of God. Not that the man climbing down from the top of the wardrobe looked much like an angel of the Lord. There was something about the American's face that made her feel uncomfortable. No laugh lines around the mouth, not even the line of a frown on the high forehead, and as for the eyes – it wasn't as if they were dead or anything grotesque like that, it was just that they were always the same, with the right eye – the one he used to peer through the sniper-scope – permanently narrowed, so that even when he was looking at her he appeared to be choosing some feature on her face as his next aiming point.

Tom slid the rifle into a tournament-size golf bag, disguising the barrel end with a numbered head cover. He added the clubs, hoisted the bag on to his shoulder, and then checked his appearance in the wardrobe's full-length mirror. There were a number of excellent golf clubs in the suburbs of BA – the Hurlingham, the Ranelagh, the Ituzaingo, the Lomas, the Jockey, the Hindu Country Club – and, dressed in a pair of dark-blue flannels, navy-blue polo-shirt, and matching windcheater, Tom thought he looked to all the world like a man with nothing more lethal on his mind than the dry Martinis he might consume at the nineteenth hole.

And, but for the fact that it was late in the afternoon and would soon be dark, he might even have played. He was a keen golfer and often used a bag of clubs to disguise the fact that he was carrying a rifle. This particular bag and the cheap set of Sam Sneads it contained (not so cheap when he remembered the *ad valorem* they'd charged him at the airport) he had brought with him from the pro shop at the Miami Shores Country Club where he usually played, and he planned to give them to Sylvia's father after she had disposed of the rifle. The old man was a member of the club at Olivos, close to where Eichmann had been living until rabbit farming took him to San Fernando and the house on Garibaldi Street from which he had been kidnapped.

'You're just going to carry it out the front door of the hotel?' asked Sylvia, closing the bedroom window.

'Sure. You got a better idea?' He thought she was looking a little green around the gills. Never seen anyone shot in colour before. Probably just a few old SS newsreel shots of Jews getting it in the back of the head. Not the same thing at all.

She shook her head. 'No, I guess not,' she admitted.

'You look like you need a cup of *mate*,' said Tom, who'd developed quite a taste for Argentina's national drink himself. A herbal alternative to coffee, *mate* was a refreshing drink as well as being considered a great remedy for mild stomach upsets.

'How can you do that?' she whispered. 'How can you kill someone like that? In cold blood.'

'Why do I do it? Why do I take down contracts?'

Tom considered the question for a moment. It was one he'd been asked many times before, mostly in the army, when he'd been more up-front about being a shooter. Somehow it never seemed to satisfy people merely to say that it was all a matter of training. Not that he usually felt much of a need to explain himself. But during the three or four days he had spent with Sylvia he had come to like her. There was something about this girl that made him want to tell her that he wasn't filled with hate any more than he was some kind of psycho. That he was just a man doing what men were always best at, which was killing other men. Never very articulate, Tom searched for a form of words that she might understand, and in doing so he shrugged, pursed his lips, bobbed his head one way and then the other, and took a deep breath through his nose before finally he answered her.

'I go to the movies a lot. I'm in a lot of strange towns, killing time, y'know?' He smiled wryly as he reflected on that particular choice of words. 'One movie I saw. *Shane*. With Alan Ladd? Pretty damn good movie. It's about this stranger that arrives in a little Wyoming town, who tries to forget his previous life with a gun. Only you know he won't be able to do that. He'll try and he'll fail and that's all there is to it. Which means that right from the moment the bad guy, Jack Palance, appears on screen, you know he's going to be shot. And that Shane is going to be the one to kill him. The guy's a walking dead man and he doesn't even know it. Just waiting to fall into his grave.

'It's the same with these guys I kill. When I take the contract they're dead already. If it wasn't me who killed them, it'd be someone else. The way I see a contract is that it's better for them it's me because I'm good at what I do. Better for them: a clean shot; better for me: I'm well paid for what I do. If it wasn't for the money I'd probably still be in the army. Money's the how and the why of just about everything in this world. Whether it's cutting a man's hair, pulling his teeth, or shooting him dead.'

Sylvia was shaking her head. There were tears in her eyes.

'You're young,' he said. 'You still believe in shit. In morals. In an ideal. Zionism. Marxism. Capitalism. Whatever. You think that stuff's any less corrosive to society than what I do for a living? Let me tell you, it's not the people who believe in nothing you gotta worry about, it's the people who believe in stuff. Religious people. Political people.

21

Idealists. Converts. They're the ones who are going to destroy this world. Not people like me, the people who pay lip service to no creed or cause. Money's the only cause that will never let you down and self-interest's the one world philosophy that won't try to bullshit you. There's a dialectic for you that'll always make sense.'

Tom smiled and shifted the golf bag on to his other shoulder. There were times when he almost convinced himself with his own bullshit. And if that wasn't politics then he was the man in the Hathaway shirt.

'Now let's get the hell out of here before someone smells our gunpowder.'

2

Quiniela Exacta

It was a hot and humid Friday evening in September when Tom Jefferson left his Biscayne bayfront home in Miami Shores and drove twenty minutes southwest, to the jai alai *frontón* on 37th Avenue and North West 35th Street. The ancient Basque sport of jai alai, though popular in Spain and France, was played nowhere in North America except Florida, reflecting the sunshine state's uniquely heterogeneous character. It had been two Cubans who built America's first *fronton* in the shadow of Hialeah, the *grande dame* of Florida racetracks, back in 1928. This edifice lasted only as long as the great hurricane of 1935. Subsequently, another *fronton* was built just a short way south of the original, right next to Miami International Airport and, until 1953, when an enthusiastic aficionado from Chicago erected a second *fronton* in Dania, the one on 37th held a monopoly on the game.

Tom followed jai alai the same way he followed baseball and football, which is to say he rarely got a chance to go, but paid close attention to the results published in the *Miami Herald*. Besides, tickets were hard to come by. Played indoors, the seating capacity of the *fronton* on 37th was just three thousand five hundred. Hugely popular among the city's Latin population, especially at the weekend, the promoters could have sold two or three times as many tickets. But for the ticket he had received in the mail, Tom, who was part Cuban himself, would never have dreamed of actually going to the Friday night jai alai. Let alone going there to discuss a contract. People who wanted other people killed nearly always preferred to meet somewhere quieter, where there was less chance of being overheard. Which meant that the mysterious Mr Ralston, who had sent Tom his ticket, was either a rank amateur in the business of killing and hence someone to be avoided, or someone so sophisticated in the purifying euphemisms of the trade that he felt comfortable talking contracts in a crowd.

The game listed was an eleven-game doubles for seven points, with all sixteen *pelotaris* who were in action coming from as far away as Cuba, Mexico, and Spain's Basque region. Tom never minded making a small bet on jai alai: the number of players involved meant that the game was hard to fix. So upon entering the *frontón*, and glancing over the players, he purchased a five-dollar *quiniela exacta* from one of the *pari-mutuel*, state-run betting machines. To collect on this ticket meant that it was necessary not only to have picked the winning pair, but also the runners-up.

When it was approaching a quarter to seven, Tom went to find his seat. This was a good one, the best Tom had ever had – right in front, next to the protective glass wall. But of his host there was, as yet, no sign. Just after seven, the four *pelotaris* already warming up on court, a man carrying a copy of the *New York Times* and a paperback novel sat down beside him.

'I'm John Ralston,' he said, shaking Tom by the hand. 'Nice to meet you. And thanks for coming.'

It was a strong handshake, stronger than the man's business-like, not to say dapper appearance might have indicated. He wore heavy-framed dark glasses, a cream shirt and tie, a well-cut beige linen suit, a folded silk handkerchief in the breast pocket, more than a hint of cologne, and a large ruby ring. The silver hair above Ralston's high, tanned forehead was a little longer than was fashionable, but neat, and from time to time he touched it as if it had been recently cut. Straight away Tom decided that the man was no amateur: Ralston was not in the least bit fearful of Tom.

'Thanks for asking me,' said Tom.

24

'Have you made a bet?' Ralston was as well spoken as he was groomed. His accent was hard to place, too, a curious mixture of Boston and West Coast.

'A *quiniela exacta* on the green shirts to win,' said Tom. 'The two Cubans are in form. And the orchid shirts to come second.' He watched Ralston study the programme for a moment or two and guessed him to be in his mid-fifties.

'You sound as if you know this game.'

'I follow it in the newspapers.'

'I've only recently started coming,' admitted Ralston. 'Since I've been in Florida. Originally I'm from Chicago, but most of my business has been in Hollywood and Las Vegas. Pedro Mir. The matchmaker? He's a friend of mine. I've been telling him that he ought to open a *frontón* in LA. Or in Vegas, maybe. With all the Mexicans living there, I think this game would go pretty well. What do you think, Mister Jefferson?'

'I don't know LA very well.'

'What's to know?' smiled Ralston. 'Raymond Chandler once said LA has all the personality of a paper-cup. But to be fair it was Bay City he really hated. Are you much of a reader, Mister Jefferson?'

'I read pretty much anything,' said Tom, noting the title and the author of the paperback lying on Ralston's lap. *Island in the Sun*, by Alec Waugh, was one book he thought he would probably never read.

'I knew Chandler when he was working at Paramount Pictures. That would have been around nineteen forty-three. Chandler and a few others besides. Lately, I've been in the fruit business. In Central America. But in those days I was in movies. Producing some, but mainly on the money side.'

'I hear that's the best side to be on,' offered Tom.

The game was starting. Played on a three-walled court approximately 180 feet long, the *pelotaris* used a curved wicker basket called a *cesta*, strapped to the hand, to hurl the *pelota* which, made of solid rubber and twice the size of a golf-ball, was covered in kidskin. *Pelotas* travelling at speeds of up to 170 miles per hour were caught in the air, on one bounce, or off the back wall before being returned to the front. Jai alai was a game that demanded power, stamina, and an instinctive ability to cover the best positions on a court longer than the width of a football field.

Ralston lowered his voice. 'Mostly I've been involved in the gaming business,' he said. 'Not the *pari-mutuel* kind, you understand. Although I can't ever see how some sports are blessed with the gambling seal of purity while others are not.'

'A dog, or a horse, or for that matter a *pelotari* is harder to fix than a game of keno,' observed Tom.

'That's what most people think, it's true. But it's not why the casino business was throttled here in Florida. The real reason is that the casino threatened the Florida state's profits from the *mutuel* machines. Not that I give much of a fuck any more. This is all ancient history as far as I'm concerned.'

He handed Tom his business card. Tom took it and glanced at the name and the LA address, which was somewhere near Sunset Strip. But it was the job title that intrigued Tom. The card described Ralston as a strategist.

'These days I'm working for the government. In a strategic and advisory capacity. Helping them to solve problems, preparing working papers for discussion groups, that kind of thing. I give those cards out, and unlike you, most people ask, "What's a fucking strategist?" And I say that a strategist is a kind of trouble-shooter.'

'Like me,' said Tom.

'Hmm?'

His eyes following the ball, Ralston didn't even acknowledge the joke. He was concentrating on the game and on himself. Reflecting that clearly these were subjects Ralston enjoyed, Tom offered up an equally provocative description of those he guessed were probably Ralston's associates.

'You're working for the agency of bright ideas and brainwaves. Also known as E Street, right?' Tom was referring to the Washington headquarters of the Central Intelligence Agency.

'The trouble with a lot of so-called bright ideas is that they simply are not very practical. Not to say hare-brained. Oh, good shot.' Ralston began to applaud.

'God save us from people with bright ideas.' Tom noted that

26

Ralston had not contradicted his suggestion that he was working for the CIA. 'That's what I always say.'

'Amen to that,' said Ralston. He handed Tom his copy of the previous day's *New York Times* which had been folded so that he could read an account of Fidel Castro's trip to New York, to address the General Assembly of the United Nations.

Tom glanced over the story, with which he was already familiar from his own paper. Alleging that they were being overcharged, the Cuban delegation had moved out of the Shelburne Hotel to stay with their oppressed black brothers in the Theresa, a run-down flophouse in Harlem that not even the poorest African diplomat would have considered suitable. The *Times* reported the mess the Cubans were accused of making in their rooms during their brief sojourn in the Shelburne: cigar burns in the rugs, chicken feathers in the rooms, raw meat left in a refrigerator. It was almost as if the newspaper was suggesting that some voodoo-communist rite had been performed there – a Marxist-Zombie created to wreak havoc on the capitalist world. Meanwhile, at the Theresa, the reporting fixed on the squalor and the number of prostitutes who frequented the place. A library picture of Castro, smoking a large cigar, appeared next to a shot of the neglected Harlem hotel front.

Ralston sighed loudly. 'But even if I told you, you simply would not believe the kind of hare-brained schemes the people at Quarters Eye have thought up to deal with our friend in the paper.'

Tom knew that Quarters Eye, on Ohio Drive in Washington, was another part of the CIA – the part that dealt with Cuba.

'Blind eye would be a better name for that place. You simply would not believe it. They've come up with everything from an exploding cigar to a dirty toilet seat.'

'Catch a man when he's got his pants down, huh?' said Tom. 'I've done a bit of that myself. A target stays steady when he's taking a dump.'

The crowd roared its approval as one of the Cuban players in the green shirts pulled off a spectacular catch.

'Shooting's one thing. Dumb ideas are another. There is too much unnecessary complication around these days,' observed Ralston. 'Too much gorp on the front of the Cadillac, so to speak. You know what I mean?'

'I think so.'

'Those bombs on the front of the fifty-three model.'

'Dagmars.'

'Devoid of utility and impossible to repair. You've got to keep things simple. That's what I'm talking about. Look at the Volkswagen. Look at the Porsche. Look at you.'

'Me?'

'What you did down in Argentina? No cigar. No bullshit. It was just match-grade, boat-tailed, high-quality loads at one hundred yards. Am I right?'

It was Ralston's turn to remain uncontradicted.

'Simple,' he continued. 'Of course, I'm not for a minute suggesting that it was an easy takedown. From what I heard it was a shot to take gold at the Pan American Games. No, the point I'm making is that what you do, what you are good at, is as reliable a method of pest control as it's always been, since way back when. Since Tim Murphy brought down General Simon Fraser at three hundred yards during the battle of Saratoga.'

Tom was impressed. The exploits of famous snipers were something that had been drummed into him twenty years earlier, during his training at Camp Pendleton, the Marine Corps Scout and Sniper School, in Greens Farm, San Diego. But he would not have said that the man sitting next to him showed any signs of having been in the military. The mob, maybe, but not the army.

'That's why I'm talking to you now,' said Ralston. 'The people I represent. People in government. They would like you to prepare a feasibility study for a job covering the gentleman in the *Times*.'

A little uncomfortably, Tom glanced around him.

'Oh, I wouldn't worry about these people,' said Ralston. 'I bet there is not a man here who wouldn't like to see the Maximum Leader turn up his toes. Besides, nobody's speaking English except you and me.'

'A feasibility study, huh?'

'Can it be done, Mister Jefferson? If so, how? And for how much? And if the Maximum Leader, then what chance his bearded brother, Raul, at the same time? You could say that's my own *quiniela exacta*, so to speak. There's not much odds in picking the winner if you can't pick the runner up too, eh? Naturally, we will cover the cost of your wager.'

Ralston handed Tom the paperback novel. Seeing Tom merely stare at it, he said: 'You should never judge a book by its cover.'

Perceiving that the book hid something of value, Tom placed it on his lap and, surreptitiously riffling the pages, discovered that it contained five one-hundred bills. Turning the book over, he glanced at the copy on the back. Appropriately enough the story seemed to be set on some fictional island in the Caribbean.

'I'm looking forward to reading this,' he said.

'Excellent. But don't take too long. I'm eager to tell my friends what you think about it.'

'I'm a fast reader, Mister Ralston. I can probably give you a reader's report within a few days.'

'Shall we say a week?'

'Fine.'

'Do you know the University Inn, in Coral Gables?'

'I know it. The place on campus,' said Tom. 'Next to the Riviera Golf Course.'

'You can leave a message for me there. Do I take it that as well as being a hunter, you are also a golfer?'

'What else is there to do in Miami?'

'No doubt I could offer you some surprises. However, I myself play at the Biltmore.'

'That's a better course. Plenty of creeks to fuck around with your game. The Riviera's okay. I mean it's well trapped, but there are no water hazards, and in Florida, well, that's like a circus without any clowns.'

'You must like losing balls. Where do you play?'

'Miami Shores. One of the toughest courses in Florida, I reckon.'

'Who's the pro there?'

'Jim MacLaughlin.'

'And what's your handicap?'

'Eight.'

'What a coincidence. So's mine. We must play sometime.'

'Yes, but where? It ought to be on neutral ground.'

'Ever play Coral Ridge, in Fort Lauderdale?'

'No.'

'Neither did I. But Lou Worsham, the pro there, he's a friend of mine. I'll arrange something with him.'

Tom smiled to himself. Ralston was obviously the kind of man who dropped names like bad golfers dropped shots. He wondered which one of the quartet of men he had met in Vegas had been the friend who'd told Ralston about the contract in Buenos Aires. Not Ilani, that was for sure: the Israeli didn't look like the type. But that left any one of the other three: Davidson, Dalitz, or Rosenstiel. He guessed Dalitz. Dalitz had more connections than GEC.

'Apparently, there's a one-shot hole they have got there,' Ralston was saying, 'with this enormous tee. Big as a baseball diamond. You can play it as a two-hundred-yard drive over a lake, or as a hundred-and-twenty-five-yard pitch.'

'It sounds interesting.'

'Then it's a match,' said Ralston.

The crowd applauded loudly as the Cubans picked up the first point. Their opponents now retired to the bench behind the eighth-place pair, to await their turn to play again. The first team to reach seven points would be the winner.

But Ralston was already crushing his ticket and dropping it to the floor. He produced a silver cigarette case and waved it at Tom, who shook his head, preferring his own brand. Lighting himself with a matching Dunhill, Ralston stood up and extended his hand.

'It's been a pleasure, Mister Jefferson.'

The two men shook hands.

'Going so soon? The game's just beginning.'

'I have a dinner engagement at eight thirty,' said Ralston, glancing at the chunky gold Girard-Perregaux he wore on his wrist. 'And if I'm not careful I shall be late.'

'I'll be in touch,' said Tom.

'Don't forget my *quiniela exacta*,' said Ralston, and then he was gone.

Tom waited in his seat for a minute or two, and then followed.

Leaving the *frontón*, Ralston walked a couple of blocks south along the

Miami Canal and didn't even glance up as a Transamerica Constellation left MIA with a shattering roar that made Tom glad he hadn't rented a house in Miami Springs. When Tom looked down again Ralston was climbing into a light-blue Cadillac Eldorado Brougham – a car that seemed to contradict everything the man had said about too much chrome and not enough simplicity. With tail fins that towered more than three feet above the sidewalk, the Eldorado was Baroque on wheels.

Tom ran back to where he had parked his own car, although there seemed little reason for haste; he thought it would have been harder following Elvis, whose own pink Cadillac drew crowds wherever it went. Finding the Chevy Bel Air, he vaulted the door, gunned the small-block V8 into life, and then sped off down 31st with an audible squeal of tyres, catching up with Ralston just in time to see him turning south on to 27th Avenue.

With the Eldorado comfortably in his sights, Tom settled down in his seat and took his foot off the gas a little, just in case Ralston was the suspicious type. At a traffic light he let a bus and a Dodge station wagon get in front of him, and lit a cigarette. Then they were moving again.

Miami was a Company town, the largest CIA station in the world, and it was an open secret that Suntan U let the spooks use its campus as a school for espionage. In any other town this might have seemed remarkable, but the CIA was a major source of city revenue, pumping more money into the local economy than all the *pari-mutuel* gambling machines put together. There were as many companies and institutions offering a front for the CIA as there were coconut palms and poinciana trees. It was one of the reasons Tom lived there. That, and the golf, of course.

For a while Tom thought they were heading to the university campus. Or maybe Ralston's golf club. But a little way north of the Biltmore, where 37th Avenue became Douglas Road, Ralston turned east on to 22nd Street, and just a few minutes later the two cars were driving over the Rickenbacker Causeway with the sunlit blue waters of Biscayne bay flickering beneath them.

Ralston drove fast, but it was no effort for Tom to keep pace with the big Cadillac. The Chevy was built for speed rather than the smooth, effort-free driving experience that characterised the Cadillac. The Bel Air was a hot car for a hot date, or so Pat Boone had implied on his weekly TV show for Chevy a few years back when Tom had bought it. Thinking about that always made Tom smile. He tried to imagine the kind of hot date that would have necessitated the handy extras Tom had with him in the car: taped under the driver's seat, a Smith & Wesson .44 Special; and, inside the trunk, underneath the spare tyre, a nine-shot .22 Harrington & Richardson revolver with a two-inch barrel. Elvis didn't look the kind of guy who would have minded that, but somehow Tom didn't think Pat would have approved.

The clock on the Bel Air's dashboard said eight o'clock by the time the blue Cadillac turned on to the exclusive Ocean Drive, where even an undeveloped waterfront lot cost as much as forty thousand, and sighed up to the front of the luxurious Key Biscayne Hotel. Tom cruised past, executed a U-turn, and drew up on the opposite side of Ocean Drive.

There was plenty of space to park even as big a car as the Cadillac, but Ralston handed the keys to the parking valet and, affably acknowledging the doorman's smart salute as though he knew the man well, disappeared inside the hotel. Tom waited while the valet drove the Cadillac somewhere out of sight. It looked very much as though Ralston was staying in the hotel.

When the valet reappeared, Tom hit the gas and turned into the hotel driveway. He parked the Chevy out front himself, walked up to the valet, and nodded back at the car.

'Am I all right there?' he asked, handing the valet an over-generous five-dollar bill.

The valet, who was aged about twenty and Irish, with a dumb Irish face that reeked of tobacco, grinned his immediate assent.

'Don't you worry, sir. I'll watch it for you. Want me to clean the windshield?'

'Yeah, thanks. Listen, I'm supposed to meet a Mister Ralston here.'

'Mister Ralston?' The young Irishman frowned. 'Ralston, you say. Is he a guest of the hotel, d'you think?'

'Silver hair, glasses, drives a light-blue fifty-seven Cadillac Eldorado? Y'know? With the built-in tissue-box, and the gold-finished drinking cups?'

'You mean Mister Rosselli, don't you sir?'

Tom smacked himself on the forehead.

'Mister Rosselli. Of course. That's the name. Where the hell did I get Ralston from?' He shook his head. 'I dunno. I guess I was paying too much attention to that car he drives.'

'He went into the hotel only a few minutes ago, sir.'

'He did, huh? Thanks a lot. You know, this could have been so embarrassing.'

'Don't mention it, sir.'

Tom went to walk through the door, then turned on his heel, grinning sheepishly.

'Pardon me. But Mister Rosselli. His first name *is* John, I suppose.'

'I believe it is, sir, yes.'

'Well, at least I got that right. John. You're sure about that?'

'Oh yes, sir. Mister Rosselli lives here. Most of the time.'

'Thanks. You've been very helpful.'

Inside the cool lobby of the hotel, chattering macaws and cockatoos added to the deliberately tropical atmosphere. Tom walked to the front desk and enquired of the pansy on duty as to Mr Rosselli's whereabouts. Miami wasn't just a spook town. It was a pansy town, too. Only in England could you be a spook and a pansy.

'You know? I think I just saw him walking into the restaurant. Would you like me to have him paged?'

'No, that's okay,' said Tom. He went into the bar and ordered a lime daiquiri.

With Ralston, or Rosselli, safely ensconced in the restaurant, Tom was half-inclined to try and search his room. As usual he carried a simple diamond pick – a piece of flat, cold-rolled steel with a barely perceptible diamond on the tip – in the cuffs of his pants, just the thing to rake the pins in a hotel door lock. But picking took time and it was still a little early in the evening to expect that Rosselli's floor – he didn't doubt that a trip to the hotel garage would have found him the keys to the Eldorado attached to Rosselli's room number – would remain quiet for as long as he would need to open the door. Because

33

he liked to know as much about his potential clients as possible, especially when they were new to him. In Tom's line of business he could not be too careful that he wasn't being set up by a cop, or a federal agent. But there wouldn't have been too many law-enforcement officers who could have afforded the Key Biscayne. Not to mention a thirteen-thousand-dollar Cadillac.

Tom decided to content himself with having discovered Ralston's real name. As he was sure it was. Maybe he had seen John Rosselli on a list of movie credits, but Tom was certain he must have heard that name somewhere before. Maybe Mary would know who he was. He would ask her at breakfast. He finished his drink and drove home.

Mary was painting her nails while watching TV, but as soon as Tom came through the living room door she put down the Revlon bottle on the boomerang coffee table and, waving her hands in the air as if she had burned her fingers, went to turn off the TV. The room darkened a little as the light given off by the illuminated white frame around the screen of the Sylvania Halovision went out, prompting her to switch on the free-standing lamp.

'You don't have to do that,' said Tom, heading toward the small wrought-iron bar that occupied the corner of the room.

'S'okay, I wasn't really watching it. It was just company.'

'You're not usually short of that,' he said pointedly, and poured out some rum. 'You want one?'

'No, thanks, I've just taken a pill.'

'Didn't expect to find you in,' he said, going into the kitchen to fetch some lime juice from the refrigerator.

Mary was a Democratic Party worker at the Miami office, and with the presidential elections less than two months away, she was often working late. Not that this was any different to how it always was. Mary liked to go out. Tom didn't. Mary liked people, too. Tom didn't. Mary was a Chigro – half Chinese, half Negro – born in Kingston, Jamaica. In her it was a spectacularly successful combination for she was as beautiful and athletic as she was intelligent and industrious. Tom had been introduced to her in Japan, while convalescing at the US Navy Hospital in Yokusaka, after his release from a North Korean POW camp. At the time Mary had been working as a hostess in an expensive Tokyo night-club. Just a few weeks later they had married. Seven years later they still got along pretty well, bound together by a powerful physical attraction and a mutual amorality, not to mention their politics.

'I didn't expect to be in myself,' she explained. 'I had a headache. I spent the whole day collating canvass reports.'

Tom found the lime juice and some ice and started back toward the living room, but checked himself in front of the cooker as he felt the heat coming off the Hotpoint oven. A quick glance inside revealed that it was empty.

'You left the oven on,' he called out to her.

'For you,' she said. 'In case you were hungry. There's a TV dinner on the worktop.'

'Thanks.'

Tom drew the tripartite foil container – turkey, gravy, whipped sweet potatoes, and peas – out of the Swanson carton and sniffed it instinctively. Nobody in Florida had forgotten the great TV dinner scare of 1955 when solvent-contaminated chicken dinners had been dumped on the market at rock-bottom prices, but this one smelled okay, and anyway, Tom was hungry. Besides, he liked TV dinners. They reminded him of being in the army. He always liked army chow. He slid the tray into the oven and went back into the sitting room to find Mary reading the novel Rosselli had given him.

'The final words of advice,' she said, reading aloud, 'given to Lord Templeton by the Minister of State for the Colonies had been, "When in any doubt produce a simile from the cricket field." His Excellency remembered that advice when he prepared the speech with which he was to announce the new constitution.' Mary smiled. 'I wouldn't have thought this was your kind of thing at all.'

'No? Well check out the title page.' Tom poured the lime juice into the iced rum and toasted her discovery of the five one-hundred-dollar bills.

'It beats an author signature, I guess,' said Mary.

Tom dropped down on the two-piece pink sofa that occupied the centre of the cherrywood floor. A couple of rattan chairs, some potted palms, and a blond-wood hi-fi console made up the rest of the living room furniture. Round the corner of the L-shaped room was the popsicle table and plastic shell chairs where, sometimes, they ate a meal together. The taste, impeccably modern, was all Mary's. Tom preferred antiques, which Mary hated as a Philistine disliked outsiders.

'Some guy wants me to do a feasibility study. For a contract on Castro.'

'A feasibility study?'

'Those are the words he used.'

'Who is this guy? Vance Packard?' Mary shook her head and sat down beside him. 'And what's he think he's going to do when Castro is dead? Check the Nielsen figures?'

Tom hadn't heard of any of those guys, but he let her talk for a moment before answering the one question he could.

'He calls himself Ralston. But his real name is Rosselli, John Rosselli.' Tom sipped some of his drink, adding by way of explanation, 'I followed him to his hotel and got the low-down from the parking attendant.'

'John Rosselli?' Mary frowned.

'You heard of him?'

'It seems like I ought to have,' she said. 'But don't ask me from where.'

'Pity. I was depending on that memory of yours.' One of the qualities that made Mary such an excellent party-worker was that she possessed a tremendous capacity for remembering names, faces, facts, and figures. Tom was in awe of her memory. She knew things he had forgotten about himself. 'Is it a bad headache?'

'Bad enough. I took some pain killers.'

'You've been working too hard.' Tom began to rub the back of her neck but she was too preoccupied by what he had told her to find much comfort in it.

'It's not that.'

'What then?'

'Every night I go to bed I wonder if any of us are going to be here in the morning,' she said. 'With all the bombs and missiles, the world is dangerous enough as it is. I mean, what would the Russians do if Castro was killed?'

'We just have to try and live our lives as if none of that matters,' said Tom.

'I suppose so.'

Tom put his arms around Mary and hugged her tight, enjoying the scent of her silky hair and her cool body.

'I love you,' he said. 'But you're going to give yourself an ulcer if you start worrying if we're going to be here in the morning and stuff like that. Don't worry about it. Life's complicated enough. Just accept that I'll be here and leave it at that.'

'Okay,' said Mary. She smiled and kissed him on the cheek. She sensed he wanted more but held herself back a little. They were both silent for a minute.

Then Tom said: 'I guess I'd better go and see Alex.'

Mary grimaced. She didn't much care for Alex, nor the interest he took in their lives. He was always turning up, uninvited, unannounced, as if he was checking up on them or something. She supposed it came with the territory – who Alex was and what he did – but that didn't make it any better. About the only thing she appreciated was that he had never tried to make a pass at her. Like most of the other guys she met. Quite a few of whom she even slept with.

'You know? I think I remembered,' she said. 'I think there's a Rosselli who is in the mob.'

Tom thought for a moment about what Rosselli had actually said: that he worked for the government. For the CIA. Absently, he said, 'I wonder if it's the same guy.'

'In your line of work, honey, I doubt that it's any Rosselli selling vacuum cleaners.'

Tom smiled at that. But there were times when he thought Mary's mouth, beautiful though it was, might be a little too smart for her own good.

Alex Goldman was an old friend of Tom's from way back, who now worked for the Federal Bureau of Investigation at the Miami headquarters on Biscayne Boulevard, in northwest Miami. Like most of the agents working there, Alex was concerned with the fight against communism. But he and Tom shared information on a regular basis, about a whole host of subjects that was not necessarily anything to do with commies. So when Tom had eaten his turkey dinner he went out again. Usually, Alex was not a difficult man to find at eleven o'clock at night. Just about every evening when he was in town he could be found in Zissen's Bowery on North Miami Avenue, only a few blocks away from the FBI building.

Zissen's Bowery was the oldest club in Miami, but the Carioca or the Boom Boom Room, it was not. Big hotels, like the Americana or the Fontainebleu, might have succeeded in stealing most of Miami's well-heeled night-club trade, but there were still a few joints that appealed to those who had to get by on a special agent's salary. Places like Zissen's, with sawdust on the floor, pretzels on the bar, and the kind of barman who had no more idea of how to mix a Manhattan than he had of making a Betty Crocker cake. The people who went to Zissen's drank beer and hard liquor, and if they happened to be people like Alex Goldman, they drank them side by side.

Goldman was bigger than Tom with fists the size of bowling balls. His grey hair was crew-cut and he wore a dark cotton suit that was too tight for him and smelled strongly of sweat and pipe-tobacco. The money clip on the bartop in front of him, made out of a silver bullet, was the neatest thing about Goldman and seemed to indicate that he was making an evening of it. Originally from New Orleans, he had the up-tempo drawl of a well-educated if easy-going southerner.

'Well, well, well,' he said, eyeing Tom through a thick cumulus cloud of pipe smoke. 'If it isn't Paladin.'

Tom didn't watch much TV but he knew Goldman was referring to a show on CBS called *Have Gun, Will Travel* that starred Richard Boone, an actor to whom Alex bore a certain resemblance. Tom wasn't in the least bit concerned that a federal agent knew what he did for a living. Federal agents turned a blind eye to all kinds of things in Miami. Especially agents like Alex Goldman, whose own activities as a member of the FBI's Domestic Intelligence Division were in the main illegal.

'How's my favourite spy?' asked Tom, clapping the big man on his Dakota-sized shoulder.

'That fucking movie,' sneered Goldman. 'I hate Bob Hope. The

Road to the Gas Chamber. Now that's one movie I'd like to see him in.'

They ordered some beers and took them to a quiet table in the back.

'What do you know about John Rosselli?' asked Tom.

'Johnny Rosselli,' sneered Goldman. 'Don Giovanni to his guinea friends. He's the mob's number one faggot.'

'He is?' Tom sounded surprised. Then he was surprised that he was surprised. Now that he thought some more about Rosselli – the cologne, the fastidious lips, the manicured fingernails, the Eldorado Brougham with the built-in vanity case, maybe even the fag at the Key Biscayne Hotel – it seemed a little more obvious than before. But he still was not wholly convinced. Sometimes Goldman just said things to provoke people, which was, after all, his main job function. Within the Intelligence Division he ran the FBI's local COINTELPRO, a counter-intelligence programme devised by J. Edgar Hoover to flush out or screw up communists.

Goldman puffed his pipe furiously. 'He was married for a while. To some movie actress broad. June Lang, I think her name was. But it didn't take. Anyway, that's why he likes it here in Miami. I'm told it can get quite hot in Vegas and LA, so it isn't the fucking sunshine that brings his guinea ass down here, you can be sure of that. Just don't go to the can with the guy, that's my advice.' Goldman chuckled his way into a short fit of coughing.

'Mob guy, huh? He told me he's working for the government. For the Company.'

'Now and then, mob and Company interests coincide and they share resources. Like in Guatemala. The Don's been in and out of Guatemala since fifty-six, fixing things for Carlos Marcello. He runs most of the things down in G City. Anyway, fixing things for Marcello also fixed things for the Company. But it's interesting that he actually said that. Give it to me again. Like his exact words, Paladin.'

'He said he was working for the government,' shrugged Tom. 'Later on, when I referred to him working for the Company, he didn't contradict me.'

Goldman nodded thoughtfully. 'I guess it would figure. Rosselli's one well-connected queer, I'll say that much for him. He's always been a kind of liaison man in Hollywood and Vegas. Between the big bosses: Meyer Lansky, Sam Giancana, Santos Trafficante and Marcello. Back in the thirties and forties he was Capone's man. Then Ben Siegel's sidekick.'

'According to Rosselli, he was a Hollywood producer for a while.'

'That's one word for it. But he was always Chicago's man out there. Him and Joe Kennedy. The Don and some other muscle took over the labour unions in Hollywood and started to put the squeeze on the big studios. Columbia. Warner Brothers. MGM. They paid up or there was a fucking strike. As simple as that. The amazing thing was that the Bureau managed to make a case against him. Rosselli and some of the other guineas involved. It doesn't happen very often. Sometimes I think Hoover must be on the take himself. That or they've got something on him. Like he's the same kind of fruit as Rosselli, for instance. Take the Bureau here in Miami. We've got two hundred agents handling the investigation of so-called communists in the city. And just three who are concerned with organised crime.

'Anyway, back to the Don, fifteen, twenty years ago. There was this guy named Willie Bioff.' Having pronounced the name 'Buy-off', Goldman grinned. 'Is that a good name for a chiselling rat who is helping to put the squeeze on you, or what? The mob had made him president of the biggest motion picture union out in Hollywood, and it was him the feds managed to put the squeeze on right back. Willie Bioff ratted on the Don and some other colourful friends of his, and then lived long enough to change his name, move to Phoenix, and get blown to pieces by a car bomb. Don Giovanni and those other movie fans, they went to jail. Not that the Don did much fucking time, you understand. Couple of years at most. Someone fixed it for him to have an early release. LAPD most likely. When Siegel got himself murdered it kind of left a vacuum for all the cops on the take. So Rosselli came out and cut himself a deal. Parker, the LA police chief, virtually fingered the Don's only rival for the territory. A Jew named Mickey Cohen. See, Parker disliked Jews about as much as he disliked niggers, and felt more comfortable dealing with the guineas.'

Goldman re-lit his pipe and blew out a long cloud of smoke.

'The Don was quite a talent-spotter, too, let me tell you. Still is. He's helped a lot of careers in Hollywood and Vegas. A part in a movie here, a season at the Sands there. A lot of big stars owe that guinea sonofabitch.'

'What is his connection with Cuba?' asked Tom.

'Cuba is to the mob what Detroit is to General Motors. And Rosselli is to the mob what Christian Herter is to the White House. The Don's kind of like a Secretary of State for the Mafia. The olive oil in the Cosa Nostra machine. Would that the Secretary of State was able to achieve so much. Christian Herter's a fucking amateur next to the Don. Lansky and Trafficante have got a problem with Castro in Cuba? Let's speak to our roving ambassador of organised crime. Maybe the Don can come up with a solution. A proposal. Some contacts. Pull in a few favours. Come up with a plan.' Goldman toasted Tom with a bottle of beer. 'I guess that's where you come in, Paladin. Who do they want dropped from the team?'

'Castro.'

'Well good for you.'

'And his brother.'

'Wouldn't that just suit everyone?' said Goldman. 'The mob, the CIA, the big corporations, the government. Everyone except the Cuban people, I guess. So the mob and the Company have cut a deal on this, have they? I guess it makes a lot of sense. If it can be done.' He paused and inspected the cherrywood bowl of his pipe before re-lighting what tobacco remained in there.

'That's what Rosselli's paying me five hundred bucks to find out.'

'Find out all you can, if I were you.'

'Sure. I'm on it. S'why I'm talking to you.'

'Can it be done, do you think?'

Tom lit a cigarette and smoked it silently, his face a study of indecision.

'Any fool can stick his fucking head in a lion's mouth,' he said finally. 'The trick is taking it out again.'

'True.'

'But, why not? It's not like Cuba's closed for business, or anything. The American embassy may have pulled down the shutters, but the ferry still sails from Key West, and Pan Am still flies in and out of Havana.' He shrugged. 'And Castro's the kind of man who likes to make a lot of public speeches. So, yeah. I'd say it can be done.'

41

'Whatever you need, just let me know.'

'Thanks, man.'

'By the way, how is Mary?'

'Not sleeping too good.'

'I find that hard to believe. She takes enough fucking pills.'

'She keeps thinking the atom bomb's going to go off while she's in bed.'

'Best place to be if it does.'

'And she's busy with the election, of course.'

'Of course. Who's going to win?'

'It'll be close.'

'Oh, for sure, but let's hope Kennedy, right?'

Tom shrugged, noncommittally.

'For Mary's sake, anyway,' argued Goldman. 'She's put a lot into this. And after November she might be well placed to get something valuable out of it.'

'Kennedy's no different from Nixon,' grumbled Tom. 'He just sweats less and owns a better razor. But Mary.' Tom shook his head, and stubbed his cigarette out angrily. 'Sometimes I think maybe she's in love with the guy. You should see her when he's on TV. It's like he's Cary fucking Grant, or something. And the rest of the time, she's breaking my balls about his style and his good looks. It's Jack Kennedy this and it's Jack fucking Kennedy that. I tell you Alex, I'll be glad when this is all over.'

'If I didn't know you better, I'd say you were jealous.'

'Me, jealous? Of Jack Kennedy? Come on.'

'Sure. Why not? She wouldn't be the first party-worker to fall for the candidate. S'probably easier for her to do her job that way.' Alex grinned. 'You really don't like him, do you?'

Tom tried to hold back a sheepish smile and then, letting it go at last, shook his head. 'I'd like to blow his fucking brains out,' he said quietly.

'Why? What is it that makes you dislike him so much?'

Tom thought for a moment and, remembering Brando's line in *The Wild One*, grinned and said, 'What have you got?'

42

3

The Big Barbudo

'Though we have a reputation for talking at great length, the assembly need not worry. We shall do our best to be brief.'

Old habits die hard, and in the event, Castro's speech to the General Assembly was, at over three hours, the longest in United Nations history. The Indian Prime Minister, Nehru, fell asleep and was woken only by the assembly president using his gavel to reprimand the longwinded speaker for saying that the two United States presidential candidates, Nixon and Kennedy, lacked brains.

Tom had read the report in the newspaper with interest. Castro's use of the royal 'we' seemed to indicate a Mussolini-sized ego. He didn't disagree with Castro's historical account of US–Cuban relations, but he did question the wisdom of referring to JFK as an illiterate and ignorant millionaire. What interested Tom most of all was the unscripted duration of Dr Castro's address. By all accounts three hours was hardly unusual for the Big Barbudo. Back home in Cuba, speeches lasting four or five hours were not uncommon. These were delivered to every kind of audience, too: sports coaches, doctors, agronomists, dentists, film-makers, and schoolteachers. It was clear that the bearded one liked the sound of his voice as much as he enjoyed a good cigar.

Tom wondered if the point of Castro's frequent speech-making was not to mobilise the masses, but to bore them into submission. Either way, a man who seized every opportunity to speak to an audience, no matter how large or small, and at such interminable length, was an assassin's dream. The wonder was that a marksman – some disaffected Batistiano, or dispossessed landowner's son – hadn't already tried. Of course Castro had his posse of revolutionary army bodyguards to protect him. But Tom, who was Cuban on his father's side, knew Cubaños well enough to guess the real worth of that kind of protection. After all, it wasn't as if the rebel army had defeated the regime of Fulgencio Batista in some great battle, merely that the old dictator's troops had refused to fight, preferring to stay in their barracks.

Tom had always felt that this was the real Cuban character: guerrillas more interested in fine cigars than sticks of dynamite, and soldiers who neglected their posts to watch the World Series on television. While about the only belief that united Cuban men was their hatred of homosexuals. Tom wondered if this was the real reason Johnny Rosselli himself wasn't in Havana making a feasibility study for a hit on Castro. Because from everything Alex Goldman had told Tom about the Don he was more than equal to the task of how and where to kill a man, having murdered as many as a dozen men during his thirty-year mob career.

Not that Tom minded very much. He welcomed this excuse to return to Cuba. He'd been too long away.

Tom felt the Cole Porter rhythm of Havana the minute he stepped off the plane at Rancho Boyeros airport. It felt good to be back in Cuba, to be speaking Spanish again, to hear the endless clamour of automobile horns, to be bargaining for his taxi fare into the centre of town, and to find himself offered a girl from a selection of photographs made available immediately he sat in the backseat by the mule-faced *jinitero* driving. Already enjoying his trip, Tom amused himself by having the driver describe each girl in obscenely intimate detail. The revolution did not seem to have changed things all that much. The Big Barbudo might have announced an end to gambling and prostitution but the taxi-driver still managed to make Havana sound like a sexual

Disneyland. No government in history, insisted the driver, had ever succeeded in putting an end to the oldest profession.

'You here on business?'

'Yes, business.'

'What kind of business?'

'If I get time I was hoping maybe to catch one of the Maximum Leader's speeches.'

The taxi-driver twisted around in his seat, his face wearing a horrified expression, as if Tom had just admitted that he was a *maricón*.

'Are you a journalist?'

'No, I'm just curious, that's all.'

Shaking his head the driver looked back at the *carretera central*. 'The most beautiful girls in the world,' he muttered, 'and the American wants to hear El Fidel give a speech.'

'Well, maybe not the whole speech,' allowed Tom. 'I hear he speaks for quite a long time.'

'That he does,' said the driver. 'And, as it happens, you're in luck, because he's going to speak on Wednesday night. Tomorrow. To tell us about what a lousy time he had in New York and all the skinny American women he fucked.'

'And where will that take place?'

'The same place as usual. From the balcony of the presidential palace. Where are you staying?'

In order to avoid paying more Tom had merely instructed the driver to take him to Central Park, on the western side of old Havana. Having a fare who was staying at one of the better hotels would have demanded that the driver try and screw even more money out of the rich *yanqui*.

'The Inglaterra,' answered Tom.

The driver chuckled sadistically as if enjoying the prospect of the penny-pinching gringo's discomfort.

'Then, without doubt, you will be able to hear every word of the Prime Minister's speech, whether you like it or not. With or without your window closed.' The driver laughed again as he thought about this some more. 'For your sake I hope he makes an early start.'

He was still laughing when he dropped Tom on Acrea del Louvre,

45

where a crowd of local youths were smoking cheap cigars and admiring a 1957 Packard that was parked in front of the Inglaterra Hotel.

Tom checked in and asked for a quiet room. The desk clerk, a short, almost dwarfish man, with a goatee beard, considered the question with a weary politeness.

'The quietest room I can give you is in the centre of the building,' he said, hardly looking at Tom.

'Okay, I'll take that.'

'But then, it has no window.'

Tom smiled patiently. Outside in the street it was touching ninety-five, with eighty-two per cent humidity.

'How about a room that's a little bit quiet but that also has a window?' he said, handing the clerk a couple of pesos.

'I think we can accommodate you very comfortably on the south side of the hotel,' smiled the clerk, and waved the porter toward him.

Tom's room, overlooking San Rafael, a busy pedestrian street, was cool and dark, at least until the porter threw open the shutters. Stepping out on to the little balcony, Tom looked down on the street with its many shops and bars and sighed loudly.

'This is a quiet room?'

'Quieter than the ones overlooking the park,' said the porter, a high-yellow, coloured boy of about eighteen.

Tom stared at the exorbitantly baroque façade of the Gran Teatro opposite and signalled his defeat with a slow nod. At each of the building's four corners was a tower, topped by a dark marble angel reaching gracefully on tiptoe for heaven, and through the open window opposite he could see a similarly hued dancer, standing beside a wall-bar and achieving much the same sort of pose.

Joining Tom on the balcony to collect his tip, the porter saw the girl and quickly noted Tom's interest.

'I know that girl,' he said. 'She's a dancer.'

'That much I guessed,' said Tom, handing over a few centavos.

'A proper dancer,' insisted the boy. 'Not like those horses in the chorus at the Tropicana.'

'I kind of like those chorus girls,' said Tom. But he continued to stare at the girl opposite.

46

'I could introduce you to her, if you like.'

'You? Know her?'

'Sure,' said the boy, flexing himself.

'What's your name, kid?' he asked.

'Jorge Montaro.'

'And her's is?'

'Celia.'

'Celia, huh?' said Tom, liking the boy's style. So far the boy hadn't promised him the fuck of his life and Tom wondered how long he could keep this particular novelty in progress. 'So what's this Celia like?'

'A very good family. A very respectable girl. An educated person, you know?'

Now he really was intrigued. This was true salesmanship. Tom smiled and handed over several banknotes. 'I'd like to. Bring her up. Bring a bottle of rum, too.'

'And for the lady? Some champagne perhaps?'

Tom started to laugh. 'Get outta here. No, wait. One more thing, Jorge. Can you find me a firecracker?'

'A firecracker?'

'You know. A cherry bomb. As big as you can get.'

Jorge shrugged. 'I think so.'

'Only don't tell anyone.'

Jorge frowned and shook his head as if he wouldn't dream of such a thing, but Tom could see that he desperately wanted to ask why the American needed a firecracker.

'It's a surprise,' said Tom, and waved Jorge out of the door.

Tom didn't watch what took place in the dance studio opposite. Instead he closed the shutters and lay down on his bed. He strongly suspected that Jorge didn't know the girl from Eve and that right now he was trying to set her up as his own *jinitera*. Assuming she needed the money – and nearly everyone in Cuba needed money: most of the American employers had left the island – then it was just possible that he might succeed. Necessity was both the mother and father of all invention in the new Cuba, and probably the aunt and uncle as well. But when it came to overcoming local shortages nothing more was necessary than American dollars. He just wished he could have heard Jorge's pitch.

Opening the carton of king-size Chesterfields he had bought at the airport, Tom smoked a cigarette and found his thoughts turning to his own Cuban father, wondering if he was back in Cuba, or still in Miami somewhere. It was years since they had seen each other.

Following the Great War, which had left most of the baseball teams with an acute shortage of players, Roberto Casas had been brought from Cuba to Philadelphia, to play ball for the Phillies. Casas had been a promising left-hand pitcher until the loss of a thumb in a knife-fight had ended his career before it had hardly started. But not before Tom's father had met and impregnated his mother, Mildred Jefferson, during the Phillies' spring training in St Petersburg. They had never married – not least because Roberto already had a wife back in Santiago de Cuba – and Tom had been brought up mostly by his mother and his aunt. Yet somehow he'd seen a fair bit of his father during his childhood. It had been his father who had taught Tom shooting and Spanish, in that order. But since the Korean War, he'd seen nothing of the old man, and from what he had heard the guy was in and out of Cuba like cigar smoke. For all Tom knew, his father was dead. And maybe for all he cared, too. He hadn't much use for a father any more. Nor for that matter a mother: on the few occasions he saw her, at the old people's home in Intercession City, he wondered that he was related to her at all.

Tom awoke with a start, and sensed that there was someone outside his door. Hearing a knock he shook his head clear of sleep, sprang off the all-too-noisy bed and went to open the door. It was Jorge, with the rum and a broad smile. He walked into the room, and was followed, at a shy distance, by a beautiful negress.

'This is Celia,' said Jorge.

'Hullo Celia. I'm Tom.'

'Pleased to meet you, Tom.'

Celia, wearing a tight, sleeveless blue dress, matching high-heels, and smelling strongly of sweat and perfume, smiled pleasantly and walked over to the window where she threw open the shutters, stepped out on to the balcony and leaned forward on the rusting wrought-iron balustrade. Tom felt his heart beat loudly. She was the most beautiful woman. Watching her stare into the studio she had been conjured from he realised that the way she was standing reminded him of something. He tried to remember. Yes, there had been a picture by Salvador Dali, a print he had seen on some hood's wall in Atlantic City. Quite a suggestive picture as he recalled it now. Something about a woman being fucked up the ass by her own chastity, he seemed to think.

Tom drew Jorge into the bathroom and handed him ten pesos, which was about a quarter of the Inglaterra room rate. Jorge pocketed the note and explained that he would return later with the firecracker. Then he left them alone.

Tom sat down in the room's solitary armchair and poured himself a drink. Celia turned and came back into the room, closing the shutters behind her. The sun painted a series of pale stripes across her light brown face so that she looked like a mulatto dancer, a *santiaguero* woman from Santiago.

Celia sat down on the edge of the bed and pressed it experimentally. 'So you like the ballet, eh?'

Tom nodded. He had seen a ballet in New York once, when he'd been tailing a guy he'd agreed to kill, and hadn't thought much of it, which was probably why he couldn't remember the name of it.

'Some,' he said.

'Like what, for instance?'

'Tosca,' he said finally.

'Tosca is an opera,' she said. 'By Puccini.' She folded her arms and shrugged. 'Not that it matters. There's not much of either happening in Cuba right now. But I try to stay in shape.'

'I know. I saw you.' It occurred to Tom that maybe he was supposed to see her; that the whole thing was meant to look like his idea, when it was actually a regular *jinitero* thing going between Celia and Jorge. Not that he really cared much either way. 'You're in pretty good shape, I'd say,' he said, toasting her with the Havana Club he was drinking.

'I'm putting on weight.'

'A man likes a little meat on the bone.'

'It gives him something to chew on, eh?'

'Makes for better eating, yeah.'

'I wouldn't know. I live on coffee, and cigarettes.'

'Would you like a drink?'

'No thanks. They put bacteria in it, you know? To give it flavour.'

Tom scrutinised his glass and then drained it.

'It works,' he said. 'How would you like to come out to dinner with me, tonight?'

'Sounds good.'

'As a matter of fact, I'd welcome your company tomorrow as well.'

'Wednesday's always a quiet day for me.'

'Naturally, I'll pay you to keep me company. How does fifty dollars sound? Twenty-five in advance.' Tom took out his dollar clip and thumbed five bills into her hand. He knew he was paying way over the local rate but he wanted to ensure the girl's loyalty, and perhaps even her silence.

'It's generous.' But Celia still handled the notes with some suspicion before putting them in her purse. 'Very generous.' She threw the purse on to the bed and before he could stop her she had stood up and hauled the dress over her head to reveal her nakedness.

Tom felt his chest tighten. Her body was even more magnificent than he had supposed. But this was not what he wanted. At least not right now. Tom didn't much care to pay for sex. Which was why he didn't mind paying too much, in the hope that it would help her to forget about money. If he did go to bed with her he needed it to feel a little less business-like, and a little more because she wanted to. A delusion of course, and an expensive one – he knew that. But what else was having money good for if not to indulge in a few expensive delusions now and again? He picked up her dress and handed it to her.

'Have you got an evening dress?'

'When the evening's worth it, sure.'

'Meet me back here at seven.'

'Is something the matter?' Celia looked puzzled. 'I thought—'

Tom smiled and shook his head. 'Nothing's wrong,' he said. 'And you needn't think I'm a *maricón*. I'm not. I'm as hard for you as the holy cross, sweetheart. But right now it's just the boat I need, not the whole fishing trip.'

*

The last time he had been in Cuba, almost four years before, he'd murdered a man. As it happened he would have murdered three if he'd had the chance. Back in October 1956 he had been contracted to kill Colonel Antonio Blanco Rico, the chief of military intelligence, as he and his wife left a Havana night-club. Tom had waited on a rooftop across the street and shot him through the heart. But when he tried to collect the balance of his fee, his clients – two senior officers in the Cuban military police – had tried to kill him, and Tom had barely escaped with his own life. The two officers, General Canizares and Colonel Miguel Zayas, had used Rico's assassination as a pretext for an attack on the Haitian embassy, where a number of Cuban opposition leaders had sought political asylum. A gun-battle had ensued during which General Canizares had been killed, leaving Tom with just the one score to settle.

Months after the revolution he had learned that Zayas had escaped being tried as a Batistiano and the inevitable firing squad that resulted from such a charge, and was now working as head of security at the Hotel Nacional in Vedado, the largely middle-class suburb of Havana where the university and most of the formerly Mafia-run hotels were situated. And when Celia showed up at the Inglaterra wearing a beautiful sequinned black cocktail dress, it was to the Nacional that Tom told their taxi-driver to take them.

He did not wear a tuxedo. In Havana those days were gone. People dressed down or got trouble. A woman could still wear more or less what she wanted, but only a man who was a fool wore evening dress. So like other Cubans who were out on the town, Tom wore a white short-sleeved shirt outside his pants, *guayabera*-style. This helped him to blend in, and to conceal a Smith & Wesson Centennial Airweight inside the waistband of his beige linen pants. Tom was expecting the evening to end with a bang. And then maybe, if he and Celia got along, the whimper, too.

Heading west along the Maleçon, with the seafront to their right, it wasn't long before they were among the cream-coloured villas and high-rise hotels of Vedado. The suburb always reminded Tom of South Beach in Miami, just as the Nacional with its distinctive twin towers and Italianate façade always put him in mind of the Breakers

Hotel in Palm Beach. Until Castro, Cuba had always looked like Florida's backyard.

Like the nearby Riviera Hotel and the Hilton – now renamed the Habana Libre – the Nacional had been seized by the revolutionary government just three months before. But back in 1956 the Nacional's casino had been operated by Meyer Lansky. Further up the road, the Capri had been run by Santos Trafficante and fronted by none other than movie tough-guy George Raft. The following year, Lansky had opened the Riviera at a cost of fourteen million dollars. Then Castro turned up. Some of the mob-run casinos in hotels like the Deauville, the Sevilla-Biltmore and the Commodoro had been destroyed by rioters celebrating day one of the revolution; the rest, allowed to remain open, but forbidden to gamblers, had just drifted into a limbo of desuetude before they closed as well.

The extraordinary thing was that the mob had taken so long to put out a contract on Castro, thought Tom as the taxi drew up outside the Nacional. There were often times when he considered organised crime was hardly deserving of the title.

Apart from the absence of an operating casino, inside the Nacional was much as he remembered it. And they still served the best daiquiris on the island. He and Celia drank several, which put both of them in a good mood for an excellent dinner of Morro crab, roast pork with rice and beans, and fried sweet bananas on the side. As soon as they had ordered candied papaya for dessert Tom excused himself and went out of the dining room.

It took only a moment or two to use the phone in the Spanish-tiled lobby and check that Zayas was in the hotel. Tom recognised the former policeman's lisping Oriente accent the minute he came to the phone. It is hard to forget the voice of a man who has done his best to destroy you. Giving his best imitation of a native Cuban, Tom told Zayas that he had Luis Rodriguez, the Minister of the Interior, calling from the Habana Libre – from where members of the revolutionary government conducted their affairs of state – and asked him to hold on for a minute while the minister came to the phone. From the lobby Tom had a good view of the Nacional's telephone operator, and it required only a glance as he passed the switchboard to see that his call had been connected to suite 919 on the penthouse floor.

Tom went along the corridor to the self-service elevator and rode up to the seventh floor. When the elevator had gone down again he walked along to the service stairs to climb the last two floors. This gave him time to take out the .38 from under his shirt. Hammerless, so as not to catch on clothing, weighing only twelve ounces, and with a three-and-a-half-inch barrel, the Airweight was the assassin's preferred choice of revolver. It fired just five shots, but each with sufficient stopping power that it hardly needed six. Tom thumbed off the safety and, peering out of the stairwell, looked out on to the ninth floor, but there was no one in sight. Suite 919 was almost immediately opposite the service elevator up to the roof terrace. Tom listened at the door and, hearing only the sound of a television set, knocked quietly.

'*Con permeso*,' he said, as if he might have been room service.

A voice answered with military vigour. '*Entrar!*'

Gun pointed, Tom slid into the room.

Telephone receiver still in hand, Zayas was watching baseball on television. It looked like a game from Cerro Stadium – the Sugar Kings versus a team Tom couldn't identify. Which no doubt explained why the Big Barbudo, a keen fan, had chosen the following night to speak to the people of Cuba. The suite was the size of a polo field with a worn leather sofa as big as a Pontiac and an enormous white jellyfish of a chandelier. The kind of suite that might once have accommodated Churchill, Brando or any of the other larger-than-life personalities who had once stayed at the Nacional.

Zayas looked surprised to see Tom and the gun in his hand. Almost as surprised as Tom was to see that Zayas was sitting in a wheelchair.

'Put the phone down,' Tom ordered.

Zayas coolly did as he was told and wheeled himself round to face his assailant. 'That was you, I suppose,' he said. 'On the phone, just now.'

He looked heavier than Tom remembered. With his thin, mascara-line moustache, coffee-bean eyes, flattened nose, and Dunlopillo belly, he reminded Tom of Joe Louis after he retired from the ring, and lost all his money. Tom had seen the boxer once working as a shill at the blackjack tables in Vegas, a burnt-out shell of the Brown Bomber who had beaten Max Schmeling in less than one round.

'Where'd you get the wheels?' asked Tom.

'I took a bullet in the spine at San Domingo. With Cantillo. Before he caved in.'

'Too bad for you he didn't cave in earlier.' Tom jerked the gun at the door. 'Get rolling.'

'Are we going somewhere?' Zayas pushed himself across the checkerboard floor. He knew better than to argue with a man like Tom. The best he figured he could do now was to keep talking.

In the corridor outside the door to his suite he paused, waiting for instructions. Tom summoned the service elevator, and when it came pushed the wheelchair and its occupant inside with the heel of his shoe. They rode up to the roof terrace.

'I thought we'd make sure we weren't disturbed,' he said, wheeling Zayas out into the warm night air. It was breezy out on the terrace and the air smelled strongly of the sea, but a six-foot-high ornamented parapet meant that there was not much of a view without standing on an overturned beer-crate.

'It's a nice evening,' said Zayas. 'Are you planning to shoot me up here? Is that your plan?'

'Could be,' grunted Tom.

'That would be foolish,' said Zayas. 'For one thing I can give you the money I owe you, with interest.' He pulled nervously at the little brightly coloured bow-tie he was wearing. 'There's a safe at my house in Varadero. Why don't we go there now? It wouldn't take long.'

Tom pulled a face and shook his head. 'I don't think so,' he said, spinning the .38 in his hand with purposeful dexterity.

'You wouldn't shoot a man in a wheelchair.' Zayas spoke with an almost confident disbelief.

Tom drew a deep breath and glanced up at the moon as if considering what Zayas had said, but merely thinking that he had eaten too much at dinner. Then he said, 'I guess you're right at that.'

Zayas smiled as if he had known it all along. It was enough of a smile to make Tom wish their conversation ended. No doubt Zayas had smiled just such a smile when he had ordered Tom's death, and the thought of that was enough to provoke in Tom an explosion of rum-fired rage. With a loud, feral curse he whipped the .38

hard across the Cuban's sweaty smiling bullfrog face, sending him sprawling on the terrace floor.

'You're not in a fucking wheelchair now,' he snarled. 'How do you like that, you cock-sucker? Hey? How do you like that? Hey, *coño.*' Tom stamped at Zayas's head. 'I'm talking to you.' He stamped again, as if he had been trying to crush a cockroach under his heel. 'Hey, *cabrón.*'

Groaning loudly, the ex-military policeman tried to protect himself, in vain.

'*Estafador,*' Tom hissed, and kicked him again, but with little apparent effect. The man's arms and shoulders were so well padded with fat, he couldn't seem to get near his head.

Zayas wriggled up against the parapet prompting Tom to put down his gun, pick up one of his victim's useless legs and drag him away from whatever protection the wall afforded him.

'*Hijo de puta.*'

Finally, Tom picked up the wheelchair, raised it over his head as if he had been King Kong, and then brought it down hard on the neck and shoulders of Zayas. He did this twice more, until Zayas stopped moving. But he was still breathing. Tom took off his shirt, laid it neatly across the parapet, and turned Zayas on to his back. It took a minute or so to manoeuvre the unconscious man into a seated position and another minute to lift him, fireman-style, on to his bare back.

'Double-cross me, would you?' muttered Tom as, standing on the upturned Bucanero crate, he managed to lift Zayas on to the top of the parapet.

Pausing for breath, he took in the ocean-side view, wondering why they didn't make the parapet a little lower. The Havana coastline curved back on itself like a crab-claw. Across the bay, the lighthouse in front of the El Morro fortress signalled its lonely vigil, as if in defiance of the vastly superior force of its enemy across the Gulf of Mexico. Once it had been the English who had wanted to control the island, and now it was the *yanquis.* Only history showed that Cubans were not so easily pushed around.

Tom smiled grimly and shoved Zayas off the parapet. The body fell ten floors, through a clump of tall palm trees at the back of the hotel, and then disappeared into the darkness. Tom spat after him and, having collected his gun and his shirt, rode the elevator down to the first floor.

Back in the lounge he paused in front of one of the show-cases that were full of imported items supposedly for sale – Radiac shirts, Brunex superfine mohair cloths, Floris soaps, Queen Ann whisky, and Mappin & Webb silverware – to check his appearance in the dusty glass. Straightening his hair he walked back into the dining room.

'You took your time,' said Celia.

Tom glanced at his wristwatch. He'd been gone for less than fifteen minutes.

'I had to make a quick telephone call,' he said, lighting up a Chesterfield.

'In Cuba?' Celia laughed. 'That explains why you were so long. For a moment I thought you'd dumped me.'

Tom smiled and kissed her hand.

'I'm not so easy to get rid of,' he said.

'I don't doubt it,' said Celia, and dabbed at his cheek with her napkin. 'Blood.'

Tom glanced at the tiny spot of red on the napkin and then wiped his face with his own.

'That's all,' she declared. 'It must have been a very heated call. And if anyone should ask? The police?'

'They're not interested in this.'

'But if they should be?'

Tom shrugged. 'I went to the men's room. I was gone for five minutes.'

'What if they ask the waiter?'

Tom glanced around the near-empty restaurant.

'What waiter?'

'You're right. He's not been near this table since you left to do whatever it was that you did.' She helped herself to one of his Chesterfields. 'Just promise me you won't tell me what that was. I'm quite scared enough of you as it is.'

'Why should you be scared of me?'

'I don't know, but I am. Instinct, I suppose.'

'Instinct?'

'I'm descended from slaves. This house-girl knows to do whatever the master tells her or risk a good whipping.'

'Is there such a thing as a good whipping?'

'Depends on who's doing the whipping, master.'

'I like an old-fashioned girl,' observed Tom. 'Shall we leave? I've a sudden urge to make you disobedient.'

The next day Celia accompanied Tom on a walking tour east of the Prado, Havana's favourite promenade. Two roads, Agramonte and Zuluetta, paralleled the Prado and sloped gently down to the waterfront and the fort of San Salvador de la Punta, and between these was a wide open park that led up to an equestrian statue of one of Castro's revolutionary predecessors, Maximo Gomez. At the south end of the plaza, beyond a semi-derelict watchtower that was a fragment of the old city walls, was the presidential palace. This enormous, wedding-cake of a building, with its domed cupola, high arched windows, gap-toothed colonnade, and Tiffany interior had been home to all of Cuba's presidents since 1917. Castro preferred to stay elsewhere: on the twenty-third floor of the Habana Libre; at an apartment on 11th Street, in Vedado, or on 22nd, in an apartment formerly owned by Santos Trafficante; there was even a villa in Miramar, and a small fisherman's cottage in the port of Cojímar. But the prime minister still spoke to his people from the twenty-foot-high balcony on the front of the palace's ornate, almost ecclesiastical façade. Even now the television cameras and radio microphones were setting up to broadcast the Big Barbudo's speech that night.

Tom's sniper's eyes took in the layout of the open plaza. Immediately to the west of the palace stood the old Corona cigar factory, a four-storey Italianate building, pale green, which was the way Tom had felt the last time he smoked a large cigar. The factory's rooftop and corner windows commanded an excellent view of the balcony, but as a vantage point it suffered the drawback of being a little obvious. Still, on the west side of the plaza, a pair of eight-storey terracotta-coloured apartment blocks immediately opposite the factory looked a better bet, with a wide variety of windows, balconies, and different-level rooftops to choose from. Further north were a pair of white office buildings, from the upper storeys of which Tom felt he could easily pick out a target on the presidential balcony. But it seemed probable that all four buildings would host a large number of spectators for any speech by the prime minister. The use of any such apartment would undoubtedly have required that Tom first kill the occupant, with all the risks that such a course of action entailed.

The eastern side of the plaza offered fewer sniping possibilities, which, to Tom's eyes, made it more interesting. The fewer possible vantage points, the less likely it would be that anyone would decide to look there first, in the event of Castro's assassination. One eight-storey apartment block – plenty of windows – stood north of a church immediately to the east of the palace. But it was the church, the Iglesia del Santa Angel Custodio, atop a rock known as Angel Hill, that interested Tom most of all. This neo-Gothic church, with its winter forest of white pinnacles, looked like a better prospect for a concealed shot at the balcony. A man might easily hide in such a petrified white forest.

Tom and Celia both crossed themselves as they passed through the entrance on Cuarteles.

'I never figured you for a tourist,' remarked Celia, watching Tom's keen eyes take in the statues and the stained-glass windows.

'Me? My middle name is Baedeker.'

'So does it interest you that José Marti was baptised here?'

'I'll make a note of that. Another revolutionary.'

Celia shrugged. 'It's what happens when you need a revolution.' She looked around the mahogany interior and sighed her admiration. 'It's beautiful, isn't it?'

Tom pointed up at the painted ceiling. 'How do we get up the tower?'

'This way,' she said, leading. 'It's not the original. That was toppled during the last century. By a hurricane.'

The two-storey tower provided what looked like an easy access to the rooftop of the church, from the rear of which Tom thought he could kneel behind one of the candle-shaped pinnacles to make his shot. He took several photographs. A distance of less than one hundred yards separated church from palace. It was not a difficult bit of shooting in the daytime. But at night, with a southerly breeze off the Gulf of Mexico – or, for that matter, a westerly off the Bay of

Havana – it was a shot that would require quite a heavy load, a bullet like Sierra's 168-grain Matchking. Probably the balcony would be floodlit, so there would be no problem with the scope; during the Korean War Tom had hit head-size targets at one hundred yards with only one second of illumination. He was confident he could make the shot. It was the set-up he didn't like.

Escaping from the church rooftop with the plaza full of G2 – the Cuban Intelligence Service – and soldiers would not be easy. Could he dress up as a priest perhaps? Unlike the mob, the Catholic Church was still free to work its racket, and there were plenty of priests in evidence throughout Havana. Surely no one would suspect a priest. Tom had some reservations about the wisdom of shooting from the church. But it looked like a safer proposition than working out of one of the apartment buildings, or the cigar factory.

Outside, on the steps of the church, Tom took some more photographs, although in Celia's eyes he seemed quite unimpressed with her hometown's famous landmarks. He used a superwide Haselblad single-reflex fitted with a thirty-eight-millimetre lens that gave a ninety-degree angle over the plaza. It was hardly a typical camera for a tourist, she thought, even an American. She began to suggest some of the other sights that were to be seen in old Havana.

'Would you like to see the Columbus Cathedral? He's not buried there any more, but it's still worth seeing. It's only a short distance from here.'

Tom grunted and took another photograph of the plaza and its buildings, his mind still fizzing with marksmanship and ballistics.

Threading her arm through his, she said, 'Or maybe you would like to take me back to your hotel room? I enjoyed it last night, although my behind is still a little sore.'

Tom smiled vaguely. 'The Hilton,' he said abruptly. 'The Habana Libre, or whatever it's called now. I think I'd like to go there.'

'You want to go and see a hotel?'

'Come on. Let's find a taxi.'

Celia shrugged and followed Tom down the steps of the church. It was true, he spoke very good Spanish, even looked a little Hispanic, but he was, she reflected sadly, still a *yanqui*, with a *yanqui*'s small horizons. In spite of all the beautiful and historic buildings Havana had to offer the tourist, he still preferred to go and see another deluxe *yanqui* hotel and no doubt marvel at the expense of such opulence and luxury. She would never understand Americans.

Just as surprising to Celia's mind was Tom's desire to hear the Maximum Leader speak in public. Like most Cuban women of her age, Celia had got over her early infatuation with Fidel Castro. Back in January 1959 she had been in the Plaza to hear him make his very first speech to the people of Havana following a meeting with President Urrutia – the only time the Prime Minister had made a short speech. If only he had held on to that brevity. Just a few months later Castro had made a speech on television that had lasted for seven hours, without a break. Life, Celia told Tom, was too short to stand around listening to a man who could rouse his audience to a state of complete indifference. But Tom was adamant.

'Besides,' he added. 'There's an experiment I'd like to conduct.'

'You're crazy,' she said, after he had told her what he planned to do. 'They'll arrest you. They'll put you up against the wall and shoot you. Me too, probably, if I'm seen with you.'

Tom shrugged. 'Then don't be. Wait for me at the Hotel Plaza. In the rooftop bar.'

'I'll be there,' she said angrily. 'But I don't expect to see you again.'

'You will,' said Tom. 'But just in case you lose your nerve waiting for me, here's the money I owe you.'

Celia took the dollars and squeezed them down the front of her brassière. Then he was gone.

'Crazy American,' she said, telling herself that now she had been paid she was under no obligation to meet him anywhere. But she was still in the fifth-floor *azotea* of the Plaza, with its splendid view of the old Bacardi building – an excellent place to hear every word spoken from the balcony of the presidential palace – when, at ten minutes after ten, the Big Barbudo began to speak.

Listening to the speech from the Agramonte side of the crowded plaza, Tom was surprised at how gentle and high-pitched the leader's voice was. He had been expecting someone who sounded tougher, as befitted a guerrilla leader and heavy smoker of large cigars. Even so, the content of the speech – which was about the ten days Castro had spent in New York – lacked for nothing in its harsh criticism of the American way of life. The United States was not the golden land of opportunity people thought it was. Blacks were oppressed. The poor were downtrodden. The press told lies. Truth existed nowhere. Everyone was motivated by money.

Tom agreed with a lot of what Castro said. When he went to the movies and saw representations of life in small-town America he sometimes wondered if any of these utopian places, with their white picket fences, beautiful children, friendly cops, and sober fathers, had ever existed except in the minds of the non-American immigrants who had dreamed them up. The real America – the America he knew, and where he had been raised – was a harder, less sentimental place than anybody ever expected, and the reality was sure to be a disappointment for the majority of Cuban refugees who went there. It was no great shakes, but at least they belonged in Cuba. Tom thought Castro was probably right to tell his people that they were better off where they were. It almost seemed a pity to interrupt him.

Tom studied the balconies and windows of the apartment buildings surrounding the plaza carefully, and found them bristling with spectators. Whereas in the afternoon he had seen these people as a potential drawback, he was now inclined to think of them as a possible advantage. With so many people in those buildings he might easily slip away and make his escape. At least he might, always supposing he had some good identity papers.

In the cigar factory most of the lights were on and there were figures moving on top of the roof. Probably security guards, he thought. So the factory was definitely out of the question.

Puffing on a large Upmann, he glanced at the crowd around him and then dropped down on to his haunches to light the fuse of the firecracker he had between his ankles. It was a small mortar bomb, the kind of thing they'd thrown at him during his army training. By the time anyone else had noticed what was happening Tom had slipped away into the crowd, heading south down Agramonte. There was a sudden push behind him as the crowd quickly parted around the mortar, adding some urgency to his progress. Seconds later, the things exploded. Quite harmlessly he was sure, although several women screamed with fright. To Tom's ears it had sounded very like a shot from a .50-calibre machine-gun.

He turned in the crowd to try to gauge the reaction. Apart from the crowd's momentary panic, nobody did very much. A couple of soldiers started to move towards the source of the explosion and then seemed to change their minds. There was even some laughter as shock turned to relief. Just as interesting was the reaction from the floodlit balcony of the presidential palace. The Big Barbudo looked like a little bearded puppet. And he hardly hesitated – even worked the explosion into his speech: the American imperialists were stupid and naïve if they thought they could defeat the revolution with their little bombs, he yelled with outrage.

The crowd cheered and began to chant: 'To the Wall! To the Wall!'

Hearing this cry taken up, Tom judged it best to be away from the scene as quickly as possible even though he was not afraid of being caught by the police. The people were more unpredictable than the security forces. To his surprise the sound of a second explosion, almost as loud as the first, was now heard, and Tom wondered if the little mortar had actually been two. Either that or some enthusiastic Fidelista had fired his weapon into the air. Not that the prime minister was at all deterred.

And he was still extemporising upon these two explosions when, some ten minutes later, Tom reached the rooftop bar of the Plaza Hotel. He figured the Big Barbudo could get at least an hour's worth of rhetoric out of the incident. Maybe even two.

4

Aloha

Johnny Rosselli swirled his Smirnoff on the rocks around his glass and then pressed it against his forehead, like a cold compress. 'Try the antipasto, Tom,' he said. 'It's the best in town.'

Tom Jefferson was meeting Rosselli at Leone's, an Italian restaurant opposite the Gulfstream Park racecourse, and virtually on the county line. Out of season it was a quiet place and Tom wondered that they had bothered to open at all.

'Celestine, *eh che se rigga? Come se va?*' said Rosselli, waving the proprietor towards him, embracing the man fondly and speaking Italian with him for the next fifteen minutes. A couple of times while they were speaking, Celestine, who was younger than Rosselli, put his hands together and rocked them back and forward in a gesture of benediction, saying, '*Sa benedica*, Giovanni. *Sa benedica.*'

Tom studied the menu and decided to have the antipasto and some gnocchi. Then he lit a cigarette and waited patiently for the *chiacchiera* to conclude, helping himself to some Chianti when that arrived, and generally wondering if the food would be better than Gerardo's on Biscayne Boulevard at 163rd Street, which was the best Italian restaurant he knew, and Mary's favourite.

Celestine took their order personally, and since Tom and Rosselli were the only people in the place, he wondered if they hadn't opened especially for the Don. When at last Rosselli sat down, he rubbed his well-manicured hands excitedly and asked Tom if he liked food.

'I like food,' said Tom.

'How about Italian food?'

It seemed a little late to be asking a question like that, but Tom just nodded back politely and said he liked Italian food a lot.

'Ever been to Italy?' asked Rosselli.

'Nope.'

'I was born there. A little town near Cassino, called Esperia.'

'Really?'

'So you might say casinos are in my blood.'

It wasn't much of a joke, but Tom tried a smile anyway, just to be pleasant. He wasn't much of a smiler.

'Take this place. It used to be the Colonial Inn, a gambling joint before the fucking puritans took over this town. That's when I first got to know it.' He shrugged. 'I've been coming here ever since. I'm like that, I guess. I stay with someone, through the good times and the bad times. You work with me, you'll learn that about me. I'm always there for my friends.'

'That's good to know,' said Tom, who didn't care much one way or the other.

Rosselli rubbed his hands some more, and then lit an Old Gold. 'Is that my feasibility study?'

Tom handed over the document he had prepared.

'If that's what you want to call it,' he said. It always irritated him the way some people tried to bury what was being said when the subject got around to murder. Just one time he'd have liked a client who came right out and asked him to kill some sonofabitch.

Rosselli put on his glasses, finished his vodka, and, pouring himself some Chianti, opened the little folder. 'What's with all this plastic shit?' He frowned. 'You trying to lift my prints or something, Tom?'

'Those are celluloid sheets,' said Tom. 'To help you to burn papers and stuff if you're in a hurry. I mean, we wouldn't want that document falling into the wrong hands now would we?'

'No, indeed,' said Rosselli. He nodded, approvingly. 'That's a neat trick. Where did you learn it?'

64

Tom shrugged. 'Just something I picked up. The way you do. I'm the real careful type, Johnny. Ava Gardner offered to suck my cock I'd probably ask what was in it for me.'

Always easy to amuse, Rosselli chuckled. 'I know Ava,' he said. 'Her and Sinatra. She's quite a girl. To be quite frank, she and I never got along that well, but we both helped Frank to get something he wanted, once.' He settled down to read the document through. Then, after Celestine had served the antipasto, he read it again. 'What the hell happened to my double? To my *quiniela exacta*?'

'Can't be done. Not with a rifle. 'Sides, it isn't exactly a double, you know. There's three of those motherfuckers: Fidel, Raul and Ramon.'

'Raul's the only one with balls, though,' argued Rosselli.

'Yeah? You're forgetting all the sisters. Anyway, Raul isn't that popular. During his May Day speech earlier this year Fidel said that if the Yankee imperialists managed to nail him, then Raul would take over as prime minister. From what I hear this didn't go down too well with the crowd. Probably on account of the fact that Raul is the real bloodthirsty banana in the bunch. Even put a few of his own rebel soldiers in front of firing squads during the revolution, for disciplinary offences. As military governor of Oriente, he shot seventy Batistianos in one day. Without so much as a trial. Cubans don't like that kind of thing. Take my word for it, Fidel is your target.'

'You're very well informed about Cuba,' said Rosselli. 'And this.' He tapped the document in his hands. 'This is very good. Very good indeed.'

'So is the antipasto,' said Tom.

'Would you come and discuss this with my associates?'

'Just tell me when and where.'

'The Fontainebleu Hotel.' Rosselli pronounced it the French way, a sure sign that he was from out of town. Without exception the locals called it the Fountain Blue. 'Five o'clock this afternoon? Just ask for the Aloha suite.'

'I'll be there.'

The Fontainebleu was the Cadillac of Miami hotels, a great gleaming white confection of modern American styling, with every conceivable extra, at an inconceivable price. Situated right on the golden beachfront, among carefully tended avenues of bougainvillaea and neatly raked gravel paths, it soared twelve storeys above an Olympic-sized emerald of a swimming pool and a series of cool cabanas where wealthy New Jersey widows and skinny Boston matrons worked on achieving the colour of aged Seminole Indians.

It all seemed a far cry from national television debates between Nixon and Kennedy, missile gaps, and a contract to kill Castro. The thoughts occupying the minds of those who occupied the Cabana Club steamer chairs in the late-afternoon orange-blistering sunshine were incessantly quotidian. Were the kids being looked after properly in the Kittekat Club? Was there time for a pre-ablutionary glass of iced tea in the Bamboo Coffee Shoppe? Should dinner be eaten in the Fleur de Lis or the La Tropicala? In the event of which, and assuming there was change out of fifty dollars a head, would they try and end the evening in the Rendezvous Bar or the Boom Boom Nighterie? Such, reflected Tom, as he made his premature entry into the hotel, was modern philosophy, Miami-style.

With ten minutes to kill before his appointed meeting in the Aloha suite, Tom went down to the hotel's Pineapple Shopping Arcade and bought a *Playboy* magazine and copy of the *Herald* to wrap it in. The front cover of *Playboy* flagged the Girls of Hollywood and Hunting for the Urban Male. Tom reckoned he knew all there was to know about hunting the urban male; with the girls of Hollywood he thought he could use a little tuition. The front page of the paper included a story about Khrushchev losing his temper at the UN General Assembly and thumping his desk during the speech of the British Prime Minister. Tom thought the Russian probably needed the company of the girls of Hollywood or maybe a few days at the Fontainebleu to unwind a little. Just passing through the lobby it was hard to think of thumping anything other than a floor button on the elevator.

He rode up to the twelfth floor and walked along the blue-carpeted corridor to the Aloha suite. It was easy enough to spot. Outside the door to the suite stood a man the size of an exhibition stand at the World's Fair, wearing a light-blue Dacron suit and beige driving gloves. Tom, dressed in a lightweight blazer, sports shirt, and slacks lifted his arms and let the bodyguard check him for weapons. Then the guard knocked and opened the door.

'Thanks,' grunted Tom, and stepped into a small lobby to find another guard and another door. Tom hardly looked at the second man, only the Colt .45 automatic he was carrying openly in his hand. Once again the door was opened for him. Muscle had better manners these days, mused Tom, and went into the suite.

Two hundred dollars a night bought you a quarter-acre of high ceiling, split-level floor, a CinemaScope-sized window with balcony, and furniture scaled long and low to encourage a relaxing frame of mind. Tom felt anything but relaxed, especially when he saw one of the men in the room. He had a good memory for faces and thought he recognised this one from a movie theatre newsreel. The Senate Select Committee on Improper Activities in the Labor or Management Field, chaired by Senator John McLellan, had been formed to investigate links between unions and organised crime. Both the Kennedy brothers had been on the committee, with Bobby its chief counsel. A number of the leading figures in organised crime had been subpoenaed to appear before the committee, including, Tom thought, the man who was standing by the window. The radiogram was playing Henry Mancini's 'Mister Lucky'.

The telephone rang and the man by the window waved at someone to get it. 'Get that will ya, Fifi?'

Tom smiled. The man who got up off the sofa and dragged his knuckles over to the Grundig could not have looked less like a Fifi if he had been wearing sixteen-ounce boxing gloves. He turned off the record, picked up the phone, listened for a moment, and then said, 'Hey boss, it's Frank.'

'What, that fucker again? Tell him to call back another time. I'm busy.'

Fifi shrugged and handed on the message. Meanwhile Rosselli, wearing the blazer but with a neat ascot this time, was coming out of the bathroom drying his hands on a towel. He smiled his smooth white smile, like a big silver fox, and placed a welcoming hand on Tom's shoulder.

'Tom,' said Rosselli. 'Here you are. Right on time.'

'Time is money. That's what Karl Marx says anyway.'

'Jesus fucking Christ. He did?'

'Not in so many words. Matter of fact it was a lot more fucking words.' Tom grinned. 'I guess more people would read him if he'd been a little more to the point.'

'You've actually read that shit? I'm impressed.'

'Some. In my line of work I have to read all kinds of shit. I even read that fucking book you gave me. I liked it.'

'I'm glad. It's one of my favourite books.'

'Hey, Johnny.' The man talking was the man Fifi had called Boss. 'Can we cut with the critic's choice and make a fucking start here?'

'Sure, Sam, sure.' Rosselli's tone became momentarily unctuous. 'Okay, Tom? Let me introduce you to everyone.' Indicating Fifi's boss, he said, 'This is Mister Gold.'

Gold was wearing an olive silk glen plaid suit, a round-collar shirt and a patterned silk tie; he looked like an older, meaner version of Frank Sinatra. Tom nodded and shook Gold's outstretched hand.

'A real pleasure to meet you, Mister Giancana,' he said coolly.

Sam 'Momo' Giancana, the boss of the Chicago outfit and one of the most feared men in America, said nothing for a moment, his weasel-like face flickering on the edge of anger before the cruel mouth spread slowly into a wry smile. 'That's good,' he said to Rosselli. 'Any man who's gonna work for me has to have balls in his pants. It's nice to meet you too, Tom.'

'I like to know who I'm working for,' said Tom. 'In my line of work it's best to avoid any opportunity for misunderstanding. Especially when I'm dealing with an organisation like yours, Mister Giancana.'

'I can understand that. And I appreciate your candour, Tom. If I use a different name it's not because I want to deceive you. Not at all. I use the name Gold because Miami is a Jew town, and a Jew name gets you the proper respect.'

'You got that right, Momo,' said Rosselli, ushering Tom toward the sofa where a trio of men were waiting to be introduced.

The first to extend his hand was a short, dark man with a receding hairline and a lawyer's sharp appearance. Tom thought he looked like a sleazier version of Bob Hope. Most lawyers looked like a sleazier version of someone. 'Bob Maheu,' he said. 'And you can relax, fellah. That's my real name.'

Next was a large, lugubrious man with a hound dog's face and the smell of a cop, none too cool in his Mister Cool sports coat, shoes just a little too clean, feet just a little too large.

'This is Jim O'Connell,' said Rosselli. 'We call him Big Jim, for obvious reasons.'

Tom caught a look passed between O'Connell and Maheu as the big man shook him by the hand. These people weren't quite used to each other, he thought.

The third man by the sofa had the face of a retired boxer – Jake La Motta after he put on weight and went on the club circuit: broken nose, small scar on right cheek, and a jaw that was as square as a box of Wheaties.

'And this is Frank Fiorucci, also known as Frank Sorges, although I dare say Castro has a few even choicer names for him now that he's working for us and not the Cubans. Eh Frank?'

Sorges took Tom's hand and grunted a greeting. Tom couldn't decide if he was smiling any more than he could tell if the man was Cuban or American.

'And the guy by the door is Fifi Buccieri,' continued Rosselli. 'You already met Butch and Chuck outside, so now you know everyone, Tom.'

'Everyone except you, Mister Ralston,' replied Tom. 'Or should I say Mister Rosselli?'

The smile vanished abruptly from Rosselli's Tanfastic face as if Tom had taken an eraser and rubbed it off.

'Better not take the fifth on that, Johnny,' laughed Giancana. 'This guy's liable to figure you for a double-crosser and use you for target practice.'

Tom reached for a cigarette and studied the faces around him. Buccieri was mob, like Rosselli and Giancana, with a real torturer's face. Maheu and O'Connell he decided were CIA, but he couldn't figure Sorges. He had a mob face and mob taste in clothes – the sports coat he was wearing was as loud as Rosselli's laugh, now restored to full volume as finally he saw the joke – but the cool, guarded manner and the close mouth was typical Company.

'Like I said,' shrugged Tom, blowing out a steady stream of smoke, 'I like to know who I'm working for.'

While Fifi Buccieri organised a round of drinks, Tom and the rest of them arranged themselves around a dining table. For a few minutes Rosselli kept on talking about nothing in particular until everyone was comfortable and looked like they were ready to come down to business. But it was O'Connell who set the ball rolling.

'I've read your report, Mister Jefferson,' he said. 'It's a fine piece of work.' He lit a Muriel Coronella from a pack of five, and continued: 'This fall-guy you're proposing to use. I mean the idea of using one. Is that something you've done before?'

'No,' admitted Tom. 'To be quite frank with you, in all normal circumstances, I wouldn't even countenance the idea. I like to work at the kind of distance and from the kind of position that makes that kind of ruse unnecessary. But this is a special situation. The plaza in front of the presidential palace provides a limited number of sniping positions. And I think that any crowd occupying the plaza would know that. And will react accordingly. Because whatever your feelings about Castro, his is a popular revolution.'

Sorges tutted loudly and shook his head.

'That's certainly my impression as a disinterested outsider,' said Tom.

'You're half Cuban, aren't you?' demanded Sorges, as if that was supposed to make him better informed about the situation.

'The half of me that's Cuban is only half-interested half of the time. The half of me that's American doesn't really give a shit. It's your best guarantee of getting the job done. I'm a professional, not a fanatic. And like I was saying, the impression I have formed is that this is a popular revolution and that Cuban public opinion will demand that someone is apprehended for Castro's murder, and apprehended quickly. I consider that my best chance of escape depends on someone else being caught.'

Sam Giancana leaned forward on the table, affording Tom an excellent view of two magnificent oval cut emerald cufflinks. The Chicago boss might be a hood, but he was a hood with good taste.

'Tom is right,' he said quietly. 'You always need a patsy. Back in thirty-three, we set up this guy to hit Cermak, the Chicago mayor. Name of Zangara, Joe Zangara. He was an ex-soldier from the Italian army. We gave him a straight fucking choice: make the hit, take the fall, pay off your debts, with some money left over to take care of

70

your family; or die real hard, and leave your family with the debts. So what could he do? He shot Tony Cermak and went to the chair for it. And because he said that he was actually trying to shoot Roosevelt, no one connected us to the killing. Matter of fact, it happened right here in Miami. Cermak and FDR riding around in an open car in the Florida sunshine, like sitting ducks.'

Tom laughed nervously. 'With all due respect, Mister Giancana, I had someone else in mind to take the rap, not myself.'

'Sure, sure. All I'm saying is that sometimes it's the guy who pulls the trigger, and sometimes it's someone else. But you're right, Tom, somebody has to take the fall for Castro. Public opinion will demand it.'

'Do you have anyone in mind?' asked O'Connell.

'No. I figured you guys would still have plenty of connections back in Cuba. To help me find someone suitable.' Tom shrugged and began to try to paint a picture of the kind of individual he was thinking of. 'It could be someone with a background in the Cuban army perhaps. A real die-hard Batistiano, with a well-known grudge against Castro. Preferably some kind of misfit, outsider type. Someone dumb. Anyone too bright might figure he was being set up. And nothing too complicated or the Fidelistas won't understand the cards they're being dealt.'

'I think we could find someone like that,' said O'Connell, raising an eyebrow in the direction of Frank Sorges. 'Frank? What do you say?'

'Anything's possible,' said Sorges. 'Sure.'

'It goes without saying that I'd want to take a look at whoever you find,' said Tom. 'Just to make sure the patsy isn't me.'

'Naturally,' said Maheu. 'Just so as you know, Mister Jefferson, I represent an industrial group seeking to recover American-owned businesses and properties that have been or are going to be nationalised by the Cuban regime.' Maheu's narrow eyes hadn't yet met Tom's. All the time he was speaking he tapped at a blank pad of paper with a Sheaffer pencil. 'I think the most pressing question my clients will have is what all this is going to cost.'

'Me too,' admitted Rosselli. 'It's the one thing that's not in your report.'

'I'd have thought there was no price too high to recover what's been lost in Cuba,' said Tom. 'Considering Meyer Lansky spent fourteen million building one hotel, I don't think you should worry about a down-payment of one hundred thousand dollars. And another hundred and fifty thousand dollars when the job is done.'

Rosselli whistled and clutched at his chest. 'A quarter mill? Jesus, I hope my Blue Cross covers me for this kind of heart attack.'

Maheu wrote down the two figures on his pad and underlined them furiously.

'Most guys figure ten thousand a year before they're thirty is setting their sights a little high,' said O'Connell.

'Isn't that just the point?' asked Tom. 'You're paying me to set my sights dead centre.'

'Two hundred and fifty thousand dollars is a lot of money, Tom,' said Maheu. 'Sinatra doesn't make that kind of dough.'

'Not last week anyway,' growled Giancana.

'A lot of money,' repeated Maheu.

'For just the one fucking Castro,' added Rosselli. 'For that kind of money we should get all three.'

'Try telling that to some of those companies you represent,' said Tom. 'Sears Roebuck, Woolworth, Remington Rand, Coca-Cola, General Electric, Otis Elevators. To say nothing of a few banks, breweries, sugar mills, chocolate companies, and department stores. I believe the *Wall Street Journal* has put an estimated figure of at least two hundred million dollars' worth of American property on the island. Under the circumstances, gentlemen, a recovery fee of point one two five per cent does not seem unreasonable.'

Maheu started to check Tom's arithmetic on his sheet of paper. 'If we recover it,' he said.

Tom watched him arrive at the same decimal figure, and said, 'I'm just the button. I leave the probable causes and effects of my actions to people like you. You want the job done? That's my fee. You think it's too much, then get someone else.'

Giancana waved an imperious hand at the others sat around the table. 'Tom is right. The money he asks is not unreasonable.' He touched his hair for a moment and Tom suddenly realised, almost with horror, that the Chicago boss was wearing a toupee. 'That fucking prick Castro's the one who's being unreasonable. But he's just a man, and a man only has to be killed once. These brothers of his, Raul and Ramon. From what I hear, they're just the dog's balls and tail. Fidel's the head and heart of the revolution, just like Hitler was in Germany and Nasser in Egypt. We cut off the head, the whole fucking dog dies. The revolution's over. We do it? We do it right. No half-measures. No penny-pinching fuck-ups.

'Bob? Jim? What your people have got to understand is that taking out a contract on Castro is like arranging your daughter's wedding. What it costs isn't really the issue. What matters most is that the thing goes off without a hitch and everything is the way it's supposed to be. I know what I'm talking about. Back in July I gave my daughter Bonnie away, right here in this hotel. She married this guy who's a congressional aide to Roland Libonati, so you can appreciate that the wedding had to be the best. No expense was spared.'

'It was a beautiful wedding,' said Rosselli. 'Real class.'

'Two hundred guests at thirty dollars a plate. And talking about decoys, I even arranged a decoy wedding party back in Chicago, just to keep the fucking feds and the news reporters off our backs. That's what I mean about doing things the right way. So I say we pay Tom what he asks and have done with this piece of shit Fidel fucking Castro. I say we approve his plan and get rid of the bastard.'

'I agree with Sam,' said Rosselli.

As if he would say anything else, thought Tom. It was plain from the way the two mobsters behaved around each other which one of them had the whip hand.

Maheu nodded. He'd taken off his coat and was looking at O'Connell. Tom guessed Maheu was the liaison between the mob and the Company, with O'Connell probably running some kind of covert operations outfit for the CIA in the same way Alex Goldman did for the FBI. Sorges, he had decided, was the local expert, probably part-Cuban like himself.

'Agreed,' said O'Connell.

Sorges said nothing and no one seemed to expect him to comment, which told Tom all he needed to know about how important he was in the scheme of things. This was a deal between Giancana and O'Connell. And once again it was Giancana who spoke.

'One more thing, Tom. I don't want Castro dead without you

hearing the word from me. And certainly not this side of the election. I don't want anything happening in the next six weeks that does that sonofabitch Nixon any fucking favours. Is that clear?'

Tom nodded. 'Sure, I understand. I'm a Democrat myself, Mister Giancana.'

'I don't think we've talked about this before, Sam,' objected Maheu. 'I mean, surely the sooner the better.'

'Not from where I'm sitting,' said Giancana. 'Listen, Trafficante can't be here this afternoon. I'm just saying what he would want. He has some narcotics deals going down in Cuba that have to be out of the way first.'

But Maheu still looked unhappy. Rosselli nodded, and said, 'Bob, you have to understand, this is Santos's territory we're discussing.' Maheu shrugged.

'Tom? Frank here will offer you whatever assistance he can,' continued Giancana. 'Both here and in Cuba, with the underground movement. He used to be Castro's Minister of Sport, so he knows all the plays. Isn't that right, Frank?'

'That's right.'

'Last year,' said Rosselli, 'Frank and the guy who used to run the Cuban air force borrowed a B-25 and flew to Havana on a bombing mission. They dropped a lot of leaflets on a convention of American travel agents that Castro had arranged to try and get the tourists back to the island.'

'Is that so?' said Tom. At last he had the measure of the man. Sorges was a cowboy, a crazy, someone who might turn out to be more of a liability than an asset. The kind of guy who wouldn't have made a bad patsy himself. 'And what was on these leaflets?'

'Only the truth,' Sorges said defensively. 'That Castro is a tool of communism. And that the travel agents were kidding themselves if they thought the tourists were going to come back and put money in the hands of a lot of fucking reds.'

'The nerve of that guy,' snarled Giancana. 'To think that he can bring the tourists back to Cuba without the casinos. Without the casinos the big hotels are dead.' Giancana leaned back in his chair and lit a large cigar. Smoking it created the impression of a man who was literally fuming about the fate of his casinos.

'That was certainly my impression,' said Tom.

'How do you want your money, Tom? Here in Miami, or somewhere out of the country?' asked Rosselli.

Tom tossed an envelope on to the table in front of Giancana. It contained details of a bank he sometimes used in Nicaragua: J.R.E. Tefel in Managua. Tom liked to bank around.

'Full instructions are in the envelope,' he said. 'When I'm advised by my bank that the first tranche of money has been deposited, I'll go to work.'

'Good. Then we're done on this.' Giancana glanced at a gold Patek Philippe watch. Tom stood up. 'Go with him, Frank,' ordered Giancana. 'Buy him a drink. Find out what he needs. Give him any help you can. Okay with you, Tom?'

'Okay with me.'

Tom nodded at the rest of the men who remained seated around the Aloha suite table.

'Gentlemen,' he said quietly, and started slowly towards the door, followed by Sorges.

Giancana was already discussing something else – something to do with his girlfriend, Phyllis, and some fucking comedian she was still seeing in Vegas and asking Maheu if maybe he could fix things there, just to make sure. Seeing Fifi open the door, Giancana glanced back over his shoulder and shouted after Tom.

'When you hear the word from Johnny, Tom. You make sure you kill that bastard. Kill him. Kill him good. Kill Castro.'

5

Air on a G String

Death was so familiar to Tom's thoughts that it seldom gave him any misgivings. Knowing it so well, he did not fear it. Indeed he had almost forgotten what it was to taste fear. Only sleep had the power to kidnap his inattentive mind and subject it to the most veracious imitation of doom. If he had a horror of death at all it was that it would be anything like sleep. The death notices in the 'Local' section of the *Herald* referred to people who 'fell asleep', as if that was a more palatable choice of words than 'met their deaths'. Not for Tom. He hoped only for complete oblivion. He did not see how anything else could suit him. Some nights were worse than others, but he had no idea why. Seconal or Nembutal stopped him from dreaming but only at the price of blurring the day that followed. And needing all his wits about him he endured the nightmares as another man, afraid of the dentist, might endure a toothache.

This particular morning he awoke with a shout, his pyjamas drenched in sweat, and reached for Mary. This particular morning, she was there.

'Was it a bad one?' she asked, wrapping his damp torso in her arms.

'They're all bad,' he mumbled.

'Do you want to talk about it?'

'Not particularly. What is there to say? If Shakespeare's to be believed, it's an occupational hazard.'

'Maybe you should see a doctor,' she said, going into the bathroom. 'Get yourself a different medication. Seconal and Nembutal aren't the only sleeping pills around. Maybe one of the other ones might suit you better.'

'What can he give me that isn't on your bedside table?' Tom lit a cigarette to steady his nerves, and followed her into the bathroom. 'Cigarette's 'bout the only thing that helps.'

'They're not so easy to handle when you're asleep,' said Mary.

'Besides, I need my edge.' He thought for a moment, considering Mary's own situation. 'I guess we both do.'

He watched her pee and then take a shower, enjoying the way she felt so comfortable around him. Humming 'High Hopes', the Frank Sinatra song that was the Kennedy campaign anthem, she washed herself with vigorous efficiency. Tom sat on the edge of the tub, handing her the soap and the shampoo when she held out her hand.

'I like you watching me,' she said. 'When a man stops looking at his wife she'd better look out. I read that somewhere.'

'I can't imagine not looking at you,' said Tom. 'That hour-glass figure of yours just makes me want to go and play in the sand.'

'Well, you can, if you want. I'm in no particular hurry this morning.'

Tom stepped out of his pyjamas and into the tub beside her.

'Why is that?' he asked, taking her in his arms.

'Because I'm going to be late tonight.' Grasping the handles on the tub, she bent over in front of him and felt him penetrate her from behind. 'JFK and Nixon are on television again tonight. Everyone at the campaign office is staying behind to watch it.'

'Sometimes I think you've got a thing about him,' said Tom, thrusting himself into his wife's body with something close to venom.

'Whatever gave you that idea?' she gasped.

'I don't know,' he said, admiring the sight of their lovemaking. Squeezing her buttocks with his hands and then pushing them apart the better to observe her penetration, he chuckled and added: 'One thing I am sure about.'

'What's that?'

'I kind of like to stay behind and watch myself.'

No. 1410 Brickell Avenue was an expensive apartment block between Highway 95 and the Rickenbacker Causeway. The place where Frank Sorges had told Tom to meet him was a two-storey house behind the main building. A suspicious-minded New York widow named Genevieve and a black cocker spaniel named Cooper met Tom at the door with a scowl and a growl.

'Who are you?'

'Tom Jefferson.'

'If that's an alias, mister, it's a mighty patriotic one.'

'Actually, it's my real name. I guess that comes as a shock to you people. Never knew so many people with different names. Frank sent me. Frank Sorges. Frank Fiorucci. Frank Sinatra for all I care, lady.'

'I know who sent you. Do come in, Mister Jefferson. And forgive me. Like most exiles, I feed on dreams of hope, but sometimes I forget my table manners. Quiet, Cooper. This man is a friend.'

Tom stepped around the dog in the hallway. Genevieve closed the door behind him and said, 'Would you like a *cafecito*? Just about everything has a Cuban angle around here.'

His quick eyes took in the stack of *Bohemia*, a Havana weekly newspaper once anti-Batista in its sympathies, but now vehemently anti-Castro, that stood in the hall; the many boxes of Montecristo cigars; a large black brassbound navy foot locker with a label that read 'Zenith Technological Services', a company Tom had earlier learned was a front, on the university campus, for the CIA's anti-Castro effort; and a furled Cuban flag.

'So I see,' he said.

'I used to be married to a Cuban tobacco grower,' she explained, thinking Tom was referring only to the cigars. 'Help yourself if you'd like a smoke.'

'No thanks. They give me a throat.'

'Me, I love them. I smoke at least one a day, but only when I'm at home. On the whole, Miami is still not really receptive to the idea of the female cigar smoker.' Genevieve pointed behind Tom. 'Well, go right on through and introduce yourself. Frank's not here yet. I'll get you that coffee.'

Tom watched her as far as the kitchen door. She was wearing a tight-fitting sleeveless black lounge suit with her initials – GS – embroidered just beneath one of her substantial breasts, of which there was plenty to see. Genevieve may have been an American but Tom thought she had that Havana look, a flirtatious style that emphasised the bust and the bottom. Tom liked that. Those were the parts he liked to emphasise himself. With both hands.

The lounge was more Palm Beach mansion than Biscayne Bay modern: a couple of Mack-sized sofas, expensive Persian rugs, antique coffee tables, Japanese lacquer screens, and Chinese vases full of flowers. Just about the only Cuban influence on the way the room looked was the quartet of macho individuals who were sitting in it. Not one of them was in charge of a moustache less than one inch thick or a cigar less than six inches long.

Tom found a cloud-free area of the room and sat down with a curt good morning largely prompted by his having recognised one of the four men, a skinny, inscrutably featured character wearing Lee slacks, a Lacoste shirt, a fur felt casual hat with a wide batik band, and hair that was the colour of his bloodshot eyes. Tom never forgot a face, nor the name that went with it, nor the reason why it needed remembering in the first place. He knew this guy from a job he had done back in Guatemala. But the man, whose name was Húber Lanz, could only recall one third of what Tom had already remembered.

'I know you, don't I?' he asked.

Tom grimaced and shrugged, but he held the bloodshot stare, as if his own eyes had been stuck to Lanz's own. Now was not the time to look shifty or evasive. 'Could be,' he allowed.

'Yeah, but where from?'

'Damned if I know.' Tom held out his hand. 'Name's Tom Jefferson.'

'Húber Lanz.' Lanz shook it, and then shook his head. 'Jefferson? No. Doesn't connect. But it'll come to me. I've got a memory like . . .' He shook his head as he tried to remember the word in English. '*Un tamiz.*'

'A sieve,' said Tom, translating. 'Sure looks like it.'

'Exactly. Anyway, this is Diaz Castillo. And over there we have Orlando Bosch. And Alonzo Gonzales.'

Tom nodded at each of them. 'Pleased to meet you, gentlemen.'

'Frank sent his apologies,' said Bosch. 'And to tell you that he'll be joining us as soon as he can.'

'You're some kind of freedom fighters, right?'

'El Movimiento Insurreccional de Recuperación Revolucionaria,' Bosch said proudly. 'However, since Miami Anglos seem to have such a problem with Cuban names, we are the M–I–R–R, for short.' He smiled. 'Although I fully expect even that to give us some problems when Christmas comes and we have little children talking about gold, frankincense and myrrh.' Bosch was well spoken, with the professional, even clinical air of a doctor or a dentist. 'Although no gift could seem as precious as the one you bring to our humble cause, Mister Jefferson.'

Hit. Termination. Contract. Feasibility study. And now a gift. Tom winced. Another rat creeping around the cheese. 'I wouldn't say "gift" describes it exactly,' he objected, with a wry smile. 'There's the not-so-small matter of my fee.'

'Since we are not paying your fee,' laughed Gonzales, 'it's a gift to us. A gift from your vice-president.'

'Does that mean you're going to vote for him?'

'Alas, no,' said Gonzales. 'We are not yet permitted. But fortunately for us it will make little difference who is president. Kennedy is also very sympathetic to our cause.'

'Frank has told us all about you,' said Bosch. 'We have been told that you're the best.'

'You've certainly priced the contract that way,' observed Lanz.

Tom shrugged dismissively. 'That's capitalism, I guess.'

'But even the best needs help to kill a man like Fidel Castro. So we have been very busy on your behalf. Isn't that right, Genevieve?'

Genevieve was laying a tray of coffees on the table. 'Very.'

'Genevieve is a great patron of our cause,' explained Bosch. 'Some people come and go, but Genevieve almost makes *el exilio* a pleasure. And because she is an American she is able to come and go, in and out of Havana, as she pleases. As a matter of fact she has just returned from a visit she made on your behalf, Mister Jefferson. But I'll let her tell you about that in a moment. She's as well connected as it's possible to be. She even entertains Cuban government officials. None of these communist idiots suspects where her real sympathies lie, of course. And why should they? She still has her seaside estate in Miramar, and her beautiful apartment in Marinao.'

Tom took the little cup offered to him and, drinking, found the coffee thick, strong, and sweet, the way Cubans liked it. The way he liked it himself.

'Alonzo there, he is in the same kind of business as yourself, only he lacks your experience. He'd never fired a gun before the revolution. Diaz is a bookmaker. Húber is a pilot. He flies a seaplane for Southern Air Transport.'

'The company's owned by Actus Technology,' explained Lanz. 'But really that's just a holding company for the CIA. You see? Another gift. People here are very generous.'

'I guess we can afford it. Especially when we're Jack Kennedy.' Tom nodded back at Lanz who, with eyes narrowed, still looked as though he was trying to recollect the circumstances of their first acquaintance. 'And what about you, Mister Bosch? What do you do?'

'Doctor Bosch. I'm just a poor paediatrician, Mister Jefferson. This kind of thing is all new to me. All I want to do is to see my country restored to democracy before it is too late. I do not approve of murder, you understand. None of us is a criminal. But these are special circumstances. Castro is an evil dictator. Many people in my country have died already. And many more look certain to die before this thing is concluded. Perhaps I will die myself. If so, I do not fear it.'

Tom nodded, and said, 'No temáis una muerta gloriosa.' This was the lyric of 'La Bayamesa', the Cuban national anthem. 'Do not fear a glorious death. To die for country is to live.'

Bosch looked impressed. 'Yes. That is it precisely, Mister Jefferson. Thank you. I can see now that you are much more than a mere assassin, as I had been led to believe. It will be an honour to help you in any way we can. So. To business. The matter of una estafa, a trick to expedite the completion of your business and a successful escape. Genevieve. Tell him what you and Diaz have rolled at your galera.'

Genevieve finished lighting her cigar, holding it by the underside, as if she had been grasping the handle of a golf putter. The reason for her seductively low voice was now plain to see. 'It's true,' she said. 'This plan has to be rolled together like a good cigar. The first smaller leaf, the *tripa*, gives the cigar its form. Then the *hoja de fortaleza* for flavour, and the *hoja de combustión* to enable the cigar to burn evenly. Last of all we have the *copa* with which to wrap the cigar. I shan't bore you by telling who is what. And I certainly don't want to make any of this seem tenuous. So let's just start with this church in the plaza. The one you photographed so well.

'The Iglesia del Santa Angel Custodio is run by a Father Xavier, a good, simple man who cares only about his church. The church itself is in a poor state of repair, but there is not much money with which to carry out the work. I told him of the existence of the Instituto per le Opere di Religione. The IOR. It's the Vatican Bank in Rome, through which funds may be sent to the Cuban church in this time of need. The IOR is run by Cardinal Alberto di Jorio, who's very old and probably hasn't even heard of Cuba. But I told Father Xavier that I was acquainted with Cardinal Spellman, in New York, who was a good friend of di Jorio's secretary, a Monsignor who also happens to be a qualified building engineer. It's this fictitious person's job to go from one poor country to another, inspecting the fabric of the church's buildings and deciding whether or not money shall be donated. Spellman is a friend of mine, from Boston. He owes me more than one favour. And naturally he hates the communists. So he'll provide any credentials we need in order to pass Tom off as this same Monsignor.'

Genevieve handed Tom a number of pamphlets and booklets to do with the Catholic Church's catechism and sacraments.

'Of course, you'll have to read these,' she told him. 'If you are a Catholic, I'm assuming, given what you do, that you're not a very conscientious one.'

'You could say that,' agreed Tom.

'Naturally we'll have a real priest to help you with the way a priest handles himself and that kind of thing. But the important thing is that, as a priest who is also a building engineer, you'll have the perfect excuse to spend a lot of time up on the church roof.'

'Sounds good.'

'And naturally you'll be supported by the MIRR in Havana,' said Bosch. 'Whatever you need to get the job done.'

'We'll take you in,' said Lanz, grinning wolfishly. 'And we'll take you out, too.'

Tom nodded, but he wondered what Lanz meant by that remark. If the red-haired Cuban had meant it to sound at all ambiguous.

'Which leads me to the next leaf in our cigar,' said Genevieve. 'The *copa*. The wrapper. The patsy. We believe we've found the perfect mark. His name is Everton Echeverria and he's a jockey right here in Miami, at Hialeah.'

'He's not so much a jockey,' interrupted Diaz Castillo. 'Not these days, anyway. He's more what we call a hot walker. An exercise boy. After races he cools down the horses by walking them around. If he had a little more nerve he might make it as a jockey, but he took a fall a few months back and since then he's lost the *cojones* for the job. Anyway, he's a real loner. Lives in a crummy motel close to the track. And he likes to gamble. Knows even less about betting on a horse than he does about riding one. He's into me for about a thousand bucks. But naturally I'm prepared to wipe the slate clean, even leave him some extra dough besides, if he's willing to go back to Cuba and do me a little favour. It's out of season right now, so there's no reason for him to say no.'

'He's Cuban?'

'*Ella cabeza*? Didn't I say?' Castillo continued. 'Yes, his background makes him just right for us. He was a soldier in Batista's army. Not a bad shot by all accounts. His father was a croupier at the Capri until they closed the place. Then he tried to leave, only, unlike Everton, he got caught and now he's in prison. His mother runs a small shop in Havana, selling sponges, mother of pearl, turtle shells. But since the revolution the business hasn't thrived. She still keeps Everton's room though. A couple of our people took a look around while she was out, and found his old army rifle under the bed. A thirty-calibre M1 Garand, and apparently still in good working order.'

Tom nodded, although he had his doubts about the effectiveness of a Second World War rifle left gathering dust under a bed in a port like Havana. All that sea air was bad for a rifle left without gun oil for any length of time. And even the best M1s had a poor trigger pull and a badly designed stock. But you didn't look a gift horse in the mouth. Finding the *copa*'s own army rifle was a real stroke of luck for them. They knew that. And they would expect him to be pleased. He said, 'With a Griffin and Howe mount, and a four-power Bear Cub telescopic sight, not to mention some gun oil, that might just do the job. And even if it doesn't, it'll be a good bit of evidence to leave for the Cuban authorities. Excellent work.'

Tom lit a cigarette and smiled optimistically at Húber Lanz, who grinned and wagged a finger back at him. As if he was warning him he wasn't going to forget to remember. Then he noticed that Sorges had come into the room while Castillo had been speaking and was now sitting in the corner. He was wearing a seersucker sports jacket and a button-down shirt. Seeing him, Tom nodded, and this seemed to prompt Sorges to bring his chair closer to the rest of them.

'Tom? How's it going? Got any questions?'

Tom nodded, but addressed his next question to Castillo: 'And what are you going to tell our friend Everton?'

'That there's a false passport for him and someone else. Someone we'd like to get out of Cuba. A political dissident. Everton's to meet this person in the church on the night you kill Castro. We'll have him wait inside the confessional. Only instead of a political dissident turning up on the other side of the screen, it'll be the murder weapon. Here's what I propose, Tom. You come down from the roof and put the gun there, on your way out. Simple as that. When Everton's arrested they'll find the rifle, the two false passports, and back at his mother's shop they'll find all sorts of other incriminating shit. Copies of *Bohemia*. Money. Maybe even some of the photographs you took of the plaza, Tom, with the balcony on the palace marked out with a neat little cross. A diary about how much he wants to kill Fidel. We have a handwriting expert to help us with that.'

Tom thought it all sounded okay, apart from the bit that had him leaving the rifle in the confessional. Leaving the rifle up on the roof would be a better option. Not that it mattered enough to say anything now.

'This Everton character,' he said ruminatively. 'I'd like to take a look at him myself.'

'Sure, no problem,' said Sorges. 'You can check him out to your heart's content. And the money, it should be hitting your account any time now.'

Tom glanced over the pamphlets. 'My mother always wanted me to be priest.'

'Not just a priest,' said Genevieve. 'A Monsignor.'

'Let's pray it works,' said Bosch. 'Because as soon as Castro's dead, the invasion can begin.'

'You really think that whoever wins the election is going to do that?' asked Tom.

'Listen,' said Sorges. 'Nixon. Kennedy. Either way we win. But as it happens, I've heard that JFK's election is in the bag. The fix is in. Momo's seen to that.'

'You reckon?'

'Sure,' said Sorges. 'Look, it wouldn't be the first time the mob delivered votes for the Democrats. Coolidge, FDR, and now JFK. What? You don't believe us?'

Tom looked less than convinced. 'I don't know,' he said. 'Somehow I can't figure the mob fixing things for someone who was on the McLellan committee.'

'That's part of the deal,' insisted Sorges. 'In return for the votes, Kennedy will call off the dogs. Leave the mob alone again. Things will be just like they were before. Here, and in Cuba. You'll see. After the election, Kennedy's going to do what he's told. Momo has an insurance policy handsome Jack doesn't even know about. Him on tape, in bed with Marilyn Monroe.'

'That's a tape I'd like to hear,' chuckled Gonzales.

'Me too,' admitted Lanz. 'How about it Jenny?'

But Genevieve was shaking her head. 'Count me out,' she said, good-humouredly. 'If I want sounds for swinging lovers, I'll listen to Frank Sinatra.'

'That pimp,' snorted Sorges. 'He's the one who introduced them.'

Tom glanced at his watch. 'Well, I've got to be going,' he said. 'Everything sounds good, though. I'm impressed with what you've devised.' He stood up and pointed at Lanz, wanting to be away from him but going along with the idea of hoping to remember where it was they had met. 'It'll come to me, where it was we met,' he said, trying to turn things so that it looked like it was him trying to remember Lanz from somewhere. 'It'll take a while, but I'll get there.'

'Yeah, you do that, friend.'

Tom shook hands all round. Even before he left the room he had decided to kill Lanz. And as soon as possible.

Outside, on Brickell Avenue, Tom waited in his car for Húber Lanz to emerge from the guesthouse. The Company seemed to have no shortage of premises. So far, with Sorges, he'd seen a suite of rooms in the Dupont Hotel, another apartment on Riviera Drive in Coral Gables, and the headquarters of the Democratic Revolutionary Front – more like a convention centre than a clandestine recruiting station – on campus at Miami University. Then there were the CIA/ Cuban-exile watering holes, such as the Waverly Inn, the ITT's Three Ambassadors' Lounge, the 27 Birds, the University Inn, and the Stuft Shirt Lounge at the Holiday Inn right there on Brickell Avenue. He was going to have a lot of information with which to tickle Alex Goldman when he returned from his trip to Mexico City.

It was another twenty minutes before Lanz emerged from the guesthouse and climbed into a 1956 De Soto. Tom followed him. At first he thought Lanz was heading to the Holiday Inn himself, but when, after a while, they did stop, they were on Ponce de Leon in Coral Gables. Lanz collected some dry cleaning, went into Boyd's Florist Shop and bought something in Engel's Men's Shop before heading back to the car. Then they were driving again, only east this time, back the way they had come, and then across the MacArthur Causeway. Just south of Collins Avenue, Lanz drove into a Burger King, picked up some lunch, and headed north up to Lincoln Avenue where he parked his car and took his thirty-nine-cent burger and his nineteen-cent shake into a movie theatre.

Tom got out of his car and walked up and down outside the movie theatre, thinking. A gun, even the .22 Harrington & Richardson in the trunk, would be too noisy in there. A knife was too messy. Finally, seeing a music shop a couple of blocks down the street, Tom had an idea. He went in and bought a guitar string. And having collected his driving gloves from the car, he followed Lanz into the movie theatre.

He had already seen the feature, a Hitchcock jolter called *Psycho*, the previous week and thought the movie was appropriate for what he was planning as it was certain to cover the sounds of a struggle. The time Tom had seen it, several women had nearly screamed the place down when Janet Leigh got her just desserts in the shower. She was a thief, after all. And he had enjoyed the movie, especially the glimpse of Janet Leigh's naked body when it was stabbed thirty times by Anthony Perkins. That part was useful, too. Lanz would be too busy concentrating on trying to see her tits and her bare ass to notice Tom behind him. He bought a ticket and went inside.

It was cool in the theatre. Cool and dark. And lonely, too. As only a matinée can be. How many afternoons had he spent alone in such places with just the movie for company? Tom sat down in the nearest seat and waited for his eyes to adjust to the black and white shades of Hitchcock's Gothic world. The movie was just starting, and seeing the opening shot again – a half-open window with the blind three-quarters drawn, in a room on the upper storey of a cheap hotel – Tom recalled how, the previous week, he'd half expected to see a sniper at work. It was just the way Tom preferred to work himself. Instead of which it was just a couple conducting an illicit affair, although just quite why it was illicit, since neither of them was married, was still lost on Tom.

By now he had seen Húber Lanz, although it would have been truer to say that he had smelt him and his hamburger. Lanz was seated about ten rows in front of Tom, right in the centre of the near-empty auditorium. There was no one seated anywhere close to him, which was one of the reasons Tom preferred matinées himself: he disliked other people. Which was an advantage for a contract killer.

Tom started to unravel his guitar string. When he'd been a kid, his father had taught him a few basic chords. He thought he probably could still play 'The Peanut Vendor' or 'Guantanamera' if someone had stuck a guitar in his hands. But most of the time he just pitied people who played the guitar. As if you didn't have enough baggage in life without a guitar as well. Even a rifle was easier to carry around than a fucking guitar.

Janet Leigh got in her car with the forty thousand dollars she'd stolen and left Phoenix, Arizona for California, which was about the time that Tom decided to move a few rows nearer to Lanz. He pulled on the gloves and tugged the G string experimentally between his fists. 'Guantanamera' was sung in G, he thought. And it was something to do with José Martí, the dead Cuban revolutionary. A nice song, but kind of miserable, too, like all *guajiras*. Tom preferred movie music. Like the movie music he was listening to now. That really touched a chord in him. Especially the slashing violins when Janet Leigh got knifed. Now that was music. Not exactly garrotting music, but then what was? He considered his own record collection, all of them LPs mail-ordered from the RCA Victor best-seller club (any five for $3.98) and came up with Mario Lanza and the soundtrack recording of his last film, *For the First Time*. Some kind of big tenor anyway. You had to have someone singing his heart out, fit to bust, to properly juxtapose a truly cinematic strangulation.

He moved a little closer as Janet Leigh pulled up at the Bates Motel. By the time she had eaten her sandwich and drunk her milk, Tom was only two rows behind Lanz, who was nervously smoking his third and probably his last cigarette.

Tom's cue to move again was when Janet Leigh removed her blouse. Lanz threw away his cigarette, too busy watching her undress to smoke now or to pay any attention to what was happening in the row behind. How much else would she show? Tom was certain that this was what Lanz would be thinking. It was what he had thought himself.

Stepping demurely into the bathtub, Janet drew the curtain and began to shower. How like Mary she looked, thought Tom as he recalled her in the shower that morning. Different hair colour of course, and Mary's skin was a little darker, but the body was the same.

Tom tightened the string and waited for the bathroom door to open, and the blurred outline of Norman Bates to appear on the other side of the shower curtain, as through a glass darkly (his favourite text in the Bible). Like a conductor steadying his orchestra, Leonard Bernstein taking on the New York Philly, Tom raised both his gloved hands in the air, and then struck the second that Bates tore the curtain aside, collaring Lanz's neck with the all but invisible string that connected them.

Gritting his teeth, Tom pulled the guitar string in two opposite directions with all his wiry strength. Lanz's cry of surprise and then pain was hardly audible under the dramatic music and Janet Leigh's piercing scream. He tried to twist around in his seat but Tom, concentrating on squeezing the blood vessels on the right-hand side of Lanz's neck rather than pressuring the airway, held him firmly with the makeshift ligature. Death from cerebral anoxia was always much swifter than by vagal inhibition. Desperately, Lanz kicked out in front of him and clawed at the wire around his neck, but to no avail. He might have somersaulted backwards over the seat and on top of his assailant except for the fact that one leg of his pants got hooked on the ashtray in front of him.

Still keeping the pressure on, Tom leaned back in his seat, putting his whole weight on to the ligature, and tried to watch what was happening on the screen: Norman Bates disappearing back up to the house and Janet Leigh slipping down the tiled bathroom wall, breathing her last few breaths. Reaching for the shower curtain there was a faint glimpse of her nipples before the curtain gave way under her dead weight and she collapsed on to the floor. Then the camera closing in on that dead eye. And the emptiness that now lay behind it. Almost as if nothing had ever been there. How fleeting life was.

Tom stayed where he was until long after Norman Bates had returned with a bucket and a mop and started to clear up, before relaxing a little and finally releasing the string that was now embedded deep in Lanz's constriction-burned neck. Then he looked around, saw that no one was paying him any attention, and checked for a pulse. Lanz was dead all right. As dead as if he'd been stabbed thirty times in a shower. Tom waited for a few minutes and then left through the fire exit. After the air-conditioned chill of the movie theatre it felt good to be back in the warmth of the afternoon sunshine. It felt good to be alive.

Back home, Tom took a bath and ate some dinner while reading through some of the instruction books that Genevieve had given him. *The Church's Seven Special Sacraments. What Every Catholic Should Know about the Catechism.* And, *Growing Up Catholic: The Seeker's Catechism.* He had been a fairly conscientious Catholic up to about the time he went into the army. But it wasn't true that his mother had wished him to be a priest. She had encouraged him to be a doctor. Anyway, after he went to Guadalcanal and Okinawa nothing religious ever made sense to him again. And saving lives looked like harder work than taking them. Tom thought if there was a God he wasn't the kind of God who looked after his friends, and that was pretty much all you needed to know. Praying a lot, living the faith, observing all the high holy days, and confessing your sins – none of it ever prevented you from stopping a Jap .25-calibre bullet in the throat at four hundred yards and taking two hours to drown in your own blood.

But the thing that really annoyed Tom was the idea of confession. Was an act of contrition really all it took to obtain absolution of sins? Because if it was then someone like him saying sorry and meaning it made a mug out of all the people who'd spent years living a decent life. It couldn't be that simple.

Tom threw the handbook he was reading aside in disgust and turned the TV on. It was nearly eight thirty and he wanted to see the debate between Nixon and Kennedy. He wondered how much of the catechism JFK himself believed in? Now that would be a fucking handbook worth reading, he told himself. *How to be President and Press the Button and Still be a Good Catholic.*

In the event it wasn't a debate at all, just the two candidates fielding questions from the news reporters in the Washington studio, and commenting on each other's answers with the polite detachment of two attorneys arguing a point of law. Nixon sounded aggressive and still looked less appealing than the cooler and more handsome Kennedy. Both men seemed overly preoccupied with the subject of American prestige abroad, but neither man seemed the obvious superior of the other. As the standing vice-president, Nixon looked and sounded more experienced. But Kennedy had personality and charm and that counted for a lot in the television age, especially in black and white. It looked like a straight choice between Playmate of the Month and the Vargas girl: one was too true to be good, and the other too good to be true.

JFK was answering a question about some remote Nationalist Chinese islands no one had ever heard of when Tom's doorbell rang. It was Frank Sorges and he looked worried. Tom could guess what about.

90

'Frank,' he said. 'What are you doing here?'

'Can I come in? I'd rather not talk out here.'

'Sure.'

They went into the lounge. Tom walked over to the bar and waved at the sofa. 'Drink?'

'Yeah. Why not? That's a pretty impressive bar you've got, Tom. You wouldn't have any Kahlúa there by any chance?'

'Coming up.' Tom opened a bottle. 'I've had this since last Christmas. I didn't know anyone drank it. Ice?'

'No, just as it comes.' Sorges shrugged. 'I just like the taste of coffee, I guess. Got the taste for it when I was in Mexico last year.'

Tom poured himself a Bourbon and sat down opposite him, but left the TV on.

'Nice place.'

Tom shrugged. 'It's okay, I guess.'

'Are you alone?'

Tom nodded. 'I was just watching the debate.'

'So I see.'

'Is there something on your mind, Frank?'

'As a matter of fact I was wondering if you had remembered where it was that you and Húber Lanz might have met before?'

'Don't you trust him?'

'I don't trust anyone.'

'And that's why you drove here?'

Sorges nodded, almost amused at the idea of it himself.

'I don't remember where we met. But then I haven't lost much sleep trying. How the fuck should I know? Ask him. Next time save yourself a journey and call.'

Sorges sipped some of the Kahlúa and stared at the TV.

'What does Lanz say?' asked Tom.

'Not much. He's dead.'

'I see.' Tom lit a Chesterfield and laughed.

'Did I say something funny?'

'Not yet. But I've a feeling you will. What the hell happened?'

'Someone strangled him in a fucking movie theatre.'

'I'm choked. And you think it was me, right?'

'Maybe. Why not? It's what you do, isn't it?'

Tom guffawed loudly. 'There you go,' he said. 'I knew you were going to make me laugh. You're Irwin fucking Corey, you know that, Frank? I'd laugh a lot louder only I'm afraid you might get the idea that I don't regret poor Húber's unfortunate demise, and suspect me all the more.'

'Do you? Regret it?'

'Makes no difference to me if he's lying next to Gerardo Machado in Woodlawn Park cemetery, or whooping it up with Anita Ekberg in Palm Beach. He's just some guy who only vaguely registered the first time I met him.'

'The way I figure it, Tom, it takes someone with a lot of cool nerve to kill a guy in broad daylight. But, like I say, it's what you do. From what I hear, do pretty well.'

'I thought you said it happened in a movie theatre.'

'In a public place, then. Either way, someone who knew what they were about. Someone who's used to killing other people.'

'Don't ever be a detective, Frank. Evidence is supposed to look a little more substantial than a lousy hill of beans.'

'Maybe. Maybe I just wanted to look you in the eye when I told you the bad news.'

'Then get closer so you can make doubly sure.'

But Sorges looked away, almost embarrassed.

'Frank, you've got more maybe baby than Buddy Holly. Maybe you think you can see into my soul, is that it?'

'Maybe,' grinned Sorges. 'Why not?'

'You're wasting your time, Frank. There's no such thing. Soul's Ray Charles or it's nothing at all.' He picked up one of the little pamphlets on the Catholic catechism and tossed it into Sorges's lap. 'I think you're the one who should read up on how to be a priest, not me.'

Sorges looked at the cover and nodded. 'There's not much I wouldn't read for two hundred and fifty thousand bucks.'

'If that's all there was to it, then you'd be in a job, I guess.'

'Maybe. But if it was up to me we'd poison the bastard. O'Connell told me he heard CIA chemists have developed all kinds of new shit. Mind control drugs. Poisons. They've got this stuff called Blackleaf Forty. Sprayed on some tobacco leaves, rolled into a Montecristo cigar and then smoked by Castro. Dead within the minute. Simple as that.'

'Poison, huh? You see, that's what I mean. You really have missed your vocation, Frank. Catholic priests always did like poison.' Tom lit another cigarette. 'How do you know O'Connell, anyway?'

'I don't really. He's Rosselli's contact. Rosselli's in the middle of everything. Him and Maheu. But Johnny's okay, you know? He loves America almost as much as he hates fucking communists. Momo says, you give Johnny a flag and he'll follow you around the yard.'

They were both silent for a long while, watching the TV. Finally, Sorges said, with contempt, after listening to one of Kennedy's smoother answers, 'Listen to him. Mister fucking clean. If people could only hear what I've heard. Him and Marilyn. Like a pair of fucking rabbits. Man, they should broadcast that and see what the man's polls are like in the morning. Mark my words, we're about to have a sex maniac loose in the White House.'

'Is that so?' And then: 'Freshen your glass?'

'Sure.'

Tom refilled their glasses and came back to the sofa.

'You gotta hand it to Kennedy though,' he said. 'If you're gonna risk your presidency to fuck some broad, she might as well be the best-looking broad in the world.'

'She doesn't pull my chain,' grimaced Sorges. 'Novak. Russell. Now you're talking.'

'Marilyn's got everything I want.'

'Take my word for it, man. You hear the tape, you wouldn't be so impressed with her. She doesn't even come when he fucks her.'

'Hardly her fault, I'd have thought.'

'Uppers, downers, you name it, she takes it. The woman is falling to pieces. Ask Momo.'

'I'd sure like to pick those pieces up. She's got something. I dunno. Star quality. Vulnerability. Charisma.'

'Well, Merry Charisma, my star-struck friend. You must believe in Santy Claus.' Sorges toasted Tom with his coffee liqueur. 'Charisma, my ass. Jack Kennedy fucks her like she's just some dumb broad he picked up in Burdine's. You ask me, it's the only way you can fuck a broad like that. Like she's nobody. Pay any attention to who you think she is, you'd never get it up her pussy, man.'

'I can't believe that.'

'Forget about it. She's just another piece of meat for him, I swear. And let me tell you, the guy owns the fucking butcher's shop.'

Tom looked unconvinced.

'Don't take my word for it,' said Sorges. 'I'll bring the tape. I can fix it. This surveillance guy? I think his name is Bernie something. He works for Hoffa and Momo. He's a friend of Johnny's. Johnny used to be a telephone man himself. Maybe I'll speak to Johnny. We can make an evening of it, hey? What do you say?'

'Sounds like fun,' said Tom. 'Sure, why not?'

'Gotta tape machine?'

Tom showed him the Phonotrix portable tape-recorder he had bought the previous summer. Almost as light as a camera, he sometimes used it for reconnaissance work.

'This is no good,' said Sorges.

'What do you mean, no good? This cost me a hundred bucks.'

'Three-inch spool's too small. I'm talking several hours of tape, here. You'd better come and hear it at the safe house. Besides, Johnny doesn't like lending it out that much. He'd probably feel happier if I kept a hold of it.'

'I can imagine,' said Tom.

'Why bother, when I can save you the trouble? That's what this is all about. After you hear this tape you won't ever have to imagine what it's like with her again. You won't want to either. You'll know, man. You'll know all there is to know. That she's a whore. That she wears a G string, or sometimes no panties at all. That she likes him to talk dirty when he's fucking her. That she likes to suck his dick. That she even takes it up the ass.'

'That's okay,' shrugged Tom. 'Nobody's perfect.'

6

The Highway of the Dead

Tom's idea was to give Everton Echeverria a trial run somewhere other than Cuba. Since he had to go to Mexico City anyway, Tom suggested that the MIRR send Echeverria down there on some kind of wild goose chase that would test his reliability. And so, on 13 October, a Thursday, the day of the third Nixon/JFK debate, Tom flew Pan American to the oldest city in North America. Around the same time, Everton Echeverria was boarding a Continental Trailways bus in Laredo, on the last stage of a long and gruelling journey from Miami. It would be another twenty-four hours before he arrived.

Tom liked Mexico City a lot, although it was fast becoming just another city of skyscrapers. The newest tallest building, the Latino-Americano, was some forty-five storeys high and it was here, at the Bankers' Club on the top floor, that Tom met the manager of the Banco de Comercio for an early lunch, before visiting the branch on Venastiano Carranza to review his account and to sign some papers. The hundred thousand dollars from Rosselli's consortium of mob and CIA had been deposited just a few days before and Tom wanted to remove twenty-five thousand of it in cash, to take back to Miami and place in his safety deposit box at the Pan American bank.

In the afternoon he arranged through his hotel, the Reforma, the hire of a chauffeur-driven car and, as was his habit – on average, Tom visited Mexico City twice every year – he went out to see the pyramids at Teotihuacan. It was one of his favourite places, with the Pyramid of the Sun, at 216 feet high, approaching Egyptian dimensions. The sides were terraced, with wide steps leading up to the summit, and Tom always made a point of climbing to the top. He liked heights, although sometimes he felt naked on top of the pyramid without a rifle. From there he had a superb view of the Pyramid of the Moon, the Temples of Tlaloc, of Quetzalcoatl and the Highway of the Dead. It was the only place that ever made Tom feel like he believed in a God.

Back in Mexico City he met up with two members of the local anti-Castro community, Leopoldo and Angel, at the cocktail bar in Tom's hotel. A member of the Intercontinental Hotel Group, the Reforma was the city's most modern hotel, and the bar one of the smartest. As soon as Tom saw the two Cubans he realised it had been a mistake to see them there. Leopoldo was tall and aged about forty; Angel was shorter and wore tinted glasses. Neither man was educated, and neither was clean. They both wore greasy polyester suits and brightly coloured Nybuc nylon slip-ons; Leopoldo's were red, and Angel's light blue, which was the way Tom managed to remember who was who. An angel in blue shoes. Neither one of them spoke any English, and they both smoked Old Gold and drank Margaritas.

'We'll meet your friend off the bus,' said Leopoldo. 'That's no problem. We meet lots of people off that particular bus. And we've booked him a room with bath at the Hotel del Comercio.' Worrying an eczematous earlobe, he laughed and looked around at the Reforma's sumptuous interior. 'Of course, it's nothing like this place. Not for a dollar a day. But Orlando said that it didn't matter. The cheaper the better.'

Tom nodded, trying to contain his loathing for the two Cubans. 'That's right,' he said. 'You did good.' He ordered another round of drinks to help loosen their tongues. You could never know too much about the scum you were working with. Even when your first instinct was to shoo them away like a pair of mangy dogs. 'But don't bring him here. He works with horses and I don't want the little punk stinking the place out. Have him wait for me at the Bottoms Up, this time tomorrow. No wait. Better make it the Florida bar. That way he won't forget where to go. Besides, I take him to the Bottoms Up and he's liable to think I'm giving him dinner.'

'Exactly what are you giving him?' asked Angel 'Orlando didn't say.'

'Just a drink and a package to take home with him. This is kind of a dry run to see if he can be trusted to perform a courier service for us in Cuba. You see, I'll know if the package has been opened, on account of the fact that he'll be real pissed off when he finds out that it contains nothing more than a couple of copies of the Beatnik dictionary.'

Leopoldo laughed. 'A mule, then. It figures. Orlando wanted us to take some pictures, too. Everton looking like he's headed for the OK Corral. Rifle, sidearm, the full Burt Lancaster.'

'Where are you going to do that?'

'Back at my place,' said Angel. 'I live in Los Remedios. It's a small town, about fifteen miles out. I've got plenty of guns there.' He chuckled. 'Enough to start another revolution.'

'If there's time,' added Leopoldo, 'we'll maybe even get Everton to hand out some anti-Castro literature in front of the Cuban embassy.'

'Why there?' asked Tom.

'Because, my friend, the CIA runs a photographic surveillance operation outside the embassy. Orlando figures him being seen handing out leaflets like that will be enough to give Everton a file. But don't ask me why. We just do what we are asked to do.'

'Are there many of you down here?'

'Enough. It's easier getting into Cuba from down here.'

'Easier getting all kinds of things in and out of Mexico,' observed Angel. 'Maybe you'd like to score some dope while you're down here?'

'No, thanks,' said Tom. 'I've always been more of a juicehead, myself.' He shrugged. 'But a man's gotta making a living. Who runs the show down here?'

'Harold Meltzer.'

'Really?' said Tom, impressed.

'It's a pretty big show.'

They talked for a while longer before Tom looked at his watch and informed his guests that he had a dinner appointment.

'Somewhere nice?'

Tom smiled. It was his turn to be pumped.

'French place on Lopez,' he said smoothly. 'The Normandia.'

'Fancy,' grinned Angel.

They all left together. Tom watched them get into a battered Oldsmobile, and then hailed a taxi. He rode it only as far as Chapultepec Park, at the end of Paseo de Reforma, just to make sure he wasn't being followed. For a few minutes he walked around under the ahuehuete trees, enjoying the fountains and early-evening air before catching another cab and telling the driver to take him not to the Normandia, but to the Cadillac Grill.

Alex Goldman finished eating and, leaning back in his chair, loosened his hand-stitched belt by a notch.

'Best fuckin' dinner I've had since I've been in MC.'

He poured them both some more red wine and stifled a belch with the back of a large hand.

'What are you supposed to be doing down here anyway?' enquired Tom. 'Aren't you a little out of your jurisdiction?'

'Yes, and no,' said Goldman, lighting his Kaywoodie pipe. 'Back in the forties the FBI built the whole special intelligence spy network in Mexico. For that matter, in the whole of Latin America. Anyway, come nineteen forty-seven, Truman told Hoover to hand over all his SIS assets to the CIA, and Hoover being Hoover didn't take too kindly to that. Nor did most of the agents down here, who suddenly found themselves working for the CIA instead of the Bureau. You got to understand, for a lot of those guys the Bureau was their whole life. So, while Mexico City may be a CIA station today – one of the biggest, too, just like the KGB – in spirit, it's still Bureau. The head of station in MC, fellow by the name of Winston McKinlay Scott, he's ex-FBI, as are most of the heads of section. Which means that Mexico Station maintains an unusually close relationship with the Bureau.

'You might even characterise it as a covert relationship, because Allen Dulles and the rest of the Company boys up in Washington know nothing about it. Officially I'm down here at the behest of the

Bureau of Narcotics to liaise with the Mexican Internal Security Police and the United States embassy's legal attaché to probe the relationship between the Mexican DFS – that's their equivalent of the CIA – and major drug trafficking organisations back in Miami. Lansky, the Teamsters, Happy Meltzer. But in actual fact, I'm down here for the usual COINTELPRO reasons.' Goldman glanced inside the bowl of his pear-shaped briar, then put it down. 'As part of the FBI's never-ending fight against the forces of international communism.' Goldman raised his glass and chuckled. 'Well, here's to it. What would we ever find to do without the Russians?'

Tom clinked Goldman's glass and looked back across his shoulder. Just to make sure he hadn't been followed. He had already told Goldman about the anti-Castro exiles he had encountered in Miami. Now he added some information about the two characters he had met in Mexico City.

'They said they worked for Meltzer,' he said, almost as an afterthought.

'And Meltzer runs things for Lansky,' shrugged Goldman. 'He smuggles most of the Mexican heroin into the United States. It's a regular fucking fraternity, that's what it is.'

'Sounds a bit like your own outfit,' observed Tom.

'Hell, they're much better organised than we are. More co-operative, too. As a rule, with our security and intelligence agencies, the left hand doesn't really know what the right hand is doing. The CIA doesn't speak to the Bureau who don't speak to the Secret Service who don't speak to the cops. No sir, not everyone's as gregarious and friendly as me. Being COINTELPRO means there's no fucker telling me who I can and who I can't speak to. Hell, I even speak to the Secret Service. Not that there's any big secret mind you. Other than the obvious one, which is that those bastards are all muscle and no brain. I mean, it's no accident they're called the Secret Service instead of something to do with intelligence like the rest of us. Last November, I had to go up to Augusta, Georgia. This was around the time Ike and Mamie were at their place there. Ike was playing golf and painting by numbers. Anyway, I met up with some of those Secret Service boys. And man, do they like to party. I'm glad they're not looking after my ass, that's all I can say.' Goldman wagged a big finger in Tom's direction. 'One day, Paladin. One day, it's all going to come unstuck, big time. I just hope I'm there to see their stupid faces when it does. That's one picture I'd like to see.

'Where is that fucking waiter? We need some more wine here.'

Not finding one, Goldman reached down and, taking off his shoe, grunted painfully.

'What?' asked Tom. 'Are you planning to get the waiter's attention with that shoe? Khrushchev style?'

Seeing Goldman look puzzled, and realising he probably hadn't seen an American newspaper, Tom related the story in that morning's *New York Times*, about how the Soviet Premier had banged his desk with his shoe when the Philippine delegate to the United Nations accused Russia of imperialism in eastern Europe.

'Communism will try and bring the world to heel, one way or another,' added Tom.

Goldman found a waiter and ordered another bottle of wine. They talked a while longer, about some of the other things that had been in the paper. Tom could tell that Goldman was going to ask him to perform a service for him. But it was only when Tom mentioned the assassination of the leader of the Japanese socialist party, Asanuma, that he finally got around to it.

'That I did hear. There was something about it on the AP and UPI wires. Some fucking right-wing student attacked him with a bayonet, wasn't it? Jesus. Typical fucking Jap, huh?'

'Yeah.'

'Listen Tom, how'd you like to go to Acapulco? Tonight. There's an Aeronaves flight leaves one a.m.'

'To do what?'

'What you're good at.'

Tom screwed up his eyes and opened them again. He looked at his watch. 'Jesus, Alex, it's ten o'clock. Why didn't you say earlier? I wouldn't have drink so much.'

'Forget about it. It's the kind of job you could handle in your sleep.'

Tom stretched and yawned. 'Looks that way.' He shook his head. 'I haven't got a weapon.'

'You think I'm expecting you to do it with just a fucking bayonet? Come on, Tom. You know me better than that. There's a takedown

Winchester seventy with a Unertl scope and a suppresser in the trunk of my car.'

'A takedown?' Tom winced. 'You want me to use a takedown?'

'Yeah, yeah, I know what you're thinking. That there's a trade-off in accuracy.'

'All those threads and surfaces and tensions,' grumbled Tom.

'But this is a good piece of kit.'

'Hex screws imperfectly torqued.'

'Listen,' insisted Goldman. 'I test-fired this weapon myself. Put it back together, refired it, and found no discernible zero shift. Believe me, this is a beautiful rifle. It comes in a nice hard-shell carrying case with a foam plastic interior. Real James Bond stuff, I swear.'

'Which book?' asked Tom.

Goldman thought for a moment. 'Doesn't he use a takedown in *From Russia with Love*?'

'Actually,' said Tom, 'it's not Bond who uses it, but the Turkish guy, Darko Bey.'

'Yeah, you're right. Where the fuck does he get these names?'

Tom hedged. He wasn't keen to go anywhere other than bed. 'Why does it have to be tonight?'

'Because tomorrow's the last day of the target's vacation. Believe me, this couldn't be easier. The guy goes water-skiing in Acapulco bay every morning at nine o'clock. I've booked you a cottage with a sea-view at El Mirador. You can make the shot and be back here by lunchtime.'

Tom poured himself another glass of wine and then thought better of it. If he was going to shoot a man at nine o'clock the next morning he would need a clear head. Instead, he lit a Chesterfield. Already he had shelved most of his objections.

'Or, if you want, you can stay on and have a good time at the Bureau's expense. There's a cat-house down there, the Casa Raquel, that I can personally recommend. A real class joint.'

But Tom was shaking his head. 'What sort of range are we talking about?'

'Four hundred yards. Five hundred max. The cottage is right on La Quebrada cliffs. From there you could hit Cuba.'

Tom grimaced. 'I hate sea-shots.'

'Oh come on. I remember you back on the island of Saipan, sitting in a rubber boat, picking off Japs at night. At night, mind. For you this is automatic pilot.'

'So who's the dead man?'

'A Russian guy.'

'A Russian?' Tom sounded surprised. 'A Russian? You are getting ambitious.'

'No, just careful. His name is Pavel Zaitsev and he works here in MC as a consular official. Pretty good volleyball player, by all accounts.'

'Not much of a reason to shoot him.'

'Really, he's GRU. Russian military intelligence. And he's been making things quite awkward down here.'

'I'll bet he's their top scorer, right?' Tom nodded. 'Okay, if you say so.'

'Attaboy, Paladin. Zaitsev's staying at your hotel, so you can't miss him. There's a funicular down to the hotel swimming pool where the Aqua Mundo boat company picks him up every morning regular as clockwork. Blue hull, twin-engined job. Zaitsev's a big fellow. Looks like Harmon Killebrew. You know, the AL home run slugger? Balding. There's a photograph of him in the takedown case. Plus an air ticket and your hotel reservation. You're going to love Acapulco, Tom. Cortés called the placed *tierra caliente*, the hot land, but after MC, the climate is actually quite pleasant.' Goldman clapped Tom on the back. 'Anyway, you can probably use the practice. It's been a while since you did a job for us, Paladin.'

Tom killed Zaitsev as easily as Alex Goldman had predicted he would. An excellent, graceful water-skier, Zaitsev presented a simple moving target. With the tow-handle coolly hooked in the crook of his arm, he had been in the act of waving confidently to the people up in the boat when Tom squeezed the trigger. Then Tom sat and waited for the boat to come around and begin the search, enjoying the sun on his face, the scent of sea air, pine groves, and cup-of-gold bushes, and the refreshing taste of some cold coconut milk. With the sky such a faultless shade of blue, it had hardly seemed possible that a life should just disappear between the waves as easily as a lobster pot.

In the boat it took them all of thirty minutes to find and recover Zaitsev's body. Through binoculars Tom watched them haul the body out of the water and saw that his shot had taken off the crown of Zaitsev's skull, like the top of a boiled egg. The boat was too far away for him to hear anything. There was just the bloody sight of a rubbery corpse and the two girls who had accompanied Zaitsev, screaming in silence.

Tom was back in Mexico City just after lunch, reflecting that he hadn't much cared for Acapulco. To him it was just another holiday resort, like Miami Beach but with better scenery. He preferred the city he was in now, once the ancient Aztec capital of Tenochtitlán, and the centre of the cult of Huitzilpochtli.

The Aztecs were people of the sun chosen by Huitzilpochtli to provide him with nourishment. His sustenance was human blood, and lots of it. As Aztec power grew, prisoners from all over Mexico were sacrificed in Tenochtitlán so that the universe and man might survive. One conquistador estimated the number of human skulls hanging on show to be 136,000. Blood was treated like holy water, and spattered over the doors and pillars of Mexican temples and houses. Mercy was an alien concept, as alien to the ancient peoples of Mexico as it was to Tom himself. The Nehuatl Indian word for sacrifice, *nextlaoalitzli*, actually meant an act of payment. This was Tom's kind of language. It was no wonder he thought he felt so very much at home there.

7

In a Boston Accent

'The margin is narrow, but the responsibility is clear . . . a margin of only one vote would still be a mandate.'

Thus spoke the thirty-fifth President-elect of the United States, having achieved a majority of less than one hundred and twenty thousand votes.

'So now my wife and I prepare for a new administration and a new baby.'

But it was what John F. Kennedy had said not to a press conference in Hyannis Port, Massachusetts, nor to the sixty-nine million Americans who had voted, but to just one American that interested Tom Jefferson more when, on the ninth day of November 1960, he left his home in Miami Shores and drove to the safe house at 6312 Riviera Drive in Coral Gables to meet Frank Sorges and to hear that much-vaunted tape. Just thinking about it was enough to give him an erection. He was actually going to hear the love goddess, the magnificent Marilyn, making love, and to no less a person than everyone's man of the moment, America's number one golden boy. It was the stuff of *Confidential* magazine and he wished Mary had been around so that he could have teased her.

These past few days he had spoken to her only on the telephone;

what with the election, the anxiety of the count – Kennedy's early lead had shrunk steadily for much of the Tuesday, 8 November, until, at around four o'clock the following morning, victory had started to look a little more certain – and then the celebrations, which seemed likely to last through until Thursday, Tom hadn't actually seen her since Saturday night. By now he was used to her irregular hours, more or less. Back in the middle of October, when Kennedy had gone to Tampa to make a campaign speech about Latin America and an alliance for progress, Tom didn't see Mary or even speak to her on the telephone for forty-eight hours. But that was okay, too. She was just doing her job. The two of them were still a team with a common interest. To borrow Kennedy's phrase, Tom and Mary were *una alianza para el progreso*. Only it was their own idea of progress. And an unusual kind of alliance.

It had been strange to see Kennedy quoted speaking Spanish. Strange and, after Orlando Bosch's forecast of an early invasion of Cuba, just a little disturbing. Not that Castro himself seemed much inclined to care. On 25 October, the week after Kennedy's Tampa speech, Castro had signed a decree nationalising those few remaining enterprises that belonged to American companies. Speaking to a group of army cadets just a few days later, Castro had challenged America to invade his country. At the same time, the Ministry of Health launched a campaign to persuade Cuban citizens to give blood. Meanwhile, thousands of miles away, another kind of launch – or at least the capacity for a launch – was being made manifest, with intent: on the day Americans went to the polls, missiles appeared for the first time at the annual parade in Red Square. A campaign speech and a rhetorical alliance was one thing; ICBMs were evidence of quite another kind of alliance, and one that Tom hoped the new President would pay attention to.

Tom was a little early for his five o'clock meeting with Sorges, so he stopped for a haircut at Johnny's Barber Shop on North West 27th Avenue. The place was air-conditioned and Johnny, a dark, balding man in his early forties, was reading the paper. 'We treat you like a friend' read a sign on the wall. That was fine with Tom, who had being going there often enough for Johnny to remember that this was

105

one friend who didn't like to talk. In the twenty minutes it took to cut Tom's hair, Johnny even managed not to mention the election.

Coming out of the shop, Tom paused in the doorway. A breeze from the west was carrying the sound of a brass band. Tom turned to Johnny and said, 'You hear that?'

'Probably the local high school,' explained Johnny. 'They got a marching band. Pretty good one, too.'

The two men stood there for a moment or two, long enough for Johnny to be able to identify the tune. '"Hail to the Chief",' he said.

'Kennedy's favourite tune,' said Tom, and started towards his car. 'Perhaps he's on his way.'

'Yeah, maybe they know something we don't.'

'From what I hear, Johnny, it's just the girls who know that much. Just the girls.'

Tom drove on, stopping again only once to pick up a bottle of Mary's favourite perfume, Lanvin's 'My Sin', at a beauty shop on Almeria, in Coral Gables. It seemed appropriate after all her hard work. Then he went to Riviera Drive.

Just south of the golf course of the same name, and overlooking Coral Gables Waterway, in an expensive palm-fringed street, the safe house was a two-storey affair with a high stone wall, a large iron gate, and a tiled roof with a little cupola. Tom pulled the bell on the gatepost, and after a few minutes Sorges, smoking a cigar and wearing a ribbed mohair V-neck and a pair of deck pants, came into the garden to let him in.

'You're early.'

'Occupational habit. Same way as when I go near a tall building I'm liable to start looking for cover.'

'What did I tell you?' Sorges clapped Tom on the shoulder. 'The Chicago poll? It was just like Momo promised. Kennedy won it by four hundred and fifty-six thousand votes. You know, without Illinois, Kennedy would have had only seven electoral college votes more than Nixon. And then the whole election could have been wide open. Might even have gone to the House of Representatives to decide. Just think about that. Four hundred and fifty-six thousand votes. That's four times as much as his final tally in the whole fucking country. When Momo fixes something, he fixes it good.'

106

Sorges ushered Tom through the big wooden door. It was cool inside the house, but this was down to the record playing on the limed oak phonola as much as to the air-conditioning: a brooding, melancholic Spanish arrangement for a solo trumpet and jazz band. Liking it immediately, Tom picked up the LP and saw that it was Miles Davis playing 'Sketches of Spain'.

'You like that, do you?' asked Sorges.

Tom thought the sound seemed to speak to him personally. And the last line on the sleeve note, from the Spanish writer Ferran, managed to characterise both the music and his own character: 'Alas for me! The more I seek my solitude, the less of it I find. Whenever I look for it, my shadow looks with me.' He nodded, and said, 'Yeah, it's nice.' Looking around, he added, 'Nice place, too. Yours?'

'Hell, no. Belongs to the Company. Or maybe Howard Hughes. Or maybe Meyer Lansky. I'm not exactly sure which. I'm just the house-sitter today.'

'Howard Hughes? What's his involvement in all this?'

'Bob Maheu works for Hughes. Before that he was with the Bureau and probably the CIA, too, for all I know. Bob's got more connections than Pan American. To be honest I'm not exactly sure what Hughes expects to gain. But I've heard he's already after a piece of the action in Vegas, so maybe he thinks to buy some of the Havana casinos from a new Cuban government. Drink?'

'Bourbon.'

Sorges collected two tumblers, an ice-bucket and a bottle of Ezra Brooks and led the way to a big leather Chesterfield. He placed the tumblers on a glass coffee table, next to a Soundcraft tape box.

'Sit down,' he said, dropping on to the sofa. 'Take the weight off your Bob Smarts.' He poured two large ones and collected his glass in a mug-sized fist.

At the same moment Tom realised who it was the big man reminded him of. Jack London. He'd seen a picture of the author in a bookstore when he'd gone in to buy Errol Flynn's autobiography.

Tom put himself down on the sofa with less aplomb and picked up his drink. Thinking Sorges was about to propose a toast, and hating to drink to anything other than a better frame of mind, he said, 'Under the circumstances, it hardly seems appropriate to drink to our new President.'

'No, I guess not,' admitted Sorges.

'Is that the tape?'

His mouth full of Bourbon, Sorges nodded, and then, 'Just don't tell your friends.'

'I don't have any friends,' said Tom, but without any trace of self-pity. It was true, more or less. He kept himself to himself. Never did much more than nod to the neighbours. Most of the people he came into contact with were afraid of him. He knew that, and it didn't bother him. Living a secret life was hard enough without having to explain things to friends.

'Your wife, then. She works for the Democrats, doesn't she?'

'I won't tell anyone,' said Tom, lighting up a Chesterfield. 'I'm not the gabby type, in case you hadn't noticed. A big mouth looks bad for business.'

'Is that all it is for you? Just business?'

'You mean, do I get any pleasure out of it?'

Sorges shrugged his curiosity. 'You said it.'

'It's just something I do, that's all,' said Tom. 'You might as well ask Truman if he got any pleasure ordering the atomic bombing of Hiroshima and Nagasaki. It was a job that needed doing. Which is the way I look at my own job. Pleasure or dislike doesn't even come into it.'

'I think I'd enjoy killing Castro,' admitted Sorges. 'We've got a history, me and him. I owe that bastard, big time.'

'Can't say that I ever enjoyed killing anyone. Not even in the war. And like I say, some of those guys needed killing.'

'Oh, Castro needs killing, all right. Make no mistake about that. There's no shortage of blood on his hands. And everything and everyone is ready to do it, too. Everton, Genevieve, Diaz Castillo, Gonzales, they're all in Cuba right now. And our people have been back to Everton's house and cleaned up that rifle, added a heavy match barrel and a flash suppressor, a leather cheek-piece and a telescopic sight. Wearing some of Everton's old clothes, including his gloves, one of our guys even fired some shots, and made sure that some fibres from his shirt stuck to the stock. They've also left some

108

other stuff in his room. Articles about Castro, old gun mags, ammunition – live and spent – and some of those photographs we took in Mexico City. It's as nice a frame as you'd see hanging in an art gallery. How are you coming along with the priest routine?'

'Pretty good,' said Tom. 'Listen.' He cleared his throat, composed himself for a second, and then began to chant: 'Si capax, ego te absolvo a peccatis tuis, in nomine Patris, et Filii, et Spiritus Sancti. Amen.' Tom made the sign of the cross with his thumb, as if anointing with holy oil.

'What is this?' asked Sorges. 'Method acting?'

Tom continued to chant. 'Per istam sanctam Unctionem, indulgeat tibi Dominua quid-quid deliquisti. Amen.' More crossing. 'Ego facultate mihi ab Apostolica Sede tributa, indulgentiam plenariam et remissionem omnium peccatorum tibi concedo, et benedicto te. In nomine Patris, et Filii, et Spiritus Sancti. Amen.'

'Hey, that's pretty good,' nodded Sorges. 'Marlon Brando couldn't have done that better. What does it all mean, anyway?'

'It's the last rites,' said Tom.

'I can see how that might attract you.'

'You see, I was thinking, suppose I shoot Castro, walk out of that church, and then someone wants a priest to grant Castro the forgiveness of sins? It would look kind of weird if I didn't know the last rites. So I thought I'd better learn it. Just in case.'

'Now there's a thought,' snorted Sorges. 'Wouldn't that be something? He'd go to hell for sure.'

'I know he's a communist 'n' all, but from what I've been reading about him, he was a pretty devout Catholic when he was a kid. Went to a Jesuit school. And earlier this year he made a speech in which he said that to betray the poor was to betray Christ.' Tom shrugged. 'Be just like the thing if he turned Catholic again at the last minute. A lot of people do, you know.'

'I guess you're right at that,' agreed Sorges. 'Better safe than sorry, huh? Well, Marlon, soon we'll take you down to Key West and have you on a boat for Havana. You can even bless the boat if it helps you to get into the part. Just as soon as we get the word from Momo.'

'Now that Kennedy's elected, what's stopping him?'

'Nothing. Nothing at all. Matter of fact Rosselli's going to call me here this afternoon. If things work out we'll have your holy ass in Havana sometime next week. As it happens, Castro's going to be making a lot of speeches in the next couple of months. So we'll have plenty of opportunities to kill him. In December and January there are a lot of landmarks in the history of the revolution. On December third we have the anniversary of the landing of the *Granma*, the boat that carried Fidel and the other revolutionaries from Mexico in fifty-six. January first we've got the anniversary of Batista's resignation. And on January eighth we've got the anniversary of Castro's triumphant arrival in Havana. But we think you may get a shot even before then. The word from Genevieve is that those dumb bastards are going to ban Christmas and Santa Claus.'

'You're kidding,' laughed Tom.

'They'll do it. Maybe you're right. Maybe they will all die as Catholics, but for the time being they intend to live as communists. Besides, food's in short supply. And money's a little tight right now. Too tight to waste on Christmas. So that means no Santa Claus. But at least Castro has a beard. Who knows? Maybe the Big Barbudo can take the place of Father Christmas. Our people think that he'll make some sort of speech about the revolutionary season of goodwill to all communists, or some such shit. Most probably on Christmas Eve. I take it you have no ethical objections to that?'

'I've no particular plans for Christmas,' said Tom.

'If you're on target my friend, Christmas nineteen sixty could turn out to be the best Christmas I ever had. Fidel Castro with a bullet in his head sure beats the hell out of a pipe-rack and a Max Factor travel trio.'

'So that's what that smell is.'

'All sorts of gladsome gifties will be coming to fill your Christmas stocking if you pull this off.'

'I was kind of hoping for a Swank electric putt machine,' admitted Tom. 'For just fourteen ninety-five it returns your ball to you after you've holed out.'

'And I'll give you the solid silver putter from Tiffany's to go with it, you blow him away.' Sorges stood up. 'Help yourself to another drink,' he said. 'While we listen to the chief executive get laid.'

He collected the tape, went over to the phonola, and lifted the stylus off the LP. Kneeling down, he started to thread the tape through the head of the Sony Stereocorder that was on the floor underneath the phonola.

'On second thoughts,' said Tom. 'You can forget the Swank and the silver putter.' He poured himself another drink. 'A night with Marilyn will do me just fine.'

Glancing across his shoulder at Tom, Sorges looked sheepish. Then he cleared his throat, and said, 'Yeah, I'm real sorry about that. But this isn't Marilyn you're gonna hear.'

Tom felt himself becoming irritated. He raised surprised eyebrows at Sorges and smiled thinly. 'It isn't?'

'Not exactly, no.'

Tom nodded, unimpressed with this development. 'Not exactly? What, you mean it's some dozy douche-bag of a ditzy blonde doing a grotesque imitation of the real thing? Or something else? Marilyn minus the sigh and the wiggle and the Spanish fly in her voice? Marilyn with a bad cold, maybe?'

Irritated, Sorges frowned back at Tom. 'I don't know who the hell it is. Just some broad Kennedy banged on the road. An actress, or a model, I think. Look, Johnny doesn't know I'm letting you hear this. I had to borrow it without his permission. So it was kind of pot luck I'm afraid. It was this one or nothing. The guy who was doing these recordings just got busted in Vegas. He was bugging Sam's girl-friend's room, to see if she was fucking some other guy. Anyway Johnny's kind of pissed about the whole thing. Blames it on Maheu for some reason. I think he's put the Marilyn tape in a safe, somewhere. So like I say, this is all there is.'

Tom gazed rudely at the ceiling and then impassively back at Sorges, as if he didn't believe a word of it.

'Look, do you want to hear this goddamned tape, or not?'

'Go ahead,' growled Tom. 'I'm all ears.'

Sorges twisted one of the knobs and the spools began to turn. There was a moment's silence, the sound of a door closing, followed by clothes rustling and some heavy breathing, and then a man's voice.

'Do you like this place?'

'I love it. I've never been to Lake Tahoe before.'

'My brother-in-law, Peter, has a stake in the place with Sinatra. I come here a lot.'

'I know, I read about the Cal-Neva in a magazine. But I never dreamed I'd be here, with you, Jack.'

'Well, now that you are, what are you going to do about it?'

Kennedy's patrician Harvard accent was instantly recognisable with its curiously flat, almost European vowels and its mushed letter 's', as if the President-elect had cultivated a lisp in an effort to sound more like Winston Churchill, who was reportedly his model in rhetoric.

In common with nearly everyone else, Tom thought Kennedy was an excellent orator. Clearly he was a man who believed in the power of words and who took considerable pride in his own real gift for eloquence. Even when, in the cold light of day, some of Kennedy's more idealistic messages seemed hopelessly unrealistic, there was still something about the way he delivered them that made people listen. So it came as something of a shock for Tom to hear Kennedy speaking not as a public figure, about the Cold War, or Indochina, or the Balance of Power, but as a private man, his relaxed, slightly intoxicated conversation studded with references to his lover's pussy, and her asshole, and what he was going to do to her pussy and her asshole just as soon as he got her panties off.

She was every bit as willing and candid as he was, her quiet voice breathless with lust and excitement as she assured Kennedy that he could do anything he wanted to her, that she would suck him, and let him come in her mouth, and up her ass, if that was what turned him on.

'Do you like me to do this, Jack? Is that how you like it?'

'I love that. Don't stop. Oh that's wonderful . . .'

The thrill of hearing the President-elect getting it on in a chalet at the Cal-Neva Lodge was as nothing beside the cold shock Tom felt on recognising the faint trace of the Caribbean in the woman's voice. Hers was a voice as familiar to him as Kennedy's own. More so. Tom swallowed hard as he tried to contain his horror and disgust. The woman on the tape was Mary. He was listening to his own wife being fucked by Jack Kennedy.

'You have the most beautiful mouth, honey. Oh that's wonderful. Just keep doing that.'

'What did I tell you?' laughed Sorges. 'Oh man, I'd love to meet this little lady. Listen to that. She's a fucking animal.'

Tom's first instinct was to tear the obscene tape off the spool and throw it in Sorges's grinning face, before strangling the man with his bare hands. But this lasted only a few seconds. Staying cool and playing a double game was second nature to Tom. And the more he thought about it the more he considered that nothing would have been served by revealing anything to the other man. He decided it was best to remain silent on the subject. So he grinned back and, steeling himself, decided to hear the tape to the end.

8

The Monsignor

Death was never very far away from Tom's thoughts, least of all when he picked up the telephone receiver in his hotel room at La Casa Marina, in Key West. Tom knew straight away that she was dead, even before the Dade County cop told him what had happened. Dully, Tom said he would drive back to Miami immediately and then replaced the receiver.

He glanced at his watch. It was nine thirty in the morning and he was dog-tired after a night on the town with Sorges and Bosch. An hour earlier, Juanita, the maid, would have let herself into the house in Miami Shores, found Mary's body and then called the police. They would have found his hotel number right by the telephone. He lit a cigarette and then called Sorges.

'Frank, it's Tom.'

'Oh Jesus, what time is it?'

'It's nine thirty-five. Listen Frank, I've got to go back to Miami. Right away.'

'Miami? What the hell for? We just got here. And everything's set. The *Flying Tiger*'s picking us up from the harbour front at eight o'clock.' The *Flying Tiger* was the name of a motor yacht that some millionaire had lent to the CIA for the purpose of ferrying Tom into

114

Cuban waters, after which a rubber boat would land him close to Oriente City. 'The Company's even cleared us with the Coast Guard.'

'Yeah, well this'll have to wait. The Dade County police just called.'

'What the fuck did they want?'

'There's been some kind of accident. Mary. My wife. She's dead.'

'Jesus, Tom. Is there anything I can do?'

'No. I'll handle it. Look, I'll call you when I get there. When I find out what's happened.'

'Okay, all right. You do that.'

Tom packed a bag and went and found his car.

Once, Key West had been Florida's most populous city and probably the richest, too. Now, with more than a quarter of the local population Cuban, the place was shabbier and altogether more foreign-looking, like an ersatz version of Havana. Grass grew through the cracks in the flagstones on Roosevelt Boulevard, while cigar factories, shrimp boats, and bordellos were the principal sources of employment. Island time ran slower than on the mainland and, except at night, when the strip-joints on Duval Street got going, no conch, as the locals were known, was ever in a hurry. Even the non-Latins spoke Spanish, ate black beans, played knock rummy, and, sometimes, ran narcotics. Life was uncomplicated, with only the hurricanes to worry about. The last big one, in 1935, had killed more than four hundred people. But for anyone walking through streets lined with poinciana, allamanda, frangipani, and coconut palms, or along the most picturesque of waterfronts with its turtle tanks, pelicans, cormorants, and twenty-thousand-dollar boats, death would have seemed a very distant prospect. That is, for anyone but Tom.

He started the Chevy, picked up some gas, and then hit the blacktop.

The road up from Key West to the mainland on the Overseas Highway was one of the most beautiful drives in the world. Henry M. Flagler had built a railway across the Florida Keys, linking one to another with bridges, like a giant and extremely expensive necklace. Opened to trains in 1912, it had been destroyed by the hurricane of 1935, and rebuilt as the Overseas Highway. With the Atlantic Ocean immediately on one side of the road, and the Gulf of Mexico on the other, sometimes it seemed as though the road was all the land there was. And crossing the lengthy span of the Seven Mile Bridge, upheld by 544 piers sunk below the water line, a car felt like a small plane. It was 156 miles back to Miami and normally, with all the cars towing boats and trailers and rubbernecking tourists, the journey took the best part of four and a quarter hours. But for some reason the route was more or less free of traffic – at least going north – and Tom did the journey in less than three hours. It was the loneliest drive he had ever made.

When Tom arrived back at the house in Miami Shores, there were a couple of police cars parked outside and a small cluster of nosey-parker neighbours gathered on the street corner. A Country Squire station wagon was leaving the scene and it was only later, after Tom had persuaded the uniformed cop on duty outside his own front door to let him inside the house, that he realised the station wagon had been carrying Mary's dead body. He was met by a detective sergeant from the Dade County police who told him that Mary's body had been moved to the County Morgue, in the Miami Hall of Justice, where she was now the coroner's responsibility.

So far, Tom had said very little, but when the detective, whose name was Joe Czernin, offered his condolences, Tom fetched himself a drink from the bar and asked how Mary had died.

'It's a little early to say for sure,' said Czernin. 'But it looks as though she may have taken an overdose of pills and alcohol. It'll be for the coroner's office to decide if that was accidental or if she . . .' Czernin hesitated for a second, his grey eyes moving quickly across Tom's face as if he was trying to judge Tom's capacity to take the unalloyed truth. Then he said, 'To decide if she committed suicide.'

Tom shook his head firmly. 'She wasn't the type.'

Czernin nodded, wishing he had a dollar for every grieving relative who said as much in these cases.

'And there would have been a note.' Tom raised a questioning eyebrow at the detective. 'Is there a note?'

'We haven't found one.'

'Well that's the end of that,' said Tom.

'I know this is difficult for you at this terrible time,' said Czernin. 'But the law is the law. Look, if you could answer some questions right now, I wouldn have to bother you again.'

Tom swallowed the rest of his drink and lit a cigarette with a trembling hand. 'Okay,' he said. 'I guess it's yet to sink in anyway.'

'When did you last see your wife?'

'Not since last Saturday. She worked at the Democratic Party headquarters in Miami. For George Smathers. She was in and out of the house at irregular times. In the final days of the campaign the whole team was working more or less round the clock. And then partying the same way when Kennedy won.'

'And when you last saw her, how did she seem?'

'Tired. And perhaps a little fearful that the campaign was lost. There was a lot of hate literature for Kennedy. And then the polls were see-sawing one way and then the other. Mary said it was too close to call. The way things turned out, Florida wasn't a landslide like Illinois, but then it wasn't a marginal either, like Nevada or New Mexico. For a while back there, they were worried. Real worried. We spoke on the telephone, you see. Even if we didn't see each other, we liked to keep in touch.'

'She was under a lot of pressure?'

'For sure. Mary was one of those people you naturally rely on a lot. And who takes more and more work upon herself.'

Czernin wore a dark suit and a pearl-grey weskit. The hat he kept turning in his hands was a low-tapered grey-felt with a narrow-brim black band. The man looked tougher than his clothes. The hands were hard and leathery and the stance nautically square, as if at any moment he expected a sudden gust of wind. Short grey hair covered his bucket-shaped head like iron filings on a magnet. From time to time he let go of the hat and stroked his hair as if it had been the nap on a piece of velvet.

They were standing by the bar in the lounge. Tom helped himself to another Kentucky Gentleman and watched the cop's eyes rack up all the liquor bottles on display.

'Did she drink much?'

'She was a social drinker. She wasn't one to drink alone.'

'What did she like to drink?'

'Cocktails. Stuff with little umbrellas in. She had a collection of those, somewhere. Otherwise champagne, mostly.'

Czernin started toward the bedroom and, sensing that Tom had

117

stayed put, turned and said in a way that indicated he wanted Tom to follow, 'Do you mind?'

'No, sure, go ahead.'

Tom pushed himself off the bar top and went after the cop, into the hallway with its director's chair, telephone table, and the three-dollar framed sunken treasure map of the Caribbean, and through the bedroom door, squeezing past a photographer who was packing up his flash lamps and his reflective umbrellas. Tom surveyed the crumpled sheets on the thin-edge bed, the clothes on the floor, her Prince Gardner key-gard, the Llama slippers, and next to them, the books she had been reading: James MacGregor Burns's biography of John Kennedy, Joseph Dineen's book on the whole Kennedy family, and *The Ugly American*, by William Lederer and Eugene Burdick, which was Mary's unread Book of the Month Club choice.

'The maid found her,' explained Czernin.

'I figured,' sighed Tom.

The cop approached Mary's swagged-leg bedside table, home to a little vase of nearly dead freesias, and picked up one of the many pill bottles that surrounded the Bonvita opalescent lamp. 'Quite a little dispensary, wouldn't you say? And all on her side of the bed.'

'We were different people, you know? Couple of Bufferin's about the only pill-popping I do.'

'Let's see, we've got Valium, Tryptizol, Nembutal, Seconal, Chloral Hydrate, you name it, it's right here. If it's not, it's in the bathroom cabinet.'

'I tried talking to her about it. But she never paid much attention.'

'And from different drugs stores, too. Breedings Drug Stores – use that one myself sometimes. Sheey's Pharmacy on Beacon Boulevard. Know that one, too. Lile's Pharmacy, in Coconut Grove.' Czernin indicated the bottles he was examining. 'If you wouldn't mind taking a look, Mister Jefferson. Just to make sure that there's nothing here you don't know about. And of course, I'll need the name and number of her doctor.'

Tom saw Mary's shoulder bag hanging on the back of the door. He took out her address book and read out the name and number, which the cop noted down. Then he glanced over the bedside table. 'It all looks familiar enough, I guess,' he said. But among all the bottles was a highball glass containing what looked like Scotch. He bent down to the glass, careful not to touch it, and sniffed.

'It's what it looks like,' said Czernin. 'Scotch.'

Tom shrugged wearily.

'Was your wife in the habit of mixing drugs and alcohol, Mister Jefferson?'

'I wouldn't say it was a habit, exactly. But sometimes, when she came home, and I knew she'd had a drink, she took pills on top. But she never washed them down with alcohol. At least, not when I was around.'

'And exactly where were you last night? In Key West.'

'Exactly?'

'We already know from a neighbour that she returned here at around twelve, last night. It would help to be able to eliminate you from the picture, Mister Jefferson.'

'Let's see. I had dinner around nine with a couple of friends. Frank Sorges and Doctor Bosch. They're both of them staying at La Casa Marina on Reynolds Street, in case you should want to speak to them.'

'What did you eat?'

'I had green turtle steak. I think Mister Sorges had Shrimp Sebastian. I don't remember what Doctor ... look, is this really relevant?'

'I think so,' Czernin said evenly. 'In my experience people are only ever vague about these matters when they're lying. Specificity is the hallmark of any proper alibi.'

'Do I need one? I mean, I thought you said she took an overdose.'

'This is a homicide, Mister Jefferson.' Czernin took out a packet of Salem and lit one quickly. 'Homicides have to be investigated. And investigations need facts. In these matters you can never have too many facts. What time did you finish eating dinner?'

'Eleven. Maybe a little after. We looked in on a couple of bars. Mom's Tea Room and Sloppy Joe's. Mister Sorges, he wanted to see Hemingway's bar-stool, only someone had stolen it. At around twelve fifteen, we went to the Mardi Gras. Not the carnival. It's a strip club on Duval Street. It's getting a little hazy after that. But I'm sure we stayed there until gone two o'clock. Probably got back to the hotel around two fifteen. Next thing I knew, you boys were on the telephone.' Tom uttered a long sigh and sat down heavily on the bed. 'Shit.'

'Sounds like you had quite a night.'

'If I had only known,' whispered Tom.

'What about B-girls? Take one back to your room maybe?'

'No.' Tom frowned.

'It's just that suicide looks better with a motive, that's all. A husband fooling around with another woman. You know the kind of thing. How about it, Mister Jefferson? Did you see other women?'

'No.'

'What about her?'

'How do you mean?'

Czernin had moved around to Tom's side of the bed and was browsing through the surface contents of the other bedside table, as if he had been a customer in a gift shop. The rifle and the priest's outfit were still in Key West. And there was nothing on the table that Tom would have found hard to explain: just a Toshiba table-model transistor-radio – the one with the snap-out portable; the little hi-hat electric clock; the English Leather aftershave that Mary had liked more than Tom; the Rubeck's leather cigarette box and table lighter; and the Catholic pamphlets. To Tom's keen eyes the pamphlets sounded an incongruous note. Did Catholics go to strip clubs?

'I mean, was she seeing anyone? Another man?'

'Not to my knowledge.'

'Do you think it might have been possible?'

'Anything's possible when people work late at the office.'

'Is that an informed guess, or your own personal experience?'

Tom stood up and went out the bedroom and into the bathroom. He tossed the cigarette end into the toilet bowl and splashed some cold water on to his face, which was still dirty from the long drive. When he looked up from the basin he found Czernin in his mirror, examining the vibrator massage belt machine that stood in the corner.

'What is this thing?' he asked. He bent towards the machine and read the name on the side of the white metal housing, answering his own question: 'The Battle Creek Health Builder. Your wife. She was a beautiful woman, Mister Jefferson. And she looked after her figure, right?'

'Her ass was never out of that thing,' said Tom.

'How old was she?'

'Twenty-nine.'

'Can you think of any reason why such a lovely young woman might want to kill herself?'

'Didn't you ask me that question already?'

'No. You volunteered the opinion that she wasn't the type.' Czernin was in front of the bathroom cabinet now. 'But you strike me as an intelligent man. So I'm sure you'll agree that people who aren't the type kill themselves all the time.' He picked out a bottle of Dandricide. 'Nothing is ever quite what it seems. Or does quite what it's supposed to do. Take this stuff, for instance. My wife buys it for me because it's supposed to keep your hair free from dandruff.' He inspected the shoulder of his suit-coat and brushed it fastidiously with the tips of his fingers. 'But it doesn't do what it says on the bottle. You see what I mean?'

Tom didn't think much of the cop's analogy, but he nodded anyway.

'I can't think of a reason,' he said firmly. 'We never had fights, to speak of. Nothing major, anyway. Like any other married couple, you know? Money wasn't a problem. As you can see we have a nice home. And her work was going well.' Tom shrugged. 'Kennedy won, didn't he?'

'That's what they tell me. I voted for Nixon.'

'So you're the one.'

'What was she going to do, now that the campaign is over?'

'I don't know.'

'Is it possible that might have been a concern to her?'

Tom swallowed. 'I suppose it's possible.'

'Wouldn't you agree, a sense of anti-climax sometimes follows a successful conclusion of that which we've been trying our hardest to achieve?'

'Yes.' Tom thought Czernin was beginning to sound like Perry Mason.

'Do you think it's possible here? That this might have made your wife depressed?'

'I suppose so, yes.'

'That this factor, combined with alcohol and barbiturates, might have made her do something silly?' Czernin nodded at the pharmaceutical evidence in the bathroom cabinet in front of him. 'That with a whole drugstore at her disposal, she might have wanted just to forget about what was going to happen to her tomorrow, and the week after that?'

Tom shrugged, and nodded vaguely, too choked to answer. He took a deep unsteady breath and sat down on the side of the tub. 'I want to see her,' he said.

'Of course. Naturally you'll have to identify the body. We can go downtown right now, if you want,' offered Czernin. 'I'll even drive you myself. Might be a good idea at that. It'll be a couple of hours before the boys are finished in here. Might be safer if I drove you, too. What with those two large ones you've had since you got back here. And on top of your evening in Key West. The last thing you want today is to have your licence revoked on a drink-driving charge.'

'I don't much care what happens to me,' said Tom.

'Maybe not today. But you will. Just see what next week's life is like without a car in this town. I know. I've walked that chalk-line.'

'What do you know?' said Tom. 'An honest cop.'

In a waiting room at the County Morgue Tom and the detective waited for the crypt attendant to come off the telephone. Somewhere he could hear the disquieting noise of what sounded like a dentist's drill being operated, and the trickle of running water. But it was the stench of chemicals that troubled Tom most, awakening depressing memories of high school laboratories and military hospitals. Another attendant came past wheeling a gurney on which lay what appeared to be a child's body wrapped in sheeting.

Czernin was talking to Tom, almost unaware of how much the place weighed on the other man's spirits.

'Unfortunately, Seconal is one of the faster-acting barbiturates, which means the fatal dose is smaller. As little as a gram to a gram and a half. In cases involving barbiturate poisoning we usually find that there is something else involved. For instance, a tranquilliser. I noticed your wife used Valium. That, or any alcoholic drink, would add to the hypnotic effect of the barbiturate, reducing the minimum

122

lethal dosage very substantially. But my money is still on the Scotch.'
He smiled sadly at Tom, who nodded back.

'You seem to know a lot about it.'

'It's the times we live in, Mister Jefferson. And maybe you can take some comfort in the knowledge that she certainly would not have suffered any pain. There are lots of worse ways to overdose than hypnotic poisoning.'

'Thanks. I'll bear that in mind.'

When the attendant came off the phone, Czernin spoke to him for a moment and then waved at Tom to follow. They went into a stark-looking crypt where the attendant – burly, red-cheeked, and generally a picture of rude health – opened a stainless-steel door and pulled out the sliding shelf carrying Mary's body, with no more grace or sensitivity than if he had been checking a roast in an oven.

Tom was surprised to discover that Mary's naked body was not covered with a sheet. Perhaps, he reflected, that only happened in the movies. But he wished he could have covered her. Because even in death she was beautiful and she might easily have graced the pages of *Playboy* magazine. If anything she was more beautiful than the average Playmate. Some of those girls were just a tad overweight for Tom's taste. He recalled thinking that Miss October, Titian-haired Kathy Douglas, supposedly under contract to a major studio, was Titian-sized, too, with an ass that looked like they were serving them in double-measures. It was no wonder that so many men had gone for Mary. A walking honey-trap, Alex Goldman had called her. And it was true, Mary had been made for love.

Embarrassed by the sight of such naked beauty, Czernin started to withdraw from the crypt. 'I'll leave you alone,' he said quietly. The attendant had already left and could be heard moving along the white-tiled corridor whistling a song from *Li'l Abner*.

Tom waited until the detective was gone before he took hold of Mary's hand. He had been intending to kiss it; instead, when he tried to lift it to his lips, her hand stayed where it was and he was momentarily horror-struck to discover that rigor mortis was already fully established. Expecting to find her arm limp, as if she had been merely asleep, he had for a moment mistaken the stiffness for strength and the thought that she might still be alive had flashed through his crapulous mind, making him start back like one who had received an electric shock. He swallowed the lump in his throat and once again approached the cold shelf where she lay.

It seemed so very unfair that her life should have to end this way. And after all she had done. Tom shook his head slowly. Their life together was over. All of that was now gone. She had deserved better than this. It seemed such a waste. To work so hard for something she believed in, only to die just as it was almost achieved. Which left him on his own, and feeling lonelier than he had ever felt before. What made it worse was that this was goodbye, too. There would be no touching graveside scene now. With Mary's death everything had changed.

Tom placed his hand upon her cold forehead and bent his own head with remorse. For a while he could think of nothing to say. What *was* there to say? That it wasn't supposed to have ended like this? That she deserved better? In life so much between them had, perforce, remained unsaid. It had been part of the contract between them. How else could they have gotten along? But, as he stood there, gradually, the apparent sanctity of their last moment together began to dawn on him until he could no longer resist the impulse to say the words that were in his head. If such a thing as a soul did exist then he could not imagine that it had yet gone from a body that still looked so beautiful. The question might have vexed theologians, but Tom spoke as the inspiration found him.

'Si capax, ego te absolvo a peccatis tuis . . .'

PART TWO

9

The Sit Down

George White, head of the Chicago Federal Narcotics office, watched his man come out of the Drake Hotel and cross the street. Leaving his car, he followed, intending to catch up with the other man, and to walk with him a while. They were old friends from the war when they had been members of the Office of Strategic Services – the forerunner of the CIA – and it was the habit of such men who had not seen each other in a while to engineer a meeting in some clandestine way that might amuse them both.

There was late-night traffic around and White only took his eyes off the man for a few seconds while he skipped out of the way of a Checker cab. But when he arrived on the other sidewalk, following his quarry's route through a pedestrian walkway that, to White's educated brown eyes, was reminiscent of the red, green, white, and yellow rectangles that characterised the modern art of Piet Mondrian, the man had disappeared. It was a second or two before White realised that the late-twenties building behind the riot of brightly coloured plastic panels was the Playboy Club, and that the man he was following must have gone inside.

White was not surprised that this assistant superintendent of the City of Miami's police department should have patronised such an establishment. His old friend had always been keen on the ladies. He was surprised, however, to discover that the front door was locked and that there was no evident sign of a bell. He had read about the Playboy Club when it had opened back in January, but this was the first time that he had attached any significance to it being a key-holder's club, and only now was it plain to see that if you were not a member, and did not hold a key, you could not go inside. That was certainly true for most people, if not for George White. Especially since it was a new and relatively simple lock.

White took out a fountain pen, unscrewed the top and emptied a lock pick on to his gnarled palm. For someone who had been bypassing locks for twenty-five years, the one on the door of 163 East Walton Street presented no particular problems. White was through the door and advancing on to the black carpet, with its golden bunny heads, in less than thirty seconds, to be greeted by a tall, buxom blonde wearing a black satin swim suit, stockings, black high heels, bunny ears, and, atop her attractive derrière, a little round fluffy tail. White considered stroking it and then thought better of this impulse.

'Good evening, sir. Could I help you with your coat?'

'You may indeed,' agreed White, allowing the bunny-girl to help him out of his hundred-dollar Barry Walt top coat. He handed over his hat and straightened his jacket.

'And the member's key-number is?'

'I'm a guest of Mister Nimmo. Jimmy Nimmo? He just came in a minute ago. I was parking the car.'

The bunny checked a board where the members' names were posted. As she bent forward to retrieve Nimmo's card White had a fine view of her enormous bosom – just the kind, he thought, to make any man with a thirst on his mouth feel more than welcome.

'Oh yes, Mister Nimmo. Here he is.' White was already walking past her and up the stairs, like he knew the place already. 'Enjoy your evening, sir.'

'Thanks.'

He climbed up to the first level and looked around a bar illuminated by backlit reproductions of gatefold Playmates and staffed by more beautiful bunny-girls. There were plenty of single men around – men who were not the marrying kind, being married already – but of Jimmy Nimmo, there was no sign.

Advancing into the bar, White caught sight of an impressive-looking hi-fidelity system that was built into a wood-panelled wall under the stairs. Next to a reel-to-reel tape deck, a record turntable, and a radio tuner, and manned by a spectacular redhead in a blue bunny costume, was something that seemed to promise an early solution to the problem of the missing Nimmo: a closed-circuit TV with controls enabling the viewer to come in for entertaining close-ups of the bunnies. The redhead showed White how to work the controls and explained that the whole system had cost Hugh Hefner, who owned the club, $27,000, and was the most elaborate custom-built rig anywhere outside the White House. White took in some more cleavages and a nice shot of a bunny in the Playboy library bending over to serve some drinks, before finally locating Nimmo on the second floor, in the living room's Cartoon Corner. He thanked the big redhead for her assistance, and added, 'If only all surveillance operations were this easy. Or this much fun.' Then he went upstairs.

Jimmy Nimmo was seated in the corner of a big leather sofa, underneath a wall covered with framed *Playboy* cartoons and outsized Vargas girls. In one hand was a full ounce and a half of Bourbon, and in the other, a Medico filter pipe that he was smoking without much enjoyment. Wearing a plaid corduroy jacket and dark brown flannels, Nimmo was a big, heavy man, and strong-looking. Like White, he was in his late fifties.

'What do you have to do to get a drink around here?' demanded White. 'Threaten someone with myxomatosis?'

'It's been tried,' grinned Nimmo. He looked hardly surprised to see White standing there after so long a time. 'You see the ones with the swellings on their chests? It's a sure sign they're already infected. Apparently, it's supposed to control the population, but it has precisely the opposite effect on me. Now I know why rabbits are supposed to fuck so much.'

'Just call me Thumper,' said White, and sat down beside him. They shook hands warmly and Nimmo waved a bunny towards them whereupon he ordered two double Bourbons on the rocks.

'The service is attractive, but slow,' explained Nimmo, toasting

White's arrival with his existing drink. 'By the time that little lady bounces back – and I mean bounces – I'll have finished this one and be ready for another.'

'Never figured you for the Playboy type,' said White.

'What about you, you old hypocrite? What the hell are you doing here? You're a married man. It's even money your wife doesn't know you're in here.'

'I didn't know I was coming myself until I followed you in through the door,' admitted White. 'But now I'm here, I can see almost all the advantages of membership.'

'Then why not join? You can bring Hoover here the next time the fat bastard's in Chicago.'

White laughed as a picture of the puritanical FBI director in the Playboy Club began to develop in his mind. 'Make a nice photograph, wouldn't it?' he said.

'And kind of an antidote to the other ones of him and Clyde.' Nimmo was referring to the rumour that Meyer Lansky possessed compromising photographs of Hoover and his deputy, Clyde Tolson.

'You believe those stories, Jimmy?'

'I'd sure like to.'

The bunny arrived back with the drinks and placed them carefully on the glass-top table.

'Thanks honey,' said Nimmo. 'Hey, you want to get up early tomorrow and we'll look for furniture?' He growled after her as the bunny-girl went back to the safety of her bar.

'Same old Jimmy,' said White. 'What brings you to the windy city?'

'My daughter, Hannah, had a kid. She and that Hiram Holliday of a husband of hers had a little boy. Roger.'

'Then here's to you, Grandpa.' White toasted Nimmo.

'Keep your voice down,' chuckled Nimmo. 'Some of these broads haven't made me yet.'

'George, isn't it? George Whayman. Is he still with the CPD Intelligence Unit?'

'Yeah. He made lieutenant last Fall. They have a nice house in Cicero. On Ogden Avenue.'

'Cicero, huh? That's nice. Very nice for a lieutenant.'

130

'You know *that* story,' said Nimmo. 'Jesus, we practically wrote it. Everyone in the CPD has one of those kinds of pensions.'

'You sound as if that bothers you. Is that why you're staying at the Drake?'

'No, not at all. He and I don't get on for all kinds of reasons, but they're nothing to do with him being on the take. I'm staying at the Drake because I know babies. This is supposed to be a vacation and I like my shuteye.'

'You couldn't get a better hotel than the Drake. Not in this city. Expensive, though.'

Nimmo laughed. 'I've got a pretty good fucking pension myself. Come on, George. What's with the dollars and cents? You know all that stuff. Being an assistant super in Miami is just a golfing scholarship.'

'I haven't played golf in a long while. Your life sounds pretty good to me, Jimmy. You're in here with these broads. Playing golf. Staying at the Drake. What more do you want?'

Nimmo pulled a face, cavilling. 'It's not New York,' he sighed.

'You really miss New York?'

'Don't you?'

'Sometimes, I guess. But Chicago's okay.'

'Let me tell you something, George. I never liked Chicago. It's a bullshit town. The place stinks. I looked up the name and apparently Chicago's an Indian name for swamp gas. What else do you need to know?' Nimmo chuckled, enjoying himself, almost hoping that one of the club's other patrons might overhear, and object, so that he could tell them to fuck off.

'It doesn't smell bad any more,' offered White.

'How can you like a city with a National League club that hasn't won a World Series since nineteen oh-eight? Another thing I hate about it? The way these swamp-living bastards have managed to shirk their responsibility for making the atom bomb.'

'How'd you work that out, for Christ's sake?'

'The world's first nuclear reactor was built right here in Chicago, in forty-two, by Enrico Fermi. But when they go off to Los Alamos, to build the damn bomb, they don't call it the Chicago Project. They don't even call it the Los Alamos Project. They call it the Manhattan

Project, like it's the fault of New York that the world's a button's push away from blowing itself to pieces. I tell you, these people are the goddamnedest liars I ever saw. You don't believe me? I'll prove it to you. Everywhere you go in this town you see a quotation by Rudyard Kipling. "I have struck a city – a real city – and they call it Chicago. Those other places don't count." You see it on matchbooks, on pencils, on tea-towels, and, for all I know, you see it on a woman's girdle, only so far this trip hasn't worked out so well on that score. It's everywhere, I tell you. Now, because Kipling is a writer I really admire – *Gunga Din* has always been my favourite movie of all time—'

'In a way, you remind me of Victor McLaglen.'

'Thanks a lot. I'm nothing like that big ape. Anyway, I decided to look up that quotation.'

'Thorough, you always were. Best Special Agent in Charge the New York Bureau ever had.'

'And what Kipling actually went on to say was this: "Having seen it, I urgently desire never to see it again. It is inhabited by savages." Well George, seventy years on, and nothing's changed. The place is still inhabited by savages. Present company excepted, of course. But however much I hate it, and I do hate it, it's still a sight better than Miami. Miami's a cold sore, George. I'm going mad down there.' He raised his glass. 'So here's to New York.'

White clinked glasses and sipped some of his Bourbon. 'I'm never sure if it's really New York I miss,' he admitted, 'or what we did there during the war. Things were more exciting then. Things were more straightforward. Winning the war seemed to be all that mattered and we were not looking over our shoulders to see if anyone didn't like the way we were doing it.'

'You don't think the communists matter?'

'Of course they do. Only now we have to be accountable to a Senate Investigation Committee telling us who is a proper person to use in waging that war. Good results don't seem to matter any more, as much as how these results are achieved. The politicians don't understand how it works. How things have to work. I guess that's what I miss most, Jimmy.'

Nimmo nodded and raised his own glass to the old days when he and White had helped to create a deal between US Intelligence and the mob, in the person of Meyer Lansky, whereby Lucky Luciano was released from prison to pave the way for the invasion of Italy. Luciano's subsequent deportation had left the diminutive Jewish gangster the most powerful organised crime figure in America.

'How is the little man?' asked Nimmo.

'What makes you think I know? He lives in Miami. So do you. And you're the one he fixed a job for.'

'Call that a job? Like I say, Miami AS isn't much more than a golf scholarship. I guess it's fortunate I like golf. Oh, there's the odd nickel-and-dime favour I do for the local teamsters. But it's not much more than that. You're the one who's still fighting the war in earnest, George. And I haven't spoken to Meyer in a long while. Unless . . .' He put aside the pipe he had been filling with tobacco and took out a packet of Lucky Strike. 'I can't get used to this damned pipe,' he confessed, lighting a cigarette.

'Unless what?'

Nimmo exhaled smoke with loud satisfaction. 'Oh, I was just thinking that maybe I'm speaking to Meyer now, and I just don't know it yet.'

'That's what you think, is it?'

'No offence intended, George. But you did follow me in here. And we are talking about old times and what a great SAC I used to be. Don't ever get sentimental, old buddy. It doesn't suit you.'

White tapped out a Newport and lit it quickly.

'You're wasted playing golf,' he said. 'Clearly.'

'What else do you do when your wife leaves home with the fucking television?'

'And it so happens that's not just my opinion.'

'Safety in numbers, eh George?'

'You're right about Meyer,' admitted White. 'He heard you were in Chicago and asked me to speak to you.'

'And he and I practically neighbours, too. I'm hurt. What does he want?'

'A favour for an old friend.'

'Who does he want me to kill?'

'He wants you to take a sit down, with Sam Giancana. You remember Sam, don't you?'

'Mooney? He's a hard man to forget.' Nimmo grinned for a moment.

'What's funny?'

'I dunno. Meyer asks you to come and meet me, to ask if I wouldn't mind meeting Giancana. Seems to me like all Mooney had to do was pick up the telephone and ask me over for a drink.'

'You know as well as I do, Jimmy, that's not the way things are done. This is Sam's town.'

'It is? I thought Tony Accardo was the big cheese on the Chicago pizza.'

'Not any more. Not for a while. It so happens that tomorrow Tony Accardo is going to walk into a courtroom here in Chicago, and be sent to prison. For income tax evasion.'

'The same rap as Capone. It's not the feds these guys have to worry about, it's the IRS.'

'Anyway, the point is this: you live in Miami, and you're a friend of Meyer's.'

'That's nice to know.'

'Which means that Sam has to go through the proper channels.'

'You know, I haven't got a thing to wear,' said Nimmo.

'Out of respect for Meyer.'

'Can't think what I can do for Mooney.' Nimmo swallowed a mouthful of Bourbon and grimaced.

'I wouldn't call him that, if I were you.'

'Maybe it's something to do with Teamsters Local three-twenty. Barney Baker, Lennie Patrick, and the Yaras brothers. They've all got Chicago connections. Dave Yaras used to be Giancana's button. Now he's a juice man with the pension fund. Gotten themselves into some heat I don't know about yet. That must be it.'

'So maybe you can help fix it. Or maybe Sam wants some advice. It's a sit down, that's all. Not the mob Apalachin meeting. A favour for an old friend. Meyer would have asked you himself, only he's a little busy right now. We've both got this thing going in the Bahamas.'

'Meyer still trying to get that free port idea off the ground, huh?'

'Gotta have something to replace Havana, hasn't he?'

'Replace Havana?' Nimmo sounded incredulous. 'They'll never replace Havana.' He shook his head. 'Certainly not with the Bahamas. Havana was more than just a few lousy casinos. Havana was an attitude of mind.'

'Don't tell me, Jimmy. Tell Meyer. Tell the Cellini brothers, Max Courtney, Trigger Mike Coppola, and Frank Ritter. Tell Sam Giancana, when you see him.'

'Maybe I will at that,' shrugged Nimmo. He glanced around the Playboy Club and shook his head, sadly. 'This place is nice, you know? But it won't ever compare with some of those Havana clubs. The Shanghai, or the Wonder Bar. Remember those places, George? Remember what it was like?'

'I remember that nigger at the San Francisco,' said White. 'Superman. I don't see how anyone could ever forget him. Certainly not the ladies he obliged.'

'Or that broad who used to do the trick with the lighted candle. What was her name?'

'Aurora Borealis.'

'Aurora Borealis,' repeated Nimmo. Finishing his second Bourbon, he sighed loudly. 'We've seen the best of it, George. The good times are gone for ever.'

'Jimmy? You don't just look like Victor McLaglen. You sound like him, too.'

The cold awakened Jimmy Nimmo. He threw off the blankets and walked to the window with the view of Lake Michigan. He closed it, and was heading to the bathroom when the telephone rang. It was Sam Giancana.

'I hope I didn't wake you,' he said politely.

'No, I was up and around,' yawned Nimmo.

'Did ya have a late night?'

'Not as late as I'd have liked.'

'The Drake's okay, but there's not much action on the magnificent mile. Unless you happen to like jazz. You like jazz, Jimmy?'

'I love jazz.'

'Then you got the Cloister on North Rush Street, real close by. Not to mention the Club Alabam. Gene Harris, who owns the place, is a friend of mine. It used to be one of Chicago's major speaks. And the food's the best.'

'I'll remember that for the next time I'm in town.'

'When are you going back to Miami?'

'First thing tomorrow.'

'Then why not spend your last night in Chicago at my own motel? It's right by O'Hare. There's a swimming pool, and the Chez Paree Adorables are really something. Chicago's number one chorus girls. I could introduce you to some of them if you have time.'

'I've always got time for chorus girls,' said Jimmy.

'It's not the Minsky show at the Dunes, but it'll do, you know? Look, Jimmy, why don't I have a car pick you up outside the Drake at eleven? Take you to the Thunderbolt Motel, and then bring you here for lunch?'

'Where's that?'

'The Armory Lounge, in Forest Park. What do you say, Jimmy?'

Jimmy smiled silently. He knew what to say all right. Before George White had turned up on an errand for Meyer Lansky, he might have had some doubts about meeting Mooney Giancana. They had met on the occasions when Giancana was in Miami, and had even got along all right, but Nimmo didn't feel he owed the boss of the Chicago outfit a thing. Meyer Lansky was a different proposition, however. Saying no to the little man from Poland was like forgetting to send a Christmas thank-you letter to your Dutch uncle. He said, 'Sure Sam, I'd be delighted to.'

By the time Nimmo was shaved and showered it was nine thirty. Ignoring the *Chicago Daily News* he brought with him to the restaurant, he ate a light breakfast and thought about Sam Giancana and the favour he would ask. His thoughts were inconclusive. Whichever way he looked at a problem involving the local teamsters it was something only Santos Trafficante, who controlled most of the organised crime in Miami, and Giancana could fix. It was going to be an interesting day.

He finished his breakfast and went to pay the hotel bill, only to discover that it had already been settled.

'By who?' Nimmo asked the desk clerk.

'We have a certified cheque from the Miami National Bank in the name of Manhattan Simplex Distributing,' explained the clerk.

'When did you get that?'

'Last night. I took it myself.'

'From a guy wearing a light-coloured single-breasted topcoat with cuffed sleeves, grey hat, glasses, mid-fifties, around a hundred and eighty pounds, right?'

'Yes.'

It had been George White. A little courtesy from Lansky. He hadn't heard of Manhattan Simplex Distributing, but rumour had it that using Lou Poller as a front, Lansky had helped the teamsters to take over the Miami National Bank, as recently as 1958.

'My uncle,' said Nimmo. Seeing the puzzled frown on the desk clerk's face, he added, 'He's a lot older than he looks. I bet you wouldn't believe it, but that guy is eighty-five. He takes monkey glands. Like that English writer. Somerset Maugham.'

At exactly eleven o'clock, Nimmo brought his own bag down, to find a black Oldsmobile waiting for him outside the hotel front door. The driver was in his early thirties, medium height, with thinning dark curly hair and tinted glasses. Nimmo had been expecting muscle in a suit but this man didn't look like he could have punched a hole in a wet paper bag.

'Good morning,' said the driver politely. He took Nimmo's bag and placed it carefully in the trunk of the Olds, which contained nothing more lethal than a tyre jack and crate of beer. Nimmo sat in the back.

They drove north, along the lake shore, and then west on North Avenue, toward the Chicago River.

'Would you like the radio on?'

'No, thanks.'

Nimmo's foot was already tapping to the jukebox that was playing in his head: Duke Ellington's 'Satin Doll'. Nimmo had a real memory for music. His brain could chew on the recollection of a tune he had heard like a stick of gum. It was an ability that had kept him amused on many a long stakeout. 'Satin Doll' was one of his favourite tunes. But gradually the policeman's curiosity to know more about his driver and, as a corollary, his host, pushed Ellington's big band sound into the back room of his thoughts.

'What's your name, fella?'

'Chuck.'

'Tell me, Chuck, do you fart when you take a honeymoon in Niagara?'

'How's that?'

'Simple question. Do you fart when you take a honeymoon in Niagara?'

Chuck shrugged and stayed silent as he tried to figure out how to answer that.

'It was a joke,' explained Nimmo.

'My wife and I took our honeymoon in Los Angeles. That was eleven years ago, in the spring.'

'Congratulations. My wife left me three years ago, last Fall. She was from Yuba City, California. Her daddy was a prune farmer up there. Well, she loved prunes. Couldn't get enough of them. Even took some on our honeymoon in Niagara. Of course, sooner or later, prunes get to you. And they got to her. She made all the wrong noises, at all the wrong times. I mean, you expect a woman's pussy to fart some after you've pumped her full of meat and air. But not her ass as well, right? And certainly not while you're minding the store.'

Chuck, the driver, was laughing now.

'You think that's funny?' grinned Nimmo. 'It's a tragedy, that's what it is, fella. Been driving long for Mooney? Or Momo? Which is it?'

'Only his close friends call him Mooney,' explained Chuck. 'As a matter of fact, I rarely ever drive for him. He has his own people do that. I run the motel.'

'What did they do? Take out a wanted ad in *Black Mask*?'

Chuck smiled a good-humoured smile. 'I guess you could say that it's a family business. Mooney's my eldest brother.'

'Pretty good catering qualification,' said Nimmo.

'As a matter of fact, the place is completely legitimate. The only thing it fronts is the River Road. I'll admit, it wasn't always that way. When it was still the River Road Motel, Willy Daddano used to run a vice racket out of the place. But I'll think you'll find it's now a very pleasant place to stay, Mister Nimmo. Sure, we have some fairly colourful characters show up there, from time to time. Friends of Mooney's. Even a few celebrities. But we have every amenity.'

'I'll bet you do,' said Nimmo. 'Hey, I was just kidding.'

'That's all right,' shrugged Chuck. 'I'm used to it. Believe me, there's nothing you could say that would bother me. I'm like Harpo, you know? I see and hear a lot, but I always keep my mouth shut.'

'I'm a Chico fan myself.'

'Hey, did you hear? Gable is dead.'

'Which one was he?'

'Clark Gable. The heart throb.'

'Jesus Christ. He couldn't have been very old.'

'He was fifty-nine. Heart attack.'

Nimmo, who was fifty-seven himself, winced. 'I guess his heart stopped throbbing,' he said dumbly. He had always thought he looked a little like Clark Gable, being tall and dark. Once, before he put on weight, he had even had the same little moustache, only people had told him he looked more like Brian Donlevy, so he had shaved it off. And now they said he looked like Victor McLaglen.

They were pulling up at the Thunderbolt and, for Jimmy Nimmo, at that precise moment, the motel was well named. The news of Gable's death had really shocked him and was to prey on his thoughts for the rest of that day.

As they got out of the Olds, Chuck pointed out a dark blue Ford Galaxie on the other side of the motel parking lot. A large man wearing a suede short coat and a tweed cap was wiping the Galaxie's hood with a car duster.

'You see that guy?' said Chuck. 'That's Joe. He'll drive you to see Mooney just as soon as I've shown you to your room.'

Nimmo followed Chuck through the motel entrance and across a black and white terrazzo floor to the elevator. They rode up to the penthouse, and a suite that Chuck proudly informed Nimmo was the best in the place.

'I'm sure I'll be very comfortable here,' said Nimmo, and threw his bag on to the bed.

'You wanna freshen up?'

'No thanks, I'd better cut along and see your big brother.'

They were coming out of the room door just as a tall and extremely voluptuous blonde, wearing a pink bell-skirt with soft box pleats, was entering the room opposite.

'Oh, hiya Rhoda,' said Chuck.

Nimmo's eyes were out on stalks.

'Say hello to someone, Rhoda. This is Jimmy Nimmo. Jimmy? Rhoda is one of our Chez Paree Adorables.'

'Hiya Jimmy.'

Nimmo took her offered hand and squeezed it gently.

'Are you gonna come and see the show tonight?' she asked him.

'I wouldn't miss it for the world. Hey, do you want to get up early tomorrow and we'll look for furniture?'

'If you like.' She smiled, and then went into her room, slowly closing the door behind her.

Nimmo nodded his appreciation. He assumed the meeting in the corridor was no happenstance. Not after Giancana had mentioned his chorus girls on the telephone. He guessed Rhoda was being laid out for him. And that was okay. He could think of worse ways of taking hospitality from a guy than to fuck one of his tame broads.

Joe said nothing on the drive from the motel to the Armory Lounge. Unlike Chuck, he had the look of a killer and, besides, Nimmo's thoughts were already frolicking with Rhoda. The Armory was in Forest Park, a leafy suburb close to Oak Park and Cicero, which was where Capone had maintained his Chicago headquarters. But even better, the place was only three or four miles north of Nimmo's daughter's home and, if things worked out between himself and Momo, he was going to ask if Joe could drive him back via Hannah's house on Ogden Avenue. Now that Rhoda was on the bill-of-fare, it might be his last opportunity to see his grandson before flying back to Miami.

'We're here,' growled Joe, steering the big Ford off Roosevelt Road, and into the parking lot.

Nimmo got out of the car and glanced around at the other cars, keeping his face in his coat collar until he was through the door, just in case the lounge was under surveillance. He was almost certain it wasn't, despite the fact that the FBI had, like in most other big North American cities, a THP – a Top Hoodlum Programme. Before receiving the call from Giancana, Nimmo had already visited the

Chicago office of the FBI on West Monroe, right in the Italian village, and found that the same Hoover-directed priorities existed in Chicago as elsewhere in the United States. Chicago may have been the spiritual home of organised crime, but the THP was under-resourced, with most of the Bureau's money and manpower devoted to the investigation of communists and other subversives. Nimmo thought *The Untouchables* was a pretty good TV show, but it dealt with the kind of Bureau that hadn't existed since the war. Nimmo had plenty of friends in the Chicago office. He'd even scored a good lunch off the Chicago SAC at the Village, one of the city's best Italian restaurants. Guys liked to talk to Nimmo and he liked to listen. It was surprising what you could learn in Chicago that might be useful in Miami.

The Armory Lounge had been a speakeasy during Prohibition. Inside, the place was done up like a New Orleans bar, with ceiling fans, murals, old riverboat photographs, soft lights, flock wallpaper, white wrought-iron chairs, and glass-top tables. In the background, a big Wurlitzer jukebox was playing a current hit – Joe Jones's 'You Talk Too Much'. Nimmo didn't recommend it. Following his stone-faced driver into the back of the thinly populated lounge, Nimmo thought there were few of these sharp-suited wiseguys who would dare to talk at all – not if it concerned Mooney Giancana. That way you ended up like Gus Greenbaum, Leon Marcus, Jim Ragen, or any one of a couple of dozen others whose deaths Giancana was reputed to have ordered. To say nothing – nothing – of the dozen or so he'd killed himself. They didn't call him 'Mooney' – crazy – for nothing. The kid brother had had the best idea. Being like Harpo was the best way to stay alive around a hood like Sam Giancana.

Joe knocked at a heavy wooden door and, after a second or two, a peephole opened, speak-style, and an eyeball rolled over their faces and their hands. Only then was the door unlocked, by another heavy-set man, wearing a pullover jacket with knit sleeves and a suede front, and carrying a light, autoloader shotgun.

As Nimmo removed his coat, his eyes vacuumed up the contents of the gangster's inner sanctum: the steel door in the back, the card table, the walnut bar-console with built-in refrigerator, the Zenith TV with the sound turned down, the rolled-up lenticular projection screen, the Elite talkie recorder-projector, the old-fashioned safe, the big wrap-around leather sofa, and, sitting on it, wearing a blue cashmere blazer, the man himself.

'Jimmy, come on in and sit down. I appreciate your coming out to the burbs. We've got an office on North Michigan, but it's kind of formal and I prefer it here. It's more private.'

'You look very comfortable, Sam,' said Nimmo, sitting down beside him, and shaking the gangster's surprisingly soft hand.

'Drink?'

Nimmo scanned the open bar through short-sighted eyes. 'Thanks. I'll have a Poland water and Ballantine's Scotch.'

'Butch.' Giancana waved at the bar, and without a word the man climbed off the tall bar-stool by the door, put the Brida down, and went to fetch the drinks.

Giancana took out a packet of Camels and offered one to Nimmo.

'No, thanks,' said Nimmo, producing a tobacco pouch. 'I'm trying a pipe.'

'How's your room at the T'Bolt? Everything okay for you?'

'I just dumped my bag and came straight down here,' he said. 'Looks nice though. And I met Rhoda. One of your Chez Paree Adorables.'

'Isn't she just?'

'Yeah. Her brassiere really has its work cut out, doesn't it?'

Giancana grinned wolfishly. 'They're all like that. Some of them used to work for me in Havana. Others are from Vegas. The show at the T'Bolt's pretty good. Best in town, probably. But it won't begin to compare with the place I'm opening in a few months. An out of town place, but real classy. The Villa Venice. You'll have to come and stay there next time you're in Chicago. It's in Wheeling, but that's not so far. Place is costing me a bundle.'

Butch handed Nimmo and Giancana their drinks and then returned to his position riding shotgun by the door.

'I hear you play a lot of golf, Jimmy. Got the weather 'n' everything. Must be nice.'

'I whack a little white ball around most days,' admitted Nimmo. 'Some days it even goes in the damned hole. You play?' Giancana nodded. 'Columbus Park. We passed it on the way here. Is that your club?'

142

'Nah. Too easy. Wide open fairways, big greens. Ray Charles could make a par on that fucking course. Riverwoods. That's where I play. Not as much as I'd like. The weather's against it up here on the Lakes. Plus, when I'm here I'm doing business, or I'm collecting porcelain. That's a passion with me. Meissen, stuff like that. Kind of an antidote to a tough business, you know?' Nimmo nodded and sipped some of his Scotch and water. 'Jimmy, I'll come straight to the point. And no offence intended. But how would you like to do some real police work again?'

'Real police work?' Nimmo grinned. 'With all due respect, Sam, if that's what I wanted to do, then I'd hardly be sitting here, drinking your Scotch, now would I?'

'You've got a point. Then let me put it another way. How would you like to do some detective work? Investigative work?'

'Private investigative work?'

'Why not? In New York, you were the soft-clothes ace, I hear.'

'Is that what Meyer told you?' Nimmo frowned and inspected his pipe. He was having a hard job keeping it alight.

Giancana was nodding. 'How did you come to leave the feds anyway?'

'On the day I was leaving the Bureau, I found myself under this big black cloud that just happened to come floating up Manhattan Island.' Nimmo grinned sheepishly and, putting aside the pipe, sipped some more of his Scotch. 'I resigned because I had to. I hit someone. Another agent. Hard. Too hard. The guy had it coming, everyone agreed, but it didn't help that I was drunk. He made a full recovery, but I was finished. Hoover doesn't care for that kind of behaviour. Actually, there's not much in the way of behaviour he does care for. Anyway, I resigned and Meyer fixed it with the Mayor of Miami for me to get the job I have now. It's not a bad job. But I'm just treading water. Waiting to collect my pension. There's a lot of that in Miami. Miami's a pensioner's kind of place. I golf, play canasta with the few friends I have down there, push some fucking papers around my desk, sign expenses, fuck this whore in Fort Lauderdale once a month, and generally plan my retirement. No one pays much attention to a guy like me. I'm part of the furniture. Some hotter days in summer I don't think they'd notice if I wasn't even there. Which means that some days I'm not.'

Nimmo put down his drink and made a couple of fists, as if he was driving a team of horses. 'But I still have it, you know?' He tapped his head and then slapped his belly. 'Up here, and in here. I'm still a good cop. Not like some of these kids they're bringing into the Bureau nowadays. Harvard graduates, some of them. They've got soft feet and nice hands. Sure they've got brains. But they don't have it here, in the belly. You ask me, it's the same as Jack Kennedy. Yeah, he's bright. He can read fast. He can comprehend a brief. But is he going to have the balls to push the button if the Russians come marching into Berlin? I doubt it. Now Ike. You never doubted the man's stomach. He was a soldier. A fucking general. But this Kennedy is just a damn college boy. A politician. A fucking bureaucrat. Same as these new kids in the Bureau.

'You ask me if I'd like to do some investigative work, Mister Giancana? I'd give my right arm to be working on a real case. That's God's honest truth. I can't figure out how else my life can have any meaning again. Just one last investigation and then I won't mind what happens, but at least I'll have my self-respect. Because when there is no dignity there is no strength. So, whatever kind of investigation it is you have in mind, Mister Giancana, I'm your man.'

Giancana nodded.

'Okay, here's how it is. A while ago, Meyer Lansky recommended a man to do a job for me and for the CIA, a job for which we would have paid him a fee of two hundred and fifty thousand dollars. But before we could give him the go-ahead, the man and a hundred Gs of that money upped and disappeared. With the help of my organisation, I want you to find that man. Jimmy? The money he took is not important. What is important is that I find him again before my new friends in the government find out that the guy has gone AWOL.

'Now after that speech you made I could probably ask you to work for nothing. But I'm a fair man, and I believe in paying a man what the job is worth to me. All I ask is a fair shake in return. I'll pay you twenty-five thousand dollars, Jimmy. Which means I want this guy found, and found quick. Ten thousand now and another fifteen when you find him.'

Nimmo whistled. 'For that kind of money, I'd find you the lost Hebe tribes of Israel and throw in Glenn Miller by way of a bonus. What's the guy's name, and when did he take off?'

'His name is Tom Jefferson. And nobody's seen him since late last Friday.'

'Friday?' Nimmo looked pained for a moment as he saw the prospect of instant enrichment begin to recede again. He thought of all the things he could have done with the money. Buy a house, a nice car maybe – he'd just started to like the idea of himself in an MGA. And a tailor-made suit.

'Mister Giancana. Eager as I am to take your twenty-five thou, that's only five days. Right now, all over this great land of America that we live in, there are red-eyed women walking into police precincts to report their no-good husbands missing. And the dumb Irish desk sergeant always tells them the same thing. Maybe the guy went on a Ray Milland and had himself a lost weekend. Maybe the lucky bastard found himself a new gal and the Dear Janet postcard from Vegas is still in the mail. But whatever the reason, a week is usually considered to be the minimum period that the average American male can go missing in this country before the police become involved. It's different for wives. For wives it's forty-eight hours. Wives get raped and murdered in less time than it takes to cook an omelette.'

'Spare me the *Naked City*, Jimmy,' said Giancana. 'I made enough guys disappear in my life to know the real thing when I see it. Coupla times I even woke up with the cats starin' at me, myself. I know dead, and I know dead drunk, and I know disappeared.'

'You'd better tell me everything.'

'I can't tell you everything,' said Sam Giancana. 'But I can tell you all I know, and then you can go and figure the rest for your twenty-five Gs. Sooner the better. This year I'd like Thanksgiving to have a red ribbon and a nigger's shine on it.'

10

Ybor City

From Miami, Tom drove to Palm Beach where he sat outside the Kennedy family estate and smoked a couple of cigarettes. There were a couple of cops, some well-wishers, and lots of news reporters standing on the road. For a while Tom joined them on the sidewalk and found that most of the talk was not about Kennedy, but about Clark Gable who had died that morning. Then he drove to the airport at West Palm Beach, for no other reason than this was where Kennedy's private plane flew in and out of, sometimes as often as once or twice a week. As soon as he saw the place Tom knew he was wasting his time.

There was a gun dealer in West PB, who was an old army buddy, and in any other circumstances Tom might have visited him, not least because the dealer supplied Tom with specialist rifles and ammunition. But since he knew that Giancana's people were likely to come looking for him, if only to get their money back, Tom decided that it would be more prudent to telephone.

From Palm Beach, by way of Fort Pierce and Lake Wales, Tom drove north-west along the Sunshine State Parkway to Tampa which, depending on whether population figures are estimated there, or in Jacksonville, is the second or third largest city in Florida. The parkway was new and wide and he could breeze along with the top down at sixty miles an hour, which helped to clear his head of Mary and Sam Giancana. He made the two-hundred-and-sixty-mile journey in just over five hours.

Ybor City was Tampa's Latin Quarter, a Spanish version of Greenwich Village, with lots of good restaurants and several cigar factories. It was from here that José Martí had plotted the overthrow of the Spanish in Cuba and where he had written the revolutionary manifesto, in 1895. Sixty-five years later it continued to be a centre for exiled Batistianos and, as a consequence, for G2, the Cuban Intelligence Service.

Tom met his own debriefing officer, Colonel López Ameijeiras, at one of the many excellent restaurants on the quayside. Ameijeiras was a sallow-faced man of about fifty whose bushy eyebrows, high forehead, and slightly slanted eyes lent him a vaguely Far Eastern appearance. If he had owned a Mao suit he might even have passed for the Chinese Premier, Chou En-lai. With or without the jacket Tom thought Ameijeiras was probably as inscrutable as any oriental politician.

Tom ordered a daiquiri and handed Ameijeiras a large manila envelope containing all the information he had gathered on the MIRR and its anti-Castro activities in Miami and Havana.

'But I don't think they'll stop trying to kill Castro just because a few of them get arrested,' he added. 'There are too many people who want him dead and who are willing to pay for it to happen.'

Ameijeiras slipped the envelope unopened into his briefcase and lit a cigarette. After a longish silence, he removed his straw hat and fanned himself with the narrow brim.

'What happened to Mary wasn't supposed to happen,' he said quietly.

'If you say so.'

'I do say so. Most emphatically.'

'So what are you going to do about it?'

Ameijeiras shrugged. 'Nothing. What's done is done.'

'Funny, but somehow I thought you might look at it that way.'

'What choice do I have? There's too much at stake to let this interfere with our plans. Right now there are other more important things to worry about. Such as whether the Americans will invade or not. Already they are sending ships and planes to Guatemala and Nicaragua. Ostensibly to protect those countries against communist-led invasion. But of course the reality is different. We may have frustrated one attempt to kill Fidel, but, as you say, doubtless they will try again. And even if they don't, they will try to invade Cuba by using what's happening in Central America as a cover. Our sources tell us that Kennedy knows all about this plan. That he even agrees with it, despite what he may say about Eisenhower's Cuban policy in public. So he has to be stopped.' Ameijeiras took a long drag of the cigarette and then added, 'You have to stop him, Tom.'

Tom's drink arrived, and he sipped it thoughtfully, avoiding the Cuban colonel's penetrating brown eyes.

'And you think this action we're taking is the best way of doing that?'

Ameijeiras replaced the hat on his head. 'Yes, I do.'

'I sure hope you're right.'

'This shouldn't be a problem for you.'

'You think so?'

'No, it shouldn't be a problem at all.'

Tom grinned uncomfortably. 'I dunno,' he said, 'I never did anything like this before.'

'It's true there are certain features that make this an unusual contract—'

'Oh, I'd say so.'

'But fundamentally,' insisted Ameijeiras, 'it's just the same thing you always do. And do very well, I might add. You've done this kind of thing dozens of times before.' The Cuban colonel handed Tom an envelope. 'Here is Kennedy's schedule for the next two months, obtained by our Russian friends. It's up to you how and where you do it. But please remember that we'd like to deliver our message before the inauguration. We don't think it's likely there will be any invasion before then.'

Tom pocketed the envelope.

'Whatever you say. This is your party.'

'Tom? It has to be this way. You do appreciate that, my friend?'

'What's the matter, López? Don't you trust me?'

148

'This has to go way beyond trust. This is life and death.'

'You've got that part right.'

'Listen to me, Tom.' The colonel's expression was sombre. 'There can be no room for mistakes with something like this.'

'I never make mistakes. That's why you're paying me so much.'

'Then we understand each other.'

'Perfectly. Where is the money?'

'The usual arrangements have been made with your bank in Venezuela.' Ameijeiras finished his cigarette and lit another. 'So, what will you do now, Tom?'

'Find the where and the how.'

'By scouting the shot?'

'Of course. But first I'll go to the safe house. Study the schedule. Do some homework. Buy some books about Kennedy. Get to know my man. Frankly it's the part I like best: the planning. I will call you the day after tomorrow with some ideas. I already read a few books. Mary had quite a little Kennedy bookshelf. Anything else I'll probably find in New York. City's got bookshops like other cities have banks. And then there's always the library.'

'Ah yes. The New York Public Library. What a remarkable institution that is. You know, in many ways, this really is an excellent country to live in.'

'Yeah? Well don't tell anyone, will you? They'll all want to come here.'

11

The Word for Death

Jimmy Nimmo felt pleased with himself. Thanks to Rhoda he had enjoyed a sleepless night. And now here he was, flying back to Miami aboard a Convair 880, with ten thousand dollars in cash in his bag. Perhaps he would postpone buying the MGA until the job was complete. But there was no reason why he shouldn't buy a colour television right away. He even knew the set he wanted: the new Fontainebleu by Andrea, with a twenty-three-inch tube, a handsome mahogany finish cabinet, and sliding tambour doors. From the airport he would go straight to Burdines and hand over $250. The rest of the ten thousand he would place in one of the safety deposit boxes the Miami National Bank had for rent. There would be just enough time to do both of these errands and make a few telephone calls before going to the Orange Bowl.

After the low fifties of Chicago, Miami was in the high seventies, and as soon as he found his car in the airport parking lot – a powder-blue Chevrolet Impala – he took the hood down. Driving a convertible was one of the few compensations for living in Miami. But not just any convertible. Nimmo saw himself driving something a little more distinctive than the Impala. Not that there was anything wrong with it. With a V8 mated to a two-speed automatic transmission, there was little to criticise in the nearly new car, unless you were driving it flat out, and then the back end had a tendency to rise up and float around a bit. But flat-out was what Nimmo really wanted. That, and some European class.

From the airport, he drove east towards the ocean, to East Flagler Street, and Burdines. After ordering his TV, and depositing the cash in the bank, Nimmo drove a few blocks south to Tobacco Road, on South Miami Avenue, where, over a couple of beers, he used the phone, calling Johnny Rosselli and then the coroner's office. Tobacco Road was a good jazz bar, although it was too early for anything other than the jukebox. Nimmo often went there when he couldn't stand his office in the Hall of Justice any longer. Or before a football game. And sometimes after one, too.

There was a big crowd to see the Miami Hurricanes play Syracuse and, for most of the time, it was a close game: 7–7 at half-time, and 14–14 in the third quarter. But then, in the last period, Ernie Davis carried the ball fifty-two yards in an eighty-yard attack to score the decisive touchdown from the three-yard line. It was a thrilling game with a last-minute drive by the Hurricanes bringing the Miami crowd to its feet, before the final whistle blew. Nimmo didn't miss a game like that for anyone.

But the next morning, Saturday, he was up early and on the case, driving the three miles that separated his home in Keystone Islands – a Keystone home for a Keystone cop, his wife had quipped, not long before he'd given her the slap in the mouth that made her pack her bags – from Tom Jefferson's address in Miami Shores. At the red traffic light on the junction of North East 123rd Street and Biscayne Boulevard, he glanced over the front page of the *New York Times* and saw that the President-elect was giving serious consideration to the appointment of his younger brother, Bobby, as Attorney-General. Nimmo lit a cigarette and grinned as he tried to picture some of the wiseguys when they read that. People like Jimmy Hoffa, Carlos Marcello, Dave Beck, and, for that matter, Sam Giancana were going to be none too pleased with the idea of their old McLellan tormentor in charge of the Justice Department. Most of those guys were probably hoping for Ribicoff or Byron White – anyone but Bobby Kennedy.

Nimmo found the address in Miami Shores and parked up the street. Then he went round the back of Jefferson's house, put on some gloves, and, from inside the fold of his newspaper, produced an improvised snap gun made from a wire coat-hanger. He inserted the sharpened business end into the doorlock, and squeezed the make-shift trigger, pulling the upper spring bracket down. Releasing the trigger abruptly drove the bracket hard up against the needle, snapping it into the tumblers, and opening the lock.

Once inside the house, Nimmo drew the blinds and switched on the television. Slowly, the set warmed up, until a silent picture appeared on the screen. It was *Captain Kangaroo*. Nimmo turned up the sound for the benefit of any nosey-parker neighbours. Felons involved in committing a burglary seldom watched early-morning television shows for children. B&E always made Nimmo nervous so the very next thing he did was use the toilet. Sitting there, in Tom Jefferson's bathroom, he quickly scanned the rest of the paper, and saw that Tony Accardo had been sentenced to six years in jail, and fined $15,000 for income tax evasion. It was, he reflected, while washing his hands, as Benjamin Franklin had observed, that in this world nothing was certain but death and taxes. Except maybe when they paid you in cash. Putting his gloves back on, he flushed the toilet, and began to search the house in earnest.

Nimmo was a thorough man, searching the house as an experi-enced book-keeper might scrutinise a set of accounts. He rifled through drawers, turned out closets, ripped up rugs, tore apart upholstery, jimmied up floorboards, and ransacked wardrobes. And when he found some small thing he thought might have significance, he placed it into an empty cardboard box: notepads, scraps of paper, matchbooks, tapes, ticket receipts, a bullet, photographs of the dead woman, maps, spare keys, library cards, newspaper cuttings, and the business cards of various local tradesmen.

After an hour had passed, and *Captain Kangaroo* had given way to *Huckleberry Hound*, the box was still two-thirds empty and it was clear to Nimmo that Sam Giancana had not exaggerated. Tom Jefferson had certainly disappeared. There was no trace of his clothing or anything of obvious importance he might have owned. No documentation, no insurance policies, no correspondence, no cheque-stubs, no address-books, no diaries – there was nothing that might have given Nimmo a clue as to where the man had gone. It was becoming increasingly obvious to Nimmo not only that Jefferson had disappeared, but that the man had covered his tracks very carefully. The attic contained nothing but dust. The bureau had been cleaned out of everything except loose change and paperclips. Even the garbage cans were empty.

Nimmo went into the kitchen and poured himself a glass of water, and it was now that he noticed the small can of kerosene behind the back door. Instinctively, he went out into the back yard and, walking its length, discovered a blackened brazier that told the story of Jefferson's last hours on the property eloquently enough. Squatting down, he removed a glove and stirred the surrounding ashes, as if he half-expected to find a phoenix or, at the very least, a salamander or two. But the ashes were quite cold. Standing up again, he placed a foot on the side of the brazier and pushed it over. It fell on to the dry grass with a dull clang, sending a miasma of dust and ashes into the warm morning air. He waited a minute until the air had cleared, and then, replacing the glove, poked at the bottom of the brazier in search of some legible fragment or informative shard that might have escaped the trail-consuming flames. But there was nothing. Zippo.

Nimmo came back up the yard and went into the garage where a blue 1950 Chrysler Windsor was parked. He searched the car and found only the few odds and ends he needed to confirm that it had belonged to Mary Jefferson.

Returning to the house, he began to pay closer attention to the small box of items he had collected. First, he listened to the tapes on a little Phonotrix portable recorder. Mostly these were recordings from television, cultural stuff like *Open End* and *Play of the Week*, but there was one tape that featured a woman reading the speeches of John Kennedy. Since Mary Jefferson had worked for the Democrats in Miami, Nimmo guessed that the voice on the tape belonged to her, although it quite escaped him why she should have wanted to record herself, or, for that matter, the speeches in this particular way. Of greater interest to him was a folded piece of paper he had found underneath the bed. On it Tom Jefferson had written ten sets of initials: W.H./P.B./H.H./B.M./G.D./S.M./M.V./H.P./N.Y./J.C.

Nimmo knew this was Jefferson's handwriting because he had another example of Jefferson's hand from a note the missing man had left beside the telephone, with the number of the La Casa Marina Hotel, in Key West.

He glanced at his watch. It was almost midday. The rest of the stuff in the box could wait. There was none of it looked like much anyway. He turned off the TV and, tucking the box underneath his arm, prepared to go and speak to the neighbours. The last thing he did before leaving the house was to fill the box with all the medicine bottles he could find on the floor, and in the bathroom cabinet, for the sake of verisimilitude: the neighbours would expect someone to be investigating Mary Jefferson's death, and the medication would add a nice touch of authenticity. Coming out of the front door, Nimmo straightened the little Stetson hat on his sweating head, and then took out the black leather wallet that contained his badge.

In the Bible it said that a lawyer had asked Jesus, 'Who is my neighbour?' It was not a question Jimmy Nimmo thought he could have answered himself. The surname of any one of his neighbours in Keystone Islands would have been a mystery to him. He even had to think hard to remember their Christian names. This apparent lacuna in Nimmo's social graces did not cause him to feel any shame, no more than it bothered him that he had so few friends. It was, he told himself, an occupational hazard. He had nothing against Jesus, or Christians, or anyone trying to live a decent life. But he figured he would have told that fucking smartass Jewish lawyer, 'Who gives a shit?' Neighbours were for regular people with three kids, a dog, and a station wagon, not for guys like him with guns and ulcers and guilty secrets.

Before he died, Nimmo's dad, a Baptist lay-preacher, had traced his family tree back to Scotland, and it turned out that his people were descended from French Huguenots who, fleeing the persecution of the Catholic King Louis XIV, had wanted to keep their names a secret. The name Nimmo was a corruption of the Latin *ne mot*, meaning no one, nothing to say, no name, fuck you and the horse you rode in on. You couldn't get more unneighbourly than that.

Nimmo was the kind of man who kept himself to himself the way some guys kept pigeons. It was as if he had trained himself not to stop and exchange more than a few words with any of his neighbours until he was back in his own coop. So he was not surprised that the Jeffersons' neighbours knew so very little about the couple except that he was often away on business, and she frequently worked late, and they were never around to get to know really, and they didn't seem to have any other friends to speak of anyway. Thirty minutes and four sets of neighbours later, and having fielded a dozen or so enquiries as to whether or not she had committed suicide, Nimmo gave up and went back to his car with what he considered was a pathetically small haul of information for several hours' work. Earning Sam Giancana's twenty-five thou already looked harder than it had seemed back in Chicago.

From Miami Shores he drove south, to Brickell Avenue, and across the Rickenbacker Causeway to Key Biscayne and the expensive hotel where Johnny Rosselli was staying. Key Biscayne was a whole world of no concerns. The ups and downs of normal life did not travel across the bridge. Or at least the downs didn't. They stayed put on the other side of Tollkeeper's hut, with the blacktop and the trash in the gutters. After New York, Miami seemed quite unreal enough to Jimmy Nimmo, but he fancied that Key Biscayners probably thought vicissitudes were a set of no-account islands in the stream, just a few miles west of the adversities.

In Rosselli's enormous ocean-front suite, the silver-haired gangster was cooking lunch in the kitchenette.

'Jesus, I thought you'd never get here,' said Rosselli. 'You want some lunch? It's linguine primavera.'

Nimmo, who knew Rosselli of old, told him he had been to Jefferson's house for a snoop around.

'Find anything?'

'Maybe,' shrugged Nimmo. 'I dunno. Not much probably. Linguine sounds good though. I could eat a wooden horse.'

Rosselli poured Nimmo a large glass of cold Frascati, and waved at another man walking in off the big balcony. 'Jimmy? Say hello to Frank Sorges.'

The two men grunted at each other. Rosselli started to serve up the linguine.

'Frank was with that sonofabitch right up until the time he disappeared.'

'So where the fuck is he?' asked Nimmo, grinning.

'Search me. I looked all over for that guy. Every fucking bar-rail in this town. At first, I thought he was just out on a bender in memory of his wife. But when I saw the guy's clothes had gone from his closet, I figured he'd lit out someplace.'

'Lit out for the territory ahead of the rest,' said Nimmo. 'Just like Huckleberry Finn, eh?'

'I never read that,' said Rosselli. 'Wish I had. I hadn't much time for reading as a kid. It was too crowded at home and I was always helling around. Not like now. I read a lot these days.'

Nimmo smiled patiently. 'He's ahead of us for now,' he said confidently. 'But we'll find him.' He snapped the head of a match with his thumbnail and held it over the bowl of his pipe. 'I'm going to want to talk to you in detail, Frank. Everything you can remember about him in those final few days of happiness you had together. What he talked about. All the news that's fit to print. Right now, however, I'd like to see that coroner's report.'

'Before lunch?' exclaimed Rosselli. 'Are you sure you wanna do that, Jimmy? I mean, there's pictures in there 'n' everything.'

Collecting a plate of pasta, Nimmo said, 'That's okay, I gotta stomach like a spit bucket.'

Rosselli smiled thinly. 'How very reassuring for your chef,' he murmured.

Nimmo held the plate under his nose and inhaled. 'Smells good,' he said. 'I remember one time I saw an autopsy surgeon open some guy's chest like it was a fucking bear trap.' And putting down his plate for a moment he clasped and unclasped his fingers for added effect. 'Five minutes later? I was eating ribs in Embers.'

'Frank, fetch him the report before he starts talking tripe and onions.'

Nimmo took his plate and his glass on to the balcony and sat down at a glass table.

'Help yourself to Parmesan,' said Rosselli.

'Thanks, I will.'

Nimmo spooned a generous spoonful of cheese and then opened

156

the thicker of the two files Sorges had placed in front of him. Rosselli brought out his own plate and sat down opposite Nimmo. He watched the other man read and eat with an appetite that appalled his more fastidious sensibilities. This was not because he knew what was in the linguine but because he knew what was in the report, for which someone in the coroner's office had been paid very handsomely to make a copy.

Nimmo read the report with growing irritation, hardly noticing when Sorges sat down and spilled a glass of wine. It always annoyed him, the way autopsy surgeons wrote their reports – the omniscience they affected to wield. Nimmo knew the truth was that most coroner's offices were understaffed and underfunded, and most autopsy surgeons were overworked and prone to depression. He wished he had a dollar for every time he had seen a croaker fold on the stand under prolonged cross-examination. But his irritation with autopsy surgeons and their findings concealed a greater hatred of scientists in general. Who else but scientists had created a world in which annihilation was only ever a button's push away? So, as Nimmo read, he growled and sneered and snorted and shook his head.

'Not this,' he said to Rosselli, jabbing a fork at the linguine. 'This is good. The fucking report is what pisses me off.'

'What's the problem with it?'

'It begs as many questions as it purports to answer, that's what's wrong with it.'

'Like what, for instance?'

'Okay. Cause of death given as acute barbiturate poisoning due to ingestion of overdose. Mode of death, probably suicide. Now then, the toxicologist says that her liver contained – let's see – twelve milligrams per cent pentobarbital. That's the chemical you find in Nembutal. Okay, now twelve milligrams is about nine or ten times the normal therapeutic dose. But she's also got Chloral Hydrate in her. Again, it's way too high – over five milligrams per cent in her blood. The CH is in another kind of sleeping pill. Maybe a little less dangerous than Nembutal, taken in excess. But she's still got ten to fifteen times the amount Mr Sensible usually recommends for normal shuteye.

'Thank you for your patience, and here's my first question. How did she swallow the drugs? Surely she would have needed a large glass of water to wash them all down. But the only glass found by her bedside contained Scotch. Now, we all know that Scotch and barbs go together like a lame horse and a broken carriage, but that's beside the point, on account of the fact that her blood contained no alcohol. However, let us give the late Mrs Jefferson the benefit of the doubt and say that she swallowed the pills with some water while she was still in the bathroom, and then went to bed.'

'What's wrong with that?' asked Sorges.

'You're committing suicide, Sherlock. Do you put the fucking tops on the medicine bottles, and then the bottles back in the medicine cabinet? The only bottles found with the tops off were by the bed, on the table, next to the glass of Scotch.'

Rosselli pointed his fork at Nimmo and said, 'What if she brought the bottles through with her from the bathroom, intending to swallow more with the Scotch? Only before she could do so, she passed out?'

'Not a bad hypothesis,' admitted Nimmo. 'Let's suppose that's what happened. A lot of pills consumed at once, like so many sweets, instead of over a longer period of time. So why didn't she vomit?' He spooned some more Parmesan on top of his linguine. 'There was no vomit found anywhere in that house. And certainly none by the bed where she was found. Barb victims don't always puke. But if they take the stuff in a rush they often do. It's that precipitate rush to wave good-bye to this cruel world that makes them barf and sometimes saves their sad, sad lives. Always assuming they don't aspirate their own vomit and choke to death.

'It is possible, however, that she took the stuff on an empty stomach,' continued Nimmo. 'That way her system would have been much more prone to rapid absorption of barbiturates, which could be the reason why she didn't have time to puke before she passed out. But that just begs another question. There's no residue of capsules in her stomach. And with that finding this autopsy surgeon ought to have considered examining her duodenum, or even her small bowel. Hell, I'm no croaker, but if the stomach is empty, that's where you might expect to find fragments of gelatin capsules. In with all her shit. Maybe even an undigested pill or two.'

Rosselli sighed, and pushed away his plate. With the smell of

Parmesan cheese in his nostrils, it was all too easy to think of vomit. 'I eat too much anyway,' he said weakly. He stood up from the table and, leaning on the balcony's handrail, took a deep breath of the air blowing off Biscayne Bay.

'So the croaker missed a few things,' objected Sorges, whose own appetite seemed undiminished. 'I can't see how that helps us to find Jefferson.'

'That's because you're not a fucking detective. Cops stepping on clues, croakers missing probable cause. Shit like that is what forensic method is all about. Look. All I'm trying to do is paint a picture. As accurate a picture as possible of what led up to him taking off like that.' Nimmo pointed to Rosselli's uneaten linguine. 'You gonna eat that?'

'I lost my appetite between the puke and the shit,' said Rosselli.

'Mind if I do?'

'Be my guest.' Rosselli watched Nimmo attack the cheesy food with alacrity, and groaned quietly. 'A spit bucket is about right.'

'My stomach only holds good for this kind of travail,' confessed Nimmo. 'And on dry land. It's no good on the water. I'm the only guy in Keystone Islands who doesn't own a boat. I get sick as a dog at sea. That's why I ended up in intelligence during the war. Because I was such a lousy sailor. Me and Jack Kennedy.'

'Jack Kennedy was a lousy sailor?' Sorges frowned.

'That PT boat sank, didn't it? And the way I heard it, the gung-ho sonofabitch shouldn't have been in those waters in the first place.'

'Don't talk to me about Kennedys,' said Rosselli.

'Yeah,' laughed Nimmo. 'I saw the paper. Frank?'

Sorges looked up from his plate.

'Let's pretend you are the most interesting guy in the world. You're a regular guest on *Ed Sullivan*. Dinah Shore wants you on her show every week so she can suck your dick while she listens to those great stories you tell. Tab Hunter just can't hear enough of you. A real raconteur is what you are my friend. You've come on TV to talk about the one person who is perhaps as interesting as you. Tom Jefferson. Well, maybe just that little bit more interesting than you, on account of the fact that he's a virtual recluse. The viewers want to know everything about you guys. No matter how small or insignificant it might seem to someone of your stellar proportions, we want you to tell us all about it.'

'Okay, I get the idea,' growled Sorges.

Nimmo took out a notebook and a pencil and prepared to write. 'Your every word, for posterity.'

Sorges shrugged and, hesitatingly, began to tell Nimmo what he could remember. He wasn't much of a talker and repeated himself a lot when there was a silence. Some of the time he looked out to sea for inspiration, and other times into his glass, which Nimmo kept filled with wine, hoping to loosen the big man's reef-knotted tongue some more. But after fifteen to twenty minutes of it, Nimmo found himself suppressing a yawn and began to cross-question Sorges about some of the things he had said.

'You told us you thought there was nothing unusual about Jefferson on that last evening in Key West, except that maybe he was a little quiet.'

'That's right. But Jefferson never did talk very much. He'd have made a pretty poor guest on *Ed Sullivan*, I reckon.'

'But you talked about something, surely? I mean, you went to dinner. You and this other guy, Bosch. The one you say is still down in Key West.' Sorges nodded. 'So what did you talk about?'

Sorges shrugged. 'Broads. Key West. Hemingway. The election.'

'I guess he was a big Kennedy fan, his wife working for the Democrats 'n' all?'

'Matter of fact I got the impression he didn't care for Kennedy at all.'

'Did he say why?'

'Nothing specific.'

'Didn't that surprise you?'

'I didn't think anything about it, at the time.'

'Okay. Broads. You talked about broads. Did he talk about his wife much?'

'Not at all. We had this ongoing argument about Marilyn Monroe. Me, I prefer Kim Novak, or Jayne Mansfield. But he liked Marilyn. One time—' Sorges stopped, seeming to think better of what he had been about to say.

'What?'

'Nuthin'.'

'I'll be the judge of that,' snapped Nimmo. 'Sam Giancana's already taken me into his confidence, Frank. I'd hate to have to tell him I thought you were holding out on me about something.' This time Nimmo caught the look that flicked between Sorges and Rosselli, and clapped his hands loudly. 'Come on guys. It's show time at Grossingers. If you've got a routine, put your fucking skates on, and let's see it before the ice melts.' Rosselli was nodding now, urging full disclosure on Frank Sorges.

Sorges told Nimmo about the JFK–Marilyn tape-recording.

'The prince and the show-girl, huh?' commented Nimmo. 'Makes sense, I guess. Sounds like some tape, Johnny. And some squeeze, too. More like a hug from a fucking grizzly bear.'

Rosselli shook his head. 'There's no squeeze. No shakedown. Not yet anyway. And Kennedy doesn't even know about the tape. No more than she does. It's what you might call an insurance policy. Just in case the President-elect doesn't deliver on a done deal. You see, Mooney helped old Joe Kennedy out of a bind with Frank Costello. Not to mention what happened during the election, when he delivered Illinois on a silver salver. The way old Joe likes things. In return, Jack and Joe promised to lay off with senate investigations and shit like that.'

Nimmo nodded grimly, drank some wine, and then pulled a face. 'Suddenly this wine doesn't taste as good,' he said. 'I'm beginning to understand why this Tom Jefferson lit out. You boys are playing some serious fucking cards here. And for high stakes. I ought to tell you to deal me out only I'd kind of like to hear what happens next. Can I hear it? The tape, I mean.'

'If you think it's necessary. Frank? Fetch the tape.'

'But it's at home,' protested Sorges. 'In the safe. Like you said.'

'Fetch it anyway.'

Grumbling loudly about a wild goose chase, Frank Sorges stood up and shuffled his bulk out of the suite.

Nimmo waited for the door to close behind him and then said, 'Where the fuck did you find him, Johnny?'

'Frank? He's a good man.'

'Yeah?'

'You remember Norman Morgan?'

'Rough House Morgan? Mob gofer from Havana?' Rosselli nodded. 'Sure, I remember him.'

'He introduced us.'

'Do you trust him?'

'We share a common interest in the liberation of Cuba from the communists. Why not?'

'I don't know. Only Mooney told me the fee you guys were paying Jefferson to hit Castro. Frank may have figured that he could do the job himself, him being part Cuban 'n' all. Maybe he got rid of Jefferson, and kept the money. Or maybe he split it with this other guy, Orlando Bosch.'

'You paint a very surreal picture, Jimmy.'

'That's my job. Bringing together seemingly unrelated fragments of life into a new reality. I do everything except soft watches.'

Rosselli glanced at his own watch. 'How shall we amuse ourselves? A little gin-rummy, perhaps? He'll be gone about an hour.'

'No, thanks.' Nimmo collected the second file off the table in front of him and burped. 'Pardon me. It's not every day I have such rich food for thought.' He opened the file and took out a solitary sheet of typewritten paper and a photograph. 'This our man?'

'Yes. The rest of what's there is rather bland fare. The make and registration of our missing gunsel's car. Foreign bank accounts, passport number, that kind of thing. Just a few odds and ends I had put together to try and make your life a little easier.'

'Thanks a lot,' Nimmo said, returning the sheet of paper and the photograph to the file. 'Tell me, did Kennedy fuck Marilyn here, or someplace else?'

'I can assure you, there are no peepholes, or hidden microphones, or anything else of that nature in this suite. I believe the recording was made at a house in Virginia, just outside Washington. Of course, there have been lots of other assignations. But you know, I think those two young people are genuinely fond of each other.'

By the time Sorges came back with the tape, a little less than a hour later, Rosselli and Nimmo were watching the basketball on television. They watched the game, between Detroit and Los Angeles, to its conclusion and then turned their attention to the tape now ready to play on Rosselli's portable Grundig.

'I forgot to tell you,' mumbled Sorges. 'This isn't actually the Marilyn tape. But it's the one I played Jefferson. I couldn't get my hands on the one featuring Marilyn. Because Johnny had hidden it away someplace safe.'

'Wait a minute,' said Nimmo. 'You mean this is Kennedy fucking some other broad?' Sorges nodded. 'How many fucking tapes are there?'

'Our President-elect,' Rosselli said smoothly, 'gets himself laid as often as eggs. When I was in Hollywood, I met some very accomplished swordsmen. Charlie Chaplin, Errol Flynn. But there never was a man for pussy like Jack Kennedy. Not that any of this excuses what Frank did. He was way out of order letting Jefferson listen to this tape at all.'

'Hey, not that he was really interested, you know?' said Sorges, switching on the tape machine. 'For him, it was Marilyn, or nothing.'

'I can dig that,' said Nimmo. He knocked out his pipe in an ashtray and set about refilling it with tobacco.

He was no stranger to material obtained from wiretaps, and, usually, most of what you heard was of a sexual nature. As someone who had worked for the OSS and, penultimately, the FBI, Nimmo had often participated in cases involving blackmail. On one occasion he had heard a tape that purported to prove that Eleanor Roosevelt and her close companion Lorena Hickock had enjoyed a lesbian relationship, but it wasn't the best of recordings and, as far as Nimmo was concerned, the jury was still out on that one. Another time he had listened to a wiretap of President Eisenhower discussing his impotence with mistress Kay Summersby. Nimmo liked Ike, but unfortunately he thought that tape had been the genuine article. It was certainly possible that J. Edgar Hoover was being blackmailed by Meyer Lansky, just as Hoover himself was supposed to have pictures and recorded material of everyone, from civil rights leaders to the Queen of England's favourite Uncle Louis. So Nimmo was only a little surprised that Jack Kennedy should have fallen victim himself to some kind of covert surveillance operation. What did surprise him, however, was that the recording should be so explicitly sexual.

Kennedy – his Boston drawl easily recognisable – was the kind of guy who liked his partner to talk dirty to him, encouraging the anonymous girl on the tape – 'Honey' was what he called her – to direct his fingers, or the way to use his tongue, or even how deep to take his cock in her mouth.

After they had brought their lovemaking to a loud conclusion – a sound recordist's nightmare, Nimmo figured – and the conversation had moved from sexual praxis to American foreign policy, Rosselli nodded at Sorges, who got up and switched off the machine.

'I hope that satisfies your curiosity, Jimmy,' said Rosselli. 'It seemed to satisfy Jack all right.'

Nimmo said nothing, just puffed his pipe thoughtfully, and frowned.

After a two-minute silence, Rosselli lit a cigarette and said, 'What's this, Jimmy? The Great Detective? Not so much elementary, my dear Watson, as alimentary. I think that girl must have swallowed a gallon of the President-elect.'

Nimmo did not hear him. But finally he seemed to break out of his thought process and, drawing a deep breath, he put aside his pipe and stood up. 'Excuse me,' he said quietly. 'I'll be back in just a few minutes.' And so saying he walked out of the suite.

Rosselli looked at Sorges and pulled a face, uncertain as to whether Nimmo had left because he was disgusted by what he had heard or not.

Sorges shrugged back and said, 'Search me.'

When Nimmo returned, some ten minutes later, he was carrying the cardboard box containing various items gathered in Jefferson's house that he had brought up from the trunk of his car.

Rosselli was watching TV again. 'Was it something we said?' He turned the set off. 'I did wonder if you were coming back at all.'

Nimmo threw Sorges one of the tapes from the box.

'Play it,' he ordered.

Sorges placed the new tape on the spool and drew the green leader through the recording head. Then he hit the play button and returned to his seat.

'The preconvention campaign is over. For the candidates, the hour of unity is at hand. We have all been friends for a long time. I know

164

we always will. We have always supported our party's nominee. I know we will in nineteen sixty.'

'Who's this, Jimmy?' asked Rosselli. 'Eleanor Roosevelt?'

'Shut up and listen.'

'For we are all Democrats – not northern or southern Democrats, not liberal or conservative Democrats . . .'

Nimmo searched their faces for some indication that they understood what they were listening to.

'Can't you hear?' he yelled. 'Don't you get it?'

'Hear what, for Chrissakes?'

'It's her, God damn it. It's the broad on the tape. The one fucking Kennedy. "You can do anything you want to me, Jack. You can fuck me up the ass, if you want, Jack. I'm your slave." Her. Jesus, haven't you morons guessed it yet? This is the same girl who was fucking Kennedy. This is Tom Jefferson's wife.'

An hour later Rosselli came off the phone to Nevada with the explanation.

'A few months ago – this would have been late May, early June – Jefferson and his wife visited the Cal-Neva Lodge on Lake Tahoe at the invitation of a guy named Irving Davidson. Davidson was fronting some Jew organisation for Meyer Lansky and Moe Dalitz, and the Shin Bet. You know? Israeli intelligence. The same guys who got together to give Adolf Eichmann a long holiday in Jerusalem. Anyway, they wanted Jefferson to pick up the contract on another Nazi war criminal down in Argentina. Only Moe and Lansky couldn't get away from some other business in Vegas. So they asked Jefferson to drive down to Vegas and pick up the contract there. To leave his wife back in Tahoe for just one night and have a good time, all expenses paid, courtesy of Moe and the others. Which is pretty much what happens. Only guess who shows up at the Cal-Neva Lodge unexpectedly and looking for some R&R? Kennedy, Sinatra, the whole fucking rat-pack.

'Skinny D'Amato, who's manager at the Lodge, is asked to fix up some broads for a party in Kennedy's chalet. And naturally he invites Mary Jefferson along. Well, who wouldn't? She's a beautiful broad. Kennedy thinks so, too. He and she hit it off big time. Next thing is they're alone in Kennedy's bedroom. Which is wired for sound, because Kennedy's partying there a lot, with all sorts of broads. Actresses, B-girls, you name it. All Skinny has to do is what he always does. Hit a few switches. Bernie Spindel, the sound man, doesn't even have to be on the scene. Well, you've heard the rest. *From Here to Eternity* with everything but the ocean and swimsuits.'

Nimmo nodded grimly. He said, 'So here's Tom Jefferson, turns up to hear a very diverting tape of our future President fucking Marilyn Monroe. Instead, what Jefferson hears, courtesy of the outfit's very own answer to *Dick Clark's American Bandstand*—'

'Hey, how the fuck was I to know?' protested Sorges.

'Is a recording of Kennedy giving it to his own wife, up the ass. Jesus Christ Frank, didn't he say anything?'

'It's like I said. He went kind of quiet and acted, well, disappointed that it wasn't Marilyn. Or at least that's what I thought he was disappointed about.'

'How much did he hear of it?'

'The whole tape. All the way through. He just sat there drinking – quite a bit, actually – smoking a lot of cigarettes and listening real close.'

'I wonder why. And you? What did you do?'

Sorges looked sheepish. 'Had some drinks. Made a few jokes, I guess. Laughed a lot. He didn't laugh at all, like he was supposed to. But then he's a shooter. You don't expect shooters to have much of a sense of humour, you know? So he just sat there, and when the tape was finished he went home.'

'This is November the ninth, right?' asked Nimmo. Sorges nodded. 'And then just two days later, you're in Key West, getting ready to go to Cuba. Which is where he more or less disappears on you.' Sorges kept on nodding. 'And then the wife is found dead.' Nimmo chuckled. 'Gentlemen, that's a chain of causation like an apple falling from a tree equals gravity.'

'Are you saying Tom Jefferson killed his own wife?' asked Rosselli.

'You've heard the tape. That kind of shit happens. Besides, it's not like this guy is Billy Graham. He kills people, all the time.'

'Yeah, but how?' asked Rosselli. 'The autopsy surgeon's report says there was no sign of bruising on her face or mouth, so he couldn't have forced her to swallow all those pills.'

'I dunno. A needle maybe.'

'Besides,' added Sorges, 'he was with me the night she died. He would have had to drive all the way back to Miami, in the dead of night, killed her, then come straight back to Key West in time for the cops to find him in his hotel room when they called with the bad news.'

'You said it,' shrugged Nimmo, enjoying their consternation. 'Maybe that's exactly what he did. Look, I don't know all the answers. Not yet. I'm not even sure she was murdered yet, and I won't know that until tomorrow.' Nimmo glanced at his watch. 'I'm going to try and get someone to go down to the morgue with me and take another look at the body. Someone qualified, but who'll keep his mouth shut. Maybe then I'll be able to answer some of these outstanding questions.'

'Kill her, yeah, I can understand that,' mused Rosselli. 'Why not? Lots of guys kill their wives. Hell, it's not exactly un-American. It's not like he was a communist, or anything. But this thing with Castro. That was for the government. It was a matter of national security. He could have killed her, and nobody would have minded. We would even have helped him dispose of the body, if he'd wanted that. He should have known that. But not seeing through the job, that was a dereliction of duty.'

'He's a mercenary, for Christ's sake,' argued Nimmo. 'What the hell does he care for duty? Look, I'll know more tomorrow morning.'

'Yeah, thanks Jimmy. Call me, okay?'

'Sure.'

Nimmo returned to his car and drove back across the Rickenbacker Causeway. Then he drove north, up Biscayne Boulevard, back to Jefferson's home in Miami Shores. Now that he had established a possible motive for a murder, he had realised there was something in the house he wanted to take another look at. It wasn't much more than a doodle on a magazine, and he wished he'd obeyed his first inclination, which had been to put the magazine in the box with the rest of the stuff he had taken. But then that was the nature of criminal investigation, he told himself: meaning was always changing, evolving in such a way that sometimes evidence seemed positively organic.

He had not locked the back door and it took only a couple of minutes to collect the magazine, which was a copy of *Time*, from 1957, before driving south again to the Luau, a Chinese restaurant on the 79th Street Causeway. Decorated like a Singapore movie set, the place was run by a couple of Jews, Joey Cohen and Jerry Brooks, who knew Nimmo as a regular patron. Even after two plates of linguine for lunch, Nimmo still had room for some sweet and sour pork. But mostly he was there to pick the brains of his Chinese waiter, Yat, as to the meaning of the doodle on the *Time* front cover.

It was nine fifteen when finally he arrived home tired and, despite all his bravado about a spit bucket for a stomach, suffering from mild indigestion. He called a medical friend about finding a pathologist to do a private autopsy on Mary Jefferson, and then settled down with a bottle of Peptobismol to watch *The Lawrence Welk Show* on television. Then the medical friend called him back to tell him that everything was fixed, and after that he watched the boxing – a middleweight bout between Henry Hank and Gene Armstrong. Five minutes after the fight ended he could not remember who had won. Five minutes after that he was in bed and asleep.

At six o'clock on a Sunday morning, Miami is as bright and empty and lifeless as a painting by Giorgio de Chirico. Hard light fills the deserted streets with sharp shadows, and there is a strange sense of departure, as if all the city's inhabitants have been consumed by a flesh-eating alien organism from another planet.

Jimmy Nimmo, sitting in the open-topped blue Chevy Impala on the corner of North West 12th Avenue and 18th Street, had flesh and its frailty at the front of his mind, not because of his location, which was in the environs of the Jackson Memorial Hospital, but because of the profession of the man he was expecting to meet. He lit a cigarette and, glancing in his rear-view mirror, caught sight of a man walking rapidly towards him from the direction of the Veterans Hospital. He watched him come and then, as the man grew closer, started up the Impala's V8 engine, pushed the automatic transmission stick into reverse, and, with a loud squeal of whitewalled tyres, growled back up the avenue to come alongside the approaching figure.

'Are you Dan Hill?' he asked, because in his eyes the much younger man did not look very much like a qualified doctor. With his cheap suit, longish hair and beard, Hill, who was also a student of forensic pathology at the Miami School of Medicine – for which Jackson Memorial was the major teaching hospital – resembled something indigenous to Greenwich Village in New York. Some kind of beatnik, anyway. It was a first impression that quickly proved to be accurate.

'That's right, man. You Nimmo?'

'Sure. Hop in.'

Hill tossed a Bonanza Air flight bag into the Impala's back seat and got into the car. 'Nice wheels, man,' he said in a whiny sort of voice. 'A real dreamboat. What'll she do if you floor it?'

'I've not had it much above eighty.' Nimmo hit the gas pedal, jolting them forward on their way.

Hill leaned across to take a squint at the speedometer on the matching blue dashboard. 'Says one twenty on the clock, so you can probably figure it's good for around a hundred.'

'You like cars?'

'Yeah. I'm tryin' to get the dough together to buy myself this fifty-six Corvette Coupé I've seen. Two point six litre, two hundred and twenty-five horsepower. A real cool car, you know?' He lit a Marlboro and flicked the match away. 'Tell me something. You ever see an autopsy before?'

'A few. Now you can tell me something. Just to check out you're a real croaker and not some night porter who's trying to make an easy buck.'

'Go ahead. But I can show you my driving licence if you like. Says there, MD. Just like Ben Casey. As to me being a pathologist, you'll just have to take my word for it until we get into the morgue. Proof of the pudding, so to speak. But Dade County's chief medical examiner just happens to be the head of my department. My teacher, if you like. But ask away, friend. Ask away.'

'There was something in the original autopsy surgeon's report. Guy named Hunt. Know him?'

'Bill Hunt? Yeah. He's a good man.'

'He said that the dead woman had been suffering from something called STD. What is that exactly?'

'An STD is what we call a sexually transmitted disease.'

'You mean like a venereal disease?'

'That's right. There are lots of STDs around. It's just a catch-all term for the Lord's host of bacterial disorders. Most women are asymptomatic, which is to say that they don't normally know when they're infected, because it's all happening inside their pussies. Men do know, because it happens on the outside. Women have to rely on their partners being honest enough to tell them. So you can see how that system falls down. An STD's easy enough to treat, though. Penicillin, usually. But left untreated it can cause infertility. There's a lot of it around, man. The more partners you have, the more likely you are to pick up an infection. Wear a sheath if you party, man, that's my advice, otherwise you could give Mrs Nimmo something nasty.' He chuckled unpleasantly.

'There is no Mrs Nimmo,' said Nimmo, conquering his first inclination which had been to smack the younger man in the mouth. He wondered if Mary Jefferson might have picked up her STD during her liaison with Kennedy. From all he had gathered from Rosselli, Jack Kennedy liked to party a great deal, and with a lot of different partners. He didn't recall any mention of a sheath being used on the tape he had heard. It looked more likely him giving it to her than the other way around.

'Ira told you the job was two hundred and fifty, right?'

'The money's in the glove-box,' said Nimmo. 'Go ahead and take it.'

Hill stabbed the lock with his forefinger, let the compartment fall open, and took out the envelope he found there. He counted the money and then nodded. 'You're aces, man. Aces. Hey, how does Ira Fellner know someone like you anyway?'

'I did him a favour once. Got him out of some trouble he was in.'

'Yeah? What kind of trouble?'

'The mind your own fucking business kind.'

'Cool with me, bro.'

Arriving at the Hall of Justice a few minutes later, the two men went down to the basement where they were met by the same autopsy assistant bribed by Rosselli to supply the original coroner's report. Under the eyes of Dan Hill, Nimmo handed over another envelope, this one containing a hundred dollars.

'Regular John D. Rockefeller, isn't he?' said Hill.

'She's waiting for you on table one,' said the autopsy assistant.

'Just like Tony Sweet's,' said Nimmo. 'Thanks a lot.'

'Deputy examiner'll be here at nine to take charge of the Sunday shift. But I want you two guys outta here by eight. Okay?'

'Cool with me,' said Hill. He put down the bag he was carrying and took out gowns, masks, and gloves. 'Put these things on,' he told Nimmo. 'Quite apart from protecting your clothes, they'll have a hard job identifying us if someone does catch us *in flagrante delicto*.'

Covered by a plastic sheet, and in a long windowless room, Mary Jefferson lay on a high stainless-steel table equipped with a water hose and drainage system. Hill pulled away the sheet to reveal her naked body, crudely stitched across the chest and belly from the previous autopsy, like some prospective bride of Frankenstein. To Nimmo's surprise, her once beautiful face was badly bruised, as if she had fought several rounds with Floyd Patterson.

'Jesus Christ,' he muttered. 'Her face.'

'Don't pass out on me, man.'

'I'm okay,' Nimmo said angrily. 'It's just that the autopsy report said there was no evidence that anyone might have forced her to swallow anything. But she looks like Ingemar Johansson.'

'Oh that. Previous surgeon, probably. The facial muscles would have been severed during the removal of her brain. The whole face gets peeled off like the skin off an avocado pear. It's quite common that it should result in this kind of discoloration. Okay man, it's your call. What am I looking for?'

'Needle marks. Look for needle marks.'

Hill searched her forearms for several minutes before paying particular attention to one of her wrists.

'Find something?'

'Not a needle mark. More like a friction burn.'

'Could she have been tied up?'

'It's possible.'

'Keep looking.'

Hill produced a magnifying glass from his bag and began to search the rest of Mary Jefferson's body for injection marks. While he studied her armpits, between her toes, her hairline, her vagina, and even under her tongue, Nimmo explained some of the problems he had with the original report.

Hill listened as he worked, and then said, 'Yes, it is possible that she could have been given a fatal barbiturate dose, by injection. But what you've said about her liver, I don't think it's very likely. The barbs would had to have been in her body for a while in order for them to be absorbed by her liver. But a shot, in the sort of quantities you've described, would have caused her to die too quickly for that to happen.' He put down the glass and shook his head. 'Besides, there's absolutely no sign of a hypodermic needle that I can find. And as you see for yourself, I've looked everywhere.' He sighed, pulled down his mask and proceeded to light two cigarettes, *Now Voyager*-style, one for himself and one for Nimmo. 'Nice-looking chick, though. Got some slope and nigger in her by the look of her. But really very striking, wouldn't you say?'

Nimmo took the cigarette and puffed it into life, grateful for the sanctuary from the smell of formaldehyde. 'She and I,' he said, 'we're gonna give the marriage another try. For the sake of the dog.'

'Go ahead and fuck her if you want, Pop. Some guys consider it a perk of the job.'

'No thanks. I like a little more life in my women, even at my age.'

Hill sniggered smoke. 'What are you, a flit or something? Just look at that body of hers, man. She's a babe. Even in death. I'll leave the room if you're the shy type.'

'You're a real pain in the ass, you know that Dan?'

'That reminds me. There is one other way in which a fatal dose could have been administered. It could have been inserted colonically.'

'You mean up her ass? Like a suppository?'

'Of course. That particular egress does not preclude entry, my friend. What does Sherlock Holmes say in *The Sign of Four*? When you've eliminated the impossible, whatever remains, however improbable, man, must be the truth. That's axiomatic for all pathologists. They virtually tattoo it on your dick when you go forensic.' Hill

172

took a last drag on his cigarette and tossed it into the sink. 'Here,' he said, taking hold of her pelvis. 'Help me to turn her over.'

Nimmo put his hands under the body's shoulder, and together the two men pushed it on to its stomach. Then Hill searched for something in his Bonanza bag, saying, 'The medication would be quickly absorbed through the anal membrane directly into the bloodstream. That would explain why her stomach was empty.' He came out of the bag holding a small set of forceps. 'Okay, Pop, you're gonna have to hold her butt cheeks open while I get the Emmetts up her ass, and have a look-see inside her anus. Think you can handle that?'

'Sure,' said Nimmo, throwing his own cigarette into the sink after Hill's. 'I hold women down for other guys all the time.' But he looked away as Hill began to inspect Mary Jefferson's anus, and then her colon.

'We'll take a smear before we do anything,' said Hill. 'In case we compromise the area. If a suppository was used, there might still be a trace of it.'

With his eyes now very firmly over his shoulder, Nimmo grunted back.

'As far as the colon itself is concerned, it does look rather discoloured,' Hill reported thoughtfully. 'The damage is quite close to the actual rectum. Looks kind of bruised and purplish. Which would be consistent with something having been shoved up her ass. And it's quite congested in there, too.'

'With shit?'

'No, with traffic.'

Underneath his own mask, Nimmo was grimacing. Things were beginning to smell bad again. Very bad.

'I'll see if I can get a sample with a Lockhart. Of course, I won't know for sure until I can run some tests in the lab, but I'd say we've hit pay dirt, so to speak. The Enema Within.' Hill coughed a little, and then laughed at his own joke. 'Did you read that book?'

'What book?' gagged Nimmo.

'*The Enemy Within*, by Robert Kennedy. All about Hoffa and the teamsters and shit like that. Pretty good book.' He paused as he grappled with the Emmetts. 'Got it. Okay, you can let go of her ass now cowboy.' Hill placed his sample carefully inside a specimen bottle, and then looked at his watch. 'We oughta tear.' Seeing Nimmo's baffled look, he added, 'We should leave. Before any of the three bears turn up looking for their porridge. We can go back to the lab, run a few tests on this little turd of hers, and the smear I took.'

'How long will that take?'

'Not long.' Hill pulled down his mask and grinned. 'You may even still make it to morning service.'

They drove back to Jackson Memorial and a laboratory in the Department of Pathology, where Dan Hill went immediately to work on the smear and the sample, while Nimmo sat and read the paper. Jack Kennedy was on the front page of the *Times* again, just like the day before. This time the President-elect was pictured at the Kennedy home in Palm Beach with Senators Stuart Symington of Missouri and George Smathers of Florida. Nimmo wondered if either Kennedy or Smathers knew Mary Jefferson was dead. Surely someone would have told Smathers. She had worked for him. Surely someone would have told Kennedy. He had fucked her. Nimmo wondered if Kennedy would have looked quite so sanguine if he had known about the tape, and if he had known what was now in Nimmo's ruminative mind.

'Your lady friend was murdered all right,' declared Hill, coming out of the empty laboratory. 'I found abnormally high levels of pure Nembutal and Chloral Hydrate in the smear and in the sample. In those amounts *ab anam*, death was quite certain, and probably reasonably quick. Couple of hours, I shouldn't wonder.'

Nimmo nodded. Good, he thought, that left plenty of time for Tom Jefferson to drive up from Key West, use the suppository on his wife, and then drive back. He tried to picture the scene when Jefferson had arrived in the dead of night. Possibly she had been asleep. Before she knew what was happening he might have bound and gagged her, forced the suppository up her ass, waited for the drugs to kick in, untied her, and then hit the road again. It was brilliantly simple. Just the way a cold-blooded killer would have handled it.

Nimmo took out his wallet and handed over some more cash.

'What's that for?'

'Your silence.'

'Man, you had that when I took the job,' said Hill, pocketing the

174

money. 'Performing an unauthorised autopsy isn't exactly the sort of thing you talk about. But thanks anyway, man. I appreciate it.'

'There is just one more thing,' grinned Hill.

'What's that, Pop?'

Nimmo punched Hill hard in the stomach, the way only a man for whom violence is a full-time job can land a blow. The punch emptied Hill of air, and dumped him flat on his behind, gasping like he had been shot in the gut.

'I don't like you calling me a flit,' said Nimmo. 'I don't like it any more than I care for the implication that I might be a fucking necrophiliac. I don't like you mentioning my ex-wife. I don't like you calling me Pop. I don't like the way you talk. And I don't like the length of your hair. However, I would like to give you some medical advice. Correction, some pathological advice.' Nimmo pulled Hill's cheek playfully. 'You got a big mouth, son. Keep it shut or you could end up catching your death. Understand?'

'And that is how Mary Jefferson was murdered.'

Nimmo and Rosselli were in Gallaghers, a restaurant run by an affable ex-Philadelphian named Joe Lipsky. Located a few blocks north of Nimmo's house in Keystone Islands, on 127th Street, the policeman regarded it as his local, eating there as many as four or five times a week. The Danish lobster tails were the best in town, but Nimmo's taste was usually more quotidian. He particularly liked the 'do-it-yourself kit' where they served a baked potato with a tray containing sour cream, chives, chopped onions, and bacon, so you could fix your Idaho just the way you wanted it.

'A fascinating story,' commented Rosselli when he had heard Nimmo out. 'And ingenious, too.'

'Yeah, you'll have to remember it for when you want to knock off some other broad. A murder weapon that dissolves itself. I checked all the medicine bottles I brought away from the house. They all had drugstore labels except one.'

'Very thorough. I'm impressed. Meyer was certainly right about you.'

His mouth full of potato and his eyes drifting on and off the football game on TV, between the Houston Oilers and the Denver Broncos,

Nimmo shrugged modestly, and then swallowed. 'So, where's that friend of Rough House Morgan's?'

'Frank? He's back in Key West. There are some problems in Havana.'

'Aren't there always? It said in the paper someone put a bomb in a department store. Los Precios Fijos. I've shopped there myself in the past. Things like this go on there won't be anything left for you guys to get back.'

Rosselli nodded. 'I tend to agree with you. If it was up to me we would restrict all our activities to the removal of Castro himself. Bombings just piss everyone off. Even the people who hate the communists.' Rosselli lit a cigarette, ignoring his own potato. There was nothing simple about his own tastes. 'So, where do we go from here?'

'You're not going to like it.'

'I'm shockproof. My middle name is Rolex.'

'If I told you Congress was gonna repeal the Sex Act, you couldn't like it less.'

'With my sex life, I'm still not worried.'

Nimmo pushed his plate away and sat back to light a Lucky Strike. Wearing the cigarette like a small tusk, he spread a sheet of crumpled paper on the table. 'Exhibit one, in the people versus Tom Jefferson.'

Rosselli collected up the paper and read it quickly. 'W.H./P.B./ H.H./B.M/G.D./S.M./M.V./H.P./N.Y./J.C. Initials. Friends of Jefferson's, maybe.' He shrugged. 'Maybe not. Too many friends for one lone wolf. But I'm still not losing any sleep about this.'

'That's what I thought. That they were initials of people Jefferson knew. You'll see that some of them are underlined, and some of them have a question mark against them. Anyway, I know what they mean now. The answer's been staring me in the face every day I read a newspaper.'

'So who are they?'

'Not who. What. In order, we have White House, Palm Beach, Hickory Hill, Boston Massachusetts, Georgetown Delaware, Santa Monica, McLean Virginia, Hyannis Port, New York, and Johnson City.'

'Okay, I'll buy that. But so what?'

176

'Jack Kennedy is so what. He's the common factor.'

'Santa Monica?'

'His brother-in-law, Peter Lawford's house.'

'And McLean Virginia?'

'Bobby.'

'Johnson City?'

'Lyndon Johnson.'

'So let me get this straight. Are you saying we'll find Tom Jefferson in one of these places?'

'I believe it's only the ones he's underlined, namely Palm Beach, Boston, Georgetown, Hyannis Port, and New York.'

'Well, that certainly narrows it down a lot,' grimaced Rosselli.

'Exhibit two, in the people versus Tom Jefferson.' Nimmo unfolded his newspaper to reveal the copy of *Time* magazine he had taken from Jefferson's home. Jack Kennedy's handsome, tanned face stared off the cover. Even back in 1957 the United States Senator from Massachusetts had looked eminently presidential.

'Kennedy's hot copy,' shrugged Rosselli. 'Always was. So what am I looking at?'

'The doodle in the centre of Kennedy's forehead is a Chinese ideogram,' Nimmo explained. 'It's *sei*, which means the number four. A very unlucky number because it means something else, too. *Sei* is also the Chinese word for death. Mary Jefferson was half-Chinese, but I think it was Tom Jefferson who wrote this. I found it with some of his things, not hers.'

'Oh, wait a minute,' Rosselli objected. 'What are you saying, Jimmy?'

'Listen to me, Johnny. I'm not some dumb Okie on *Play Your Hunch*. This is me, Jimmy Nimmo. The nearest damn thing to Daniel Boone there is. Make no mistake about it, these are fucking tracks. I don't need to see this guy's private journals to know what he's planning to do. He's a hitman, and a damn good one. Paid to kill Castro by the mob acting in conjunction with the government. Then he finds his wife has been nailed by the President-elect of that government and, what's worse, that she's been recorded on tape so everyone can share in the experience. His wife is murdered and he disappears, leaving one contract on Castro hanging in the air. Now you add all that to exhibits one and two, and you've got John Wilkes Booth in Ford's fucking Theater.'

'That was a long time ago. Presidents are a lot better protected these days.'

'You're forgetting McKinley. Shot in Buffalo, September sixth, nineteen oh one, by Leon Czolgosz, an anarchist. And when Tony Cermak got shot here in Miami? When was that? Thirty-three? The guy who did it. Zangara. He could just as easily have shot and killed Roosevelt who was sitting right alongside Cermak. Besides, Kennedy isn't President yet. So long as he's not living in the White House, he's an easier target for any nut with a gun. Right now, he's a Secret Service nightmare, all over the place, putting his cabinet together, basking in the glow of his mandate. It's his honeymoon with the American people. Why should he believe anyone would hate him enough to kill him? He hasn't done anything yet. Not even something wrong. Except maybe fuck the wife of a top contract killer.'

'You don't shoot the President of the United States just because he happened to fuck your wife.'

'Johnny, I'll tell you something. Of all the reasons I ever heard for why one guy shoots another, they don't come any better than that. Just because one man is the President doesn't make him any less of a man. A simple motive like he fucked my wife? That you can trust. You don't have to look for anything more complicated than that. Not in this case. Oh, I dare say Jefferson might arm himself with all kinds of extra reasons. Kennedy's soft on communism. He likes niggers too much. He's going to sell us out in East Asia. But the bottom line is still the same. I'm convinced of it.'

Rosselli ran a worried hand through his silver hair. 'I'm still not convinced, Jimmy. Your evidence, it's all very circumstantial.'

Nimmo shrugged. 'Attendant facts, small details, the state of a man's affairs, conclusions which might be inferred from the logical surroundings of a man's actions and character – these are the things that put a man in the electric chair. More often than not, the DA doesn't have a star witness, or a murder weapon. If real hard evidence wasn't so difficult to obtain, do you think cops would work so hard to beat confessions out of people? Circumstantial evidence is the bedrock of our system of justice. Without that you'd be throwing people in ponds to see if they sink, or pricking them with needles in search of the devil's mark.'

Nimmo finished one cigarette and started another. He had made a decision to give up the pipe. So long as he had this case to handle he was going to require a serious amount of nicotine.

'You don't have to be convinced, Johnny. You just have to be worried. A lot worried. It's just like Mooney said to me. About finding Jefferson before your friends in the CIA find out that the guy's gone AWOL. All I'm saying is that it's that, times a hundred. Look, suppose I'm right. Suppose Jefferson is hunting Kennedy. Suppose he does manage to shoot and kill him. And then suppose he gets caught. What happens then is that the shit really hits the fan for you guys. Because the newspapers will be looking for some reasons why. Presidents don't get killed because the President fucked someone's wife. You said so yourself. There'll be talk of conspiracy, of John Birch, of Minutemen, of communists, and of the Mafia. The FBI will start an investigation into why Jefferson killed Kennedy. And before you can say McLellan, they'll find a trail that leads straight to Sam Giancana, Moe Dalitz, Lansky, Frank Costello, Trafficante, and you my friend. Your CIA friends will disappear into the ether leaving you to take the rap. The feds'll say the plot to kill Castro was just a smoke screen. All along the intention was to hit Kennedy. That's how it will be, Johnny. Think about it. How shockproof are you feeling now?'

'When you put it like that, I guess.' He shook his head. 'Sam's gonna go mooney when I tell him. What are we gonna do?'

'It's my guess that sometime between now and inauguration day, January twentieth, Jefferson will make his move, most likely at one of these underlined locations. After that, we can maybe relax a little if we haven't caught up with him. Until then we've got a manhunt on our hands. With all the law enforcement agencies working together we would still have a job on our hands to track this guy down.'

'There's no way we can involve law enforcement, Jimmy.'

'I know, I know. All I can suggest is that I'm going to need all the available resources of organised crime to try to bring about the same result. The whole fucking outfit.'

'The mob looking after the President? It's a weird idea.'

'You gotta better one? I'm going to need some kind of an office, with several phone lines, and the active co-operation of all the bosses in the United States. New York, Boston, Florida, Vegas, LA, New Orleans.'

'There's a safe house in Coral Gables, on Riviera Drive. It belongs to Lansky. We can use that.'

'I'll need a couple of mob gofers to help me out on a permanent basis. Not Frank. There's something about him I don't trust. Someone sharp. And someone else who's tough.'

'There's a cousin of Trafficante's. A lawyer. Recently graduated from somewhere. Paul Ianucci. He's been taking a year off, playing tennis, and fucking girls before going to work for his uncle. He's a smart kid.' Rosselli snapped his fingers as he thought of someone else. 'For muscle, you can have Licio the Elephant. He's tough as they come. And he's got this special skill that might come in useful. He used to be a memory man, counting cards in Atlantic City before the casinos figured it would be cheaper to give him a job looking out for scams. He was a pit boss at the Capri in Havana before the revolution. Since then, he's been kicking his heels.' Rosselli lit another cigarette. 'What else?'

'Money. Cash. People talk easier when they're seeing green. Transport. A driver. A cook. Make sure she doesn't speak English. A coffee machine. Groceries. Toiletries. An AP wire. Stationery.'

'No problem.'

'I'll give the feds some story about Jefferson being a communist. Nothing too grand or they'll start to get nosey. Just enough so we can trace his car. Assuming he's still driving it.'

Rosselli had taken out a pad and was writing now. 'Anything else?'

'More money. I'll need to bribe some people. Cops. Feds. Secret Service guys. Make it small bills, tens and twenties. Those kind of people don't trust anything larger than a fifty in case they're being set up by Internal Affairs.'

'Okay. What else?'

'Tomorrow I'll call the Police Department and tell them I need to take some leave, or something. Not that anyone will give a shit. Those bastards think I'm just hanging on for my pension.' Nimmo grinned as if he was enjoying himself. 'If only they knew, huh?'

*

180

Sunday afternoons in Miami were quiet, almost as quiet as Sunday mornings. That is anywhere except the beach, or the resort hotel swimming pools. Government offices were closed of course, so there was little Nimmo could do except report Jefferson's car stolen, and then move a bag of things over to the house on Riviera Drive that was now the headquarters of the search for Jack Kennedy's potential assassin. With anyone but Johnny Rosselli it might have taken days to arrange extra telephone lines, an AP wire, and a cook at an hour's notice. That was the advantage of having the Teamsters' Union in your pocket, not to mention the Laborers' Union, the Hotel and Restaurant Employees' Union, and the Longshoreman's Union. Having the 'Bad Four' major unions meant there wasn't much that couldn't be fixed at a time when most families were collecting their children from Sunday School.

When Nimmo arrived in Coral Gables he found a telephone engineer already at work. And twenty minutes later a woman turned up in a van from the Fontainebleu Hotel with a coffee machine and several bags full of groceries. Nimmo spoke a little Spanish and was able to comprehend that her name was Tintina, and that Señor Rosselli had told her to come. Having made several storeys of sandwiches, filled the refrigerator, and set up the coffee machine, Tintina, who looked as though she never ate anything herself, told Nimmo she would return at seven o'clock in the morning to make breakfast.

It was six thirty in the evening when the engineer finally left, by which time Nimmo was becoming better acquainted with Lansky's large and airy house. It was a little too Miami-modern for his taste and for Lansky's too, he supposed – all high ceilings with fans, plantation shutters, wooden floors, rattan furniture, and enough big plants to hide a small army of Japanese die-hards. It was difficult to imagine that Meyer Lansky had ever lived here. But as safe houses went it was a pleasant one, and Nimmo thought he and the two wiseguys Rosselli was delivering with the morning milk would probably be very comfortable in it. There were several large bedrooms, each with an en-suite bathroom, and a sizeable meeting room with a long table – now with several phones and a wire – where Nimmo had decided to base their activities.

After a bath, he collected a plate of sandwiches, and the photograph of Jefferson provided by Johnny Rosselli, and settled down on one of the big sofas to watch *Ed Sullivan* on TV. Seeing Jerry Lewis, Sophie Tucker, and Connie Francis guest on the show it was hard to credit the possibility that they were living in an America where a professional killer was already stalking the forty-three-year-old President-elect, whose victory at the polls was still only eleven days old. A young Senator with a beautiful wife, two lovely children, and a baby on the way. What kind of America was it that could have produced such a situation?

Nimmo looked forward to collecting his money, but the stakes were more important now. He hadn't voted for Kennedy himself, didn't even like him much, but he wasn't about to see the man get shot and killed. Jack Kennedy certainly didn't deserve to die for anything he had done in the bedroom. The very idea of preventing an assassination made Nimmo feel quite public-spirited again – loyal and true to his country and its institutions, the way a decent citizen was supposed to feel. He hadn't encountered that kind of feeling in himself since the war.

Now and then, Nimmo looked away from the TV and searched the face of the man in the photograph, like General Montgomery studying the picture of Field Marshal Rommel, as if some clue to the man's psychology and his probable next move might be found in those quiet, dark eyes. Jefferson didn't look much like a killer, but then not every gunman was as obviously a murderer as Jacob 'Gurrah' Shapiro, or Albert 'The Mad Hatter' Anastasia. Nimmo didn't have much faith in physiognomy, but he still believed that, in time, he might get to read a face just as a good poker player could spot whether another guy had a tell or not. It was going to take a while, but he was going to learn everything he could about Tom Jefferson – the way Jefferson had, in all likelihood, already learned everything he could about Jack Kennedy. Nimmo's resolve was sharpened by the certainty that if he failed, the unremarkable face in the photograph on his lap might turn out to be one of the most infamous faces in history.

12

The Iceman Cometh

Tom did not linger in Tampa. In other circumstances he'd have tested himself on the Palma Ceiba Golf Club. But the city was the centre of all Mafia activity in Florida and controlled by the Trafficante family, which had put up a good part of the money for the hit on Castro. So the day after meeting López Ameijeiras, Tom sold the Chevy Bel Air and boarded a train for Jacksonville, ignoring the temptation to go and visit his mother who lived near Orlando, in Intercession City. There seemed little point in making a detour since her mind was gone and she could no more have recognised her son than she could have told him Eisenhower's nickname.

From Jacksonville, he flew to New York and was back in his Riverside Drive apartment in time to catch the six o'clock news on NBC, which reported Kennedy meeting Allen Dulles and Richard Bissell from the CIA, at the Kennedy estate in Palm Beach that same morning. Kennedy's press secretary, Don Wilson, said that Dulles and Bissell had brought two large folders of maps and charts and had discussed the uprisings against the pro-American governments of Guatemala, Nicaragua, and Costa Rica. Which meant that Ameijeiras was probably right. An invasion of Cuba was definitely in the wind, with or without a Castro assassination.

Tom spent the remainder of the evening studying Kennedy's forthcoming schedule and watching television – from *Jim Backus* at seven o'clock, right through to the end of *Mr Adam and Eve* at eleven, when he went to bed.

The next morning he rose early. He had breakfast at Rosenbloom's Kosher Deli on Broadway, near 100th Street, and read the *Times*, which headlined with Kennedy considering his brother, Bobby, for Attorney-General. It was beginning to look as if the Kennedy brothers would be every bit as clannish as the Castros.

After breakfast Tom walked across Central Park. The city was cool after Miami, although mild by the standards of a New York November, with the temperature in the mid-fifties. A westerly wind was blowing leaves from the trees, which always left Tom feeling blue. He crossed to the Upper East Side, to survey the Kennedy family's Park Avenue addresses. He had already looked at the family estate at Palm Beach on the drive up from Miami, and by lunchtime he had rejected two of the four possible locations where he considered an assassination might feasibly be staged.

After lunch at Liborio, a Spanish restaurant on 53rd, he bought some books at Rizzoli, his favourite New York bookstore, on 5th, and then visited the De Witt Wallace Periodical Room on the first floor of the New York Public Library, where he consulted some back issues of the *Congressional Record*, the *New York Post*, the *Saturday Evening Post*, *McCalls*, the *Boston Globe*, and the *Boston Herald*. Then he went bowling at the City Hall Bowling Center on Park Row, opposite the Woolworth Building. In lieu of golf, Tom often went bowling when he needed to think. Apart from the weather, that was the only major disadvantage about living in Manhattan: the limited golfing opportunities.

Once again he spent the evening alone, studying the books he had bought and watching more TV. *Gunsmoke* was pretty good, as always, but *The Iceman Cometh*, with Jason Robards, was not, as billed in the *Times*, 'the finest play ever seen on TV', just depressing – all those alcoholics only reminded Tom of his own father – and Tom soon found himself heading to bed, to listen to a Schumann piano concerto on radio. It was the kind of music Mary had liked a lot.

The next morning he left the apartment early and caught the

express train to Boston. A couple of days later, following trips to Cambridge, to the Irving Street home of Professor Arthur Schlesinger, to MIT, to the Boston Public Library, to Kennedy's Boston home on Bowdoin Street, and to the State House on Beacon Hill, Tom telephoned López Ameijeiras from the Copley Plaza Hotel, where he was staying, and – his voice on the edge of excitement, for Tom was pleased with what his own extensive research had revealed – outlined a draft plan.

13

The House on N Street

'You'll have to drop whatever you are doing. Everything. And forget about Thanksgiving. There's going to be no holiday for any of us until we've found Tom Jefferson.'

For almost thirty minutes Nimmo had briefed the two men Rosselli had brought to Lansky's safe house on Riviera Drive and, until now, they had listened in silence.

'My wife's not going to like that,' objected Licio Montini. 'She's got the turkey bought and everything. All the trimmings. I tell her I'm not going to be there for dinner she's liable to stuff me and not the fucking bird.' Licio the Elephant was the Jackie Gleason type, big, but light on his toes, with a large handkerchief in his pudgy gold-ringed fingers to wipe the sweat from his heavy, anxious face. He looked to Rosselli for an adjudication on the matter of Thanksgiving dinner, but it was Nimmo who answered him.

'Listen, I'm not going to come between any man and his dinner. Least of all a man like you. All I mean is that as soon as you've eaten it, you're back here instead of watching football on TV. Okay?'

Inside his grey pinstripe seersucker suit, Montini nodded with a show of gravitas, as if he wanted everyone to see that he thought this was fair, and said, 'Okay.'

186

'Paul?'

Paul Ianucci, a second, or even a third cousin of Santos Trafficante's – Nimmo was not quite sure which – and only half the size of Licio Montini, had twice the polish. With his dark curly hair, twinkling brown eyes, and casual virility he looked like a younger Dean Martin, a stellar impression that was enhanced by the lilac Ford Thunderbird that was parked outside.

'That's fine with me, sir,' he said in an educated voice that belied his Italian underworld antecedents. 'As a Catholic I never did see the point of observing a Protestant acknowledgement of divine favour.' He palmed a handsome Tiffany's gold cigarette case from the pocket of his Ivy Jacket of Indian Madras and fetched a cigarette to his perfect smile. 'I'm as keen to see that nothing happens to Jack Kennedy as the next man. But where the hell do we start?'

'Paul? I want you to track down some documentation for this guy. We've got a passport number. It's probably fake but check with the Miami Passport Agency. Try the Office of Vital Statistics, too. That's in Jacksonville. The Division of Driver's Licences, in Tallahassee, and the Department of Defense in Washington. We think Jefferson may have been in the Marine Corps. I want next of kin, a mother. Even the son of God had a mother. I want to know who and where she is.'

'I'm on it,' said Paul Ianucci, and sitting down at the boardroom table, he picked up the phone and called the operator.

'Licio? I want a list of hitmen, button-guys, shooters, assassins, whatever. Maybe somebody worked with Jefferson. A cross-fire contract, I think they call it. If someone did work with him then maybe he'll know Jefferson's *modus operandi*. Who he gets his guns from, how he likes to work, that kind of thing.'

'Right,' said Montini, and sat down opposite Ianucci. 'What about me? What would you like me to do?'

It was a mark of how seriously he took the situation that Sam Giancana had flown in from Chicago the previous night. But his take on Nimmo's book of revelations was much more pragmatic. As soon as he had arrived with Rosselli and the two others, Giancana had taken Nimmo to one side 'to put him in the picture', as he said, 'with a cross and a fucking halo around your head'.

'Here's how it is, Jimmy,' Giancana had told him. 'The election cost me a bundle. In the Chicago wards I control, Kennedy got eighty per cent of the vote. And it's still costing me now. Which is why Nixon's not going to demand a recount. We're gonna repay the thirty-five grand that walkin' five o' clock shadow still owes on the mortgage on his place in Wesley Heights. It all adds up to a pretty substantial investment in one Irish sonofabitch. And I'm not about to see it flicked off by some kook with a grudge and a rifle. Back in Chicago, Jimmy, I said I'd lay twenty-five grand on you to find this fuck. Well I'm doubling that. Fifty grand, Jimmy. That means water into wine, and cripples up on their dogs and running around like it's Christmas morning. You stick to this job like it's Duco, you hear? Find that fucking *cetriolo*.'

'Sam. Depend on it. The guy's next week's Dead Sea Scrolls.'

Now, as Nimmo considered Giancana's request for some kind of investigative task, he found himself unable to see how he could order around the boss of the Chicago outfit like Montini or Ianucci. Giancana saw the idea troubling Nimmo and came to his aid.

'Just like I'm one of the soldiers, Jimmy, okay?'

'Okay, Sam.' Nimmo shrugged. 'It's like I said to Johnny. Maybe you could call around the heads of the various crime families. Impress upon them the need to find Tom Jefferson for all their sakes. If the most powerful crime organisation in the world can't get some kind of lead on this guy then my name isn't James Bywater Nimmo.

'In the meantime, I'm going to Washington DC, to see if I can't persuade someone to give up Kennedy's schedule. If we know when and where he's going between now and the inauguration, then maybe we can second-guess our shooter.'

'Just like that?' sneered Giancana. 'Who the hell's gonna give you Kennedy's schedule?'

'The Secret Service.'

'How are you gonna fix that?'

'You fixed the American election, Sam. I think I can fix the President's outfield.'

As soon as he was in his room at the Georgetown Marbury, in Washington, Nimmo picked up the telephone, and dialled NA 8-1414. As requested, the White House Signals board relayed the call to

188

Murray Weintraub, in the East Wing of the Executive Mansion. As he waited for the connection, Nimmo stared out of the window of his comfortable but gloomy room, at the hotel courtyard and the Chesapeake and Ohio Canal that lay beyond it. Already Georgetown lay on his soul like a dead weight. How could anyone live in a place like this?

Another couple of minutes passed. He twisted the tiny cap off a miniature of Scotch, applied the whistle-sized neck to his mouth, and drained the bottle's contents, as if it had held nothing more potent than antiseptic mouthwash. There was something so ersatz, so baubling about spirit miniatures, like something you might find in an outsized doll's house, that he found it hard to take them seriously as containers of real alcohol, almost as if the effect of the spirits ought to be somehow in proportion to the size of the bottle itself.

When Murray Weintraub finally came on the phone their conversation was brief and to the point.

'I'm here,' said Nimmo.

'Okay. My shift ends at ten. I'll meet you in front of the Marbury at ten twenty.'

The Georgetown Marbury was a small colonial-style hotel of red brick, like most of Georgetown, and Weintraub was outside the M Street doorway on the dot of the appointed time. The two men were old friends. The Secret Service was part of the Treasury Department and, before joining the presidential detail, in 1952, Weintraub had worked in the Secret Service's New York office, which was where he had met Jimmy Nimmo. Together, Weintraub and the former FBI SAC had helped solve a big counterfeiting case involving bank-workers and, it had even been alleged, Albert Einstein. Hoover suspected the physicist of having invented a machine capable of rendering perfect copies of dollar bills, with the aim of undermining the whole edifice of American capitalism. It was just one of many preposterous charges secretly levelled against Einstein that Hoover had wanted to believe were true, but which were never proven.

It was a moist, chilly night. The cobbled, tree-lined streets of Georgetown, covered with November leaves, were treacherous underfoot. Both men wore sensible shoes, warm raincoats, and felt hats.

Often, it is said that dogs and their masters, or any two creatures living in symbiosis, come to resemble each other. It was the same with Murray Weintraub, who looked very much like President Eisenhower – or at least a younger Eisenhower, the Eisenhower who had been appointed Supreme Commander of the Allied Expeditionary Force back in 1943. Weintraub had more hair, which was fair, the same broad nose, prominent ears, ruddy complexion, and wide, dyspeptic mouth. A fit forty-eight-year-old, he had the older man's erect military bearing too. They headed west, in the general direction of the university.

'So how is life in the Secret Service?'

'Not good. Possibly it's a corollary of the service's command structure. After all, how many countries have a Secret Service that's commanded by a businessman, instead of a policeman or a soldier, anyone with intelligence experience? We have the Secretary of the Treasury, George M. Humphrey, former president of the Mark A. Hanna Company of Cleveland. A nice enough guy. He and Ike get along pretty well. But he knows nothing about the world of intelligence. But then neither do we. Right now, we're living on our reputation, and even that's in danger of going to the dogs. Procedures are slack and old-fashioned. A lot of the time we have to rely on local law enforcement officers, and that means we're usually only as good as they are, and sometimes just as bad. Did you know that the NYPD is the only municipal force we're posted on?'

'Things are that good, huh?'

'They're worse. I tell you, if the American people knew how slack things had become there would be a fucking outcry. When Ike went on his South American tour, back in February, some of the guys on the detail were so tired from all the partying that was going on, they couldn't keep up with the presidential limo. One guy had such a bad hangover, he actually puked up during the parade in Rio. What's more, we let Ike sit up on the back of the goddamn car, like a fairground target. The idea of a human shield to protect the President? Forget it.

'Take the cars. In FDR's day, most of the cars had running boards. Modern cars don't. They look stupid with running boards. Danger-ous, too. The last presidential car to have boards was retired seven years ago. And as for the drivers, they don't know shit. They've no driving skills to speak of. No getaway techniques. James Dean was a better driver than the guy behind the wheel of Ike's fucking car.'

They walked past Francis Scott Memorial Park where a flag hung limply in honour of the Washington attorney who had penned the national anthem. It seemed a noisy place for a park, so near to Key Bridge to their left, conducting streams of traffic south across the Potomac River. The two men turned north toward the quieter heights of Georgetown, and arrived at the foot of a seemingly interminable Jacob's ladder of stone steps leading up into the darkness of the November night. They began their ascent.

'Hell, agents don't even have to take a yearly medical,' complained Weintraub. 'If you did, then they'd retire me for sure. The truth is that I can't cut it any more. I'm getting too slow. If I could afford to retire, I would.'

'You seem fit enough to me,' puffed Nimmo. 'Talk about John Buchan. How many goddamn steps are there, anyway?'

'Almost twice as many. Seventy-five, to be precise.'

'About as old as I feel right now.'

'You know how much overtime I work? Seventy, sometimes eighty hours a month. There's some public law that says you don't get overtime unless you exceed your shift by twenty-six hours a month. I can't remember the last time I did as little overtime as that. Nobody can. We've all of us got wives and families. I just got this new apartment in Silver Spring and I need every dollar. Overtime makes me an extra thousand dollars a year. Of course, the more overtime you do, the slacker you get and the more tired you become. If they paid us a decent wage in the first place, I dunno, maybe things would be different. But if this system didn't exist, no one would be stupid enough to invent it. Thank God Ike's not more active. He's been real easy to guard since the heart attacks.'

They reached the top of the steps where Nimmo felt obliged to lean on the wall of some old federal building just to catch his breath. Inside his thick chest his lungs felt like two hot kippers. 'Don't mention heart attacks,' he gasped, and lit a cigarette to help him concentrate on recovering his breath. 'You're a lot fitter than you think.'

'Thank you, sir.'

Turning right, they began to walk east, along N Street.

'It could be worse,' continued Weintraub. 'It could be President De Gaulle we were guarding. In May we were in Paris with Ike and I tell you those French boys have their work cut out. De Gaulle's a regular fucking Geronimo. Seems like everyone wants to shoot him.' Quoting Eisenhower's campaign slogan from 1952, he added, 'I like Ike. And fortunately so does everyone else. But Little Boy Blue? That's what Ike calls Kennedy. I wonder. Some of the guys on Kennedy's detail tell me he likes to party a lot himself. He certainly likes to meet people, and that's going to be a problem. A big problem. Bodyguards don't get on with the body politic.'

'As a matter of fact, that's what I wanted to talk to you about,' confessed Nimmo. 'Kennedy's security.'

Weintraub pointed up the street. 'Take a look up there. You're about to get a closer look at his security. Do you see those lights? They're TV lights. And they're outside Kennedy's house. Which means he must be home.'

'I knew it was around here some place.' Nimmo stopped to light another cigarette with the butt of the one he had just smoked, and then looked around. There was no one in sight at this end of N Street. 'So that's where he lives.'

'Until January twentieth. After that, he'll be in the White House. So. What were you going to say about Kennedy's security?'

'Unlike you, Murray, I'm in no hurry to retire. Despite what anyone might think when they see me in Miami. Fact is, I miss the Bureau. Well, for a while now I've had this scheme that I figured might put me in good odour with Hoover again. There's this guy I know in Miami who's part of the local Teamster. Fellow by the name of Dave Yaras. He's a hood, Murray, a real fucking villain, and connected to a lot of mobsters. Jake Guzik, for one. Santos Trafficante, for another. Anyway, I've been developing Yaras as an informant for George White at the FBN. Remember George?' Weintraub nodded. 'There's nothing official, you understand. I mean, if I ever registered Yaras as an informant it'd be like cutting his throat myself. Chicago's riddled with corruption. Even the FBN. It's not that I don't trust George. But some of the people around him are really fucked up. However, to come back to the main point, I've been hoping there'd be some kind of a big narcotics bust, and George would put in a good word for me.

'Then a couple of days ago,' Nimmo lied smoothly, 'I had a drink with Yaras, and we both got a little tight, and he told me that some guy, a friend of Jimmy Hoffa's, was going to take a pop at Kennedy, and that this would happen sometime before inauguration day. It's no secret Hoffa hates the Kennedys, after the way they went after him. He may have beaten those indictments, but he's smart enough to know there'll be others. Especially if Bobby becomes Attorney-General. Yaras said that Hoffa believed the quickest way to prevent this was to kill Jack, not Bobby. That Bobby would be nothing without Jack. Thus the contract.

'Murray, my first instinct was that this was just a bunch of bullshit. Big talk from Yaras and this pal of Hoffa's. But when I rang Yaras to talk about it again, the next day, he seemed real scared, and clammed up. Wouldn't say another damn word about it. I could go to Hoover now, only I'm pretty sure he and those other boys on the fifth floor at Justice would just laugh me all the way down Constitution Avenue. Sure, someone wants to shoot the President-elect dead, they'll say. Same as they want to kill the Vice-president. During the campaign a mob of Dallas housewives spat at LBJ, for Christ's sake. They could just as easily have sprayed him with acid. And that was his home fucking state. Threats come with the job, they'll tell me, like the use of Air Force One and the executive toilet in the Oval Office.

'But then they'll want to know why I'm drinking with the likes of Dave Yaras. And I don't think George White's the kind of friend who'll be there to back me up. Maybe it is all bullshit. I hope it is. But I voted for Kennedy and I wouldn't like to see anything happen to him, you know?'

'So what is it you want from me?' enquired Weintraub.

'I was thinking. If I knew more about where Kennedy's going to be in the next few weeks, then I might be able to bluff Yaras into the belief that Hoffa's hitman doesn't stand a chance – that there are Secret Service agents waiting for him in Palm Beach on the first of December, and at Hyannis Port on the fourth. So he might as well tell me everything he knows. I figure then I can get a fix on this guy, and tip off the local Bureau with some information that's A-one-A, and not some gangster's vodka Martini say-so.'

'You're not asking much, are you?'

'I swear I wouldn't ask if I didn't think this was on the level.'

'I should say, no. You know that, don't you? And even if I said yes, and called the President-elect's office, at the Senate Office Building, and spoke to Kennedy's personal secretary, Mrs Lincoln, and you can't get more respectable than that, she'd be well within her rights to tell me to go to hell. The President-elect's schedule is highly confidential. Of course, I could tell her that the Protective Research Section of the Secret Service have asked me to liaise with her, in order that they can avoid doubling up on the checks made in advance on the places both Ike and Jack are gonna be. That's what I could tell her. And like I said, I should say no. I could get in trouble. But it so happens I need a favour myself, Jimmy.'

'Whatever I can do, Murray. You only have to ask.'

'I was telling you how I'm getting too old for this job. Forty-eight isn't old. But it's too old for this job. Only I can't afford to retire. Not only can I not afford to do it, I don't want to be sitting on a veranda, picking my feet, and reading the paper from one cover to the other. I'm still a young man. I could do something. Most guys get jobs in the Treasury. The lucky ones join Western Union, or some place where they pay good money. A few even go to big hotels. Head of security, something like that. I was thinking, you being in Miami, you must know a lot of people who own hotels.'

Nimmo nodded. 'Or maybe a casino. In Vegas.'

'Vegas. Yeah. I hadn't thought of that. Vegas would be nice, too.'

'Sure, I know lots of people who could use a man with your background and experience. Leave it to me, Murray. I'll speak to someone on your behalf, tonight.'

'Thanks a lot, Jimmy. I really appreciate it.' They started to move again. 'Did you know that it isn't anything other than a straight murder felony to kill the President of the United States? In England, they call it high treason if you kill the head of state, Queen Elizabeth. But not here. Imagine if the President got shot on a trip to the Yukon? Shit, they'd have to try the killer's ass according to local state law, in Juneau, which, I'm sure you know, is the capital of Alaska.'

'So what's wrong with that? They'd have to try the guy somewhere. Juneau'd be as good a place to do it as any place else, what with all the witnesses and all.'

'Except that they don't have the death penalty in Alaska. They abolished it in fifty-seven. Some fucked-up Alaskan gold-miner shoots the President of the United States and all they do is put him in jail for the rest of his natural. Seems hardly just, now does it?'

They stopped outside 3307 N Street – Senator Kennedy's Georgetown home. It was a flat, red-brick building of three storeys, with a walled garden out back. To Jimmy Nimmo, it seemed a small sort of house for the President-elect to be living in. The lights were on, and no doubt Kennedy was inside choosing another member of his cabinet. It appeared unlikely that he'd be fucking some big-breasted actress with so many reporters and TV cameras parked outside his front door. But then maybe there was a back door, too. And maybe Kennedy was the type to get off on that kind of risk.

Standing there, watching the house, searching the windows for some sign of the President-elect, Nimmo began to understand how easy it would be to kill the man. He himself was carrying a six-shot .38 in a shoulder holster. It had taken just one shot, from a .44-calibre Derringer, to kill Abraham Lincoln. Ford's Theater – the scene of the assassination – wasn't more than three miles away. Killing the President was probably straightforward enough, provided you were willing to be executed for it – or be shot trying to escape, like John Wilkes Booth. But to be shot by a fucking actor. That was plain embarrassing. No wonder they had tried to prove that Booth had been part of some great Confederate conspiracy. Important people – gods – just weren't supposed to die that way.

Of course, the autopsy hadn't helped any. Fucking autopsy surgeons. Early confusion centred on the fact that Booth had approached President Lincoln from the right, but the bullet had entered his head from the left. This obfuscation persisted until the trial of the conspirators – despite the fact that Booth had indeed acted alone, the United States government still managed to hang several others for the crime – when one witness gave evidence to the effect that just before the fatal shot was fired, Lincoln, hearing a noise in the auditorium, had turned his head sharply to the left.

Nimmo turned his own head in one direction, and then the other. The buildings facing the Kennedy home belonged to other senators, or were owned by the federal government. It was hardly sniper's terrain. This would not be where Jefferson made his attempt, that much was clear to Nimmo. Shooting a man with a handgun and then getting caught was hardly the style of a professional marksman.

Weintraub took Nimmo by the arm and led him away. 'I'll see what I can do for you, Jimmy. I'll call you, in your hotel room, tomorrow morning.'

Nimmo breakfasted alone in his room, and waited for the phone to ring. He watched *The Today Show* with Dave Garroway, on TV. Then an old movie, just because Peter Lawford, Kennedy's brother-in-law, happened to be in it. Nimmo had heard the stories about Lawford. Rumour had it that Lawford, a boozer and a womaniser, was also a nasty piece of work. The movie was *Picture of Dorian Gray* and, for a while, Nimmo thought that Lawford would have made a more convincing Dorian than the actor who did play him. But, by the time the movie was over, Nimmo had come to the conclusion that Jack Kennedy would have made an even better fist of the role. Who better than Kennedy, with his handsome good looks and easy charm, to play the part of a destructive hedonist whose own attractive features hid a shocking story of moral degeneration and sexual depravity?

He was watching *Morning Court* when finally the phone rang. It was Murray Weintraub. He said, 'Okay, you first.'

'I spoke to my friend,' reported Nimmo. 'Seems like they could use someone with your abilities at the Riviera Hotel and Casino, in Vegas.'

'I always wanted to go to Vegas.'

'The way you play your cards? I had you down for a regular, Murray.'

'I think you'll be happy with what I have for you, too, Jimmy. Meet me for lunch at Duke Zeiberts, seventeen-thirty L Street. That's two doors west of Connecticut Avenue. Twelve o'clock.'

'I'll be there.'

After spending most of the morning cooped up in his hotel room, Nimmo decided to walk the mile and a half to the restaurant. There had been a shower of rain but the sun was shining now. It was a typical late November day. Thanksgiving holidays were being planned. Pumpkins were piled in front of grocery stores. Shop windows were posted with Thursday opening hours. America looked a peaceful place to be living in, prosperous and responsibly governed. For all but one citizen abroad on the streets of Washington that 22 November morning, the murder of a President, especially one who had yet to take the oath of office, would have seemed a very unlikely scenario.

14

Edith Quadros

Ever since he was a boy, Tom Jefferson had been fascinated by American presidents. When Tom was in New York he used the name Frank Pierce, after Franklin Pierce, the fourteenth President of the United States. If he was moving among the buxom, blithe, and barely bedecked cocktail waitress set – somewhere like Chez Joie, on Broadway – then he called himself Marty Van Buren, after the eighth President. But mostly he stayed at home in the apartment, especially when Edith turned up pretending, for the benefit of the doorman in Tom's building and his nosey neighbours, to be his half-sister.

Edith Quadros was Nicaraguan, estranged – since she was also a communist – from a very rich family who were close friends of Luis Somoza Debayle, the Nicaraguan President. Working alongside Tom was to be her last assignment for the Cuban Intelligence Service before returning to Managua and helping Carlos Fonseca to found a Nicaraguan revolutionary movement. She believed in the Soviet Union – which she had visited – in the Cuban revolution – which she had assisted – and in Fidel Castro – whom she had bedded – as much as she believed in the evil of Standard Fruit, the CIA, and the Somoza regime. And she believed in the expedience of what Tom and Ameijeiras were planning.

Tom liked Edith immediately, not least because she was as intelligent as she was beautiful, and they were quickly lovers, for theirs was the kind of secret work that promotes an easy intimacy. She knew something of the plan already from Colonel Ameijeiras, and although Tom described it again in greater detail, he could see that it made her nervous. He would have been surprised if it had not. So he tried not to discuss it too much with her, which was easy since there was little to do until the week before Christmas, except rent an apartment and buy a car in Boston.

And in the week up to Thanksgiving, he concentrated on showing her a good time in New York. He took her bowling at Pinewood Lanes on West 125th, and to dinner at Le Vouvray on East 55th. He even took her clothes shopping at Korvette's and Ohrbach's. Gradually, as he got to know her better, Tom realised that he had mistaken nerves for impatience to get on with the job, since Edith was quite resolved to go through with her part in the plan which, in its way, was almost as difficult as his own. And it became clear to him that she disliked Kennedy in the same way Tom did.

'He's a playboy,' she said dismissively. 'I've known the type all my life. I can't stand playboys. Being the President is just like having another expensive toy his father has bought for him, and an opportunity to sleep with more women. I don't understand why America would elect such a man.'

'The reason's simple,' said Tom. 'Richard Nixon. Nobody wanted a bum like him for President. He was the one candidate worse than Jack Kennedy.'

'You're right,' she laughed. 'I never thought of it that way.'

One day, after they had returned from another shopping trip to Stern's on West 42nd Street, Edith lit a cigarette and coolly asked him what might happen if they got caught.

'We won't get caught,' insisted Tom.

'Please, Tom. I want to know. What method of capital punishment do they use in the state of Massachusetts?'

'We're not going to get caught,' he insisted. 'Believe me.'

'All the same,' she smiled, 'I should still like to know.'

'Very well. Not that it matters much, since it just isn't going to happen that way.' Tom shrugged. 'They use the electric chair.'

Edith nodded. She had thought it was the electric chair, only she knew that there were some states still using the gallows, and a few now using gas. She grimaced and shook her head. The electric chair seemed so peculiarly American. She muttered, 'Yes, of course. I was forgetting Sacco and Vanzetti. They went to the electric chair in Boston, didn't they? Myself, I think I should prefer to be executed by a firing squad.'

'Don't even think about it. It's not going to happen. Besides, even if they did catch you, which they won't, the most that would happen to you is that you might go to prison.'

'Why do you think so?'

'Because you're a woman.'

Edith laughed bitterly. 'Tell that to Ethel Rosenberg.'

'Edith, that was during the Korean War. Things were a lot different then.'

'It was only seven years ago.'

'Look, this whole thing has been planned too carefully for any of us to get caught.' Even as he said it, Tom knew this simply was not true. Much remained still to be done. And there were considerable risks, but Edith's risk still seemed smaller than his own. 'Don't worry,' he insisted. 'I've thought of everything.'

'Something always goes wrong. That's to be expected.'

'It won't. So let's change the subject, shall we?'

'Okay. Tell me about your wife.'

'López told you about her, did he?'

'And what happened to her.' Edith stubbed out her cigarette and smiled. 'Tell me about her. About how you met.'

'We met in Tokyo, after my release from the Korean POW camp. It was Mary who showed me how capitalism needed to live up to its own principles of liberty and equality, and that socialism was the best way of achieving this. Neither of us was a communist. She said that it was an accident of history that being a socialist in America was as bad as being a communist. Which was why she had been helping the Russians, although not in any important way. Just passing on the odd bit of information that came her way. Soon after bringing her back to America as my wife, we both came to the conclusion that we might as well be hanged, or electrocuted, for a sheep as for a lamb. And I started to work for the KGB. This wasn't difficult. I never had a problem killing fascists. Still don't. But things became harder when Mary became more actively involved. Her sleeping with other men – important politicians, government officials – wasn't so easy to accommodate.'

'Evidently.'

'Of course, once the KGB has you, they have you for ever. There's no going back. The best we can hope for now is to help defeat the fascist counter-revolutionaries in Cuba. And that would seem to require something singular.'

Tom took Edith's hand and added, 'That's what really scares you, isn't it? It's not the electric chair. It's the idea that you'll end up like Mary.'

'Will I?'

'Believe me, Edith. I wouldn't ever let that happen.'

15

The Other 0.1

'We're in the wrong fucking place,' snarled Sam Giancana, his mouth a rictus of hoodlum distaste.

It was Wednesday morning, 23 November, and Nimmo was back in Miami, at the safe house on Riviera Drive. Seated around the board-room table, examining the details of Jack Kennedy's pre-inauguration schedule, were Nimmo, Giancana, Rosselli, and Paul Ianucci. Licio Montini was away, on the trail of another contract killer who might once have worked with Tom Jefferson.

'Look at this,' Sam Giancana continued, in a rough note of complaint. 'Kennedy flies to Palm Beach tomorrow. For the weekend, says the note. Then he flies back to Washington on Tuesday, for a meeting at Dean Acheson's house. Then, hey whaddya know? It's back to Palm Beach, Thursday, the first of December. I mean, this guy's supposed to be getting ready to run the fuckin' country, for Christ's sake. But most of the time he's sunning his ass by the pool, at his old man's hacienda. As far as I can see he's only in Washington for two nights a week.'

'Sunning his ass, some of the time, maybe,' objected Nimmo. 'But not all the time.'

'Saturday third, tenth, seventeenth, he's playing golf at the Palm Beach Country Club.'

'The Everglades Club is a better course,' reflected Rosselli. 'If it comes to that, it's a better club. I wonder why the Kennedys don't belong.'

'They wouldn't have Joe because he was a fucking crook,' explained Giancana. 'Then the old bastard put out that he was joining the Palm Beach Country Club because he didn't like the Everglades' anti-Semitism. But everyone knew Joe was the biggest Hebe hater of the lot.'

'Look,' said Nimmo. 'He doesn't have to be in Washington to do the job of President-elect. He can pick his cabinet anywhere. For example, he's meeting Dean Rusk in Palm Beach, on Monday the twelfth.'

'Why are all these Washington types called Dean anyway?' grumbled Rosselli.

'Because their Harvard daddies wanted them to grow up to be the head of something,' said Giancana. 'Only punks are called Johnny.'

'Maybe so, but I heard of a President called Tom Jefferson.'

'Being called Dean is like being called Dulles,' said Ianucci. 'It's the right kind of handle for being some crappy old politician. Everyone knows there's dull, there's duller, and there's Dulles.'

'That's what a college education gets you,' said Rosselli. 'A smart mouth. You're going to make a great lawyer, kid.'

'It looks to me,' said Giancana, 'that after his meeting with the British Ambassador in Washington, on the sixteenth – Sir Harold whatever his fucking name is – that Kennedy is in Palm Beach right through New Year. Seems I've spent an awful lot of money to put a fucking playboy in the White House.' Giancana counted his way down the list of appointments for the President-elect that Murray Weintraub had provided. 'And since he's there for thirty days out of the next forty, it leads me to suppose that Palm Beach is the more likely venue for a hit, given what you've said, Jimmy, about how hard it would be for a sniper to go after Kennedy outside his Georgetown home. In which case, maybe we should be there, too.'

'He flies to New York on January second,' said Rosselli. 'He's there until the night of Wednesday January fourth, when he flies to

Washington. Thursday the fifth he's back in New York. Then on Sunday evening he's going to Boston to make some speech on the Monday at the Board of Overseers, then right on back to the Big Apple.'

'Wouldn't Boston be a good place to try to take him down?' asked Ianucci.

'Listen to him,' snorted Rosselli. 'Anyone would think he'd made his bones, instead of a promising career. Don't let your Uncle Santos hear you talking like that kid.'

'Overseers? In *The Ten Commandments*, an overseer was a guy with a whip and a naked broad at his feet,' laughed Giancana. 'Sounds like Jack's kind of party.'

'I think it just means a kind of superintendent, or supervisor.'

'I know what it means, kid.' Giancana grinned patiently. 'Besides, it's more of an opportunity for a handgun than a marksman, I'd have thought. But you're right, Pauli. A public speech is a target standing still. Maybe we should try to check the place over. See what opportunities it might present.'

'But apart from that, Mrs Kennedy,' quipped Rosselli, 'how did you enjoy your husband's speech?'

'Let's hope this sonofabitch Jefferson isn't moved by historical parallels,' said Giancana. 'What month was Lincoln shot?'

'April fourteenth,' answered Ianucci, 'eighteen sixty-five.'

'The State Legislature. Is that the building with the big golden dome on Boston Common?' asked Nimmo.

Rosselli, who knew Boston well, said it was. 'Pauli's right,' he said. 'This is a good place for a shot. What is more, as the state Senator for Massachusetts, Kennedy has had to maintain a voting address in Boston. According to our schedule his apartment is number thirty-six, at one twenty-two Bowdoin Street, which is right around the corner from the State House. And he'll be going there to make a last visit to his old apartment before moving into the White House. Chances are he'll walk to, or from, the State House.'

'That's something even Jack Kennedy can do for himself,' said Giancana. 'I'd better get it checked out. You can leave that to me, Jimmy. I'll call some people in Boston. Howard Winter.'

'That fucking mick?' objected Rosselli. 'I wouldn't trust that cocksucker to send flowers to his own mother.'

'It's a fucking mick town, ain't it? I'll have him send someone down to take a look and advise on that other f word you're always using for the CIA, Johnny.'

'Feasibility.'

'You ask me, it's a major fucking mistake for the President to walk anywhere,' commented Ianucci. 'I mean, it is kind of naive, isn't it? Look at what happened to Andy Jackson back in eighteen thirty-five. Poor sonofabitch walks out of the Capitol to light his fucking cigar and some limey fires two pistols at him. Lucky for him they misfired.' Seeing the way everyone was looking at him, Paul Ianucci shrugged defensively. 'What?'

'Where does he learn language like this?' sighed Giancana.

'No, I've been reading up about this kind of thing. Most American presidents get shot from a distance of less than six feet, and what is clear to me is that all the Secret Service agents in the world won't stop someone who is really determined to do it. Teddy Roosevelt got shot in Milwaukee, standing up to acknowledge the cheers of the crowd. He got it in the lung, but lucky for him the bullet velocity was spent, having passed through his coat, his spectacles case, and, thickest of all probably, a folded manuscript of his speech. Garfield wasn't so lucky. He got shot in a Washington railroad station, not by some obvious criminal, but by an attorney, Charles Guiteau.'

'Attorneys?' said Giancana. 'They're the worst fucking assassins of the lot. When you're dead, you don't even feel it.'

'As a matter of fact, Garfield was on his way back to Massachusetts when it happened. And he had lots of protection. So did McKinley. He was shot by a man who had concealed a thirty-two inside a handkerchief. Shot him at point-blank range. It's like I say. The Secret Service won't stop you from getting shot.'

'The Secret Service saved Harry Truman's ass, as I recall,' said Rosselli. 'Remember those Puerto Ricans who tried to whack him in fifty-one? It was a long time before that dumb bastard could wear the pants of that white suit again, I can tell you.'

'We're getting away from the point here,' said Giancana. 'Which is that Kennedy's going to be spending a fuck of a lot of time in Palm Beach.'

'Sam's right,' said Nimmo. 'I oughta drive up there, and check it out.'

'If you do.'

Ianucci began to search through some of the papers that were piled in front of him. Since arriving at the safe house the man who looked like Dean Martin's younger brother had spent hours on the telephone, dealing patiently with the most dauntingly Gordian knots of red tape that American bureaucracy had ready to confound the unsuspecting interlocutor. He was tired, but he was still full of an investigative zeal that Nimmo applauded.

'If you do go, Mister Nimmo,' he repeated, finding the paper for which he had been looking, 'there is something else you might like to check out at the same time. I've got a friend, from when I was in the army, who is now attached to the Fourth Army hundred and twelfth Military Intelligence Group, at Fort Sam Houston in Dallas. On my behalf, he's made some enquiries about Tom Jefferson with the hundred and eleventh MIG here in Miami.' He shrugged apologetically. 'I didn't know anyone there, I'm afraid. That's why the long way around.'

'No, you're doing good, kid,' said Nimmo.

'Well, sir, it turns out that Jefferson's army file is classified. But I was able to glean the following information.' He glanced down the page and began to read the notes he had taken of his telephone conversation. 'Tom Jefferson, born St Petersburg, Florida, nineteen twenty. Father Roberto Casas, a Cuban-born baseball player, natural-ised American, mother Mildred Jefferson. Status, illegitimate. Brought up by his mother and his aunt, in Miami. Attended Miami High School, graduating second in his class, National Honor Society President, blah-blah. A runner-up in the National Rifle Champion-ships when he was just nineteen years old. Enlisted United States Marine Corps, nineteen forty-two. Training at Camp Pendleton, and Marine Corps Scout and Sniper School, Greens Farm, San Diego. Served Guadalcanal, Okinawa, decorated, blah-blah, ended war with rank of Gunnery Sergeant.

'Now then, here's where it starts to become really interesting. The official story is that he was attached to the United Nations between forty-seven and forty-nine. But what he was really doing is classified. Well, how can that be? We do know that he was a member of US Armed Forces in Korea in June nineteen fifty, when North Korean troops crossed the thirty-eighth parallel. And we do know he was captured at Pork Chop Hill, in January nineteen fifty-three. Repatriated August, when he retired from the army, after which nothing about him is known officially. I'm still trying to locate his parents, but I have been able to trace one of Jefferson's old army buddies from Greens Farm and Korea. Someone else who trained to be a sniper, just like our boy. Name of Colt Maurensig. And guess what? He's now running a gun dealer's shop, in West Palm Beach.'

'Good work, Paul,' said Nimmo.

'What the hell is there to shoot in Palm Beach?' grumbled Rosselli.

'Burglars, intruders,' grinned Nimmo. 'People like you and me. Anyone who's worth less than a million dollars.'

'You speak for yourself.'

'In Palm Beach, it's not just Jack Kennedy who needs a bodyguard.'

'Jimmy's right,' agreed Giancana. 'A lot of nervous money lives there. The kind that needs a castle door and a gold inlaid forty-four Magnum in order to sleep at night.'

'Sam?' said Nimmo. 'Who can you call in Palm Beach?'

'You mean made guys?' Nimmo nodded. 'Nicky "Mothballs". Bobby "Sunshine". They're part of Louis Trafficante's family. Why?'

'We're going to need someone in Palm Beach. To help us keep an eye on the Kennedy place. In case Jefferson shows up. So, I was thinking, I might as well meet them when I'm up there.'

'No problem. When?'

'This afternoon. Tell them to meet me at the Breakers. It's the only place in Palm Beach I know.'

'A charmed life you lead,' muttered Rosselli. 'I'd better come too. Make the introduction. Pay the price of their fuckin' help. Buy whatever it is they'll want to sell.' He shrugged at Nimmo, and by way of explanation, added, 'I've met these two characters before.'

'Okay. I'd enjoy the company.'

Rosselli laughed, as if to say he didn't feel like he was much company, and said, 'You drive.'

'Suits me.'

'Can I come too?' asked Paul Ianucci.

'Your Uncle Santos would kill me if I got you involved in something,' said Giancana. 'Be a fuckin' lawyer, kid. That's the best way of not getting involved there is.'

It was a sixty-five-mile drive north from Miami to Palm Beach, along US1. Jimmy Nimmo liked to drive with the hood down. America was at its most American seen from a convertible. Driving a car that way made him feel deracinated, rootless, floating, conditions which he thought were probably those that most defined what it was to be an American. Like John Wayne riding the range. These days you had to be in a car to be reminded of what a vast, lonely country America really was. The Impala's powder-blue bonnet was short, by the standard of a Cadillac, but for him it was an essential feature in the appreciation of his country's geography. Rosselli seemed more interested in the copy of *Life* magazine he had brought along for the journey, than female pedestrians, and the occasional blue riband view of the ocean.

'What are you reading about?' asked Nimmo.

'Adolf Eichmann. He says his job fascinated him.'

'Be happy in your work. That's what I always say.'

'I was in effect a travelling salesman for the Gestapo,' Rosselli quoted, 'just as I had once been a travelling salesman for an oil company in Austria.'

'Excuse me, ma'am,' said Nimmo. 'I wonder if I might interest you in getting rid of your neighbours. For only five dollars a month, we'll arrest them, torture them, and then shoot them. We'll even dispose of their bodies, at no extra charge.'

Rosselli was shaking his head, not much amused. 'Don't talk to me about arrests,' he said darkly. 'Some of our anti-Castro people have been picked up by G2, in Cuba. Alonzo Gonzales. Genevieve Suarez. One of our guys, Luis Balbuena, escaped to Guantanamo base by the skin of his teeth. But the arrest of Genevieve is especially unfortunate. When they arrested her, they found two secret rooms underneath her swimming pool. In one room were some Castro government defectors, and in the other a large weapons cache we've been building up for a while.'

'That's too bad. Will they shoot her?'

'Very possibly. Frank and Orlando are devastated. Genevieve was a good friend of theirs. Comes to that, she was a good friend of mine, too.'

'What happened?'

Rosselli shrugged. 'How do these things always happen? Poor security. Big mouths. You know, back in the twenties, when I made my bones, I took an oath of silence. *Omertà*, we called it. That's a blood oath, and when Sicilians take a blood oath, to keep their mouths shut, they mean it. I'm not sure if some of these fuckin' Cubans understand what it means to keep silent. If it comes to that, I'm not sure the people I've met from the CIA understand that either. Thanks to assholes like McCarthy, Kefauver, and McLellan, people no longer have respect for silence. If you refuse to answer, you're guilty. Silence is now a very underrated quality in a person, Jimmy. But you should never forget how important it is. *Capisce?*'

It irritated Jimmy a lot that Rosselli had said that. He thought of himself as a man who was as mindful of his tongue as Prometheus had been about his liver.

'One thing I've always been good at Johnny, and that's keeping my fuckin' mouth shut. I don't even know a dentist. I can't sing, and I never learned to whistle. I might even still have a wife, if I'd ever licked her pussy. But that's something else you can't do if you keep your tongue in check. So don't tell me about keeping my mouth shut. I'm breathing through my fucking nose for you people.' Nimmo slammed the steering wheel hard with the heel of his hand. 'Don't ever tell me that. My name is Helen fucking Keller for you guys. Jesus Christ, I won't stand to be compared to some blabber-mouthed fucking Cubans. Me, I'm Burt Lancaster's dumb friend, Nick Cravat. You got that? Don't ever mistake me for a fucking rat, Johnny. I've never squealed on anyone.'

The rest of the drive was completed in silence.

Palm Beach is a narrow sandspit, thirteen miles long, and three quarters of a mile wide, and separated from the mainland by Lake

Worth. The lake is well named, for there is a gulf of financial difference between the inhabitants of Palm Beach, secure in accumulated wealth and accustomed privilege, and those of its more plebeian neighbour to the west. Palm Beach is quiet and contemptuous, with the kind of declarative housing – mostly bogus French chateaux, ersatz Florentine palazzos and phoney Spanish haciendas – which, in the twenties and early thirties when most of them were built, cost several Lindbergh ransoms – small fortunes, even judged by the more obviously prosperous, you've-never-had-it-so-fucking-good standards of the Eisenhower years. Created to serve its beautiful but snooty millionaire sister to the east, West Palm Beach is bustling and friendly, but with lots of shops, high-rise office buildings, small factories, even a dog track, this is one Cinderella too ugly to merit anything but a wrecker's ball. One hundred yards apart, these two Palm Beaches are two side-by-side worlds as different as Manchester and Monaco.

The Breakers, on County Road, was Palm Beach's oldest and grandest hotel, a palatial Italian Renaissance structure surrounded by expansive lawns that looked as if someone trimmed them with nail scissors. Nimmo parked the car in front of the main entrance where, in a marble fountain, a gang of ill-advised cupids were wrestling a whole shoe factory's supply of alligators. It looked an unequal struggle of the kind that only the ageing reptiles who lived on the island, behind high, rust-free iron fences, among carefully tended jungles of tropical growth, might have enjoyed.

Inside the hotel's cool lobby there was more marble than a Medici mausoleum, with some frescoes thrown in for those few guests whose eyes were still keen enough to see as far as the ceiling vaults. Nimmo, Rosselli, and, seated on a chintz sofa by a Chinese porcelain table lamp, Nicky 'Mothballs' Mazarini and Bobby 'Sunshine' Solegiatto made an incongruously robust foursome among the decrepit denizens of the Breakers Hotel.

'Hey, Johnny,' brayed Mothballs. 'How ya doin'?'

Both the men from West Palm Beach wore dove-grey Cricketeer Shirtweight suits, with white shirts and black ties. Despite their well-pressed clothes, the two of them looked as pugnacious as a pair of battered boxing gloves. Neither man was particularly tall, but what each lacked in height he made up for in breadth and front, displaying more attitude than a regiment of cavalry officers.

Rosselli made the introductions, and then they sat down in a quiet corner and ordered some coffee. He told them that a renegade associate of San Giancana's and Meyer Lansky's had gone nuts and was threatening to kill the President-elect, and that Sam saw it as his patriotic duty to make sure that this did not happen. To which end, he wished to enlist the help of his friends in West Palm Beach, for which he would be forever in their debt.

'Anything to help Sam and Meyer,' Mothballs said after an expletive declaration of vicarious outrage. 'We're glad you thought of us.'

'Thanks a lot, boys. I appreciate it a lot. And you know, I was wondering, is there something we can do for you?'

Mothballs and Sunshine exchanged a vacillating look, as if there really was some doubt as to what kind of favour they were about to ask. Then Mothballs, who seemed to do all the talking, looked at Rosselli, and said, 'You know us, Johnny. Generally we stick to what we know. Vice, gambling, narcotics – what the fuck else is there to do in Palm Beach, right? But we got this new thing going. A real sweet thing that we figure is going to make some real dough. Only we'd like your help, and Sam's help to get the thing off the ground. Let me tell you, Johnny, this scam is the future of the scam. This thing is gonna be universal in its use. It's a miraculous piece of cardboard. Show him, Bobby.'

Bobby Sunshine held up a wallet and let fall a ladder of square plastic holders each one of which contained a Diners Club credit card.

'February twenty-eighth, nineteen fifty,' said Mothballs proudly. 'It's the day they killed cash. We got someone on the inside of Diners Club head office in New York. He can get any number of these we want, in whatever fuckin' names we like.'

Rosselli took one of the oblongs of cardboard from its plastic holder and scrutinised it carefully. 'I've been thinking of getting one of these,' he said thoughtfully. 'I'm told you can charge up to a thousand dollars' worth of merchandise to one card, is that right?'

'That's right.'

'And this John Doe's name and address, they're a fake?'

'All you have to do is sign it. This is the future of fraud, Johnny. We're certain of it. Only Louis can't see that. All he understands is dollar cash money. In God We Trust, he says, like what we was proposing was some kind of fuckin' blasphemy. But you and Sam and the Little Man, you're always thinking about the future of business.'

'This is a great fuckin' idea,' grinned Rosselli. 'Can I keep this one?'

'Keep 'em all,' said Mothballs. 'Show them to Sam and Meyer. We got a box load. Like fuckin' Christmas cards. We figure you can sell 'em out for a hundred bucks apiece. Maybe more.'

'What's our cut?'

'Forty per cent.'

'Fair enough.' Rosselli shook his head at the simplicity of their scheme. 'Sam's gonna love this.'

'Great,' said Mothballs, rubbing his gnarled, murderous-looking hands together. 'Okay, let's go and take the ten-cent tour.'

They paid their bill, in cash, and then left in Sunshine's car, a copper-coloured 1959 Pontiac Bonneville Sports Coupé. In closer proximity to Mazarini, Nimmo easily understood how Mothballs had come by this nickname, for he smelled like a balloon-sized chunk of naphthalene. But his gloomy-looking associate's nickname was harder to understand as anything other than the crudest irony. So far he'd hardly spoken a word.

'Nice car,' Nimmo told him.

'Thanks,' grunted Sunshine.

'Why do they call you Sunshine anyway? It wasn't for your disposition, was it?'

'Solegiatto. That's my name. It's Italian for sunshine.'

They drove north, up County Road, with the ocean on their right, or at least what they could see of it between the ship-sized houses.

'Then I guess you're in the right place, Sunshine,' said Nimmo. 'Just look at these fuckin' houses. This place looks like they own the patent on good weather, as well as everything else. How the other half lives, huh?'

'The other half?' Mothballs twisted around in the front passenger seat and laughed harshly. ''Sa matter, pal? Something wrong with your math. Jesus, there isn't more than nought point one per cent of the fuckin' country lives the way these people do. Heaven's gonna look mighty disappointing when they die.'

'Heaven?' snorted Nimmo. 'I don't think so. There's only one place for people as rich as this to go when they're dead. It's not hell. It's worse than hell. It's Canada.'

'When we get to the Kennedy place,' said Mothballs, 'you'll see that there ain't much to see. Leastways not from the road, anyway. There's a better view from the ocean. But we'll take the land side first and then go pick up the boat.'

The Kennedy house, at 1095 North Ocean Boulevard, was as easy to spot as his home in Georgetown. A group of pink-faced tourists and a parboiled cop were grouped on the sidewalk, opposite the front of the house, although, as Mothballs had predicted, there was very little to see. Just an archway in a big white wall, with a heavy oak door and, beyond a courtyard, the glimpse of a white stucco corner, and a red-tile roof among a whole coconut plantation of wind-bent palm trees. The house looked as private as a camera-shy clam.

Sunshine pulled up a way short of the entrance and turned off the Pontiac's throbbing engine.

'Whad I tell ya?' said Mothballs. 'Place is real private and, you might also say, modest by comparison with some of these other joints. I ain't ever been inside but I know people that have. Peter Lawford for one. He likes to score some weed off me when he's in town. Anyway, he told me that old Joe paid a hundred grand for the place back in the early thirties, and another twenty thousand bringing the place up to par. It was called La Guerida back then. But now it's just the Kennedy house. But some people have already started calling it the winter White House, for obvious reasons. Mind you, the weather's only part of the reason Jack comes down here so often, without Jackie. The other half is his next-door neighbour, Florence Smith. Her old man, Earl, used to be ambassador to Cuba. Jack's been fuckin' Flo since fifty-seven. You wait and see if Jack doesn't appoint Earl ambassador to somewhere else a lot further away than Cuba.'

Nimmo smiled. Listening to Mothballs was like listening to a reporter for *Confidential* magazine. He said, 'This is better than any ten-cent tour I ever went on.'

'We aim to please. Anyway, you can see for yourself that the boulevard's hardly the place for a sniper. A drive-by maybe. You know? Capone style. But not a marksman. But we'll stake it out for ya. Wait a minute. Who's this?'

A black, flat-top Cadillac drew up outside the entrance to the house. As a tall man got out of the car and moved towards the door, one of the tourists shouted, 'Where's Jackie?' The man smiled, and gesturing that he had no idea, he disappeared through the door.

'Was that a Kennedy?' mused Nimmo.

'Who the fuck knows?' commented Mothballs. 'There are so many of those mick fuckers. We've got Kennedys in Palm Beach like Sanibel's got fuckin' pelicans. Okay, let's go and get the boat.'

Driving south to get on to Flagler Memorial Bridge and across Lake Worth, Mothballs pointed out an undistinguished church near the junction with Royal Poinciana Way. 'St Edward's,' he said. 'If you wanna shoot Jack Kennedy on a Sunday morning, before he confesses a whole Saturday night's worth of sins, then that's the place to go. Seven a.m. mass every time he's in town. And believe me, he's got a lot to confess. Mattress Jack is what the local girls used to call him. Man's been laid more times in this town than a fucking dinner table. Word is he even married some Palm Beach broad back in the forties. Durie Malcolm was her name. But old Joe got it annulled. Yes sir, Jack's a regular in confession. And somehow God always forgives Jack's sins. So I guess we'd better keep an eye on this place, too.'

Across the bridge, in West Palm Beach, they turned north on to Broadway. A few minutes' steady driving put them in Riviera Beach, and on Blue Heron Boulevard where they boarded a Tupperware sports fisher and headed out to sea, past Peanut Island and through the Lake Worth Inlet. Almost as soon as they were on the open blue mosaic of the Atlantic Ocean, Sunshine steered the boat south, along the Hesperidean coast of Palm Beach, affording his nefarious crew a clear and uninterrupted view of a plurality of plutocratic homes and gardens containing golden apples, ambrosia spurting fountains, and three-headed attack dogs. After only a few minutes he throttled back, and let the boat drift around in the eddy from its own screws.

'There it is,' announced Mothballs, and handed a Nimmo a pair of binoculars that were as large as two Coke bottles. 'That's the Kennedy

214

place. If it was me planning to whack the guy, this might be where I'd choose to do it from.'

Nimmo lifted the binoculars to his beetle-brow and quickly focused on the house. The main part of the house was a two-storey affair, about one hundred feet long, with a guest bungalow or pool-house immediately to the south. Bracketed by palm trees shaped into parentheses by the prevailing Atlantic breezes, and lush vegetation that evidenced a contempt for the cost of gardeners, the place was set atop a concrete dock that was twice the length of the house, and about fifteen feet high. Nimmo thought it an impressive-looking house although, by the more opulent standard of a Flagler, a Post, or a Widener, Addison Mizner's pseudo-Spanish design was quite plain – even a tad Boston conservative.

Nimmo enfiladed his way along the winter White House, taking in details like the two dozen windows, the white picket fence that nearly hid the swimming pool from the ocean, and, moored to the dockside, the coastguard's launch from which two blue-shirted men wearing life-jackets were staring back at him through equally powerful binoculars.

'They say Jack's got a secret entrance, to let him get out on a pussy hunt with no one seeing. But don't ask me which one of those doors it is. If Kennedy was here now, those coastguards would be patrolling this area and moving nosey-parkers like us on our way, for sure. Not that Jack gives much of a fuck who sees him in his swimsuit. No sir. Sometimes he even swims in the ocean. There are sharks, but he doesn't seem to give a fuck. But then I guess Jack's the biggest shark of them all.'

'You add those coastguards to the swell under this boat,' said Nimmo, 'and you've got a tough shot to make. How far do they come out from shore, Mothballs?'

''Bout fifty, sixty yards, depending on the weather.'

'Jefferson would probably have to put another hundred between himself and the coastguard. That's a minimum of a hundred and fifty yards to shore. Yes sir, that's quite a shot to make. He'd have to hope for a nice smooth sea. Not to mention the most important thing, which is getting a sight of Jack. The pool area's quite well hidden. Seems to me it's all just a little unpredictable.'

'He's a professional,' said Rosselli. 'That's what you pay him for. If any schmuck could do it, you'd do it yourself. That's the way these things work. Maybe he'd do it at night. Some of those windows get lit up they'd make quite a target.'

'You wanna shoot Jack Kennedy?' growled Sunshine.

'Nimmo grinned. 'Not especially, no. I think you're missing the point, Sunshine. We're trying to prevent that from happening.'

'Then you wanna do it on the fuckin' golf course.'

'Yes, there's a thought,' agreed Rosselli.

'Man plays early Saturday morning,' Sunshine continued in his Buddhist chanter's bass monotone. 'At the Palm Beach Country Club. S'about half a mile from the house. Shooter waits in a bunker, or something. With his gun in a golf bag. Makin' like he's tryin' to wedge his way out of the sand, right? Only he'd have to make it the nine out. Jack don't often complete the nine home.'

'Sunshine's a real keen golfer,' confirmed Mothballs. 'Gotta handicap of six.'

'Is that all?' Nimmo grinned.

'I seen him play a few times,' continued Sunshine. 'Got a friend who's a member at the PBCC. It wasn't right him makin' those remarks about Ike playin' golf all the time, specially when he likes to play himself. Mind you, Ike's better. May be an old man, but he's good. Good enough, you know? Kennedy'll hit some nice shots. But he's too stiff around the waist. And he ain't got the patience to get his game right.'

'I'll remember that tip if I ever play him,' said Nimmo. 'Come on, let's get out of here. Before the coastguard asks us to open our bags.'

'Where to now?' asked Mothballs.

'Colt Maurensig's place, on Gun Club Road.'

'It figures,' said Rosselli.

Colt Maurensig's Gun Shop, in West Palm Beach, was a pueblo-style building of pink concrete near a liquor store and a do-it-yourself centre. Maurensig had used his Christian name and the prefix and suffix of his surname to make an acrostic featuring three popular makes of gun: Colt, Mauser, and Sig. Parked on the near-empty car lot, in front of the shop, was a 1957 Chevrolet Stepside pick-up truck bearing the same design as the gun shop window.

The four men in the Pontiac Bonneville pulled up and sat in the shade of the pick-up, waiting to see if anyone went in or came out of Maurensig's store. Finally, when Nimmo decided there could be no customers in the shop, he said, 'No one says a fuckin' word except me. You all got that?' Nods all round. 'Mothballs? You and me'll go in first. Johnny? You and Sunshine give us ten minutes, and then come in, and when I give you the nod, close the store up. Okay?'

A bell rang as Nimmo and Mothballs went through the door of the gun shop. Behind a wide glass counter that was home to an extended family of automatics and revolvers stood a man the size of a gun safe, with red hair and a beard, and forearms that were the colour and shape of two rifle stocks. The man, who was on the telephone, looked part hillbilly, part baresark Viking. Mothballs hung back by the door, browsing some cartridge belts.

Nimmo went up to the counter and, as the man came off the call, flipped open his old FBI shield, the one he had told the Bureau he had lost. Sometimes it came in handy, and this was such a time. He didn't want to get into an argument with this guy about being out of his proper jurisdiction: it was fifty years since Palm Beach had been part of Dade County.

'What can I do for the FBI?'

'Is your name Colt Maurensig?'

'Yes, it is.'

'I'd like you to take a look at this picture, sir.' Nimmo showed him a photograph of Tom Jefferson, and said, 'We're checking gun dealers throughout the state to see if anyone recognises him as someone who might have come in and bought something.'

'I keep good records here. If you've got a name for that face, I can look him up and check if he purchased a firearm.'

'No, we don't have a name,' lied Nimmo. 'Not yet. If you could just look at the picture, sir. And tell me if you recognise him.'

Maurensig took the picture in his fingers and shook his head slowly. 'Nope. Can't say that I do. What's he done, this fellow?'

'He's an assassin. A marksman. He uses a rifle with a scope to shoot a man in the back, like a dirty stinking coward.' Nimmo pointed at the rack of rifles behind Maurensig's broad back. 'Same as one of those rifles probably. Winchester. Springfield. He's not particular how he murders someone.'

'I just sell 'em, mister. Where they point them is their own affair.'

'Take another look, sir. I'd appreciate it.'

Insolently, Maurensig looked at one side of the picture and then the other. Handing it back to Nimmo, he said, 'He could be the Sliphorn King of Polarou for all I know, mister. I've never seen him before in my life.'

Nimmo nodded wearily and pocketed the picture. 'Well, thanks a lot for your time, sir. I appreciate it.' He rubbed the back of his head and sighed. 'I didn't mean to be short with you. Only, so far, we're not getting very far with this inquiry. It's been one of those days. Thank God it's a holiday tomorrow.'

'I'm working. Thanksgiving tends to be a busy day for us. Some folks like to go over to Okeechobee and shoot duck, hogs, or wild turkey.'

'On Thanksgiving? Seems kind of late in the day to be shooting your turkey, doesn't it?' Maurensig shrugged like he didn't care if they shot the last passenger pigeon. 'Listen,' said Nimmo, 'you couldn't do me a favour, could you? I'd pay you, of course. You see, I carry a Military and Police Smith and Wesson nineteen oh-five Model thirty-eight-calibre revolver. Would you mind if I showed it to you?'

'Be my guest. Always happy to help the John Laws.'

Nimmo took out his weapon and laid it on the counter. 'As you can see it's a five-inch barrel. Now my partner over there, he carries a thirty-eight Special. The shorter barrel makes it easier to draw. Lighter, too. I was wondering if you might be able to cut this down to a two-and-a-quarter-inch barrel for me, while I wait. I'd sure appreciate it.'

'As you can see, I'm none too busy this afternoon. I guess I could do that for you. Just cut the barrel, right? Only, to turn this firearm into a thirty-eight Special, I'd have to rechamber it to accept thirty-eight Special ammunition. And that's a lot of effort, for not much result. 'Sides, you can't change the diameter of the cylinder.'

'Sawn off and smoothed up would be just fine,' said Nimmo.

218

'Okay,' shrugged Maurensig, and took the gun into the smithing shop in the back.

'I really appreciate it,' said Nimmo, following. 'Strictly speaking, agents aren't supposed to customise a weapon. Otherwise I'd have one of our own armourers doing it. But everybody does.'

Maurensig sat down in front of a bench, unloaded the revolver, and then fixed it into a vice. 'Wish I had a dollar for every one of these I've seen,' he said. 'Largest-selling quality revolver ever produced.'

'Never let me down yet.'

Sniffing the Sweet's Solvent out of the air, Nimmo started to look around. The smithing shop was littered with all kinds of specialist equipment: reloaders, case-cleaners, case-media separators, eliminator scales, and rifle rests.

'Thirty-eight Special ammo's smaller in diameter, but slightly longer than standard. Maybe a little more accurate over a distance, but less stopping power.'

'Oh, I'll trade stopping power for accuracy any day of the week.'

Nimmo's keen eyes alighted on a single bullet that was lying at the back of another workbench. Careful not to be observed by Maurensig, he picked it up and examined the sharp end of what turned out to be a 30.06-calibre cartridge, closely. Until 1954, the 30.06 had been the official US military cartridge, which made it as ubiquitous as Fords. Only this particular cartridge had been modified, and by someone who knew what they were doing. Most likely Maurensig himself had removed the original bullet and fitted a small red plastic shoe, or sabot, in order to hold a smaller-calibre slug inside the larger shell casing. Using an accelerator was, Nimmo knew, an old sniper's method for achieving a vast increase in a bullet's velocity and striking power. From his coat pocket, he took out the 30.06 bullet he had found in Tom Jefferson's house. It had the same red plastic casing as the one from Maurensig's workbench.

The bell in the shop rang again. Nimmo knew it was Rosselli and Sunshine, but he let Maurensig get up from the bench and go back out front. It gave him time to reclaim his thirty-eight, and reload it. Having holstered his weapon, he followed Maurensig into the shop.

'What can I do for you, gentlemen?'

Nimmo caught Rosselli's eye and nodded. Rosselli turned the

open/closed sign around in the door, saying, 'Here, let me do it for you. You're closed for the afternoon.'

Sensing trouble, Maurensig was already reaching for the weapon he kept handy under the counter. Nimmo saw him. The little flat slapper he carried inside his jacket, which was a leather-covered lead billy with a spring just above the handle, was, even now, swinging through the air. The first time on Maurensig's outstretched wrist. The second time against his elbow. And the third time, on the back of his thick neck. The gun dealer hit the floor like Terry Molloy diving for the short money and a one-way ticket to Palookaville. Even before he stopped moving, his hands were cuffed behind his back. Rosselli, Mothballs, and Sunshine were all made men, which is to say that they were men who had killed other men, but even they were impressed by the speed and dexterity with which Nimmo had handled the big man.

'I'm glad he's not holding my rap sheet,' Mothballs told Johnny.

'Come on,' said Nimmo. 'Let's take him in the back.'

In the smithing shop, they found some rifle straps, tied the unconscious man to his chair, and waited for him to come round.

'So what happens now?' asked Sunshine.

Nimmo did not answer. He lit a cigarette and smoked it silently, thinking how he always hated this kind of thing, which was making someone tell you that which they didn't want to tell. It was not that he was a cruel man. He himself thought it was simply that he had little or no empathy for other people. It was as if something inside him had been switched off, disabled, in the same way that some people were colour-blind or tone-deaf. Of course, he had questioned men before. Many times. And often he had been brutal with them. More often than he cared to remember. Usually, the inflicting of pain was the result of a simple lack of time. Mostly you were in a hurry for information and that meant there was only one possible solution to your dilemma: pain. Lots of it, too. The way Nimmo saw it, for both parties' sakes it was best to go in hard, as soon as possible. That way they knew that you were not fucking around, and it wouldn't get any better from then until they convinced you they weren't holding anything back.

Maurensig groaned and, hearing this, Nimmo pulled his beard hard a couple of times to hurry him up to the surface. When Maurensig's Tabasco eyes finally opened, Nimmo lit another cigarette and placed it between the gun dealer's already well-chewed lips. He said, 'Okay, beard, listen up. Here's the I-know-you-know dialectic.

'Now I know you know Tom Jefferson. I know you were in the army with him. For quite a while. And I know you're a friend of his otherwise you wouldn't have told me that you'd never seen him before in your hitherto pain-free life. I know you made this bullet. Exhibit one.' He held up the sabot he had found on Maurensig's bench. 'Which is the identical Toni twin of this bullet I recovered from Tom Jefferson's house. Exhibit two.' Nimmo held that one up too. 'So, now you know that I know that you must have supplied it to him. Which means now I know you know things I don't know. Quite a fuckin' lot, I shouldn't wonder. And the way I see it is that with your ass at a position of extreme disadvantage, I shouldn't have to wonder at all. Not any more. Not with what you are about to receive for which the Lord won't make you truly thankful, amen. So I'm gonna make you a real friendly invitation to bring me up to speed on what you know. And please try to bear in your red-haired mind that this invitation is strictly RSVP. That's French for you respond or vous gets pain. Wherever pain hurts most.'

Maurensig closed one eye against the smoke that was curling into his eye from his cigarette and said, 'What kind of a fuckin' fed are you anyway, mister?'

'The worst fucking kind there is. The venal kind. The vicious and degraded kind. The impatient kind. A drunkard, a liar, and an adulterer by an enforced obedience of planetary influence. Evil by a divine thrusting on. A villain and a bastard.' Nimmo paused and bent closer to Maurensig's face. 'Where, my hog-tied friend, is Tom Jefferson to be found?'

'I don't know anyone by that name.'

Nimmo stood up and sighed. 'I'd forgotten. You were a soldier, were you not? You've got the will to heroism. But only because your body isn't in a panic yet. Or maybe it's that you think there's a creator, who's going to save your soul, even if he can't save your lardy ass.'

'I don't know who the fuck you're talking about, mister.'

Nimmo shook his head. 'Watch out. That's two denials. You deny your friend a third time and we're gonna be looking around for a fuckin' rooster, Colt. Look what happened to St Peter. Cock-a-doodle-do spells big trouble. Old Peter, they crucified his ass. That's what the Bible says anyway, if you believe that shit. Those Christian martyrs could take the New Testament's amount of pain the Romans put them through because they had faith in an immortal soul. But you and I know different, Colt. If there's one thing the twentieth century has taught us, it's that this frail flesh is all there is. We know what happened during the war. And there ain't any such thing as the peace of heaven. So, I'm going to ask you one more time. Real friendly. Like we were outside the gates of Jerusalem, and I was one of those maids of old Caiaphas himself. Where the fuck is he?'

'How the hell should I know? I haven't seen him in a long—'

Before Colt Maurensig could complete his third denial, Nimmo had snatched away his cigarette and had thrust his fingers into the other man's nostrils, twisting them hard like a farmer attempting to control a maddened bull. Maurensig opened his mouth and bellowed with pain. Coolly holding Maurensig's nose with one hand, Nimmo fed the cigarette between his own lips, quickly puffed it aglow, and then popped it into the other man's wide-open mouth, before pulling the gun dealer's lower jaw tight shut on the burning hot end. Maurensig's whole head turned magenta, and his body flexed as if he had been in the hot seat at Sing Sing and the New York State executioner had just thrown the switch to send him on his way with twenty amperes at 2,400 volts. From behind Nimmo's hand, clamped tight across his mouth, Maurensig screamed a long, muffled shriek of choking pain that sounded like a whole pitful of devils.

'Come to where the flavour is,' breathed Mothballs. 'Jesus.'

Sunshine sneered a cruel laugh and lit one for himself. Experimentally he tapped the lighted end at a callus on his hand and, discovering that this hurt more than he had thought it would, he tried to imagine what it would be like to have a hot cigarette inside his own mouth. Since Maurensig was still screaming like a burning heretic, this was easy enough, even for an intellectual somnambulist like Bobby Solegiatto.

After ten or fifteen seconds, Nimmo removed his hand and let

222

Maurensig spit, gag, and retch the still-burning cigarette end from his wretched mouth.

'Colt?' Nimmo tried to get the weeping man's attention. 'Colt?' Now he took hold of the beard again. 'Listen to me, Colt. The next time, I'll make you swallow it,' said Nimmo. 'Like Portia, the wife of Brutus. And by the way, she didn't make it. So what's it to be, Colt? Some answers, or a last cigarette? Smoking'll kill you pal, and that's a fuckin' promise. Mothballs? Fetch hotlips here a glass of water so he can talk his way back into our affections.'

Mothballs brought a glass of water and helped Maurensig to drink. Wincing with pain, he swallowed the water and then mumbled, with Quasimodo's care of diction, 'He's got. A safe house. In New York. I don't. Know where. But that's where. It is.'

'When did you last see him?'

For a moment, holding cold water inside his branded mouth seemed to afford Maurensig some relief. Then he shook his head and swallowed uncomfortably.

'Not in a while. But we spoke. On the phone.'

'When?'

'Mid-November some time. Maybe the eighteenth?'

'What did he say?'

Maurensig looked as if he was suffering from the most excruciating toothache, and every answer was like cold ice-cream on a raw nerve.

'Only that he was going. To New York.'

'To do what?'

'That's where he. Does his research. When he's planning. A hit. Finds out about people. Targets. You want to find him. Try the New York Public Library. Maybe. You'll find him there.'

'So why did he call you?'

Maurensig sucked some cool air into the auto-da-fé that was the inside of his mouth. He'd seen someone hold a cigarette inside his mouth when he was in the army. A party trick. It was a trick you obviously had to learn with an unlit cigarette. Maurensig found it hard to imagine that anyone would have risked feeling the kind of pain he was in to impress a few dumb broads in a bar.

'He said he was going to be gone for a long while. And that his next job. Would probably. Be his last.'

'Jesus Christ,' muttered Johnny Rosselli. 'Jesus fucking Christ's ass.'

'He say who it was that he was planning to wing?'

'Never tells me nuthin'. Not like that. I just supply ammo and guns, is all. Or a scope.'

'But not this time, right?'

'No. Give me some more water. Please.'

Mothballs, still holding the glass of water, looked at Nimmo, who nodded back. Maurensig leaned toward the glass like he was dying of thirst.

'And what did you say?' asked Nimmo. 'When he told you that this New York thing would be his last?'

'Not what he said. Listen. New York's just safe for him. Plans the job there. Then he goes someplace else and does it. Miami. Dallas. Vegas. You name it.'

'Palm Beach?'

'Wherever the contract takes him.'

'So what did you say? On the telephone.'

'I asked if he was retiring. He just said that he had enough money. To live well for the rest of his days. To get out of the country. If he had to.' Maurensig shook the tears out of his eyes. Nimmo guessed that the smoke inside his mouth had done that. 'He said something about how the John Laws might make it difficult for him to stick around. That he'd have to get himself a new ID. Shit like that. Because lots of people were gonna come looking for him.'

'Christ's ass and balls,' said Rosselli. 'Looks like you were right, Jimmy. I must say I had my doubts. But not any more. The crazy fucker's really planning to do it, isn't he?'

'Yeah, but where?' said Nimmo.

'Could be here. Could be New York. According to your schedule, our friend is supposed to fly to New York on January second. And stay there a coupla days.'

'Tell me, Colt,' asked Nimmo. 'Could he shoot a man from boat to shore at a distance of, say, two or three hundred yards?'

Maurensig spat blood. In his pain he had bitten his tongue and cheek quite badly. 'He could shoot almost any damn thing, mister. Chappo Flat Range at Camp Pendleton. Jefferson fired two-three-six. Out of a possible two-fifty. Highest score of any enlisted man in the

224

First Marines. Best man with a rifle I ever saw. Man, with his head in a bag he's still Davy fucking Crockett. Look, mister, that's all I know. Honest. You've got to believe me.'

'That's for damn sure,' chuckled Mothballs. "'Less you want to take up smoking again.'

'Look. I knew him, okay. But he wasn't a friend. His kind doesn't make friends. If I'm not telling you much, it's because I don't know much. Not since we left the army.'

Nimmo lit another cigarette which Maurensig regarded as Winston Smith might have regarded a rat in Room 101. The worst thing in the world. 'You said New York. Have you any idea where in New York?'

'No, I honestly don't.'

Nimmo regarded the tiny fireball at the end of his cigarette with detachment. 'Are you sure about that?' Now he blew on the end with sadistic meaning.

'Honest mister,' pleaded Maurensig.

Nimmo grabbed the man's nostrils once more, hauled them towards his tear-stained eyes, and then held the cigarette about an inch away from the exposed mollusc, grey with numerous livid red spots, that was Maurensig's branded tongue. 'I don't think that's true,' yelled Nimmo.

'There's a piece of paper,' screamed Maurensig. Nimmo let him go. Maurensig shook his head and added, 'It's just some places, he recommended me to go, if ever I was in New York. Places he used to go himself. That's all.'

'Where is this piece of—'

'In the shop, under the counter, there's an American guide. It's in there.'

Nimmo went back into the shop and, under the counter, next to a twelve-gauge semi-automatic shotgun, was a whole pile of books. The American guide was sandwiched between *Grant Moves South* and *A Stillness at Appomattox*, both by Bruce Catton. In the New York City section, he found a folded sheet of paper with the names and addresses of some night-clubs and restaurants, most of which he knew himself. Chez Joie up on Broadway, west of High Bridge, was a late-night joint where the waitresses wore not very much and, if you paid them, even less when they took you home. A little further south, also on Broadway, the Prelude was a pre-prandial cocktail bar that was favoured by a better class of B-girl. Nimmo had not heard of La Barraca on West 51st, but he knew Basin Street East on 48th Street, and the Five Spot on Cooper Square, as good places for jazz. Liborio, on 8th, was the west side's smartest restaurant, the kind of place where you took a girl to satisfy your interest in the finer things in life, such as her silk underwear. Nimmo thought there was nothing much wrong with Tom Jefferson's taste, since it seemed to coincide pretty much with his own.

Back in the smithing shop, Nimmo grabbed Maurensig by the nose. 'This better be according to Hoyle, or I'll use your crotch as my ashtray. You understand me, fat boy?'

'It's on the level,' insisted Maurensig. 'I swear.'

'Sunshine? Keep an eye on him. Johnny? Mothballs?' Nimmo jerked his head toward the shop. 'We need to huddle.'

Back out front, he said, 'I don't know if we kill this guy, or not. Thing is, if we leave him alive, then maybe he'll warn Jefferson.'

'He said he didn't know how to contact Jefferson,' offered Mothballs. 'And I believed him.'

'A phone works two ways, Mothballs. Maybe Jefferson'll contact him again, and then he'll be warned. What I can't figure is if it's best that Jefferson knows we're after him, or not. If he does know it, then maybe he'll figure to call off the hit on Kennedy. On the other hand he may not stand down, just get more careful. Right now, the one thing we've got going for us is that he doesn't know we know what he's planning, and that we're on his trail. So if the outfit sends some people in New York to stake out the places on this list that Maurensig gave me, not to mention the New York Public Library, then maybe he'll show up. In which case they'll spot him.'

'I don't know that they've ever seen the inside of the New York Public Library,' said Rosselli, thinking out loud. 'But the Gambino family can take care of things for us in New York.'

'But if he's spooked,' said Nimmo, 'he'll stay away from these places like they were plague pits. Maybe even leave New York altogether. We might never catch up with him.'

'I don't like it when someone takes me for an idiot,' said Rosselli. 'As I see it, getting Jefferson is paramount. Everything else comes

226

after that. Nothing should jeopardise that. Putting him off doesn't do it for me, and I don't think it'll work for Momo. Tom Jefferson is a dead man breathing air.' He jerked his thumb in the direction of the smithing shop. 'And so is he, if he stands a chance of getting in the way of making that happen.'

Nimmo shrugged. 'Who's going to do it?'

'This is my territory,' said Mothballs. 'Let me handle it. S'not a problem. 'Bout twenty minutes' drive west of here is Loxahatchee. It's a refuge, if you're the national wildlife, but it ain't much of a sanctuary if you drink beer and watch TV. Place is two hundred square miles of sawgrass marshland. Fuckin' snakes and alligators everywhere. Not a good place to be without independent transportation. A man might never find his way out of there. Specially if an alligator found him first. Me and Sunshine'll stick him in the trunk and drive him out there after dark, pop one in his hat, and leave him for the critters. You won't have to worry about Colt Maurensig no more.'

'Thanks a lot, Mothballs,' said Rosselli.

'Not a problem. It's not just cash we kill, y'know?' Mothballs opened his William Bendix reject face and laughed uproariously at his own joke. 'Soon as the job's done we'll get to watching Kennedy's ass for you. From what Lawford's told me, it might make interesting viewing. Hell, I voted for that boy and I wouldn't like to see anything happen to him. Even if he is the biggest tail-chaser since Errol Flynn played Don Juan.'

'So you voted for him. You are one of the nought point one per cent.'

'Come again?'

'I worked it out. Sixty-eight million Americans voted. Kennedy won by one hundred and twelve thousand. That's point one per cent of the vote.' Nimmo grinned. 'Nothing wrong with my fucking math pal.'

16

A Man's Word

When Alex Goldman arrived at Tom's riverside apartment it was the first time the two men had seen each other since Mary Jefferson's death. Edith was out, having her hair done at the Beacon Beauty Salon on Broadway, for which Tom was glad. He and Goldman had a lot to talk about. Tom poured them both a Scotch and waited for Alex to speak first. Goldman looked around at the large and well-appointed apartment with its high ceilings and fine view of the river, and then toasted him silently.

'Nice place.'

Tom nodded. 'Of course. It's the first time you've been here.'

'Very classy. Rented?'

'Of course.'

'Very different from your place in Miami.'

'Lots of things are different from Miami.'

Goldman sipped his drink silently, and fumbled awkwardly for his pipe.

'Did you have to kill her, Alex?'

'What did you think I was going to do?'

'You said you would take care of her. I didn't figure that meant you were going to kill her.'

'And *you* said they had a tape of her and Kennedy.' Goldman shrugged. 'I took no pleasure in it. But what choice did I have? She was compromised. You said so yourself. Close to being blown. And, therefore, so were you. We couldn't risk that. Not with what we're planning for Christmas.'

'After. Monday, January the ninth, to be precise.'

'Whenever.' Goldman found his pipe and began to fill it with tobacco. 'I'm sorry, Tom. Really I am. But there was no alternative.'

'Was it your idea, Alex, or did the Russians tell you to do it?'

'Tom, I did what I had to do. It wouldn't have made any difference if I'd asked them. The result would have been the same. You know that. I liked that little girl. I liked her a helluva lot.' Goldman gulped the rest of his drink down and got up to help himself to another. 'But I did what I had to do.'

Tom nodded sombrely and watched Goldman carry his refreshed drink over to the big window. The view from there of New Jersey was worth a look.

'Just like I had to get rid of that guy down in Mexico. Shit, he was a friend of mine. But he'd fallen under suspicion, and when he found out what we had planned for Kennedy, that was it for him. He had to be killed.'

'I thought you'd just get her out of the country or something,' persisted Tom. 'A new passport. Maybe even Russia. She always wanted to go to the Soviet Union.'

'It was nothing personal, like I said.' Goldman frowned. 'Come on, Tom. What can I say that I haven't said?'

Tom shrugged and lit a cigarette.

'She wouldn't have liked Russia at all. Nobody does. Not even the Russians.'

Tom just kept on smoking.

'Look, Tom, are we okay? I don't see how we can do this job if you and I are not okay.' Alex held out his hand. 'What do you say?'

After a long moment, Tom stood up and grasped it.

'Yeah,' he growled. 'We're okay.'

'Good. By the way, where's the broad?'

'Edith? At the beauty parlour.'

'What's she like?'

'Good. She'll be fine.'

Goldman nodded. 'López Ameijeiras speaks very highly of her. I hear she's quite a looker.'

'We'll need another girl.'

'Same deal?'

Tom nodded.

'Want me to fix it?'

'No, Edith is going to speak to Ameijeiras. She reckons she knows someone who fits the bill.' He took a deep draw on the cigarette and blew the smoke towards the Jersey coastline. 'She thinks you're going to kill her when this is done.'

'Whoever gave her that idea?'

'Not me. It was Ameijeiras told her about Mary.'

Goldman tutted loudly. 'Bastard. Why'd he want to do a thing like that?'

'I imagine he has some very old-fashioned ideas about party discipline.'

'Sounds like.'

'Anyway, I told her that you had no intention of killing her.'

'Good.'

'And that's what she believes.'

Goldman nodded.

'I am right, aren't I? You don't intend to kill her when this is all over?'

'Of course not.'

Tom held out his hand.

'Your word?'

Goldman grinned and took Tom's hand. 'Sure. Why not? I give you my word.'

17

Giving Thanks

In 1621 Captain Miles Standish, the leader of a group of religious fanatics from England, who believed in the imminent arrival of Armageddon in Europe, invited a local tribe of Algonkian Indians, the Wampanoag, to join them for a dinner celebrating the good fortune that had seen their immigrant community established in New England. Since this had more to do with the charity of the Indians than the Christian God, or happy accident, it would have been churlish not to ask them. Especially since it was the Indians who supplied the food. Two years later, things looked even more secure for the New Englanders, and Mather the Elder's Thanksgiving sermon included a special thanks to Almighty God for the plague of smallpox that had destroyed the tribe of Wampanoag who had been their immediate benefactors.

For these Indians, Armageddon turned out to be rather closer to home, and Americans more or less forgot about the destruction of the world until 23 September 1949, which was the day when Joe 1, the first Soviet atomic bomb, was successfully detonated. Since then, and since 29 December 1955, when Bulganin announced that the USSR had developed a rocket that could carry the H-bomb four thousand miles, Thanksgiving has had perhaps as great a meaning for

Americans as it has ever had in the three hundred and forty years since the Pilgrim Fathers sailed across the Atlantic Ocean.

Not that this holiday, traditionally the last Thursday in November, has ever lost its meaning. The importance of the holiday in the American calendar is evidenced by the fact that George Washington's 1789 Thanksgiving Proclamation was the first presidential proclamation ever issued in the United States. This proclamation, mislaid for 132 years and rediscovered in 1921, says nothing about those Wampanoag Indians, which is a pity. No more does it mention family food, or football, or the Macy's Thanksgiving day parade, sponsored by the Lionel Corporation and Ideal toys, and watched by Jimmy Nimmo, in colour, on NBC television, at his home in Keystone Islands.

He was alone. Reluctantly he had conceded that there was little of practical investigative use that could be achieved on a public holiday. Except perhaps one thing.

And so it was that, after watching the parade on his new television set, followed by the game – the Green Bay Packers versus the Detroit Lions – and a TV dinner, and then a nap in his favourite chair that took him through *Edge of Night*, and Leonard Bernstein and the New York Philharmonic in West Berlin, followed by a couple of beers and a sandwich during the *Seven o'Clock News* and *Bat Masterson*, he got into his car and drove back to Palm Beach.

It was after eleven by the time Nimmo got there but, according to Jack Kennedy's schedule, he was early. So he had a drink at the popular Bradley's Saloon on Royal Poinciana Way, near the intracoastal waterway, before driving across Lake Worth to the airport in West Palm Beach. He was still early when he joined the crowd of reporters and well-wishers who were there to see Kennedy fly in from Washington National Airport. Nimmo wanted to see if the airport in West Palm Beach was the kind of place Tom Jefferson might choose to make an attempt on the life of the President-elect.

With no jet aircraft, and only turbo-prop planes, mostly private, flying in and out, it was not a large airport, so there was not much to see – just a landing strip and a building handling passengers and air traffic control. Looking around, Nimmo decided that the best place to position himself would be where Tom Jefferson would probably

232

choose, and with all the people and cars around, he figured that would be somewhere higher up.

Getting out on the roof of the airport building proved easy enough, and he might have been more alarmed at the excellent potential it offered a marksman, had it not been for the two Secret Service agents who were up there already. The square jaws, right-angled haircuts, buttoned, lozenge-shaped coats and sensible black shoes gave their game away in less time than it would have taken them to show Treasury badges and Big Brother attitudes.

'Who are you?' asked one of the agents. 'You're not supposed to be up here.' Both men walked quickly towards Nimmo as, somewhere in the deep purple sky, a plane began its final approach to the runway.

'I thought I'd get a better view up here,' Nimmo explained. But what he really thought was that it might be awkward to be detained and questioned by these two bozos, who looked as if they had every intention of searching him. 'I'm sorry, I didn't mean any harm.' But meaning a great deal of harm was exactly what he intended as he flattened the first agent's nose with a rock-breaker of a punch. The second man went for his gun, which was fastened securely in a holster underneath the elastically controlled waistband of his Goldenaire pants. By the time the agent had his hand on the .38, Nimmo's sap was on his skull.

Leaving both men sprawled on the rooftop in the darkness, Nimmo returned to the inside of the building, his question about a shot from the highest point in the airport answered. And out on the tarmac, he mingled with the two hundred people who, even near midnight, were gathered to applaud the man of the moment, and to wave their banners: 'Welcome to Palm Beach' and, rather prematurely, 'We Love you Mister President'. Nimmo glanced at his watch and concluded that the four-engined plane taxiing noisily towards the building could hardly be John Kennedy's Convair. According to the schedule his private plane left Washington at eight thirty p.m., on a flight that took four hours. The two men standing right in front of Nimmo were real convention types – liquored legionnaires – who knew all the answers. This was not the first time they had welcomed Jack Kennedy into Palm Beach airport.

'That's the press plane,' explained the fatter, more sober, uglier of these two Democrats, whose asinine, stupid, stubborn faces reminded Nimmo why a jackass was the party's symbol. 'It left Washington around the same time as JFK, but s'got four engines, see? That makes it faster than *The Caroline*. Which is what JFK calls the two-engined plane he owns. After his beautiful, two-year-old daughter. Just like her mother, too. Matter of fact, they're all beautiful. Don't you think? We love Jack Kennedy. I think everyone does, don't you? Even the folks who didn't vote for him.'

During this explanation, Nimmo recoiled from the Floridian's florid breath. This one was a real Cracker. His conversation smelled of fish, grits, and humbug.

'I guess so,' agreed Nimmo, pretending to blow his nose.

The plane began to disgorge the fourth estate and its baggage, and started refuelling. Twenty-five minutes passed with the two Crackers discussing some of Kennedy's cabinet appointments, and how a new dawn was on the horizon for the people of the United States. Nimmo listened patiently, hardly worrying about the two agents he had left insensible on the rooftop. It had been dark, and besides, Secret Service agents were usually coy about their mistakes. He wondered what the two Crackers might have said if he'd told them only half of what he had learned from Mothballs about Mattress Jack. But at last a plane was heard and, at twelve thirty a.m., with the crowd cheering enthusiastically, a smaller plane landed.

It was the first time Nimmo had seen Kennedy in the cupreous flesh. The policeman's eyes saw a six-foot Caucasian male, weighing around 170 pounds, with code six eyes (blue), code four hair (reddish brown), and in his early forties. He wore a blue-grey two-button suit, a dark-blue tie, and a white shirt with narrow grey stripes. Not wearing a hat helped to make the young Senator look even younger – too young to be the President-elect of the United States. Too young, the old cop would have said, to be the President's press secretary. But for the private plane, the European cut of the suit, the Palm Beach tan, and the shit-eating grin, Nimmo would have marked Kennedy down as the kind of B-movie actor you would get to play the DA in some gritty courtroom melodrama: Dana Andrews harassed by Lee J. Cobb. Except that for once the grin was gone. And something was clearly wrong. Senator Kennedy walked rapidly from his plane into the airport building, hardly slowing to acknowledge the applause of the crowd or to shake any of the supplicant hands.

'The hell's the matter with him?' complained one of the Crackers. 'On a goddamn holiday, too. Might have stopped to say hello. Wish us a happy Thanksgiving. Who the hell does he think put him in the White House in the first place?'

'You can bet he would have stopped if there'd been niggers waiting in line,' suggested the other. 'Gettin' his picture taken, shakin' hands with a nigger. Too good an opportunity to miss.'

'Too dark,' laughed the first. 'Picture wouldn't ever come out. Just be him shakin' hands with two eyes and a happy smile. 'Sides, if that's all he wants he just has to go down to Montgomery and get on a goddamn bus. I just can't get over his behaviour. On a goddamn Thanksgiving holiday, too.'

Nimmo paid little attention to their disappointment. Instead he wondered if the Senator's concerned demeanour might have had anything to do with the incident on the airport building rooftop. Maybe the Secret Service had advised Kennedy to get his ass indoors as quickly as possible, in case some nut with a gun was out there.

Nimmo was just starting to think of going home when Kennedy came out of the building again, and marched quickly back to his own plane where he spoke to one of the pilots for a moment. Then he walked fifty or sixty yards to the press plane, and climbed aboard.

'Maybe Cronkite's on board that plane,' speculated once of the Crackers. 'And he wants an interview.'

But a few minutes later the press plane finished refuelling and started up its four engines. By one a.m. the President-elect was airborne again, leaving some very puzzled people back on the warm ground in West Palm Beach.

Nimmo drove back to Miami, went to bed, and got up late to learn that not long after Kennedy had flown out from Washington, the pregnant Jackie had started haemorrhaging. She had been taken to Georgetown hospital where she was delivered of a son, by Caesarean section. Kennedy had simply taken the faster plane back to Washington to be at his wife's side.

One thing was now obvious to Nimmo. Jack Kennedy would be

spending a lot less time in Palm Beach and a lot more time in Washington than anyone had thought.

The next two weeks passed without any action, or leads. It was a difficult time for Jimmy Nimmo and everyone who was associated with the investigation. An increasingly anxious Sam Giancana flew to New York to square things with Carlo Gambino. As a result, outfit men were sent to keep an eye on all the places on Colt Maurensig's list, and a few others besides, just in case Tom Jefferson decided to reconnoitre these locations, too: the Carlyle Hotel, on Madison Avenue, where Jack Kennedy owned a penthouse apartment and where, sometimes, he met Marilyn; Joe Kennedy's apartment at 277 Park Avenue; and the building the Kennedy family owned at 230 Park Avenue where, in suite 953, old Joe had offices that had been the Kennedy campaign headquarters during the election. There was nothing on the schedule that showed Kennedy was planning even to visit New York before the New Year, but Giancana did not want to leave any possibility untried.

'Besides,' he said, 'it'll be next year before you know it. After January second he's there for the best part of two whole weeks. Seems to me that New York's as good a place as anywhere to hit Jack Kennedy.'

The only light relief to be had for the Chicago gangster was a telephone call from a plainly terrified Joe Kennedy who, having noticed the muscle that had started hanging around his Park Avenue addresses, now concluded that Frank Costello still bore him a lethal-sized grudge. Giancana, an old friend and admirer of Costello's, tried to reassure Bootlegger Joe that Costello was more or less retired after the Genovese family had shot him in the head, some four years earlier. But Bootlegger Joe was not persuaded, and shortly afterwards flew to Palm Beach for the rest of the month.

There was some good news from another area, however, and for which the Chicago boss gave a loud thanks in the shape of a party in New Jersey for a couple of dozen wiseguys.

In November 1957, right in the middle of the McLellan Committee hearings, the mob had held the largest sit down in Cosa Nostra history, at the one-hundred-and-fifty-acre estate of Joe Barbara in

Apalachin, New York. The sit down had been raided by New York State police and US Treasury officials. Many of the leading figures in organised crime were arrested, although quite a few, including Sam Giancana, escaped. Those arrested were subpoenaed to give evidence to a Grand Jury on the purpose of the meeting. This had been a peaceful one – to avoid a war in the wake of the attempt on Costello's life, and the murder of Albert Anastasia – but no one was talking. As Johnny Rosselli had told Jimmy Nimmo, *omertà* was more than just a word to these men. As a result of their refusal to do anything but take the Fifth, Russell Bufalino and nineteen others were indicted and convicted of conspiring to obstruct justice. They were sentenced to prison terms of three to five years, and each was fined $10,000. On bail, they appealed, and on 28 November 1960 the judgement came down from the United States Court of Appeals for the Second Circuit, reversing the conspiracy conviction for want of sufficient evidence. Giancana was jubilant.

Meanwhile, the search for Tom Jefferson continued, slowly. Paul Ianucci and Nimmo found Tom Jefferson's Chevy Bel Air with Peter Rooney's Used Cars in Tampa, and then his mother at the Elderflower Home for Elder Citizens in Intercession City, near Orlando, in Osceola County. Mildred Jefferson was not yet seventy, but she did not know what month it was, or even who had won the election. Barbara Zioncheck, the nurse in receipt of Nimmo's ten dollars and who, on a promise of ten more, agreed to call if anyone came to visit the prematurely old woman, told him that no one had and no one would. But since the retirement home's bills were paid by Tom Jefferson's bank in Mexico City, it remained a possibility that had to be covered. Just like the bank itself, which was now watched round the clock by the same team of Cuban anti-Castro exiles whom Jefferson had met while he was there.

Barbara Zioncheck recalled her last coherent conversation with Mildred Jefferson, and thought she remembered having heard something about someone called Roberto, Tom Jefferson's father, who was now living permanently in Cuba. Nimmo came away from Intercession City almost certain that this particular avenue of inquiry was now terminated. Just like N Street, back in Georgetown, which the local police had now closed to the public – everyone, from those who wished mother and child well, to those who wished only harm to the father.

Nimmo had thought Kennedy would remain in Georgetown, next to his recuperating wife, for a long time, but he was soon proved wrong. One of Jack Kennedy's girlfriends, Judy Campbell, a Jackie look-alike from Los Angeles, was, through Frank Sinatra, also a girlfriend of Sam Giancana's. From Campbell, Giancana learned that Kennedy had invited her down to Palm Beach for the first weekend in December, staying at the Breakers Hotel, in a complimentary suite that Kennedy kept reserved for weeks at a time. After spending two or three nights sneaking out of La Guerida and into the back entrance of the Breakers – which kept Mothballs and Sunshine hugely amused – the President-elect returned to Washington for a meeting with President Eisenhower, on 6 December. Then it was back to Palm Beach again, only this time he was accompanied by Jackie and their two children, Caroline and John. Photographed on the runway at Palm Beach airport, they looked like any other happy family worth a hundred million dollars. Jackie, glamorous as always, seemed well rested, with no concerns other than the ones that afflict any new mother who has had a child delivered by Caesarean section.

It was ten o'clock on Saturday morning when Mothballs telephoned the safe house in Coral Gables. 'I'm not sure, but I think we could have a situation here,' he told Nimmo. 'There's some guy in a car with a New Hampshire licence plate who keeps coming back to park outside the Kennedy place. He's not John Laws, and he's not a Secret Service agent. And I'm pretty sure he's not Tom Jefferson, unless that was a very old photograph you gave me. No, this guy is old, about seventy years of age, and kind of rough-looking, too. Unshaven. Very not Palm Beach. The car's covered with dust, like he's been driving a way. And he does nothing but stare at the house, like he's waiting for something, or someone. And I got thinking, I know you didn't mention it, but it occurred to me that Jefferson might have some kind of accomplice. You know, a partner. For instance, you said he had a father, who might be around this guy's age. Either way, I've got a bad feeling about this fucking character. Maybe you should come and take a look for yourself.'

Nimmo thought for a moment. It did not sound like Tom Jefferson's MO, but could he afford to ignore the nose of an experienced criminal like Mothballs? He said, 'Where's Kennedy right now?'

'On the golf course. Bobby Sunshine's keepin' an eye on him. After that, Sunshine'll be in the boat on the other side of the house.'

'Have you got the licence number of this guy's car?'

Mothballs gave it to him.

'Sit tight. I'll be there as soon as I can.'

Nimmo telephoned police headquarters for a DMV check and any rap sheet on the driver, and then took off for Palm Beach. It was lunchtime when he arrived but, before driving up to the north of the island and the Kennedy house, he found a payphone and rang headquarters again. It turned out that the car was registered to a Richard Paul Pavlick, aged seventy-three, from Belmont, New Hampshire. Pavlick had no criminal record to speak of but, according to the Belknap County Sheriff's office, he had been treated at a local mental hospital. More disturbing was the news that Pavlick had written to a local attorney, Maurice P. Bois, threatening to kill Jack Kennedy. Bois had reported the threat to the police who had formed the conclusion that Pavlick, a retired postal clerk, was a harmless crank.

Mothballs was sitting in a grey Chrysler Imperial on North Ocean Boulevard, about forty yards north of the Kennedy house. Outside 1095 were the usual well-wishers, braving the heat in the hope of catching a glimpse of glamorous Jackie, and the usual cops shepherding them. The truth was that no one in Palm Beach wanted to see him as much as her. Nimmo parked beyond Mothballs' car and got into the Chrysler's passenger seat alongside him. The Palm Beach mobster looked hot and tired and smelt like he was badly in need of a bath. He pointed to a dirty-looking Ford parked about ten yards in front of him, on the opposite side of the baking boulevard.

'That's him there,' he said, handing Nimmo his binoculars. 'Just sits there and watches, like a cigar store Indian. Gives me the spooks.'

Nimmo took a closer look. Pavlick seemed to be in no hurry to do anything now that he had driven all the way down from New Hampshire. He was round-shouldered, grey-haired, bespectacled. Having seen the guy for himself, Nimmo's first inclination was to agree with the New Hampshire police. The guy looked harmless enough.

Nimmo said, 'He's a loony. I had him checked out. Seems like he's spent some time in a mental institution.'

'Only a loony would sit out here in this fuckin' heat,' Mothballs said pointedly. 'So that figures.'

'On the other hand.'

Even as he spoke the dusty Ford started up its engine, and moved gently away, heading south, down the Boulevard.

'I think maybe he heard you,' observed Nimmo. 'C'mon, let's follow him.'

'What the fuck for?' objected Mothballs. 'He's a loony, ain't he?' But he started the car anyway and set off in slow pursuit of Pavlick's Ford.

'I was thinking,' explained Nimmo. 'Maybe the New Hampshire cops got it wrong. I mean, it's over fifteen hundred miles between here and there. And that's a fuck of a drive for anyone, let alone a loony. And another thing. He's a smart enough loony to know that he'd be wasting his time sitting outside the Kennedy place in Hyannis Port. Massachusetts is a lot nearer Belmont, New Hampshire. Seems to me that if I was a loony, that's where I'd have headed. No, this guy knew Kennedy would be here in Palm Beach, because he reads the newspapers. And how loony is that?'

'Depends which paper,' said Mothballs. 'Okay, you made your point. It was you that mentioned he was a loony in the first place. To me he looked like a guy trying to get up the nerve to do a drive-by. I know what that's like. I've sat in that car myself. Okay, you're thinking, I don't look old enough to have pulled that kind of *Untouchables* shit. But I started early in this business.'

They trailed Pavlick across Lake Worth to one of the many no-frills motels along Dixie Highway, close to the junction with Southern Boulevard. Between the cheap motels were stores selling sub-tropical plants, honey, citrus fruits, and kitsch souvenirs made of coconut shells, conch shells, and cypress knees. If they had driven further south on Dixie Highway the road would have been lined with signs advertising the merits of various jungle gardens, Indian villages, mineral springs, alligator farms, and lion ranches. It was a depressing area replete with half-assed schemes and disappointed dreams, and so many neon proclamations of 'Vacancy' that it was as if blank minds and absence of thought were the recommended orders of the day. Nimmo considered it an unlikely place to choose to stay in for anyone who was looking to give his mentally disturbed life some desperately needed meaning and significance. Substance and expression fled from the Dixie Highway like a breeze blowing through the bluish-green Australian pines, and out towards the empty ocean.

'I do believe that the Secret Service agents guarding Mattress Jack are billeted in one of those flop-houses,' observed Mothballs.

'Jesus, it's no fun being the Kennedy help, is it?'

Pavlick turned into the parking lot of a faceless, innominate motel and, watched by Nimmo and Mothballs from the other side of the highway, got stiffly out of his car, as if he had been sitting in it for quite a while.

'Now what do we do?' asked Mothballs.

Observing that Pavlick had taken nothing with him from the car and into the motel, Nimmo said, 'One of us should take a look at that car. See if he's carrying a piece, or something.'

Mothballs turned off the engine and pulled on the parking brake. 'Like I keep saying, this is my territory, so let me handle it. If there's any trouble, I know all the cops around here. But you they don't know, and they don't owe. I reckon you of all people will understand what I mean by that. Besides, I used to jack cars when I was a kid. Grand Theft Auto was all I could spell until I looked up masturbation in the dictionary. Told you I started early.'

Nimmo shrugged as Mothballs pushed open the car door and got out. 'Okay. Whatever you say.'

Mothballs threw the door closed, then opened the back door, took out his jacket, and put it on. 'A unit like that heap of shit he's driving,' he said. 'S'not a fuckin' problem. Only, I always wear a jacket when I'm doing something of this order. You can get away with a lot if you look respectable in this town.'

His arms and body hardly moved at all as he ran across the street, just his legs below the knee, so that with his bulk and in his black suit, he looked more like a bowling bowl, rolling slowly toward Pavlick's car, than anything that might be described as respectable. True to his word of his own expertise, though, he was inside the car in seconds, checking the glove box, and then the back seat, and last of all the trunk with the innocence of a travelling salesman from Honor, Michigan.

He was back in the Chrysler, alongside Nimmo, in just a few minutes, his broad, sweating face flushed with fear and excitement.

'He's a fucking loony, all right. He's driving a bomb around, and I don't mean no fuckin' Edsel. The trunk of that car is filled with fucking dynamite, and several cans of gasoline. There are all sorts of wires going in and out of the driver's compartment, and a kind of switch thing under the dashboard that looks as though it might turn this whole street into Bikini fucking Atoll if you rocked it. I really think he means to do it, the crazy sonofabitch. To kill Kennedy.'

'Wired up, you say?'

Mothballs wiped his face with a handkerchief. 'Wired. There are blasting caps, detonators, wires, sticks of dynamite, everything except the cheap clock and the Jew accent.'

'Did you touch it?'

'Do I look like a fuckin' Jap general? I wanna kill myself I'll take an overdose of pussy, not go screwin' around with a fuckin' bomb.' Nervously, Mothballs lit a cigarette. 'What do we do now?'

'Call the Secret Service.'

'What about the cops?'

'They'll involve the FBI. Do you want to spend the rest of the weekend answering their questions?'

'Not now you come to mention it.'

'Besides, I owe someone a favour. Someone in Washington. I need to call long distance. Can we pick up my car and then go to your place?'

Mothballs gunned the engine. 'I'll be glad to get out of here.'

'I don't get it,' said Nimmo, switching off the TV in the corner of Mothballs' living room. 'There was nothing at all about Pavlick or his bomb on the eleven o'clock news.'

'Hey, forget about it,' yawned his host. 'They're probably still questioning the guy. And you know how they are with the newsboys.

They don't want to tell 'em what fucking year it is. Come on. I'll show you to your room.'

Mothballs' home in Lake Worth was a modest Cape Cod-style house with a kitchen, a living room, two bedrooms, a bathroom, and a carport, in a Levittown-like development of uniform, unidentifiable, pre-fabricated properties. Mothballs was perhaps the only unmarried man in the street.

The bed was comfortable, but Nimmo hardly slept. Every half hour he would start out of a light doze to recall the details of what he had told Murray Weintraub, worried that he had somehow failed to impress upon the Secret Service agent the full gravity of the threat posed to the young President-elect. The fourth or fifth time he woke up, Nimmo wondered if perhaps his insistence on not wanting any credit for the collar after all might have confused Weintraub, or even made him suspicious.

'I don't get it,' Weintraub had said. 'I thought you said you wanted this collar. To get back in Hoover's good books.'

'I changed my mind. I'd prefer to remain anonymous.'

'Anonymous tips have to be verified before we can act on them, you know that, Jimmy.'

'I already thought of that. You can call the cops in Belknap County, New Hampshire. And there's an attorney, name of Maurice P. Bois, who originally reported this character. He'll verify that Pavlick threatened Kennedy.'

'Good enough.'

'Just leave me out of it.'

'Why so coy all of a sudden? This is on the level, isn't it?'

'Like it was built by Frank Lloyd Wright, Murray. Look, let's just say that I was somewhere I shouldn't have been when I found out, okay?'

'Same old Jimmy.'

'If you're quick, you might just catch him in his motel room.'

Now Nimmo sat up in bed and looked at his watch. It was five fifty-five on Sunday morning, a whole fourteen hours since he had reported Pavlick and his car bomb. Surely they would have put out something to the press by now. He got out of bed, went into the living room, turned on the Pilot Soloist radio-phonograph and, as soon as the tubes had warmed up, searched the tuner for a six o'clock news broadcast. But to his irritation and discomfort, the news was still dominated by events in Algeria and Congo. As if anyone cared about shit like that. There was nothing about a plot to kill Jack Kennedy.

Nimmo was not a man to sit around and do nothing. He dressed quickly and, leaving Mothballs snoring like a lawnmower, he went out to his car.

From the house in Lake Worth, it was a straight drive north up Dixie Highway into West Palm Beach. Pavlick's car was gone from outside the motel but it was immediately clear to Nimmo that its absence had nothing to do with the Secret Service, or any other law enforcement agency. If Pavlick had been arrested the motel would likely have been closed while the bomb squad boys went over his room, just in case there were any other sticks of dynamite or booby traps inside a hollowed-out Gideon Bible. At the very least, the county sheriff would have posted a couple of men in the parking lot. Clearly something had gone very wrong.

Nimmo looked at his watch. It was now six thirty a.m. Jack Kennedy would be getting ready to go to seven a.m. mass at St Edwards. Suddenly Nimmo saw Pavlick's obvious course of action in all its simple lethality. Detonating a car bomb in front of La Guerida might only injure the President-elect. The Kennedy house looked substantial enough to withstand a decent-sized blast. The only certain way of killing the President-elect with such a device would be if Pavlick were to crash his car into the Kennedy limousine, and then to hit that switch underneath the dash. In just a few minutes Kennedy would be getting into the back of his car for the short drive to St Edwards Church. There was no time to lose thinking twice.

Nimmo stamped hard on the gas pedal and, with a strident caterwaul of hot rubber on warm blacktop, the Chevy Impala sprang forward, as if pursued by a whole pride of hungry lions. Driving like a man who is late for the Indianapolis 500, Nimmo careered east over Flagler Drive and on to the Royal Park Bridge, across Lake Worth. The car snaked from side to side as it held the left turn off Royal Palm Way on to South County Road. Touching sixty miles an hour, he sped past another church – Bethesda-by-the-Sea – cursing himself at the top of his voice for what he might have to do. How the hell did you stop one car from crashing into another except by crashing into that one car yourself? And not just any fucking car, but a car filled with dynamite. He would probably be lucky if they found enough bits of him to put in a lousy shoebox.

Rounding the Palm Beach Country Club on to North Ocean Boulevard, Nimmo slowed a little. It was six forty-five and a dark limousine was already parked outside La Guerida. As he passed the front doorway he had an excellent view of Jack Kennedy himself coming through the oak door and on to the Boulevard, followed closely by his daughter, Caroline, and Jackie, who was carrying their new baby, John. It was then that Jimmy Nimmo saw Pavlick's dust-covered Ford, parked about thirty or forty yards to the north of the house. The Ford was already creeping slowly forward, like a wild animal stalking its prey. There was no need to crash into it.

Nimmo accelerated again, spun the wheel to the right, and then hit the brakes, which was more than enough to cause the Impala's uncertain back end to sweep across the whole road like a pastel-coloured turnpike, blocking the path of Pavlick's explosive-filled car.

The dusty Ford jerked to a halt. Richard Pavlick looked as surprised as a jack rabbit to see Nimmo blocking the Boulevard in front of him. Any chance of driving into the Kennedy limousine was now gone. Surprise quickly turned to fear as Nimmo, gun in hand, leaped out of his car and lurched towards the bonnet of the Ford. Momentarily he lost his footing and went down on the blacktop, scraping his knees. Almost immediately, Pavlick began to reverse away from Nimmo, gaining speed all the time, and by the time the policeman had picked himself up from the ground, the Ford had all but disappeared. Nimmo got back into his own car and turned the key, intending to pursue the bomber, only to discover that the stalled V8 engine was also flooded.

With his own car now blocking North Ocean Boulevard, the only way for Pavlick to reach St Edwards would be to go all the way to the north of the island and then drive south down the western shore of Lake Worth on Lake Way. Meanwhile, thirty yards away to Nimmo's right, quite oblivious to what had just taken place, Jack Kennedy and his Secret Service detail had already departed for mass, waved off by his equally oblivious family.

It was another ten minutes before Nimmo was able to restart his car. He drove quickly south to St Edwards, but of Pavlick's car there was no sign. But he still sat outside long enough to see Kennedy come out of the church, shriven and absolved, and get back into his limo. Nimmo followed the unwitting Senator safely back to La Guerida, and then drove back to Mothballs' place, thanking the Almighty God he no longer believed in for having delivered them both – himself and Jack Kennedy – from a violent death.

After all he had gone through, it seemed incredible to Nimmo that Mothballs was still so soundly asleep in his Cellini bedroom suite. It was as if, during some ramble in the Kaatskill Mountains, the gangster had met some strange people dressed in the old Flemish style playing at ninepins, and taken a draught of their Hollands.

Nimmo placed another long-distance call to Washington and, speaking once again to Murray Weintraub, told him what had happened. Weintraub swore that Nimmo's information had been passed on to the PRS – the Service's Protective Research Section – but was at a complete loss to explain why that information had not been acted on. An hour or so later Weintraub telephoned Nimmo to confirm that a search for Pavlick was now properly underway and that he would soon be in custody. But his private account of what had happened in Palm Beach upon receipt of the original red alert signal would have appalled the Chief of the Secret Service, one Mr U.E. Baughman.

'You're not going to believe this,' said Weintraub. 'It seems as if Jack Kennedy himself overruled the detail chief. Kennedy said it was just another crank threat and that there was really no need to overreact to what was really a common enough situation for the President of the United States. The fact was, he knew that a PRS red alert would have grounded him last night. And that was the last thing he wanted. You see, after Jackie went to bed, Jack slipped out the back way for a midnight swim in his next-door neighbour's pool. Florence Smith. Well, what can you say, Jimmy? You are dealing with a young, horny guy who is not yet ready to behave like old FDR, Harry Truman, or Dwight Eisenhower. In short, a security fucking night-mare. What can you do when the future President of the United States tells you to ignore signals from the White House Communications

Agency? You remember what I said? That politics and protection don't mix? Change that. It's not politics, it's promiscuity. Promiscuity and protection don't mix. JFK carries on like this, he's going to find himself in trouble.'

Nimmo heard Weintraub out and agreed that the Secret Service had a difficult job on its hands. But four days later, when he was in New York, he decided that it was not all Kennedy's fault. Four days. That was how long it took before Richard Pavlick was finally apprehended. And not by Secret Service agents, either. Still driving his car around Palm Beach as if it was nothing more lethal than an ice-cream van, Pavlick was arrested by a Palm Beach patrolman, for driving over a white line.

18

Harvard Yard

On Monday, 12 December 1960, New England had its heaviest snow in years: thirteen inches fell, and for a while the whole region slipped and skidded to a halt. In Cambridge, Massachusetts – Boston's intellectual younger brother, although the two cities are so close that they are more usually thought of as twins – freshmen students emerged from the dormitories of Harvard Yard, and an unusually vigorous snowball fight ensued.

Snow fights were always a serious affair in Massachusetts. The Boston Massacre of 1764 had started thus when inexperienced British soldiers found themselves pelted with snow and ice, and returned fire not with snowballs but with musket-balls. On a cold December morning two hundred years later, there was but one symbol of authority to be found in all of Harvard Yard. Within Johnson Gate, the elderly gatekeeper charged with offering advice to visitors, directing vehicles, and generally keeping an eye on things for the Harvard University Police Force, wisely stayed inside his tiny beige-coloured guard-house, which was more like a sentry box, and poured himself a cup of hot coffee from a thermos flask.

Harvard Yard is almost always open to the public. On any day you can see several groups of tourists pausing in front of the statue of John

Harvard, and hearing the same old nonsense about his not having founded the university at all. On that particular morning there was but one visitor to the Yard's western quadrangle, recently arrived from New York, and he soon found himself involved in an icy battle that was probably as much action as the Yard had seen since George Washington stationed some of his troops there. Good-humouredly, the visitor gave as good as he got, although he was more than twice the age of the mostly male students – two or three hundred of them – who fought a running, laughing, yelling battle between the leafless American elm trees and the handsome eighteenth-century buildings.

Anyone watching the snowball fight from the comparative safety of an open window might have noticed the older man's keener eye and more accurate aim, for nearly every missile he hurled left a fresh young face stung or bruised with snow and, likely, even fresher than before. Few would have paid attention to the visitor's expensive-looking thirty-five-millimetre Nikon camera, which had an Auto Nikkor telephoto zoom lens, nor to the Telectro portable tape-recorder that he had been carrying over one shoulder, although there could have been very few tourists that came to Harvard who exhibited a desire to particularise and describe the university's architectural treasures in such close detail.

Only minutes before joining in the fight, which had obliged him to place his camera and tape-recorder behind the statue of the much-maligned John Harvard, close to the steps of University Hall, which had been his vantage point, the stranger's interest had been focused on those dormitories that constituted the western side of Harvard Yard's first quadrangle, these being Matthews, Massachusetts Hall, Harvard Hall, Hollis, and Stoughton. Indeed, there was really but one of these buildings that interested him, enjoying, as it did, a view of the University Hall steps that was almost uninterrupted by the branches of the elm trees, and that was Hollis Hall.

There was nothing remarkable about Hollis, in the sense that it was nearly a facsimile of Stoughton and Holsworthy, the dormitory that constituted the northern side of the first quad. The Harvard Book will tell you that Hollis is one hundred and three feet long, forty-three feet broad, and thirty-two feet high. On both façades, the line of the four-storey building's roof is broken by an ornamental pediment, in the centre of which is a common window, with a circular window on each side of it. But it was the four tall rectangular-shaped windows on the top storey's southern side that the solitary visitor had been most concerned to photograph. And not just the windows, but the occupants of the rooms that lay behind them. A supply of snowballs had been carried up to the fourth floor of Hollis to be hurled out of the open windows, and the visitor had obtained several good photographs of the two pairs of students occupying these rooms. It was more than he could have hoped for on his first visit to Harvard.

Finally quitting the frozen fray, the visitor collected his expensive belongings and, wet but laughing, returned to his car, a Rambler Station Wagon he had bought in Norwood, and, thankful that he had enjoyed the presence of mind to spend an extra sixty-five dollars on snow tyres, drove back to the three-room apartment he had recently rented on nearby Center Street, at a cost of one hundred and fifty dollars a month.

Once inside the door of the centrally heated hallway, he pulled off his boots and his wet outer clothes and placed them in the bathroom, close to the hot-water tank, before going into the laundry room he had turned into a darkroom, to develop his black and white film and make some enlargements. When these prints were dry, he spread them on the kitchen table so that he and Alex Goldman could examine them in detail.

Tom Jefferson lit a cigarette and said, 'These are all taken from the steps of University Hall, where Kennedy will leave the building after the meeting of the Harvard Board of Overseers. That's Grays to the left of the quadrangle, which is too far for our purposes. Then we have this rather more Gothic-looking building, which is Matthews. We have plenty of good windows to choose from there, but I'm not happy about all these trees. Those branches could easily spoil a good shot. Then we have Massachusetts Hall, which also has some nice windows, but it is where the Harvard president has his office, so there are likely to be a few Secret Service agents, cops, what have you, coming in and out of the place. Besides, I don't like the proximity of the balcony you see above the arched windows on Harvard Hall, opposite. Or that little cupolaed bell-tower on Harvard Hall's roof. I figure those are two places you can expect to see some Secret Service agents, and they might very well see a gunman who was positioned in a window of Massachusetts.'

'Agreed,' said Goldman. 'They're bound to position a man with binoculars in that bell-tower.'

'Coming out of Harvard Yard for a second, on the other side of the Johnson Gate, we've got the First Unitarian Church.' Tom paused. 'What the fuck kind of church is a Unitarian one, anyway?'

'It's a numbers thing. I don't think they like the Holy Trinity, or some shit like that. How the fuck should I know? I'm a Jew.'

'Well, whatever the fuck it is, it's possible we could get into that spire, take out some window panes. But it doesn't look too comfortable. In these kinds of temperatures, I'd like to suggest we forget all about using this building.'

'I agree.'

'I'd also recommend we forget all about Harvard Hall. One, it's used for lectures and tickets for Harvard sports events, so people will be coming and going at all times. And two, we both agree there will probably be an agent in the bell-tower. That leaves Hollis, which is this one, and Stoughton, between Hollis and Holsworthy. Holsworthy's too far, same as Grays. Stoughton's good, but Hollis gives us longer for a shot. Especially if we can gain access to one of these windows on the top floor, to the side. Thirty-two feet high, plus a hundred and fifty across the yard, to the steps of University Hall.'

Tom pointed to a photograph of a building whose grey granite was in contrast to the red brick of all the others.

'Kennedy comes out of this door, on the steps here, to the left of the statue of John Harvard. Anyway, according to Pythagoras, that's a range of one hundred and fifty-three feet.' He pointed to the white balustrade atop University Hall's three-storey façade. 'Figure on a couple of Secret Service agents up here, on the roof of University Hall. They'll command quite a good view of the whole quad when looking down. But not such a good view of the top floor on the southern side of Hollis, when looking up. Which they'll have to do. Hollis is a whole storey higher than UH. Just as good is the fact that you cannot see any of these four windows from the bell-tower.'

Tom removed the photograph of University Hall and replaced it with some wider shots of the whole western quad.

'By the way, we're lucky those aren't evergreen trees,' he said. 'If they were, we wouldn't even be having this conversation. If it was the other side of UH, in the eastern part of Harvard Yard, we'd almost be in as much trouble. There's a pine tree in front of the chapel, and a smaller one in front of Boylston Hall.' Tom puffed his cigarette and shrugged. 'So I hope the information from your Russian comrades is good. The car only drops him at the back door of UH, right? But he leaves from the front, on the western side, which is where we'll be.'

'That's right. Ten thirty a.m., January ninth. He'd be out of the car for ten seconds at the most before going inside. Not much of a window. Not compared with the front door. He'll come out of there at midday, with the rest of the overseers, and then they'll stroll across the Yard, and then the Square, to Brattle Street. They're planning to have lunch at the new Loeb Drama Center. If he wants drama, we'll give him a drama.'

Tom nodded. 'Depending on the number of people in the Yard, I figure it will take him at least three or four minutes to walk between University Hall and Johnson Gate. For seventy-five per cent of that time we'll have a clear view of him from Hollis.'

'Three or four minutes. That's more than enough time.'

'All you have to do is figure out a way for us to get into one of those rooms in Hollis,' said Tom.

Alex Goldman grinned back at him. 'I'm in the FBI, aren't I? Shit, no one argues with the FBI, especially when it's some eighteen-year-old kid who's fresh out of school. You can relax and leave the talking to me, Paladin. After nearly five years working COINTELPRO ops, I eat bullshit for breakfast.'

The following Tuesday evening, at around five o'clock, and wearing dark suits and ties under their G-man type raincoats, Goldman and Tom drove along Massachusetts Avenue to Harvard, in the Rambler Station Wagon. They parked in Harvard Square, alongside the Old Burying Ground, where early settlers and revolutionary soldiers – not to mention Harvard University's first eight presidents – are interred, and walked across Peabody Street, through Johnson Gate, with Harvard Hall to their left. There, they turned on to a path now cleared of snow, and paused before the southern side of Hollis Hall for a brief moment.

Observing that there were lights in all the fourth-floor windows, they came around front and walked coolly through the first of two entranceways, called Hollis South. Immediately to their left was a staircase which, like the walls surrounding it, was painted white, so that the interior of Hollis looked almost as if some negligent student had left the front door open to the elements. And certainly it was none too warm inside, even with the door closed.

The two men proceeded up three flights of stairs, ignoring a couple of young men carrying green cloth bags, apparently full of books, who ignored them right back. There were five plain wooden doors on the top landing, four of them numbered, and one, at the back of the building, an unoccupied bathroom. Somewhere they could hear the sound of a record player – Elvis Presley singing 'Are You Lonesome Tonight?' Immediately at the top of the stairs, at the back left of Hollis, was room thirteen. Down the hall, on the front left, was room fifteen. Rooms fourteen and sixteen, having no side windows, were of little interest to Tom and Goldman, beyond the names of the two roommates posted on a piece of paper that was taped to each of the doors.

'Okay,' said Goldman. 'In room thirteen we have John McMurry and Michael Salant. And in room fifteen we have Chub Farrell and Torbert Winthrop. Good Ivy League names, if ever I heard them. Okay. It's your call, Paladin. Which of these two pairs of roommates is going to receive the benefit of a real education in the university of life?'

'Fifteen,' said Tom.

'Fifteen,' repeated Alex. 'Tonight's winning number is fifteen.' He knocked softly on the door. 'They don't know how lucky they are.' Both men took out FBI identification – fakes from one of Alex's COINTELPRO ops, but indistinguishable from the real thing – and held them up to the scrutiny of the young man who threw open the door. 'FBI,' growled Goldman. 'I'm Special Agent Christopher. This is Agent Rutter.'

The student's mouth opened and then shut again, several times, as if he had been thinking of spitting out some butter that would not melt in there. He was tall, red-haired, with large ears, and a face that looked as though it had fallen off the side of a church. Finally, he stammered, 'Wow.'

Goldman grinned. 'Can we come in for a minute, son?'

'Sure,' said the young man, and stepped politely aside as if he had been standing in a ballroom full of debutantes. 'Please do, come in.'

Tom and Goldman advanced into a large but cosy room that was approximately thirty feet square. A fireplace with a roaring fire jutted out about two or three feet into the room, on either side of which was a single bed. Elsewhere in the room were two dressers, two closets, two desks, two desk-chairs, two sets of well-stuffed bookshelves, and two library chairs. A large, heavily stained Bokhara rug covered about half of the uneven hardwood floor.

'Chub?' The tall, red-haired fellow closed the door and, springing nervously from one foot to the other like a dancing bear, attempted to get the attention of his roommate who, seated at his desk, had yet to look up from the book in which he appeared to be thoroughly absorbed. 'Hey, Chub. Get up. It's the FBI.'

'The FBI. Sure it is,' muttered the boy at the desk, still not looking round. 'Jerk.'

'I'm not kidding, man.'

Chub leaned back in his chair, glanced around wearily, and then did a Stan Laurel of a double-take as he saw Goldman and Tom, and the badges they were still flourishing. 'Jesus Christ, Torbert,' he exclaimed loudly, jumping up from his chair. 'What the hell did you do?'

'We're sorry to disturb you two gentlemen,' Goldman said smoothly. 'No one's in trouble. No one's done anything. So there's absolutely nothing to get alarmed about. This is just a routine background security check we're making, in advance of Senator Kennedy's visit to Harvard, next month.'

Chub Farrell frowned. 'Jack Kennedy's coming to Harvard?'

Tom laughed wryly and walked over to the windows, of which there were four, each about three feet wide by six feet high, with wood-panelled window seats, and two pairs of matching shutters. There were no drapes. He stamped gently on the floorboards a couple of times, and spent the rest of his time staring out of the two windows that looked immediately on to Massachusetts Hall. These two windows remained his favoured place for a rifleman's position. From either one it was possible to cover the whole quadrangle, from the snow-covered steps that led down from University Hall to within only a few yards of Johnson Gate.

Chub's roommate, Torbert Winthrop, was remonstrating with him wearily. 'Don't you read the newspapers?' he demanded. 'Jack Kennedy's on the Harvard Board of Overseers. That's why he's coming. For the January meeting.'

'That's right,' confirmed Goldman. 'January the ninth, to be precise.'

'He is? What do they do?'

'They talk about a whole lot of stuff. Committee report on things like the performance of the football team.'

'Hell, that sure won't take long,' snorted Chub. 'The team's lousy. What else is there to say?' Chub was shorter than his lanky roommate, but better-looking, with longish fair hair and a pale complexion that seemed to indicate he needed to spend more time outside the Widener Library. Like Torbert, Chub wore a Harvard pullover, a cotton shirt, grey flannel trousers, and a pair of stiff English brown brogues. 'The team plays like it's in aspic.'

'The university police,' continued Goldman, unperturbed by this interruption, 'are co-operating with the FBI and the Secret Service to make sure that next month's visit goes as smoothly as possible. I'm sure we all want that, don't we?'

Goldman glanced around the room in an attempt to make a quick appraisal of the two young characters with whom he was dealing. There was a pair of skis sticking out from under each boy's bed and, taped to the walls, were pictures of naked girls and sportscars. In the corner, resting on a Knickerbocker beer crate, was a Motorola television set, and there was even a small Christmas tree, atop of which shone a toy sheriff's badge. Torbert's desk was home to a copy of *Atlantic Monthly*, a flashlight, some family photographs, and a new briar pipe, while Chub's desk revealed interests as Catholic as *Playboy* magazine, Marx's *Das Kapital*, a *Ben Hur* souvenir movie programme, and a French edition of Charles Baudelaire's *Intimate Journals*. Goldman thought Chub and Torbert looked like what they were: a couple of polite young men in a hurry to be older ones. That was good. That was very much to his purpose. With what Tom had in mind for them, they were booked on a DC-8 bound for Manhood.

'Sure, I guess everyone wants Kennedy's visit to be a success,' agreed Torbert. 'But how can we help you, sir?'

'Yes, of course, anything,' said Chub.

'I'm sure you understand that sometimes we have to check people out, just to make sure they're not the enemies of democracy.'

Goldman picked up the copy of *Kapital* and turned the pages with a show of disapproval. It was a long time since he had read it himself – at least twenty years. Things had seemed clearer back then, in the thirties, when he had decided that the best way of serving the cause of anti-fascism had been to work for the Soviet Union. For a long while after the war, when he had learned the true facts about Stalinist Russia, he had doubted the wisdom of that original choice: political conscience, instead of loyalty to country. But, more recently, his communist faith had been restored by the revolution in Cuba. And by a determination to prevent the forces of American fascism from destroying Castro and his popular revolution, by any means necessary. Those were his orders from his KGB controllers. And he intended to carry them out. Even when those orders sometimes involved carrying out an assassination. No matter who it was.

Silencing the two Nicaraguan girls, Edith and Anne, after this was all over, would be tough enough. A lot tougher than merely ordering Tom to kill an old friend who had been about to defect from the GRU in Mexico City. But hardest of all had been killing Mary Jefferson. Goldman had liked her, and even his degraded sensibilities had found the means of her murder quite abhorrent. By comparison with what had happened to Mary, planning John Kennedy's assassination looked like a picnic.

Chub Farrell was looking nervous at the amount of interest the FBI was showing in his choice of reading matter, and, flushing bright red, said, 'I was just reading that, sir.'

'It's only a book,' said Goldman.

'We both were, as a matter of fact,' added Chub. 'For Economics.'

'But *you* bought it,' accused Torbert.

'Thanks a lot, Tor.' Then, to Goldman, 'Economics is one of the subjects we're studying this year. That's the only reason I'm reading it. I'm not a communist. I don't even like Economics.'

'Dismal science, huh?' Goldman tossed Marx aside and, collecting *Playboy* off Chub's desk, idly thumbed through its pages. 'What are the others?'

'History, English, French. French is my worst.'

For a moment, Goldman's eyes lingered over a pictorial tribute to Marilyn. Then he smiled and said, 'What are you majoring in? Good-looking broads?'

'Government, sir. With an emphasis on international relations.'

Goldman thought the better of making a remark about sexual relations being more likely in government, especially if Jack Kennedy was anyone to go by. Replacing the magazine, he took out a notebook and a pencil.

'Where do you live, son? When you're not here and studying hard?'

'New York, sir.'

'Address?'

Chub gave an exclusive-sounding address on New York's Upper East Side.

'What about you, son?' Goldman asked Torbert.

Torbert's address in Boston sounded equally patrician.

'Now then. Can you each verify the other's good character?'

'Oh yes sir. We were at school together. At Choate.'

'Cho what?'

'It's an Episcopalian school in Wallingford, Connecticut,' explained Torbert.

'Where Jack Kennedy went to school,' murmured Tom.

'That's right, sir.'

'And now you're both Harvard men.' Goldman looked like he was impressed. 'It all sounds very promising. Who knows? Maybe, in twenty years or so, it'll be you who's coming to attend a meeting of the Harvard Board of Overseers. Now wouldn't that be something?'

'It sure would, sir,' agreed Chub.

'Okay. That's about it for now,' said Goldman. 'The Secret Service might be along sometime nearer the big day, to check over the immediate scene.'

'That's the easy part,' said Tom.

'They leave the background checks to us. It is possible your parents might get a visit over the holidays, just to find out if you are who you say you are. But, like I said before, it is nothing to be alarmed about. Just routine. By the way, when do you boys break up here for the holidays?'

'Winter recess begins on Friday the sixteenth,' said Torbert. 'We're both back for the Winter Reading Period on January second.'

Tom got up from the window seat. 'What are you boys doing for Christmas?' he asked innocently.

'Studying at home.'

'Me too.'

'We've got mid-year examinations starting on the sixteenth of January.'

'We'd stay here and study, if we could, but you can't. It's not allowed. Winter recess is the one break when you have to leave the Harvard campus.'

'And you can't come back in after you've left. The dorm is all closed up.'

'Good luck with the exams,' said Goldman. 'And I want to thank you both for your time and your co-operation. Oh, there is one more thing, gentlemen. I'd be really grateful if you would refrain from discussing our visit with anyone. And I do mean anyone. Not just Thold and David in room fourteen, McMurry and Salant in thirteen, and Boyd and Costello in sixteen, but anyone at all. Girlfriends, teachers, even the university police. You see, in matters affecting the security of the President, or the President-elect, we usually find that it is best if our involvement is treated in a vacuum, as it were. Just in case a foreign power or enemy agency should discover how we handle these matters. Now I would be within my rights to ask you both to sign an executive order, binding you to confidentiality, which forbids the unauthorised disclosure of anything that might reasonably be expected to cause damage to the national security. Such as our investigative procedures in the FBI. But you being Harvard men, I'm only going to do what I've done with your friends along the hall there. All I'm going to do is ask you on your honour not to discuss this matter. Not even with each other. Okay?'

Exhibiting the kind of gravity normally reserved for the Grand Jury,

258

or presidential inaugurations, the two Harvard students came to attention and gave their solemn oaths to Alex Goldman.

'Good enough,' he said, shaking each by the hand. 'Good enough.'

Tom opened the door and walked silently into the cold white corridor. He had always wondered what it might be like to go to Harvard, and now he knew. It was high school with good shoes and a historic view. Goldman followed him along the hall, and down the stairs.

'Seemed like a couple of polite young fellows,' he said.

'Yes, they did.'

'Bright, too.'

'Bright, they always are. Did you know that Ralph Waldo Emerson and Henry David Thoreau were once residents of this dormitory?'

'No.' Goldman stopped and looked at the staircase beneath his feet, as if some physical trace of their poetic presence might still remain. 'You know, I always did like Thoreau. And now that I've seen where he lived at Harvard, I can understand why he wanted to go and live by himself in a log cabin at Walden Pond. I wouldn't much like the idea of sharing a room with you, Paladin. Or anyone else for that matter.'

Outside Hollis Hall, they walked across the quadrangle to the steps of University Hall where, next to the statue of John Harvard, they mounted the steps and turned to face the building whence they had come. For a minute or two both men stood in silence, their eyes fixed on the lights that shone from room fifteen, unhindered by tree branch or lamp-post. Finally, Goldman glanced up at Tom and said, 'So what do you think of their room, Paladin?'

Tom's nod was full of shrewd deliberation. 'Perfect,' he said. 'You couldn't get a more perfect position for a shot than that. Not if you were Alfred Hitchcock himself.'

19

Manhattan Walks

After the word went out about Pavlick's Model TNT, Palm Beach was wrapped as tight as Lariat, Texas. The Secret Service doubled the detail on La Guerida and almost everywhere else Senator Kennedy was likely to go – at least those places he was supposed to go. Agents who had never seen the inside of a Catholic church overcame three centuries' worth of conservative American protestantism and learned that the Scarlet Woman played no part in a mass, not even one attended by Mattress Jack. The golf course at the country club never saw so many good walks spoiled by so many men in sober suits. And not one, but three coastguard cutters went sharkspotting off La Guerida's private beach. Despite getting himself arrested for loitering close to 1095 North Ocean Boulevard, first thing on Monday morning, no one was more relieved to see this general improvement in Senator Kennedy's security than Mothballs. It meant that Nimmo could take Mothballs and Sunshine out of commission, and let them get back to more obviously felonious activities.

Friday, 16 December, the day Pavlick was finally picked up – he told newsmen he wanted to take Mr Kennedy's life because of 'the underhanded way he was elected. Kennedy money bought the White House and the presidency. I had the crazy idea I wanted to stop

Kennedy from being President' – Jimmy Nimmo flew to New York, with a few crazy ideas of his own. Friday, 16 December 1960 was not a good day to fly into New York, however. Two inbound planes – a United Air Lines DC-8 from Chicago and a Trans World Super Constellation out of Columbus, Ohio – collided over New York City harbour, killing 127 passengers and crewmen. The DC-8 jet crash-landed in Brooklyn, killing five people on the ground; the Super Constellation crashed on Staten Island, eleven miles to the southwest. It was only the next day, when Nimmo saw the report in the *New York Times*, that he realised his own plane had been airborne over New York at around the same time.

Despite the accident, and the cold, and the early snow that lay thick on the streets of Manhattan, and the certainty that he would probably have to spend Christmas alone, he gave thanks that he was back in New York. Instead of a beach with neighbourhoods, he was in a real city. It was the biggest city in the world, a great ship of living stone, but Nimmo, whose positive thinking owed nothing to the best-selling book by the Reverend Norman Vincent Peale, was confident – nay, he had faith, not in the God of Abraham and Isaac and Oral Roberts, but in himself – that if he could find Tom Jefferson anywhere it would be in little old New York. According to his schedule, Kennedy would leave Palm Beach on 2 January, and fly to New York where, apart from brief trips to Washington and Boston, he would spend the first two weeks of January. The inauguration of John F. Kennedy as thirty-fifth President of the United States was now just thirty-four days away. Time was not just running out, it was hitching a ride in a fast car.

New York is all the cities. The opinion city. The style city. The financial city. The radio city. The TV city. The cultural city. The immigrant's city. If, post-Copernicus, the geocentrist view could persist anywhere in the enlightened face of heliocentrism, it would be in cynosural New York, the dog's tail containing the North Star that is Manhattan Island. The wonder is that New York had to fight hard to persuade the United Nations to make its headquarters there. Paris may be more beautiful, but it lacks impact. London may be larger, but it fails to overwhelm. Rome may be eternal, but it does not thrill. But

New York is its own model, the supreme expression of all that is good and bad in contemporary civilisation, whatever that is. The city is an extraordinary achievement, and although there is nothing pedestrian about New York, in the pejorative sense of that word, nevertheless the pedestrian is king. One need not be mounted on Pegasus, either to appreciate its architectural treasures, or to travel down its magnificent avenues or across its ornamented streets. All sorts of native Gothamites go walking in New York: bankers, lawyers, publishers, librarians, store assistants, waiters.

And cops. No one knows more about walking the streets of New York City than a cop. Five years before, as the Special Agent in Charge of the FBI's New York office, on 3rd Avenue at 69th Street, Jimmy Nimmo had walked a lot in Manhattan. He reckoned he knew the Upper East Side as well as he knew the guy he saw every morning in his shaving mirror. And, even in winter, with side streets banked high with dirty levees of gritty grey snow, Nimmo knew that the best way to find someone in a city as large as New York was to get on his dogs. Only first he needed to be dressed for something colder than a box of Florida fruit preserves.

He went to Macy's overcoat sale in Herald Square and walked out of the place street smart for only eighty dollars: a British woollen overcoat for sixty bucks, a pair of Hahn Ripple shoes for thirteen bucks, and pigskin gloves with stretch sidewalls for seven. And of course he wore his hat. In New York, going without a hat in winter was like the joke people used to tell about Harry Truman: 'Would you like a Truman beer? You know, the one with no head.' To err was Truman, but not wearing a hat during a New York winter was plain stupid.

Nimmo stayed at the Shelburne, on Lexington, because he had stayed there before, and because it was close to the New York Public Library, where he would frequently begin or, sometimes, end his daily search of Tom Jefferson's alleged haunts. Indeed sometimes he thought that it was a little like looking for the ghost of a man who had never existed, when you didn't even believe in ghosts. The hotel was not particularly luxurious, although quite comfortable for Nimmo's bachelor needs, being an above-average mid-town choice of interim lodging for newly relocated executives. Despite its proximity to the

United Nations, however, the Shelburne did seem an unusual choice of lodging, interim or otherwise, for UN Secretary-General Dag Hammarskjöld to have made for the Cuban delegation back in September. Soon after he arrived, Nimmo made a joke about Fidel Castro to Mr Spatz, the hotel manager, who said that the hotel would burn in flames before he ever took another Cuban guest again, whatever his politics.

Prometheus bringing fire to man was the story contained in just one of the many murals that were to be found on the ceiling and walls of the New York Public Library. Built of marble in the beaux arts style, and around two inner courts with an immense reading room occupying a half-acre of floor space, the library opened from Tuesday to Saturday, and from ten or eleven o'clock until six or seven thirty. Thomas Jefferson's own handwritten copy of the Declaration of Independence was among the treasures that could be seen in the library, although Nimmo thought it unlikely that Jefferson's homicidal namesake would be influenced to go there by something as cute as that. Colt Maurensig's asseveration that Jefferson went to the NYPL to research the backgrounds and probable praxis of his more important targets looked a much safer bet.

Nimmo himself had once been a frequent visitor to the library, especially in summers when a walk of twenty-seven blocks had seemed less of an effort than it did now. The FBI HQ on 3rd had a library, of sorts, but nothing to compare with the resources that were to be found in John Jacob Astor's building. Hoover, it was said, was impervious to all kinds of culture, and his favourite reading matter was *Reader's Digest*. But Nimmo appreciated libraries, and this one, with its atmosphere of scholarly calm in the huge, high-ceilinged reading room, above all others. He thought it just the place that a man like Tom Jefferson would use as his intellectual base of operations, since by now he had formed a better idea of the man's character. For as well as Rosselli and Sorges, Nimmo had spoken to Orlando Bosch, Irving Davidson, and Moe Dalitz. He had even spoken to another contract killer named Lucien Sarti with whom Tom Jefferson had performed a contract in Houston, the previous year.

In 1959, 1,094 people were murdered in Texas, twice as many as New York, which has seven million more people, with Houston narrowly outstripping Dallas as the state murder capital. Whichever way you look at it, Texas is not a state to have someone bear you a grudge, or even displeasure, as the much-spat-upon Mr and Mrs Lyndon B. Johnson could no doubt testify. Local gun law being what it is, and lenient Texan juries (unless, of course, you are coloured) being what they are, Texans are mostly inclined to shoot you themselves. A man's gotta do what a man's gotta do, runs the single entry in *Webster's Familiar Texan Quotations*. But on this particular occasion, Houston's second-largest oil shipper wanted Houston's largest oil shipper permanently out of the port and, as is the way in this rich state, was prepared to pay handsomely for it.

'This fellow was so determined, he paid double to have not one, but two sharpshooters, to make absolutely sure,' Sarti, a Corsican-born killer, had explained to Nimmo and Licio Montini. 'Jefferson, he planned how we do it. To catch our target in a crossfire, I would be on top of the Rice Hotel, while Jefferson, he is on top of the Gulf Building. Pffft. It was simple. We shot the guy right on Main Street, as they say in the cowboy films. I got him in the throat, and Jefferson hit him in the back of the head. We were in Houston for only a couple of days. Less than thirty-six hours. I would not say I got to know him very well, except to say that he is an excellent shot. The best I have seen. And that he is a quiet man. He liked to read, always reading, and to play golf, he said. He liked to play *boules*, also. The American *boules*, you know? One other thing. He was a late bird. Not sleeping very much. You might almost say nocturnal, like a bat.'

There were twenty-eight bowling alleys in Manhattan, and most of them were open twenty-four hours a day. Nimmo could see no point in visiting them all, so what he did was to try and construct a little probability theorem he hoped that in time he could prove. It worked like this: Chez Joie, the topless joint on Maurensig's list, was at 3740 Broadway, and the Prelude was at 3219. Close to these spots were three bowling alleys: Pinewood Lanes, on the corner of West 125th Street; Harlem Lanes, which was a little further along 125th near Seventh; and Lenox Lanes, which was up on 146th. Detective work! A dark, inscrutable workmanship that reconciles discordant elements, and makes them cling together in one society Imagination! Insight!

Amplitude of mind! Reason in her most exalted mood! Gut feel! Hunch!

In the two weeks up to New Year, Nimmo got into an investigative routine he was certain would yield a result. Perseverance was an essential quality in a detective, as were obstinacy and fixity of purpose. They were the very same characteristics that helped him to ignore Christmas and, as a corollary of that joyful season, his complete and utter loneliness. Not that he saw it that way at all. He knew the difference between solitude and separation, and convinced himself that he was armed with solitude's self-sufficing power. He was like Moses gone up into the mountain, Christ sent by himself into the wilderness, or Luther fasting to draw nearer to his God.

Which was why he avoided calling those few old friends he still had in the city, and stayed away from his former favourite bars and restaurants: P.J. Bernstein's Delicatessen on 3rd near 71st, the Café Hindenburg on East 86th, and the Red Hackle on 2nd near 88th. He even stayed away from the Luxor Baths on West 46th, figuring that the more he denied himself, the more focused he would be on tracking down Tom Jefferson, and the sooner he could get back to his normal life. That was what he told himself. And that was what he came to believe. He forgot that he had taken the job from Sam Giancana, not just because of the money, but to give his normal life some meaning. Walking the streets at night, looking for someone who may or may not have been there, passing the time, talking to himself, or to the four walls of his hotel room, alone with his thoughts, exchanging a few words here and there with total strangers – this was his life, and it was no more normal than the Flying Dutchman's.

Every day he would drop into the library and wander around the main reading room and the periodicals room. Sometimes he would sit there and read a book, or a newspaper, or a magazine, but, as in an art gallery, he was always more interested in the people around him, their studious, bookish faces themselves a whole Frick of portraits by Gainsborough, Reynolds, Titian, Holbein, Rembrandt, and El Greco. But a crowd is not company, and at noon Nimmo would head out of the library to one or other of the two lunchtime addresses on Maurensig's list. This was no great hardship. Liborio on 8th Avenue, between 52nd and 53rd, was an excellent Spanish restaurant. Le

Vouvray, on East 55th, was an equally good French restaurant, but with the added attraction of a shapely proprietor, Yvette, who was soon welcoming Nimmo as if he had been one of her long-standing customers. After lunch, Nimmo would head back to the hotel for a short nap.

Around five o'clock he would return to the library for an hour, or less. At six o'clock he would walk up to West 51st and La Barraca, drink a couple of very dry Martinis, and listen to a pretty good Flamenco guitarist they had playing there, a guy by the name of Arnaldo Sevilla. Sometimes, he even stayed for dinner, but never if he had been to Liborio that day. You could have too much of a good thing when it was *paella* or *arroz con pollo*. On Liborio days, he would leave La Barraca and walk down to Basin Street East on 48th, and have dinner there. The food was Chinese and not so good, but the jazz was first rate, and he saw Johnnie Ray, George Shearing, and Quincy Jones, but never Tom Jefferson. Nimmo's thoughts on leaving the Basin Street East were always the same: if Jefferson really was a jazz fan, then how could he miss hearing the Prince of Wails do 'Cry'? Maybe Johnnie Ray was a faggot and a junkie, but he could still sing the pants off anyone but Sinatra. Or the nigger covering Ray Charles and Count Basie? The blind limey he'd never heard of, but he was good, too.

Around ten to ten thirty he would catch a cab up Broadway, and try the Prelude, or Chez Joie. Naturally he preferred Chez Joie because there was more to look at, such as the half-dressed waitresses, especially the one with the forty-four-inch bust who looked like a Vargas drawing. The place was run by one Joie Dee, a snub-nosed, gap-toothed, lascivious blonde beauty of indeterminate age, who wore only a little more than the girls who worked for her, and who much appreciated the way Nimmo handled his money in her club, which was none too carefully. Upstairs in the Chez Joie was a Gay Nineties bar, where the girls wore next to nothing at all, and were not too bothered where or on whom they sat. You could only get upstairs with Joie's blessing, which the free-spending Nimmo soon had, and with holy oil. There was no minimum cover charge, but Nimmo always bought champagne for Joie and the girls, and never looked too closely at his check. He hoped that one night Joie would like him well enough to take a look at the picture of Tom Jefferson he carried in his wallet.

Chez Joie closed around one thirty a.m. A few times he took one of the B-girls bowling, or, if she was hungry, to La Luna restaurant, on the corner of 140th and Broadway, where you could eat a beef dinner until five a.m., or on to the Prelude, which was open until four, and did a pretty good burger plate for a dollar twenty-five. A couple of nights before Christmas he even persuaded one of the girls, a big, tall, kraut-looking blonde named Lisa, to spend the night with him, but the night ended none too satisfactorily when he caught her taking a twenty from his coat pocket, which was on top of the twenty he had given her already. Any other time he might have slapped her in the mouth and kicked her fabulous ass out on the street, but it was the season of goodwill to all men, and women – even Nazi-faced B-girls who dipped your pocket. So he let it go with just a slap in the mouth.

Lenox Lanes on West 146th, near Lenox Avenue, never closed. There were thirty-four lanes, all wood, with a bar and a luncheonette. It was fifty-five cents a line, and fifty cents for shoe rental. The house balls were the latest thing, being plastic instead of rubber, and the pins, also plastic, flew, but not normally into each other, and Nimmo had lots of tens. Some nights the floor was a mess, but he usually played after a league, and he knew the guy that ran the place, Quinton Hindrew, was trying. Nimmo figured that Jefferson would almost certainly prefer Lenox Lanes to Harlem Lanes, where there were papers in the settee area, old league standing-sheets, sticky tables, and dirty toilets; or Pinewood Lanes, where the pins were old and did not have much left on them, so that he only ever had a few light hits that carried.

Nimmo was not much of a bowler, but his ex-wife, Hannah, had been a real anchor. When they had still been living together in the Bronx, on Aqueduct Avenue, close to where she worked as a midwife at University Heights Hospital, they used to take a bus across the Harlem River and go bowling at a bowl on Dyckman Street. Hannah could bowl a straight line like the ball was on rails. The Christmas Eve he went to the Dyckman Bowlway was also the night he went to see his old neighbourhood and his old apartment building – a sentimental journey that left him feeling hollower than a dugout canoe in a dried-up riverbed.

Nimmo never saw Tom Jefferson at any of the places he visited. A couple of times he went to the Kennedy family addresses on Park and Madison, and spoke to the guys from the Gambino family crew who were watching the front doors from parked cars, reminding them that Jack Kennedy was due to arrive in New York on 2 January, and to keep on their toes. He told them the closer they got to January, the more likely Jefferson was to show up, but some of them didn't look convinced that their obviously tedious assignment was anything other than a waste of time. With Nimmo sitting in the back of their grey Oldsmobile convertible, the two watching the Carlyle on Madison made no secret of their opinion that Jack Kennedy was a *minghia*, which is Sicilian for a prick.

'And not just him,' explained the older of the two men, whose white head, wrinkled brow, and crooked jaw put Nimmo in mind of Moby Dick. His name was Antimo Gelli, and he spoke in a rasping, barking, pungent way that sounded as if at any moment his larynx might throw up a cloud of volcanic ash. 'Him, his smartass brother, his cock-sucking father, the whole fucking family. They're all a bunch of Irish pricks. *Buttiga devilo*, I don't care if someone does shoot that sonofabitch. *Te jura anima futa.* He's no friend to us. Momo's wrong if he thinks you can make deals with these fuckers. You mark my words. These assholes don't play by the same rules as the rest of us. Momo isn't from New York. He didn't have to work with Joe Kennedy. That guy has no fucking honour. You could ask Longy Zwillman, if he was still alive. Longy was one of Kennedy's bootlegging partners in the twenties, until someone ripped off a shipment. Kennedy always figured it was Longy. Only it was some other guy. Anyway, Longy committed suicide last year, because he was facing a subpoena from that Senate Rackets Committee the Kennedy boys were on. Grudge work for their old man. That's what I mean about no honour. *Maronna mia*, I'd kill them myself, cut their fucking throats like chickens, if I thought I could get away with it. You hear me, Nimmo?'

'*E calma, Dio cane*,' the wiseguy's partner had said to him. And then, with an apologetic shrug, to Nimmo, 'I'm sorry. No disrespect to

Momo, you know. But Timo's not in the best of moods, right now. Christmas always gets him this way.'

Nimmo walked away thinking Kennedy was a dead man if his life depended on the likes of Antimo Gelli. But at the same time there was something in what Gelli had said: if the Kennedys were going to use the mob to deliver votes, to raise money, to get Castro, whatever, they were going to have to play by the mob's rules. Only somehow he didn't see that happening.

20

A Liberal Education

On Saturday, 17 December, Chub Farrell took the Red Line train to Boston's South Station, where he caught the nine a.m. express to New York. The journey lasts about four hours and, even in unreserved seats, it provides a comfortable view of the New England countryside which, in winter, is especially beautiful. Like most young men of his age, Chub had never been much interested in countryside and, after reading all about the Brooklyn air crash in the newspaper, was intending to make a start on Baudelaire.

Chub was a polite, courteous young man and he tried hard to respect the privacy of the woman who was seated next to him, a dark, auburn-haired beauty in her mid-thirties, who reminded him of Sophia Loren (August, *Playboy*) and was just about the most stunning woman he had ever seen. He tried not to look at her fabulous, sibilantly stockinged legs which she would keep crossing, nor to notice when she scratched at one of her large breasts. He tried hard to ignore her seductive perfume, and her beautifully manicured finger-nails, and her perfect smile, which was surely just her being pleasant, because women of her age and beauty and obvious sophistication were not supposed to be attracted to young men like Chub Farrell. That kind of thing only ever happened in books and movies. But when she looked at him with her fantastic violet-coloured eyes and smiled her smile of smiles, he felt his young heart skip a beat, and his brain empty of all thoughts that were not fuelled by pure testosterone. To his delighted surprise the woman, whose name was Edith, seemed keen to talk, first about Baudelaire and then about anything at all, and by the time the express reached Mystic, Connecticut, which was about halfway to Grand Central Station, Chub thought he himself was probably halfway to paradise.

Edith told Chub she was Venezuelan, from Dutch Curaçao, that she was the wife of an American oil executive, and that since he was away in the British North Sea, exploring for new oil deposits, this was to be her first Christmas in New York, alone. Edith approached her task with some pleasure. She enjoyed sex, a lot, especially with young men, and since no harm was likely to befall Chub – or Torbert, when the time came for her confederate, Anne, to become involved – she felt, like Alex, that she was doing Chub a favour, giving him the kind of education she thought would matter more than Economics and French.

Having finished her own schooling in Switzerland, French was just one of several languages that she spoke fluently, and, as the train journey progressed to its conclusion, she suggested that she might give Chub French conversation at her Riverside Drive apartment over the Christmas holidays. Chub, who had been expecting and dreading a quiet and thoroughly studious vacation with his parents, accepted with alacrity. He thought French conversation was really all that could and would happen – and, after all, French was his weakest subject – but, even as she extended her invitation, a small part of Chub started to enjoy a lubricious fantasy in which Edith would add some much-needed love lessons to their Christmas curriculum.

In this harmless fantasy, Chub was not disappointed. It took him only a few days to fall hopelessly in love with Edith. A small part of her knew she would break his heart, but since there were, she knew, worse things for a nineteen-year-old boy to suffer, she gave the matter little or no thought. A broken heart is its own education. The first time Edith went to bed with Chub, which was two or three days before Christmas, they had sex several times, after which the young man slept the smug, self-satisfied sleep that is the inevitable corollary of

271

male virginity's loss. While Chub dozed contentedly, Edith borrowed Chub's keys, and gave them to Tom, who was waiting patiently, and without any apparent jealousy, in the next room for her to execute this part of their plan. Tom's lack of feeling was a disappointment to her for, in her own way, and despite knowing almost nothing about who and what he was, Edith was falling in love with him, although she knew he did not love her. But a display of some feeling would have been nice.

From Riverside Drive, Tom took the keys to All Over, a twenty-four-hour locksmith on Lexington, near 80th Street, and had three sets of copies made, returning the originals to Edith in time for her to replace the keys in Chub's pocket, before he left the apartment at around eleven thirty, in time to be home before midnight, as his parents had dictated.

The following day, Goldman, Tom, and Edith met in the Riverside Drive apartment where they admired the short-wave radio Tom had bought to listen in to Secret Service radio traffic when they were in Boston. After that, Goldman flew to Mexico City, to collect some final orders from his KGB controllers before returning to Miami, on Christmas Eve, having supposedly recovered from the bout of cholera that had apparently kept him south of the border.

Edith and Tom spent Christmas Day together, before he too left New York for Cambridge. They exchanged small gifts, enjoyed a delicious Christmas lunch that Edith cooked, went for a walk by the river, watched TV, and then made love. Neither of them mentioned John Kennedy, although, like that nagging Bobby Vee song about a rubber ball, he was always on their minds.

21

Blowback

The CIA had its offices in some twenty-five buildings all over Washington, with most of the departments housed in a sprawl of wartime-built wooden structures on the Foggy Bottom bank of the Potomac, near the Reflecting Pool in front of the Lincoln Memorial. The agency headquarters was the old OSS complex at 2430 E Street, which comprises four brick buildings with Watt Ionic columns, located between the State Department and a roller-skating rink. A little further along E Street was an abandoned gasworks and a brewery, that gave the already damp air a strong malt flavour and a smell like a bad hangover. It would be another ten months before the first CIA employees would move into the new CIA 'campus' across the Potomac, at Langley – a project that was CIA director Allen Dulles's all-consuming interest.

On a cold, blustery morning a couple of days before Christmas, Colonel Sheffield Edwards and Jim O'Connell left the old and run-down naval barracks on Ohio Avenue known as Quarters Eye, where the JMARC 'war room' was headquartered, and walked across the Polo Grounds towards the Reflecting Pool. A stiff westerly breeze, off the tidal basin to their right, bent the cherry trees and Edwards nearly lost his hat. Outside the dingy hut that was simply known as

'K' they collected a dark-blue 1956 Pontiac Start Chief four-door sedan and headed north on to 23rd Street, across Virginia Avenue and Washington Circle. On L Street they made a right, and parked close to Duke Zeibert's Restaurant where, after the meeting in the DD/P, they planned to have lunch.

Richard Bissell's office was on the corner of the building, overlooking L Street, an unadorned, slightly shabby room, with felt-covered pinboard walls, peeling linoleum, a threadbare Aubusson rug, and, around a refectory-style table, a junk-shop of wobbly chairs. On one wall was a large framed photograph of a yacht – a fifty-seven-foot yawl named *The Sea Witch* – which was Bissell's pride and joy, while on an overstuffed set of bookshelves were piles of paper weighted down with an assortment of auto parts.

The owner of the office and his deputy were what was known as 'P Source' – 'P' meaning someone who had been a professor, or who had attended an Ivy League university. Richard Bissell was both. A Yale man, he had spent the war running the Shipping Adjustment Board, planning the comings and goings of American merchant shipping. After that, he had taught for a while at MIT, before being recruited by Averell Harriman to help set up and run the Marshall Plan in 1947. It was 1953 before Bissell finally joined the CIA, since when his rise had been spectacular. A technocrat, rather than a professional spy, Bissell had developed the U-2 programme before being appointed to the DD/P to succeed Frank Wisner as head of the CIA's clandestine service. Tall, about fifty years old, wearing a double-breasted English worsted suit, a Yale tie, large heavy-framed glasses that did not quite seem to fit over his ears, and with a large truffle of a nose, Bissell looked and sounded like a slimmed-down version of Sydney Greenstreet.

Tracy Barnes had gone to the same school – Groton – and university as his boss. They were the same age, but Barnes, noticeably more athletic, was the professional spy. During the war he had joined the OSS and been parachuted into enemy-occupied France, on a mission for which he had won a Silver Star. After practising law, the Korean War saw him back in the service and, following an unsatisfactory time spent with the Psychological Strategy Board, he found himself working for his old school-friend as ADD/PA. A handsome, noble-looking man, with Alpine cheekbones, an eagle nose, and wearing amber-framed spectacles and a Yale bow-tie, Barnes looked like the cleverest Indian on the reservation.

Bissell and Barnes were already seated side by side at the table when Bissell's secretary, Doris, ushered Edwards and O'Connell – about whom it was impossible to say more than that they looked like they had been pressed from the same military mould, like a rifle part, a helmet, or a mess-tin – through the door of the office. Edwards and O'Connell were closely followed by two younger men.

'Sheff, Jim, sit down,' said Bissell, indicating a choice of seats. 'You remember Jim Flannery and John Bross, of course. From the last time?'

Edwards and O'Connell nodded quietly. Flannery, a combat veteran from World War Two, was Special Aide to Bissell, but bore more of a resemblance to Edwards. Bross, on the other hand, who was Bissell's old classmate from Groton and now the DD/P's Planning Officer, was very definitely 'P Source'. Barnes's own secretary, Alice, brought up the rear with a tray of coffee and, after a short exchange of lights for cigarettes, and Georgetown gossip, the meeting commenced in earnest.

Handling a small inhaler which from time to time he would thrust into his nostrils like a tiny rocket, to clear his problematic sinuses, Bissell's patrician, Connecticut tones brought the meeting to order.

'Sheff?' he said. 'For the benefit of John and Jim, why don't you take us through the chain of causation that has caused us to be brought here on this cold and windy morning.'

Edwards nodded, and cleared his throat.

'Yes sir, I will. Back in late October, the thirty-first, to be precise, in the Riviera Hotel in Las Vegas, a maid walks into a hotel suite and finds the room filled with a sophisticated array of sound equipment – tape-recorders, amplifiers, tuners, speakers, and boxes of Soundcraft tape. She starts to dust the furniture, and the tape-recorder, and, inadvertently, switches on the machine's play button. At least that was what she said. Anyway, she hears the sound of a man and a woman talking about how much they love each other. It seems like a very intimate conversation, except for the very obvious fact that it has been recorded by the gentleman whose suite she is cleaning, and whose name, according to the housekeeper's guest list, is Mr Arthur Balletti. The man on the tape's name is Dan. The woman is called Phyllis. Her suspicions aroused, the maid calls hotel security who, suspecting that someone might be trying to defraud the hotel casino in some sophisticated, highly technical way, call Sheriff Lamb's office, and Balletti, a private investigator from Miami, Florida, is subsequently arrested. The charges were a little vague, since wiring another man's room and telephone are not in violation of Nevada state law. But when that man is Dan Rowan, and the woman is Phyllis McGuire, then you can bet your sweet bippy that Sheriff Lamb can be forgiven for arresting Balletti first, and then looking around for some kind of crime with which to charge him.'

Dan Rowan was half of the popular Las Vegas comedy duo Rowan & Martin, and Phyllis McGuire was one third of the even more popular close-harmony trio The McGuire Sisters. In 1952 they successfully auditioned for television's *Arthur Godfrey's Talent Scouts* and a series of hit records soon followed. 'Sincerely', written by Harvey Fuqua and Alan Freed, was their first million seller, in 1955. That stayed at number one for ten weeks. But the song that everyone remembers them for was, of course, 'Sugartime', which had been a big, big hit for the McGuires in 1958.

'Balletti calls Jimmy Cantillon, a Los Angeles attorney, who telephones Johnny Rosselli, who arranges for a local gambler, one T.W. Richardson, to turn up at the sheriff's office and post the thousand-dollar bail. By now, the sheriff has decided to use Balletti's place of origin and the 1934 Federal Communications Act as sufficient reason to dump the whole matter in the lap of the FBI. And that, more or less, is the official version of the Dan Rowan wiretapping affair. The truth is somewhat different.

'Back in 1958, the girls were appearing on *The Phil Silvers Show*, *Red Skelton's Show*, and topping the bill at Las Vegas, which was where Phyllis found herself being introduced by Frank Sinatra to Sam Giancana. To quote a couple of McGuire hits, "It May Sound Silly" but Sam Giancana found his hard old heart going "Ding Dong" whenever he thought of Phyllis. And to do it a third and last time, that "Lonesome Polecat" began to lavish her with expensive gifts: jewellery, furs, cars, a ranch in Vegas, an apartment in Manhattan, a condo in Beverly Hills, extensive stock and bond investments, even picking up the tab for her gambling debts.

'Sam was almost happy. Except for one thing. He was haunted by the suspicion that Phyllis was continuing to see her former lover, Dan Rowan, to whom she remained, in fact, secretly engaged. So Sam called our old friend Bob Maheu, who promised to fix things in Las Vegas, so that Sam Giancana would know for sure if Phyllis and Rowan were still together. He agreed to install some electronic eavesdropping equipment in Dan Rowan's room and to bring Sam the tapes.

'Now this particular pair of star-crossed lovers were both playing the Riviera Hotel in Vegas, which is owned by the Chicago outfit. Nothing happened at the Riviera without the okay from Chicago. But fear of Chicago was just one of the reasons that stopped Maheu from handling the wiretap on Dan Rowan's hotel room himself. Maheu spoke to an ex-FBI man, Edward Dubois, who ran a private detective agency, not in Vegas, which would have made more sense, but in Miami. And for a fee of five thousand dollars, Dubois took the job and dispatched Balletti to Vegas to handle it. Dubois and Balletti were old hands at this kind of wire-work, and they frequently employed Bernie Spindel, who's been something of a pioneer in the field of electronic eavesdropping. During the war Spindel did a lot of work for the OSS. After the war he did a lot of work for Jimmy Hoffa, advising him on how to defend himself against eavesdroppers like the FBI and Bobby Kennedy. Our information was that at first it was just Bobby he was spying on. But then they started to set up fuck recordings involving Jack Kennedy, too.

'Of course, by now, Bob Maheu was also involved with our plot to kill Castro.'

The notion of using the mob as a cutout to kill the Cuban Prime Minister had been Bissell's idea. He and his Assistant Deputy Director of Plans for Action, Tracy Barnes, had brought in Colonel Sheffield Edwards of the CIA's Office of Security to set up the contract. Edwards had contacted his Operations Chief, Jim O'Connell, an ex-FBI counter-intelligence expert, who had worked with Maheu. O'Connell had brought Maheu on board to develop the liaison between Rosselli and Colonel Edwards. These men had supported

Nixon for the presidency, perceiving Kennedy as being too weak ever to get tough with Cuba. Moreover, plans to invade the island, codenamed JMARC, had been drawn up well in advance of the election, and Dulles and Bissell were of the opinion that the then Vice-president Nixon was best qualified to give the plan the presidential go-ahead after preparations were completed. But when Kennedy looked like winning the election, members of the JMARC group began to look for some insurance.

'After Kennedy got the better of Nixon in the first of the television debates,' continued Edwards, 'the necessity for ensuring JMARC continuity started to look much more urgent. We saw Giancana's asking Maheu's help in establishing the loyalty of his girlfriend as an opportunity, not only to put pressure on Giancana finally to sanction Castro's assassination, but also to use the mob as a cutout in putting pressure on Kennedy himself.

'On October thirty-first, it was not Riviera Hotel security that called the sheriff's office, but one of our people. And it was also one of ours who suggested to Sheriff Lamb that he use Balletti's Miami origins and the Federal Communications Act's ban against wiretapping to bring in the FBI, who were themselves already trying, illegally, to bug Giancana in Chicago. The squeeze was almost invisible. We told Giancana we could make anything disappear in the name of national security, even the FBI. It was the same thing we told Bernie Spindel. Help us to get a hand on some of those tapes you have made for your friends Hoffa and Giancana, and we will keep you out of this mess with Dan Rowan you've gotten yourself into. Spindel agreed, and ten days after the Halloween bust, he handed Security Office agents copies of some of the more sensational recordings he had made of Kennedy and a whole series of women.'

The Security Office existed within the CIA's Directorate of Administration which was the largest department, and when most people thought of the CIA – opposing other spy agencies, tapping telephones, organising security clearances for government personnel, handling defectors, and carrying out polygraphic tests – they were usually thinking of the Security Office.

'It was two or three weeks before anyone in the Security Office got around to organising transcripts of the honeymooners' tapes,'

278

explained Edwards. 'And it was another fortnight before we managed to read all the transcripts. Only then did we realise that we had an extra, Ralph-sized problem. I now draw your attention to the transcripts before you. To Kennedy's fuck with one girl in particular. Most girls just fucked the guy. But this little lady wanted to talk. More important, she had questions she wanted answered.'

Bissell took another loud snort from his inhaler and then used the kind of hyperbole that was typical of him.

'All presidents are whores,' he declared. 'They change their policies like panties and sell themselves to whoever will vote for them. The purpose of this meeting, however, is not to determine how much whoring Jack Kennedy has done to get elected, but exactly who he has been whoring with, in his own free time, so to speak. If I may bowdlerise Dorothy Parker, you can lead a whore to the skipper, but she mustn't be a pink. So the question before us is just how much of a pinko the lady is, Colonel Edwards having drawn our attention to the fact that one of the President's ladies, with whom he has been recorded *in flagrante delicto*, evinces a much greater interest in the President-elect's foreign policy than in his very remarkable sexual prowess. In particular, Jack Kennedy's future policy vis à vis Fidel Castro and Cuba.

'Now, if I may generalise for a moment, gentlemen, most people's post-coital small-talk is just a little more routine than that which lies before us. Call me old-fashioned, but I would not expect a B-girl I had just picked up in a Nevada hotel-casino, and who had just pleasured me orally, to sound like Walter Cronkite, viz. page eleven, line six, "Do you think it likely that there will be a US invasion of Cuba within the next twelve months?"; and page fifteen, line twelve, "Why don't you just take Castro out? You know, have him assassinated?"; and page sixteen, line nineteen, "If the Russians marched into West Berlin, would you really press the button? Could you stand to have that on your conscience?"'

Bissell threw the transcript down on the table in front of him and exclaimed, 'And if all that wasn't bad enough, the dumb sonofabitch goes ahead and answers her, too. Sweet Jesus, if only his suspicions were aroused as easily as his goddamned libido.' Bissell snorted loudly. 'Well, Sheff? What's the verdict? Who the hell is she, and is she a goddamned spy?'

Edwards answered Bissell quickly. There were some who thought Bissell a cold-blooded person, but Edwards was not one of them. He knew the DD/P to be a warm and courteous person, whose cool demeanour concealed a personal tragedy: one of Bissell's children, Will, was retarded and had been recently institutionalised. Edwards thought that must have been especially hard for someone as intellectually bright as Richard Bissell. If the DD/P did have some faults they were his impatience, and a tendency to high-handedness.

'Well, sir, her name is Mary Jefferson. Correction, was. Mary Jefferson was found dead just a few days after the election, and although the police were not initially inclined to treat her death as suspicious, it now seems she may actually have been murdered. Until her death, Mary Jefferson was a dedicated Democratic Party campaign worker in Miami, where she lived with her husband, Tom Jefferson. She was half-Chinese, half-coloured, from Jamaica, and, until nineteen fifty-three, she held a British passport. Her maiden name was Swithenbank, and she and Tom Jefferson met in Japan, after his release from a Korean POW camp. She had been working as a hostess in a Tokyo night-club, but prior to that she was doing the same in Hong Kong, and it's possible she was indeed a prostitute.

'I've checked with the British in Jamaica and Hong Kong, and it would seem that prior to her going to Hong Kong, Mary Swithenbank was quite active politically. She was a member of the Jamaican Labour Party and the Bustamante Industrial Trade Union, but there's no evidence that she was ever a communist. The British say they don't know anything about what she was doing while she was in Hong Kong, but our own station chief, John Horton, says that for a while she was the girlfriend of a guy by the name of Hugh Wilberforce, who worked as a secretary to the British Governor of Hong Kong. In fifty-two Wilberforce suddenly resigned from the foreign service, without any explanation. At least none that was made public, and Horton says that he often suspected that the British may have found something in Mary Swithenbank's background which led them to think that Wilberforce had been compromised. Anyway, it was after this that Mary Swithenbank left Hong Kong altogether and went to Tokyo.'

'I'm beginning to smell a rat,' observed Barnes.

'The smell gets worse, I'm afraid,' said Edwards. 'During the war, Tom Jefferson was a highly decorated US Marine sniper. After the war he did the odd job for the Pickle Factory.'

'Sweet Jesus,' muttered Bissell. 'You mean he's one of ours?'

'Not exactly. More of a freelance. In nineteen forty-seven he handled a wet job for General Gehlen's Org in Austria, at our recommendation. In forty-eight he did a job for us in Greece. In forty-nine he did another job for us as part of Operation BGFIEND in Albania. Then there was the Korean War, of course. He saw some pretty distinguished service before being captured. After Korea, we continued to use him. The French had him hit someone in Vietnam, I believe. Then, in nineteen fifty-four he carried out an assassination for us in Uruguay. I'm not exactly sure who that was. Some local commie. But in fifty-seven he assassinated Carlos Armas, the President of Guatemala. By then he was also doing work for the FBI's COINTEL-PRO programme. But mostly, he was working for the mob. There were a couple of hits in Cuba—'

'Wait a minute, Sheff,' said Bissell, whose agile mind had already leapfrogged over the back of Edwards's exposition. 'You're not going to tell me that this Jefferson's the guy that Giancana and Rosselli put up to do the contract on Castro?'

'I'm afraid he is, sir.'

'Sweet Jesus, Sheff.'

'Yes sir,' said Edwards, who had decided not to mention that his own Operations Chief, Jim O'Connell, had met and vetted Tom Jefferson at the Fontainebleu Hotel in Miami, with Maheu and Rosselli. At this particularly delicate stage of his explanation, that one detail seemed a little more than Bissell needed to know.

'And this is the guy who's now quit the contract and disappeared, right Sheff?' asked Jim Flannery.

'That's the way it looks,' Edwards admitted uncomfortably.

'Do you think Tom Jefferson murdered his wife?' asked Bissell.

'The Miami police don't seem to think she was murdered,' said Edwards. 'And that's the way the coroner judged it. He returned a verdict of accidental death. But our friends in TSS will no doubt tell us that there are ways of doing it that won't leave a trace. Jefferson's a professional. My guess is that it is certainly possible he was responsible, sir. But I don't know how. And Rosselli and friends aren't saying. In fact they're not saying anything at all. I think they're a little embarrassed at this turn of events. Rightly concerned about how this will look in our eyes. Just as importantly, I think they're worried how it makes them look in the eyes of their underworld colleagues. I mean, this guy took a hundred thousand dollars from them. That was the kill fee. A part of it, anyway.'

'Let's say he did murder her,' suggested Bissell. 'Did he murder her because he heard the tape, and found out that another guy was screwing her? That other guy just happening to be Kennedy. Or, did he murder her because he heard that tape and maybe thought she was a Russian agent, the same as we did?'

'Her background seems to hint as much,' said Bross. 'There can't be many women in trade unions who decide to become hookers. And then the British thing.'

'More likely it was a combination of both those reasons,' said Barnes, who thought he knew women. 'He was jealous, sure, only I don't think that would be enough of a reason on its own. But if he thought she was a spy, as well.' He shrugged.

'There is another possibility, sir,' said Edwards. 'Suppose Jefferson is a Russian agent himself. Maybe while he was in that Korean POW camp the commies got to work on the guy. And sheep-dipped him.'

'Yeah, like in that book,' said Bross. '*The Manchurian Candidate.*'

'That's a damned good book,' said Bissell.

'Made one of ours into one of theirs,' continued Edwards. 'He wouldn't be the first. Six months they had him. I checked with the one hundred and eleventh MIG in Miami. Apparently Jefferson was one of the very first prisoners to be released. Within just a few weeks of that he married Mary Swithenbank, and brought her back here to the United States. Maybe she was his controller. Maybe she was supposed to be a sleeper. To get herself deep into the political machine.'

'You sure couldn't get deeper than what she was doing with the President of the United States,' remarked Barnes.

'While she sleeps with the odd Democratic Party senator, picking up information, here and there,' said Edwards, 'Tom Jefferson resumes his old trade. He works for us, and for the FBI's anti-communist programme. That must have brought him some good intelligence. Could be that some of the people he killed for us and for the feds were actually people the Russians wanted out of the way themselves.'

'I'll buy that,' said Bissell. 'Wasn't Carlos Armas, the guy we put in power in Guatemala, to replace the commie guy, Jacobo Arbenz?'

'Yes sir,' explained O'Connell. 'The trouble was that Armas was a man of considerable probity. He wanted to get rid of the casinos in Guatemala, and place our man, Ted Lewin, in jail. So we agreed to let the mob kill Armas, and put up someone else to replace him. Miguel Ydigoras Fuentes.'

'If I may continue sir,' said Edwards. 'Suppose that when the communists took over Cuba and we started planning Operation Pluto, Tom Jefferson's masters decide to use him as another dangle, to penetrate American-backed opposition to Castro. He wouldn't be the first one of those we've had, either. Now suppose that he hears the tape—'

'But why would Rosselli be dumb enough to let him hear it?' demanded Bissell.

'Maybe it was a mistake. Maybe Rosselli didn't actually think that it was Tom Jefferson's wife who was on the tape, but Marilyn Monroe. Could be that Rosselli had been bragging about how he had something that was going to give the mob a stranglehold on the White House. And the tapes got switched. Or the Marilyn tape wasn't available. It might be that Tom Jefferson heard that tape and realised that, sooner or later, someone in the Pickle Factory might get to hear that tape, and wonder why Mary Jefferson liked to talk politics instead of pussy. Imagine it. He'd know right away that she had been compromised. And that she had to be silenced before we caught up with her and started asking questions.'

'Why not just take the tape?' asked Barnes.

'Because he knew it was just a copy. Same as ours.'

There was a longish silence.

'Sheff? You've got a whole gutful of supposition there,' said Bissell. 'I'm not saying I don't think there's anything to it. But have you got any evidence to support what you've been talking about?'

'Well sir, I don't have any U-2 overflight reconnaissance photo-graphs from seventy thousand feet above Miami, if that's what you mean,' he said pointedly.

'Touché,' chuckled Bissell. 'But?'

'But I do believe I have some circumstantial evidence to support what I've been talking about.'

Sheffield Edwards paused to light a cigarette and savour the moment. It made a very pleasant change for the P Source to be on the back foot like this, and hanging on to his every word. He knew the kind of jokes they made about the Security Office at their Alibi Club cocktail parties – the how-no-one-in-the-Security-Office-could-read-a-report-without-moving-their-lips kind. Let them think that if they wanted, but so far he had not needed to read anything to get their attention. Maybe it was mostly conjecture, but that was the corner-stone of good intelligence.

'Come on, Sheff,' Bissell said impatiently. 'What I want is facts.' He was quoting Charles Dickens now, not that he thought anyone would notice. 'Teach these boys nothing but facts. Facts alone are wanted in life. Plant nothing else, and root out everything else.'

'Very well sir. It's like this. Just a few days after collecting the AMTHUG contract from Giancana, Jefferson met several members of a WH/4 group in Miami. Cuban exiles who were part of the big Operation Pluto picture. One of them, a guy by the name of Húber Lanz, was murdered the very same day. He was found strangled with a length of wire, in a Miami Beach movie theatre. Now Lanz had worked for G2, until the Cubans worked out that he was on our side, and tried to arrest him. Lanz barely escaped with his life. My guess is that Jefferson recognised him and killed Lanz before he could remember Jefferson and inform the other members of the group. Since then, two other members of the group have been arrested in Cuba. No one knows who betrayed them to G2. One of them is dead, and the other, an American woman, Genevieve Suarez, was sentenced to ten years in prison just a few days ago. How am I doing?'

Bissell nodded. 'I think you're right, Sheff,' he acknowledged. 'We need to speak to this Tom Jefferson.'

'The mob has someone co-ordinating their efforts to find him,' said

Edwards. 'An ex-FBI Miami policeman named James Nimmo. I think they have high expectations of him.'

'And if he finds Jefferson? What are his orders?'

'The mob doesn't like to be crossed, sir,' said O'Connell. 'They'll kill him for sure.'

'That would be a pity,' said Barnes. 'I'm sure Jefferson could tell us a lot.'

'Any ideas, Sheff?'

Edwards looked meaningfully at O'Connell. He said, 'Big Jim?'

O'Connell shifted forward uncomfortably on his creaking chair. Bissell's departmental budget was rumoured to be in the region of a hundred million dollars. It seemed almost absurd that a few hundred dollars of it was not being spent on some new office furniture.

'As you probably know, sir,' he said, 'the Office of Security has a lot of guys who used to work for Hoover.'

'Or were fired by him,' snorted Barnes.

O'Connell smiled thinly. 'I was FBI myself for a quite a while. It so happens that the Miami COINTELPRO is run by an old friend of mine. A SAC by the name of Alex Goldman. Goldman has used Jefferson to do some wet work in the past. Now I'm more or less certain that neither the mob, nor this Jimmy Nimmo guy they've got trying to find Jefferson, know about COINTELPRO, or Goldman. So, I was thinking, maybe I could have a word with Goldman. See if he has any better idea than Nimmo about where we might catch up with Jefferson. Maybe even go after him for us himself. That would help to keep us at arm's length, and make any search for him that we initiate more or less legitimate.'

'Have the feds do our dirty work for us?' Bissell nodded. 'It would certainly avoid any more blowback than we already have here now. I like the sound of that, Jim.'

'Of course, I'll have to offer him something in return.'

A sedulous John Bross said to Bissell, 'Sir, we have some active lines of credit with the Teamsters' bank in Miami. The Miami National. We could use one of those to compensate him.'

'Goldman operates right on the edge of his remit, sir. And he likes to be creative with his operations. Innovative. I was thinking more along the lines of having the Technical Services Staff give him something for Christmas, sir.'

'A toy?' Bissell nodded. 'Good idea, Jim. But let him ask for it. Don't suggest anything. Maybe there's something electronic he wants from Santa Claus. If he's heard of it, then the chances are it's not the family silver.'

O'Connell nodded, and then leaned back in his chair, trying to second-guess what someone as well informed as Alex Goldman would ask for. He thought of some of the things that TSS came up with. Eavesdropping devices, poisoned cigars, handkerchiefs treated with deadly bacteria like the one they had sent to Colonel Mahdawi of Iraq, but which got lost in the mail. Now that using a gunman to kill Castro was more or less defunct, the chances are that it would be down to TSS to come up with a way of assassinating AMTHUG.

Barnes looked at his watch. 'Christmas,' he muttered. 'I haven't bought one damn thing.'

'Me, I'm tired of it already,' said Bross.

'You know it's finally Christmas when you see the Easter eggs in the stores,' laughed Barnes.

Bissell gave a loud snort, like the sound of a heavy table leg being dragged across a wooden floor. 'All storekeepers,' he declared sourly, 'should be hanged.'

A couple of days after Christmas, Jim O'Connell was collected from Miami Airport by Ted Shackley, the Miami station chief who was running the local JMARC programme. Bissell had telephoned Shackley from Washington and told him to put O'Connell in touch with Alex Goldman.

'That's easy enough,' said Shackley, driving O'Connell to the FBI building on Biscayne Boulevard. 'Normally Goldman's a little more difficult to track down, but I believe he's been ill.'

'You sound like you know him,' observed O'Connell.

Shackley shrugged. 'Enough to know that Goldman's behind most of the red baiting and subterfuge that goes on in this town. I think he must have invented the concept of the *agent provocateur*. That guy would use his own grandmother to screw the communists. If I can give you some advice? Watch your step with him. Guy's a real slim customer, you know? Anyway, he is expecting you. Be sure to let me know if there's anything else I can do for you while you're in Miami. I wouldn't want the Barons to think that we didn't know how to run things down here.'

The FBI building was just north of the Julia Tuttle Causeway, and Goldman's office was on the fourth floor, overlooking a Biscayne Bay that was as blue as the blue on the CIA roundel. It was an otherwise unremarkable room with a desk that was handsomely set up for smoking: a leather pipe rack with a series of Kaywoodie matched-grain pipes lay between a miniature ship's binnacle made of heavy brass, which held cigarettes, and a removable lighter, and a crystal ashtray that was as big as a car hubcap. There were two books on the otherwise empty shelves – *The Intellectuals* by George B. de Huszar, and Harry and Bonara Overstreet's *What We Must Know about Communism* – and an eight-hundred-dollar Bolex Rex cine camera that O'Connell, a keen amateur movie-maker, greatly coveted. The Bolex had everything: auto-threading, tri-turret lens system with corresponding telescopic viewfinders, a built-in exposure meter can lap dissolve, and, best of all, a fantastic Pan Cinor zoom lens.

Goldman was thinner than O'Connell remembered, which also made him seem taller. And his normally robust New Orleans voice, which always made him sound like Burl Ives playing Big Daddy, had been reduced almost to a near whisper, as if it had been boiled off in a saucepan. He was recovering from a heavy cold, only the story he had given out at the FBI, in order to account for his several absences from the office, was rather less prosaic.

'I've had cholera,' he explained, in response to O'Connell's polite enquiry after his health, and after they had exhausted the compliments of the season. 'Just a mild dose, but a mild dose is bad enough. Picked it up when I was down in Mexico City. The whole of Central America's lousy with it. Taken me over a month to recover. You ever had cholera, Big Jim?'

O'Connell recalled a dose of *turista* he had had in Guatemala which had seemed bad enough to warrant being called something more serious than plain diarrhoea, and said, 'I don't think so.'

'Oh, you'd know if you had. It's the stomach cramps that really fuck with you. And the stink of yourself. Until you have cholera you never know what bad company you can be.'

'So, how are you now?'

'Not too bad, I guess. So what can I do for the CIA?'

'Tom and Mary Jefferson. I was wondering if you could tell us anything about them.'

'She's dead, I can tell you that right away.'

'That much we know. We would very much like to speak to him, now. As a matter of some urgency.'

'We're off the record here, right?'

'Record?' O'Connell smirked. 'What the hell's that? What with Eisenhower's committee to keep the CIA under policy control, we're not much interested in paperwork at the Security Office.' O'Connell glanced over the empty bookshelves, and smiled wryly. 'I can see you have the same free-thinking attitude as we do.'

Goldman lit his pipe and said, 'Keep it all in your head, huh? Damn right. It's the only really secure place I know.' He puffed a nimbus cloud of smoke across the office and, with pipe clenched between his discoloured teeth, like Popeye, leaned back in his chair and stared at the ceiling for a moment. Then he said, 'Back in fifty-four, the FBI in Miami received an anonymous letter, most probably from one of Jefferson's neighbours, to the effect that Mrs Jefferson was half-Chinese, and might therefore be communist. I'm pretty sure this was around January of that year, and it was certainly before Joe McCarthy went and let Ed Murrow make an idiot of him on television. I guess maybe he was an idiot, but that's another story. It wasn't exactly the height of the red scare, but the witch hunt was still on, and there were some prominent people who had to be burned. I think it was another few months before Oppenheimer got stripped of his security clearance.

'The letter received here was fairly standard Salem stuff. You know the kind of thing: Mary Jefferson was an atheist, she was a passionate Democrat, she was clever, she thought housing discrimination against coloureds ought to be outlawed, she thought there ought to be state-regulated house insurance, and she wore a lot of red. I guess maybe there'd been some coffee morning at which Mary Jefferson spoke her mind, and wore a red scarf. Seems strange, but even a few years ago, some of those things were enough to arouse the suspicions of ordinary citizens. And this office received hundreds of letters like the one about Mary Jefferson. I think Hoover probably wrote a lot of them himself.

'At that time, it was my job to check out this kind of thing. So I went around to where the Jeffersons lived and met them both. She was a beautiful, clever woman, maybe a little liberal, but no more of a communist than Harry Truman, or Dean Acheson, or you, or me. I remember now. A couple of days after I was there visiting with them, we got another letter from the same source, this time saying that a suspicious character wearing a black hat had been at the Jefferson's house. The letter gave the licence plate of this Rooskie spy character's car, which turned out to be my own. A lot of people thought that was very funny, I can tell you.

'For all that my first inclination was to close the file, instead I decided to keep tabs on her. This was for two reasons, neither of them anything to do with any national security threat that she might have posed. One was that she was gorgeous and I thought, married or not, she might be turned on by me being in the FBI. Faint hope. The second was that I wanted to maintain contact with him. Because by now I had checked him out and was aware of his army past, and how some of what he had done was classified. Over the next few months I got to know him pretty well and found out that he was a highly decorated marksman. He always had plenty of money and, without an obvious source of income other than a private detective agency he ran out of a box number here in Miami, and which didn't seem to have any clients, I began to wonder if he was now working for the CIA.

'So then, nineteen fifty-six. The FBI's counter-intelligence programme, COINTELPRO, is initiated and I'm asked to handle it here in Miami. At first it was just harassment and disruption of people who were considered to be subversives. Ruining careers, bankrupting businesses, planting stories, smearing reputations, fucking with people's lives, all routine intelligence stuff. But then, the following year, we got this secret directive from Constitution Avenue to make things a lot rougher, so I began to look around for guys to help me handle that kind of thing.

'In early fifty-eight, we decided to take out Ernesto Pereira. He was a communist friend of Jacobo Arbenz, the deposed Guatemalan President, who we suspected of trying to raise money to bring down whatever right-wing spic it was you guys had put in there. Tom Jefferson did the job for us right here in Miami.'

O'Connell nodded, but said nothing about how the CIA had employed Jefferson around the same time, to assassinate Carlos Armas, the army colonel who had taken over from Arbenz. This was Goldman's show.

'The following year, he assassinated an Indonesian businessman, a friend of Sukarno's, who was selling narcotics for guns, down in Key West. Since when, he's done a couple other jobs for me, not to mention his having become an excellent source of information. He worked for me down in Mexico City as recently as October, when he took out a Russian by the name of Pavel Zaitsev. Zaitsev worked for the Russian embassy in Washington which, as you know, handles Florida as part of its consular and spying jurisdiction. Zaitsev was in and out of Miami like a fucking pelican. Flying to Cuba a lot. That was okay, we kept an eye on his comings and goings. But when he started meeting up with leftist Chileans from the Popular Action Front in Miami, and in Mexico City, we decided to get rid of him permanently. Tom did that job, too. He's a good man.

'That was when I got sick. Not long afterwards I heard that Mary was dead and that Tom had gone away. He often did that, and I presumed he'd be back when he was over it. Until you showed up, that is. Now that the Security Office of the CIA is visiting with me, I'm not so sure. Look Jim, my cards are on the table. I think it's about time you did the same. What's this all about?'

O'Connell shrugged. 'We think it's possible they were both working for the communists.'

'What? Bullshit. I vetted them myself. She never liked me all that much, but if she was a communist I'll eat my hat. And some of those people he killed. They were communists themselves. How do you work that out?'

'He was in a Korean POW camp. We think it's possible they turned him while he was there. And we both know that killing other communists has never been a problem for the Russians. Look at

Hungary. Recently, there have been a number of betrayals in our local anti-Castro organisation. Cuban agents who got picked up in Havana. It looks very much as though it was Tom Jefferson who betrayed them. Maybe he's G2, maybe he's KGB. We're not sure. That's why we want to find Jefferson and speak with him.'

'Well, I guess he is half-Cuban,' admitted Goldman.

'Yeah, but which half?'

Goldman puffed in silence. 'Is that all you have?' he said pointedly.

'Isn't it enough?'

'Like I said before, Tom was a pretty good informant, too. He told me about this Castro hit you have planned with Rosselli.'

'He told you that, did he? Do you think he told anyone else?'

'Come on, Jim, you're really not telling me very much. If I am going to help, I'll need a little fuckin' more than we think that it's possible, and maybe.'

'Okay. The mob has put a guy on Tom Jefferson's tail. A local cop by the name of Jimmy Nimmo.'

'The assistant police superintendent?'

'You know him?'

'Not personally. But I've heard of him. He used to be a fed, didn't he? Just like you.'

'Not like me. He was New York SAC for a while. Pretty damn good agent until he got drunk and hit someone. During the war, he ran an operation with Lansky and Luciano, which is how he's connected down here. Probably always was. The mob has pulled out all the stops on the organ to help him find Jefferson. And when he does I don't think he's planning to buy Jefferson lunch. You see, Rosselli and co., they're taking this thing very personally. They wanted to fix the problem before we found out that they had one. Not to mention the fact that your pal disappeared with a hundred grand of their money. So, now we do know about it, we'd like to catch up with Jefferson before this Nimmo guy does. Maybe even use him ourselves. Turn him back.'

'Why not just speak to Johnny Rosselli and have him call off his dog?'

'There's no point in doing that if he's on Jefferson's scent. By all accounts Jefferson's not so easy to find. Nimmo may actually be the best chance we have of finding him ourselves. Unless you have any bright ideas, Alex. That's really why I'm here.'

Goldman inspected his pipe and went over to the window. 'Where's Nimmo now?'

'That's about the only thing we do know. A month ago he told his office he needed to take some personal leave. Then, about ten days before Christmas, they heard that he had to go to New York. And that if they needed to get in touch with him, he would be staying at the Shelburne Hotel.'

Goldman turned and leaned on the sill. 'I guess he's on the scent, all right. Tom used to go to New York a lot. He had a safe house somewhere.' Goldman sighed as he tried to remember. 'I'm not exactly sure where, though. Was it the Upper West Side, or the Upper East Side? My brain's like shit since this fucking cholera. But I reckon it'll come to me. I'll call when I do remember.'

'Do you think he still trusts you?'

'Why shouldn't he?'

'Then we were thinking that maybe you were the one to bring him in.'

'For you guys?' Goldman laughed and, returning to his desk, knocked out the pipe in the crystal ashtray. For a moment it hummed like a bell. 'Hey, I'm only just back on my feet, you know. Until just a few days ago, my throat led straight into my asshole. You want me to go to New York for you, and find Jefferson before Nimmo does?'

'If that's where he is.'

'I reckon it is. Tom always did like New York.'

'ASAP.'

'What's the all-fired hurry?'

'I'm not sure I understand your question, Alex.'

'The mob is pulling out all the stops, you said. Now you guys. So he's got a hundred grand. So he's fucked up your plan to kill Castro. You are telling me everything, aren't you?'

'Unless he's planning to kill Santa Claus, that's really it, Alex. If there's any urgency on our part, it's because we don't like Russian spies running around the country, maybe finding out things they shouldn't. I can only imagine Rosselli feels much the same way. He may be a mobster, but he's a patriotic kind of guy.'

'What's my deal?'

'Your expenses.'

'Natch.'

'Signed without scrutiny.'

Goldman made a face. 'For pulling your nuts out of the fire? Goes without saying.'

'He was your agent, Alex. I'd have thought you'd be quite glad to avoid any potential embarrassment.'

'There might be some heat on me, it's true. But nothing I can't handle. If his cover did include killing commie scumbags, then I'd say I was pretty much in the clear, Jim.'

'Okay,' shrugged O'Connell. 'Name your price.'

Goldman grinned. 'Now you're talking, Big Jim. You know, this is a pretty weird town. We've got all kinds of Cuban scum, commies, looney tunes, niggers, homo fucking sexuals – this town is lousy with fags, Jim – goddamned radicals, you name it. I'm supposed to fuck them around with not much more than my imagination, and lately that's been getting just a little tired. I need some new ways of provoking some of these mothers. They need to be encouraged a little before you can nail their asses. Their violent, irrational, embarrassing, and crazy ways need a little enhancement, so that the proper action can be taken against them. Anyway, I've been hearing this rumour that some of the mad scientists who work in your TSS Chemical Division have come up with this mind-control drug. I don't know what it's called. MKULTRA is all I know. But I was hoping you could get me some supply. It would sure make a change from anonymous letters and telephone wiretaps.'

'That stuff can send you nuts,' objected O'Connell.

'Then it sounds like exactly the sort of juice I'm looking for, Big Jim. Something to radicalise the radicals, and agitate the agitators. Just the thing to make 'em do something that'll put them in jail where they belong.'

'I'll have to clear it with Bissell,' said O'Connell. 'He's kind of interested in that MKULTRA shit. Anything scientific or technological, he's hot for. Now that your friend Jefferson has let us all down with the plan to hit Castro, Bissell's got all sorts of weird ideas about how to fix the Big Barbudo without risking security. MKULTRA's just one of them.' O'Connell shrugged. 'Hell, I don't see why not. Matter of fact, that might work out rather well, that is if you are going to New York. One of the places they've been testing the stuff is in a cathouse in Greenwich Village. The hookers give the stuff to their johns, and our guys film the results through a two-way mirror. I'm told it's turning into quite a home movie.'

Goldman nodded. 'One more thing. Suppose I do catch up with Tom Jefferson. And suppose I do persuade him to speak to you guys. What then?'

'Our New York station will give you any assistance you need, Alex.'

'What about Jimmy Nimmo? Suppose he doesn't care to be pushed out of the picture? Chances are he's on a fat finder's fee from Rosselli. I don't think he'll just calmly walk away from that, do you?'

'If he gets in your way, then deal with him. Use your own discretion. Take a management decision.'

'He's a cop, Big Jim.'

'He's a bent cop. If necessary, New York station will help you to dispose of the situation.'

Goldman nodded and said, 'New Year in New York, eh? It'll sure beat Christmas Eve on the toilet.'

22

On the Trail of the Assassins

As soon as Jim O'Connell, from the Security Division of the CIA, left FBI headquarters in Miami, Alex Goldman went home and called Tom Jefferson in Cambridge. He told Tom about how Giancana and Rosselli had contracted a Miami cop who was ex-FBI to try to find him and kill him, and how the CIA had, it seemed, finally woken up to what Mary Jefferson's purpose had been when she went to bed with Jack Kennedy.

'I'm not sure they know exactly how many times he fucked her, but either way, since she's now dead, it means they're kind of anxious to speak to you, Paladin. Because the fact is they still don't know shit. They seem to think that I might be able to help them to find you, before Nimmo does it for the mob, on account of the COINTELPRO work you've done for me in the past, and to bring you in for the CIA. Since Nimmo's currently in New York, I believe, then it's even possible that he may actually be on your trail.'

'What trail?' asked Tom. 'I've been careful. There's no way he could have trailed me here.'

'Yeah, well, they must know something. The mob is real good at finding people. I'm flying to New York tonight to try and find out exactly how much he knows. The good news is that the CIA don't seem to mind if Nimmo gets taken out of the way for good. They really don't want any harm to come to you. Now, isn't that comforting? Like I say, I'll try to find out what he knows, if anything, and then kill him.'

'If you do that, won't the CIA figure you know where I am after all?'

'Not necessarily. I'll probably tell them that I met Nimmo, who told me that you were already dead. That he'd killed you. After all, that's what he's supposed to do. Giancana's kind of pissed at you, taking his money like that. Rosselli, too. Pissed and embarrassed. They don't want anything upsetting their thing with the CIA, because the CIA's going to get them off the hook with the FBI, and McLellan. That's what they believe, anyway. Besides, I'm not actually going to put a gun to Nimmo's head. Nothing so crude. I leave that kind of thing to you, Paladin. No sir, Mister Nimmo is going to have an accident. I'll simply tell O'Connell that I was supposed to meet him somewhere, but that he never showed up. The way I'll pitch it, things will sound like maybe the mob killed him because he was getting greedy. That he wanted a lot of money to keep his mouth shut about Castro, and stuff. They're real paranoid about that, let me tell you.

'So Paladin, you just relax and leave everything to your Uncle Alex. Let me do my job. If this guy Nimmo was really on your case, he'd be in Boston, right? Anyway, none of this shit will matter after January nine. You'll be out of the country, spending some of that money you've got saved. People like Giancana, Rosselli, Nimmo, O'Connell, Kennedy, they'll be just a fucking memory to you. You will have earned a well-deserved vacation. Not to mention a lot more money. We both will. So, take it easy and I'll see you on January five. Okay?'

'Yeah, okay. And a Happy New Year to you, too.'

23

Nocturne

After spending his own Christmas Day alone at the Shelburne, Nimmo's lack of success began to seem oppressive. Giancana kept calling to remind Nimmo of what he already knew, which was that Kennedy's arrival in New York was now just a few days away. A lot of the time he stayed out of the hotel to avoid having to tell Giancana about his lack of progress. He decided it was time to show his hand.

At Lenox Lanes he handed Quinton Hindrew the picture of Tom Jefferson and told him that he was a private investigator working for a smart firm of Miami attorneys, who were looking to pay Jefferson a substantial legacy. But even with a free buck in his greasy pocket, Hindrew just shook his head and swore he'd never seen the guy in the picture before, which was enough to make Nimmo think he was lying. He tried the same thing with Joie Dee, but with a sawbuck that was supposed to be for a lot of other things as well. Joie said that Jefferson's was an interesting face, being completely symmetrical, like a Rorschach ink blot, she said, and that it didn't remind her of anything or anyone, but if she did see anyone who looked like him – how much was that legacy? – then maybe she'd tell Nimmo, and out of gratitude Jefferson would marry her, because she could sure use a rich husband. With the accent on use, she laughed.

New York was a very different city at night. But contrary to the popular prejudice, in most parts of the city it was easier to talk to strangers by night than by day. People had more time. The all-night deli owner would stop cleaning his chill cabinet to discuss Kennedy's cabinet choices. Was Bobby really up to the job of being Attorney-General? The twenty-four-hour baker would put down a tray of fresh-baked bagels and tell you why he thought Penn State beat Oregon so overwhelmingly in the Liberty Bowl: Dick Hoak was, and always would be, a better quarterback than Dave Grosz. Even a cop who, irritably spinning his night-stick like a bandleader's baton, might tell you to move on by day, would walk a block with you by night, to show you the 66th IRT subway stop, or simply shoot the breeze: Broadway is not theatre now, it's movie lines.

Nimmo spoke to them all. He knew he was taking a risk that word of his search might reach the invisible ear of Tom Jefferson, and spook him to run for cover. But Nimmo was desperate now. Giancana was right. There was not much time. Kennedy was flying to New York on 2 January. Nimmo was desperate enough even to contemplate going back to Lenox Lanes and maybe beating some information – any information – out of Quinton Hindrew. Besides, he did not think that Jefferson running for cover could make much of a difference. The man could hardly remain more hidden than he was already.

It was a risk he had to take and, fortunately for Quinton Hindrew, it was a risk that, all of a sudden, seemed to pay off. A cab driver outside the Prelude recognised Jefferson from the picture Nimmo showed him, and said that just before Christmas he had taken him from Reid's Barber's Shop on Lenox to an electronics store on Broadway. In Broadway Radio, near 77th, a Mr Lewis looked at Jefferson's picture and said that a guy very like him had come in the day before Christmas, and bought a radio.

'And not just any radio,' Mr Lewis explained. 'A Hallicrafter. That's probably the best short-wave receiver you can buy. It's got a waveband that goes from fifteen-fifty kc to thirty-four mc. With that kind of width you can eavesdrop on just about anything, or anyone, you want. Mind you, this level of sophistication doesn't come cheap. They retail for almost one seventy-five, but I can do you one for a hundred and sixty bucks.' Seeing Nimmo's incredulity that anyone would pay that kind of money for a radio, Mr Lewis added, 'For twenty-five cents I can let you have a record that shows you just how good a radio it is, if you want.'

Nimmo took the record and looked at the sleeve of 'The Amazing World of Short-Wave Listening' narrated by Alex Drier, radio-TV *Man on the Go*: 'Hear these authentic recordings of dramatic events. The President's voice from outer space! Actual capture of a desperate criminal! Radio amateur at Little America! Ships at sea! Aircraft in action!' He handed over his quarter. The record sleeve had told him all he needed to know about why anyone would have bought this kind of radio, but the information seemed worth at least twenty-five cents. Nimmo grinned. His luck really seemed to be changing.

'He had money to spend, that guy. Cash money.'

'Did he say why he was buying it?'

'He said it was a Christmas present, to himself, because he knew his wife was getting him socks and handkerchiefs.'

'Socks and handkerchiefs sounds okay to me,' confessed Nimmo, who knew he would not be getting anything, except a telephone call, and maybe a card, from his daughter. And probably only because he had sent his grandson a Teddy bear from FAO Schwarz.

'Anyway, I said he must have been a good boy this year, if Santa was bringing him something like the Hallicrafter, and he laughed and he said he'd been a very good boy indeed. You ask me, mister, he doesn't need any legacy. He paid cash. New bills, too, from a fold in his back pocket that was as big as a paperback.'

'You know what they say,' remarked Nimmo, having thanked the man for his help. 'To them that have, yea more shall be given.'

Nimmo had something himself now, almost as good as socks and handkerchiefs: the certainty that he was not in New York on some wild goose chase. Tom Jefferson was here. Maybe New York was where he planned to make the hit, after all. It was not much, but having been given this, he was quickly given more. Perhaps it was the good mood this small break had put him in, but that night he ended up in Chez Joie spending even more than was usual. And pleased to see such a display of largesse, Joie Dee was moved to respond in kind.

'Let me see that photograph again,' she said. Joie was wearing a dress of compelling interest, consisting of some thoroughly transparent netting and a few sequins, just to make sure you didn't miss the high points of her voluptuous figure. Nimmo handed it over and let her make a show of pretending to remember the face, although it was obvious that she had known the face all along. 'You know,' she said, 'now I come to see it again, it seems that perhaps I do recall this guy. About two or three times a year, I think he's a regular here for maybe a week to ten days. Then he's gone again. He told me he was some kind of salesman, but he didn't look the type to be going door to door with brushes in his hand, or pushing memos around a desk. And his name wasn't Jefferson, it was Van Buren. Martin Van Buren.'

'Van Buren?' Nimmo frowned. 'Are you sure?'

'I know my American presidents. Hey, the guys who come in here give themselves all kinds of names and claim they're in all sorts of professions. Actors, doctors, movie producers. We get a lot of them. We even get the odd guy who claims he's a private investigator. Anyway, Marty was quiet, polite, well behaved and generous with his money. Just the way I like them. He never said very much. And there was one girl he seemed more fond of than most. Summer McAllum. Summer was a really beautiful girl. He liked to party with her, and only with her. A lot of guys in here used to feel that way about Summer McAllum.'

'Used to?'

'I had to kick her ass out of here. For one thing and then another. It's just possible that's why Marty hasn't been back here. Which is a shame, because he was a good customer. You know, if I was looking to find him, Summer'd be the one I'd want to speak to.'

'Do you know where I can find her?'

'Someone told me, someone I consider to be reliable, that she was working in the lower mid-town area. At the Britania Café. That's on Eighth Avenue and, I think, Twenty-eighth. She's a belly dancer, if you follow my meaning.'

'Oh I do, but what makes that different from what happens here, upstairs?'

'I employ waitresses and hostesses, not street-walkers. All I do is pay them to talk a little and wear less. If they want to arrange a party with a customer, that's their own affair, not mine. Their own money, too. People expect more from a girl on Eighth Avenue. Like maybe twenty per cent.'

300

Nimmo glanced at his watch and saw that it was well past midnight.

Joie said, 'Most of those places are open until four a.m. Tell her I said hello, and she's welcome back here if she's straightened herself out.'

'How do you mean, straight?'

'The kind of straight that doesn't have a spoon on the table and a tie around its arm. But not so as you'd notice. Summer looks like the all-American girl, with big rosy cheeks and everything. And I mean everything. Summer has it all. Six feet tall, with red hair, emerald green eyes, porcelain skin, and more impressive curves than the Taj Mahal. Oh yeah, and she always wears long black gloves and smokes with a long cigarette holder. If all this sounds like Ernie Kovacs on *Take a Good Look*, it's because you'll have to be a little careful with the Q and A down on Eighth. But I guess it's okay to ask around for Summer. Most guys do, weather we've been having.'

For a few blocks on 8th Avenue, Nimmo half expected to see Isabel Bigley, who played the Salvation Army sergeant in *Guys and Dolls*. It was a neighbourhood that cried out for redemption, but not so as anyone would have heard above all the noise. Most of the guys who were around – a lot were sailors ashore for a few nights and a lot of beers – had dolls in mind, although luck had nothing to do with the kind of ladies they expected to find on 8th. And if any of these girls did trust in God it was only because that was what was printed on a dollar bill. The guide books that dared to mention the girls on 8th at all referred to them as belly dancers.

It was not a bad euphemism for what went on. In more automobile-oriented cities such as Dallas or LA, girls with hearts of gold drove cars and were known, less romantically it is argued, as 'mechanised girls'. But like almost everyone else in New York City, the 8th Avenue broads walked, or, to be more accurate, sashayed along the street in an ostentatiously sinuous and lithe manner, as in some bogus biblical epic involving seven veils and a severed head. Thus the terpsichorean reference. Many of the establishments they and their clientele patronised – the Ali Baba, Arabian Nights, Egyptian Gardens, Grecian Palace, Istanbul, Port Said – did present some tenuous Middle Eastern connection, but on the whole there were many more belly dancers than there were shish kebabs and baklava.

With no spectacular redheads on show at the Britania, Nimmo asked around and was directed to an ice-cream parlour called Dial-a-Doll on 9th and 29th, where the *schtick* was a network of telephones connecting all the tables and, therefore, all the guys with all the dolls. Nimmo could tell his luck was changing. A young nymph answering Summer McAllum's description was sitting in the back, wearing a black harem-panelled silk-print dress with cognac-coloured roses, and the trademark long gloves Nimmo figured she probably wore to hide the needle marks on her arms. For all her obvious attractions, Summer looked tired, as if autumn was just around the corner.

Nimmo sat down at an empty table, ordered a coffee and a sundae, and then called Summer on the telephone. A few seconds later she was seated opposite him, smiling a well-polished smile and wielding her cigarette holder with the sophistication of one who might have finished her schooling in Switzerland instead of Hoboken. It was, she breathlessly explained, ten dollars for an hour, or twenty-five dollars for all night, which Nimmo paid, thinking that she was more likely to relax if she assumed she had earned her keep for the evening, and more likely to talk if she was relaxed. Besides, now that he had seen her, he badly wanted to have sex with her.

They jumped in a cab and she told the driver to take them to the village, on the corner of Bleecker and Cornelia. The cab dropped them close to a twenty-four-hour bakery – Zampieri Brothers. The store was closed, but Summer knocked at the side door and, uttering a few words in Italian, received a bag of fresh-baked rolls for ten cents.

'Breakfast,' she explained, leading him up the steps of a federal brownstone.

'Seems like a friendly neighbourhood,' Nimmo small-talked nervously.

'It's the Sargasso Sea as far as I'm concerned,' she remarked, opening the front door and leading him through a dim and creaking corridor that belonged in an old tea-clipper. 'Things may look alive round here, but they're not. It's a biological desert. And me, I'm just another derelict ship, bobbing around, entangled within the mass of floating weeds.'

302

'That's a happy thought,' said Nimmo, following Summer's oxbow curves along the corridor.

'Round here,' she said, with a wry smile, 'Happy's just the name of some canyon in Oregon.'

It was just a little studio apartment that occupied the parlour floor, with a Murphy bed, an ice-cube of a bathroom, and a kitchenette that was the size and colour of an avocado pear. But it was clean and comfortable, with two eight-foot-high windows that overlooked a garden in the back, a TV, and lots of books. When she took off her gloves, he saw the Band-aids on her arms and, seeing his eyes linger there, she volunteered the information that the cat had scratched her.

'You've gotta cat?'

'Not so as you'd notice,' she said, peering out of the window, and then pulling the drapes. 'He comes and he goes, which is pretty much the way it is for all the guys around here.' There was, thought Nimmo, a bitter edge to almost everything she said, but still she kept on smiling as she said it.

'Sorry,' said Nimmo.

'Don't be,' she said, pulling down the Murphy. 'It's the laws of physics. Like gravity or the speed of light. Things are the way they are. There's no other way of looking at the world.' She paused. 'You want something? A drink? Dexamyl, maybe?' Nimmo shook his head. 'Keep you going? Make sure you get your money's worth?'

He kept shaking his head. 'I'll risk it.'

Summer shrugged off her dress and hung it carefully on a hanger, in a closet full of clothes. In a second or two she was naked, and standing close enough for him to smooth her cool bottom like the quarters of a very fine horse.

'You're beautiful,' he said. 'There's sure no other way of looking at that.'

'What?' she said, taking his hand and cupping her sex with it. 'You mean this? Why thank you.'

'And Summer. That's a beautiful name, too. How'd you come by it?'

'The same way as most people. I had parents. But being Summer is sometimes a little tiresome in the winter, you know. Like that Laurel and Hardy film. When they're playing a bass and harmonium combo in the snow? And the tune is "The Good Old Summertime".'

Nimmo grinned. '*Below Zero*,' he said. 'That's a good one. You like Laurel and Hardy?'

'Two men sharing a bed? Sure. It's quite the thing round here.'

He pressed his face close to her belly. 'I couldn't love anyone who didn't like those guys.'

'In the circumstances, I'd say that was fortunate, wouldn't you?'

When it was over, not very long after it had started, and she was lying beside him, she said, 'Did you enjoy that?'

'Very much. Thank you.'

'Just tell me when you want to go again.'

'You must be thinking of some younger guy,' he said. 'I'm more like a play than a movie. It's just the one performance a night, I'm afraid.'

'Not even a matinée?'

'Not even a rehearsal.'

'Told you, you should have had that Dexamyl.'

'But there's one thing you could do,' he said carefully. 'It would make you another twenty-five.'

Summer jerked her head up from Nimmo's vested chest. 'Look mister, with me it's straight sex. No whips, no chains, no enemas.'

'Relax, it's nothing like that.'

'Like what, then?'

'Like some information.'

'You a cop?'

'Hell, no. Private investigator. I'm trying to find a guy.'

'If that's all there is to it, then I must be Nora Charles.'

'You'd sure make a lousy Asta.'

'Twenty-five, huh? Who's the guy?'

'Martin Van Buren.'

'Marty? I haven't seen him in a while. Is he in trouble?'

'No, his parents died in a car crash, and left him some money.'

'Jeez, some guys have all the luck.' Summer sat up and lit a cigarette. 'I'll bet you're on some kind of percentage. Like a recovery fee. So what do you wanna know?'

'Everything there is.'

304

'For five bills? Haven't you heard? Everything costs more these days.'

'Then that would be everything including an address, for maybe a little more.'

'I'm not sure I can write you an envelope with a zip code. But for fifty I could do the next best thing. Take you there. You see, mostly, Marty would come here. I only went to his apartment once.'

'When was this?'

Summer shrugged. 'The summer, sometime. Seems like a long time ago, anyway.'

'And where?'

'Somewhere on Riverside Drive.'

'You're not telling me much, are you? Have you got a cross street, or were you planning to look for footprints?'

But Nimmo was grinning. His chest was tight with excitement, just the way it had been when Summer had taken his finger and put it inside her. This not-so-stupid little street-walker actually seemed to know where Tom Jefferson lived. It was beginning to look as if New Year was going to be a lot better than Christmas.

'It was close by the Ninety-sixth Street viaduct. I'm almost sure I'd recognise the building again.' She finished her cigarette and stubbed it out in a little glass ashtray. 'So? Have we got a deal?'

'Okay, deal. Another fifty on top of the twenty-five I already gave you. Half up front. The rest when you show me the building. That's seventy-five dollars in total.'

'You do have another fifty, don't you, mister?'

Nimmo gave her another five bills from the fold he was carrying.

'Good.' Summer pulled up Nimmo's vest and began to kiss his chest, then his stomach, and, finally, his penis. Looking up for a moment, she said, 'Would you care to make that an even hundred?'

Tree-lined Riverside Drive is one of the city's loveliest and longest streets. Between 72nd Street and Inwood Hill Park, which borders the Harlem River and separates Manhattan from the Bronx, Riverside Drive runs for almost ten miles along the banks of the Hudson. Much of the dignity and elegance that characterised the drive when first it was built has gone, but it still rivals 5th Avenue as one of the most fashionable addresses in town.

Later that morning, Summer McAllum took Nimmo to a spot a little south of the 96th Street viaduct, to West 93rd where, on a slight crest overlooking Riverside Park, stood the Joan of Arc memorial statue.

'She is the reason why I remembered where it was,' explained Summer. 'Joan of Arc. I've always identified with her. On account of the fact that French was always my favourite subject at school. Also, when I was fifteen, I nearly burned to death in a house fire. I used to come here a lot when I was working at Chez Joie. The pedestal underneath the statue contains fragments from Rheims Cathedral, and the Tower at Rouen. They were places in France that were important to Joan.'

Nimmo tried to affect interest in the rather Gothic-looking statue, and the charismatic life it memorialised. But it was bitterly cold. An icy wind blowing off the Hudson River sharpened his desire to finish his search. Hard as he tried to imagine the horror and injustice of it, an enormous pile of burning faggots heaped around a nineteen-year-old virgin could only feel attractive to his freezing fingers and numb nose.

'That's the building, there,' she said, pointing across the drive. 'Number two hundred. I remember now. The apartment was on the tenth floor, I think. Only I don't recall the number. But it had a good view of the Palisades. And that Spry sign, of course.'

Nimmo took hold of Summer's arm and, walking her across the road, and past the large building that was 200 Riverside Drive, he glanced in at the doorman, wondering if Jefferson was living there as the third President of the United States, or the eighth, or something else again. Zachary Taylor, perhaps. But for the fact that Paul Ianucci had checked his identity with various government departments, he might have wondered if Tom Jefferson was a real name at all. He kept walking them north along Riverside Drive, and then east, on to Broadway. In the Adlo Book and Card shop on the corner of 106th, he bought two large envelopes and two copies of the *New Yorker*. He stuffed the magazines into the envelopes, sealed them, and then wrote out two addresses, one in the name of Mr T. Jefferson and the other in the name of Mr M. Van Buren. Then they walked back to 200 Riverside Drive, and went inside the building.

It could, he thought, have been his own grandfather standing there, behind the little redoubt that was the doorman's desk, an impression enhanced by the memory that upon his retirement George Nimmo had been a doorman at the long-forgotten Pabst Hotel, on 42nd Street. This was now the New York Times Tower where, in a matter of a few hours, enormous throngs of revellers would gather to welcome in the New Year.

Nimmo took out his glasses and, with pen poised, made a little pantomime of getting ready to complete the addresses on the two manila envelopes.

'Pardon me,' he said in an effete, Mittel-European accent of the kind that is heard a lot on the Upper West Side, in places like Eclair, an excellent Viennese pastry shop on West 72nd. 'But I cannot remember the right apartment numbers. Could you help me, please? Which number is Mister Jefferson?'

Putting down his cigarette, the small, elderly doorman, whose face was smoked back to the skull, frowned. 'Jefferson? No sir, there's no one of that name here.' For a moment he was distracted by two people exiting the elevator and heading towards the door. He nodded to one of them and smiled.

'Strange,' said Nimmo. 'Well then, what about Mister Van Buren?'

'There's no one of that name either, sir. I'm sorry.'

'Are you quite sure of that?'

The doorman kept on shaking his head. He said, 'I've been the doorman here for eleven years, sir. I know everyone in this building.'

'How very odd,' exclaimed a perplexed-looking Nimmo, and politely handed the doorman both envelopes. 'Tom Jefferson? Martin Van Buren? You see, their names are written here.'

'Not so odd, sir,' said the doorman. 'These are addressed to number two hundred and ten Riverside. This is two hundred.'

'It is?'

'Yes sir.'

'How very stupid of me,' sighed Nimmo. 'I'm very sorry to have wasted your time.'

Outside the door, Nimmo confronted Summer McAllum with Van

Buren's non-existence. 'You wouldn't be trying to take me for a sucker, would you?' he asked.

Summer shook her head. 'I swear, this is the building. I don't remember there being a doorman. But it was late when we came here, after midnight, so it wasn't like he had to use his name, or anything. There wasn't even a night man. I remember we took a self-service elevator up to the tenth floor. And I do remember the statue. And the place he took me for breakfast, in the morning.'

'Breakfast? You didn't mention that before.'

'Rosenblum's on Broadway. I got the impression he went there a lot. They seemed to know him. And that's all I know. Honest. Can I have my fifty bucks now? Please. I'm cold. I'm tired. And I want to go home.'

'What, and miss out on a nutritious breakfast?'

Rosenblum's Kosher Deli on Broadway, near 100th Street, was large and full of people, most of whom were fat and old, which was why they probably remembered someone as young and beautiful as Summer McAllum.

'Nice to see you again,' said the obviously enamoured waiter. 'Miss . . .'

'Goldberg,' she said, without missing a beat. 'This is my boss, Mister Meyer.'

'Nice to meet you, Mister Meyer,' said the waiter, hardly taking his eyes off Summer.

'I told him about this place,' she said spiritedly. 'He's one of those Stage or Carnegie people, you know? But I told him what a friendly place this is. And how good the pastrami is.'

'Your other friend certainly thinks so,' said the waiter.

'Who?'

'Who. The guy you were here with last time. How could I forget? What am I saying? The guy who was here with you, that's who. Franklin Pierce.'

'Oh, Frankie,' gushed Summer. 'Of course. Now I remember. It was him who brought me here, wasn't it? Frankie's the guy I was telling you about, Mister Meyer. How is Frankie? I haven't seen him in ages.'

'He was in here just before Christmas, on his way down to the library, I think.'

'I'm sorry to have missed him. Tell him I said hello.'

After they had ordered breakfast, and when the waiter finally left Summer alone, Nimmo said, 'You missed your vocation, honey. You should work for the FBI. Better still, the CIA. A quick-thinking broad like you would make a swell honey-trap.'

'Ugh,' grimaced Summer. 'I hate honey.' Nimmo got up from his seat. 'Don't take it personally. Where are you going?' she asked.

'I need to make a quick call,' he said, but in the phone booth in the back of the deli, his fingers raced through the phone book until his nail was underlining an F. Pierce at 200 Riverside Drive, Apartment 1010, New York, New York, Telephone RI 9-3359. It was like his numbers had come up. He took out a matchbook and scribbled down the address and telephone number.

'You look happy,' she observed, when he came back.

He sat down and, handing her fifty dollars under the table, said, 'It's going to be a great New Year.'

24

It's a Wonderful Life

Having paid off Summer, Jimmy Nimmo returned to the Shelburne Hotel to take a shower and change his clothes. While he shaved, his mind tried out various permutations of his next course of action. By the time he was in the shower, the possibilities had come down to his entering 200 Riverside Drive after midnight when, according to Summer, the doorman went off duty, and taking the self-service elevator up to the tenth floor, where he would let himself into the apartment of Franklin Pierce and, at gunpoint, have the occupant call Johnny Rosselli on the telephone, before blowing his brains out on the carpet. No one would pay much attention to the sound of a gunshot on New Year's Eve – not even the sensitive folks who lived on Riverside Drive. He even knew where to get hold of Rosselli. The gangster was planning to spend the evening in the Fontainebleu's La Ronde Supper Club, with Sam Levenson, Ben Novack, and Dick Shawn. Nimmo thought it was just possible that with a .38 pressed against his ear, Jefferson might say how and when and where he planned to assassinate Jack Kennedy, although by now Jimmy Nimmo had sufficient respect for the marksman to conclude that he would be doing well if he got through the door to Jefferson's apartment, and shot him dead. With a professional killer such as Tom Jefferson, it was probably best to keep things as simple and straightforward as possible.

And if Jefferson should be out somewhere, celebrating New Year, then so much the better, thought Nimmo: he would wait for him, settle down with a drink, and sap the guy as he came through the door. Then he could tie him up and try a little Q and A. Because whichever way he looked at it, just to know the details of Jefferson's plan would have neatly cauterised the stump of any bleeding doubts that might follow on from Jefferson's amputated life. They were probably the same doubts that might make Giancana forget to be grateful, and maybe inhibit him from paying Nimmo the remainder of his money. Money that was going to buy him a pretty good retirement.

Nimmo came out of the shower and dried himself vigorously. For the first time in a long while Duke Ellington was back in residence inside his head, and there was a big band swing in the way he moved across the room to answer the telephone.

It was the Massachusetts State House in Boston whom Nimmo, posing as a member of the Secret Service Protective Research Section, had telephoned the previous day to enquire about the Board of Overseers that Kennedy was possibly scheduled to visit on 9 January. Kennedy's trip to Boston had seemed almost unimportant beside New York, but he had felt it necessary to explore every possibility. The person with whom he had spoken earlier, a Mrs Hichborn, had adamantly told Nimmo that there was no such thing as a Board of Overseers in the new State House or, for that matter, the Old State House, which was a very different building. There was just the state legislature, formally named the Massachusetts General Court, and the House of Representatives. In her near English accent that reminded Nimmo of Eleanor Roosevelt, Mrs Hichborn explained how she had been racking her brains to solve Agent Nimmo's mystery, and that she had made a special journey into the office on a Saturday morning because she now believed she knew what must have happened.

'I've worked here for seventeen years, Agent Nimmo, and sometimes, like Oliver Wendell Holmes, I tend to think of the Boston State House as the hub of the solar system. So I hope you'll excuse me if I wasn't more obviously helpful when you telephoned yesterday. Last night I thought and I thought, and I said to my husband, "I simply cannot believe that the Secret Service would make something like this up. There must be a Board of Overseers somewhere in Boston." Well, my husband, Allen, works in the Widener Library at Harvard University, and he said that there's a Board of Overseers at Harvard, of course, which is the senior governing board of the university, and which holds a bimonthly meeting in the faculty room of University Hall. Well, of course Senator Kennedy, who's an old Harvard man, is, like three other Harvard men who were President of the United States, a member of that same Board of Overseers. He has been since nineteen fifty-seven when, Allen tells me, he was elected to the board with the largest vote ever obtained by a candidate, getting over seventy per cent of votes cast by Harvard alumni the world over.

'By all accounts, Senator Kennedy takes his administrative obligations very seriously. The next meeting of the Harvard Board of Overseers is ten thirty a.m. on January ninth. If the Senator does come here to the State House – and it's still by no means certain that he will, I might add – it won't be until the late afternoon, possibly around five thirty p.m., when he'll make a speech to the whole two-hundred-and-eighty-member Great and General Court. If he does come, then we'll be very honoured of course, not least because it will be his first formal speech since his election on November eighth.'

When Mrs Hichborn finally stopped talking, and Nimmo had got through thanking her for coming in on a Saturday morning to tell him her news, and apologising for his stupidity in making such an elementary mistake, he got dressed, walked quickly out of the hotel, and more or less ran to the public library, where an assistant helped him to find a reference book on America's universities.

Harvard's Old University Hall, where the Board of Overseers were scheduled to meet, was in Harvard Yard, which comprised two enormous quadrangles of lawns and trees surrounded by various undergraduate dormitories. One look at the photograph of Harvard Yard told Nimmo all he needed to know about where Tom Jefferson was planning to shoot John F. Kennedy. With the front of University Hall overlooked by no fewer than three or four hundred windows, not to mention ten rooftops, and a bell-tower, it would have taken an army of Secret Service agents to have made the Yard safe for the President-elect to walk in. Harvard Yard looked like a sniper's alley, with John F. Kennedy a sitting duck. It was true, there were plenty of tall buildings and windows on Park Avenue, but in New York Kennedy would be out of a building and into a limousine in the blink of a sniper's eye. Not much chance for a shot there. Going back to Harvard University, however, would be like a Roman general accorded a triumph. Surely Kennedy would want to savour the moment. Surely he would want to shake a few hands, maybe even speak to some students. College students were an undisciplined lot even at the best of times. How could the Secret Service ever hope to deal with them? Harvard had to be the place where Jefferson would strike.

'Excuse me, Mister Nimmo?'

Nimmo looked up from the book he was examining and into the face of a largish man, with crew-cut grey hair, and wearing a tan polar-style coat, with a wool-faced lining and hood, and a hefty zip that was open to reveal a three-piece grey-green plaid suit.

'Who wants to know?'

The man doffed his hat and, grinning, shook his head. 'I was waiting in the lobby of your hotel, sir. But when you dashed out, well, I'll tell you, you caught me by surprise, sir. I only just managed to see you duck in here, and then I'm afraid I lost you for a while.' The man took out a little wallet that he opened for Nimmo's inspection. 'My name is Goldman, sir. I'm with the FBI. I was hoping that I might have a quiet word with you, sir.'

'This is as quiet as it gets in New York,' said Nimmo.

Goldman glanced around uncomfortably, affecting disinterest in the book about Harvard that Nimmo held open in his hands. 'Perhaps,' he whispered, 'this is a little too quiet. There is something about a library that doesn't exactly encourage free and frank conversation. Look, what do you say we go across the street and go find ourselves a cup of coffee?'

Nimmo looked at his watch like a man getting ready to time a race. It was eleven thirty, and he had nowhere special to go. But just about the last thing he needed now that he was so close to finding Tom Jefferson was to end up down at the FBI's offices on 3rd and 69th, answering a lot of awkward questions. So he winced and said, 'I'm afraid that I have a lunch appointment.'

'Come on. Please. Look, you used to be in the job. You know how it is. Just a few minutes of your time and then I'll leave you alone.'

'All right,' agreed Nimmo, closing the book. Just a few minutes sounded about right. It couldn't very well be anything too awkward if that was all the time Goldman required of him. Following the burly FBI agent out of the reading room, he added, 'But it would help if I knew what it was about.'

'Sure, sure,' said Goldman, zipping up his polar coat against the last cold day of 1960. 'Let's try Grand Central, shall we?' he suggested, and led the way down and across 42nd Street.

Inside the station they crossed the cavernous main concourse with its zodiac ceiling, and walked away from the three giant windows, towards the first coffee shop they saw. Goldman put a cigarette into his mouth and pointed to an empty table.

'Take a seat. I'll get these,' he said.

A minute or two later he brought the coffees, the cigarette still unlit in the corner of his clumsy-looking mouth like a forgotten thermometer. Goldman placed a cup of coffee carefully in front of Nimmo and then, making a collapsing noise as if he had been on his feet for a long while, sat down opposite. He sipped his coffee gratefully.

'You're a hard man to keep up with, Nimmo.'

'What happened to "sir"?' asked Nimmo.

Goldman grinned. 'You're here now, aren't you? We can cut through all that bullshit and get down to business.'

'I'm all for that happening,' Nimmo said patiently.

'What it's about,' Goldman said, with tantalising cunctation, 'is a whole lot of things, as a matter of fact.' He was searching his many pockets for a light and, deciding that the best way of moving their conversation forwards would be if Goldman could actually begin smoking, Nimmo handed him his book of matches. 'Thanks a lot,' said Goldman, and, having puffed himself into action, he handed back the matchbook, adding, with eyes narrowed against the smoke, and perhaps the impression he had of Nimmo, 'Things must be going all right for you since you left the Bureau, I guess.' He nodded at the matchbook. 'Liborio. Friends in Riverside Drive. Staying at the Shelburne. New coat. Nice gloves. Yes sir, they must be going all right.'

314

'You don't miss much, do you, Agent Goldman?' said Nimmo, carefully replacing the matchbook – the one on which he had written Tom Jefferson's address when breakfasting in Rosenblum's Deli – in his pocket.

'Me?' Goldman grinned good-naturedly. 'Oh hell, I miss my fair share. In our business everyone misses something sometime, don't they? It's an occupational hazard.'

'If you say so. Look, what's this all about?'

'Johnny Rosselli is what. We've been trying to get a handle on that guy for a while now.'

'What makes you think I can help you?'

'You do know him, don't you?'

Nimmo sipped his coffee and found it surprisingly good. 'Sure I know him. It's hard to be in a position of any civic responsibility in Miami and not run across Johnny Rosselli from time to time.'

'How about Rafael Gener? "Macho" Gener to his friends. Ever come across him?'

'Never even heard of him.'

'He's a Cuban friend of Rosselli's. Judy Campbell? How about her?'

'Heard of her. But I've never met the lady.'

'Doesn't matter. It's Rosselli we're really interested in. Did you know he plays golf with Joe Kennedy?'

'You know more than me.'

'It's always possible. What about women?'

'What about them?'

'What I mean is, do you think that Rosselli is a fag?'

Nimmo found himself grinning. 'A fag? No. The few times I've seen him socially, he always seems to have plenty of girls around. There was an actress I believe he was involved with. Ann Corcoran. And before that it's my information that he was married to another movie actress. June Lang.'

'Yeah, but that was twenty years ago.' Goldman's nose wrinkled. 'Besides, it only lasted, what? A year and a half?'

'Like I said, you know more than me. I'd like to help you, Agent Goldman, but to be quite frank with you, Johnny Rosselli's sexuality is a closed book to me.' Nimmo sipped some more coffee and smiled. For a moment back there, he had actually been concerned that the

Bureau and its THP might be about to pose some awkward questions. But the idea that the feds were investigating Rosselli's sex life was almost hilarious.

'Ever go to his apartment in LA?'

'There you go again. I didn't even know he had an apartment in LA.'

'Twelve fifty-nine Crescent Heights Avenue. Near the Strip.'

Nimmo shook his head.

'Would it surprise you to learn that on some weekends, when he's in LA, Rosselli brings boys from a local Catholic orphanage to swim in his pool?'

Nimmo laughed out loud. 'Yes, as a matter of fact it would. I didn't know he was much of a Catholic.'

'That's not what I meant.'

'I know what you meant.'

'Look Nimmo, Rosselli's a hoodlum, but he's a hard sonofabitch to nail, as a racketeer. So then, in the same way that we nailed Capone, not as a racketeer, but for income tax evasion, we're looking to nail Rosselli's ass for a fruit. I just thought you might be able to shed some light on whether you thought any of these women you've seen him with were beards. You know, girls along for the show, to make him seem more like a real man around his mob pals. Those guys dislike pansies even more than most. I mean, can you think of one of those wiseguys who's been a fucking faggot?'

'Nope, can't say that I've ever thought about it much.'

'The underworld is a man's world. It's a crooked world. But it sure isn't a queer one.'

'Look,' grinned Nimmo. 'He's Italian. He dresses nice. He wears cologne. He's polite. For a racketeer he's even, you might say, polished. Good manners. I think he's even nice to his mother. Sends her money back in Boston. But none of those things makes you a pansy. I think Rosselli would talk to Bobby Kennedy before he would let you guys charge him with being a lousy pederast.'

'Bobby Kennedy? Well, he's queer, too.'

Nimmo laughed out loud. It was as good a laugh as he had had since coming back to New York. Bobby Kennedy a queer. Goldman was funnier than Milton Berle and Jack Benny, and certainly more original.

'You think this is funny?'

'You're damn right I think it's funny,' said Nimmo. He sipped some more coffee, leaned back in his chair, and put a cigarette in his mouth. 'Bobby Kennedy, queer.'

'It is kind of funny, isn't it?' grinned Goldman. 'I just made that up, actually.'

By now, Nimmo was thinking Goldman looked a fairly decent sort of guy. His face was as big as it was open, which made it the wrong kind of face to have if you were in the FBI. Hoover did not like grinners. Once, Nimmo had overheard the director telling Richard Hood, then head of the FBI's field office in Los Angeles, to fire an agent because he smiled too much. And now here was one of Hoover's men – Hoover, whose own sexuality was open to question – trying to find out if Johnny Rosselli was queer. It seemed just too funny for words.

'Why don't you see if Hoover has any personal knowledge of Rosselli being a pansy?' Nimmo suggested playfully. 'Or maybe he'll have some expert ideas on how to catch Rosselli with his pants down. Maybe Hoover might even care to volunteer to put his own ass on the line. You know, like a honey-trap.'

Nimmo flicked a match with his thumbnail and watched it fire up like a tiny yellow flower. Everything was looking good to him since he had discovered Tom Jefferson's address, and where and when he was planning to try and kill Kennedy. Even the matches he was scraping into being.

Grinning hugely now, like a Red Indian witch doctor's mask Nimmo had once seen in the Museum of Natural History, Goldman said, 'Perhaps I will at that, the old faggot.'

'That's the idea, Agent Goldman. Goldman. What's that, a Hebe name?'

'Something wrong with that?'

'Naw. Could be worse. You could be a goddamn faggot. Like Hoover.'

'Next Passover, I'll try and remember that.'

Nimmo laughed. 'You do that.'

'You seem like you're in a pretty good mood.'

'It's New Year's Eve. Why not? I had the lousiest Christmas on record. But nineteen sixty-one is shaping up very nicely.'

'I'm glad to hear it.'

Nimmo finished his coffee and, taking a deep, unhurried drag on his cigarette, watched the smoke curl away from his face. He was in no hurry now that he knew Goldman was after information about Rosselli's sex life.

Smiling wryly, he said, 'Matter of fact, I got laid last night. Which no doubt explains why I'm feeling so good about myself. Best-looking broad you ever saw. I mean, really beautiful. Her name was Summer. Sounds corny, I know. But all those gals give themselves crackerbarrel names. Her hair. Her hair was fantastic. The colour of that light over there.' He pointed over Goldman's shoulder to the light that was flooding the main station concourse. 'Good mood? Hell, I'm walking on air this morning.'

'I hear that'll do it,' said Goldman, still grinning broadly at Nimmo. 'Getting laid.' But the FBI agent's intensely green eyes seemed to burn into Nimmo's face, as if he was still curious about something.

'You still look like you have an important question to ask, my friend.'

'Just one.'

'Just the one? Jesus, what's the Bureau coming to? Just the one question. Ask away.'

'It's about Tom Jefferson.'

'Are you sure you mean him and not Franklin Pierce?' snorted Nimmo. 'Or Martin Van Buren? Or, Jesus I don't know.' Nimmo pulled a name down from the mote-filled air. He actually tried, physically, to reach for one. 'Millard Fillmore?' Laughing now, he added, 'Rutherford Hayes?'

'Who else knows where he is living in New York?' Goldman asked levelly.

'How do you mean?'

'Does the mob know where he is yet?'

Very much to his own surprise, Nimmo found himself saying, 'No, just me.' And now that he considered the question in more detail, it really did not seem to matter all that much. 'I only found out myself this morning,' he sighed. 'He and I are going to celebrate New Year's Eve together.'

'A party?'

'Yes, you could call it that. Except that it'll be just him and me. No one else is invited. Not even you. Tom and I will see the new year in with a bang. Quite a loud one, I shouldn't wonder. Yes sir, we'll paint the whole room red.' Nimmo frowned. 'Talking of colours, that's quite a suit you're wearing there, fellow.'

'You like it, huh?'

'It looks great. What the hell kind of material is that?'

'English plaid. Cost me eighty bucks.'

'Hell, you could have got a new one for that,' chuckled Nimmo. 'But no, worth every penny of what you paid, I'd say. It really is incredible. I can see every living fibre.'

'How about Harvard? Is that where he's going when he leaves New York?'

'Harvard?'

'The book you were reading in the library?'

'Oh yes. Now I remember. He's on the Board of Overseers. I was in the bath when I suddenly thought, like Archimedes, Eureka! I've found it!'

Everyone in the coffee shop looked around to see who it was that had shouted so loudly.

'And I dashed out of the hotel and into the library, and found the right book, and I just knew as sure as eggs is eggs that he was going to Harvard University.'

'Must be a clever guy.'

Goldman was standing up now, and putting on the polar coat. He seemed taller than Nimmo remembered. And the polar coat was not tan-coloured but golden, so that it almost seemed as if, like Hercules, Goldman was putting on the skin of lion. Then he was helping Nimmo on to his feet.

'Come on,' he said. 'It's time we were moving.'

'Are we going somewhere?'

'We're all going somewhere.' For the benefit of the rail passengers in the coffee shop, he looked around and said, 'Just a little early New Year's Eve celebration, folks. Nothing to worry about.'

'Happy New Year,' shouted Nimmo.

Goldman ushered him out on to the station concourse. 'Are you okay? You seem a little hysterical.'

'Hysterical?' Nimmo grinned. 'I never felt better in my whole life. My God. Will you just look at this place? I never really looked at this building before. It's fantastic.'

'Grand Central? It sure is something, isn't it? They really knew how to build something back then.'

'And this is the way it really is. This is the way you ought to see it, always. On a day like this. With the sun streaming through the tall windows on to the blonde marble floors.' Nimmo wrestled his arm away from Goldman's grasp. 'Look at that. It's a giant ladder up to the heavens, that's what it is. If Jacob, the son of Isaac, was here now, why he'd climb up that ladder and speak to the Lord himself. Of course. Look at that. Yes. That must be how it was. That must be how it happened. For Jacob, I mean. A ladder of fiery sunlight. I must have been in this station a thousand times, and I never really looked at it before. It's enough to make you believe.'

'In what?'

'In God, of course. In everything. Heavens above.'

Nimmo was staring up at the ceiling now, with its illuminated constellations of the zodiac. They looked quite different from when he had come into the station some thirty minutes earlier. If a station was what this place really was. Surely, he thought, a building such as this one, made of gold and filled with lights, must be some kind of secret temple wherein the elect were shown things that not everyone could see. Why else could he see, and not the others who were walking around with nothing more transcendent than a train on their minds? It was inspiring and it was humbling at the same time: that he, of all people, should have been given the privilege of seeing such a wonder.

Nimmo shook his head in awe and whispered, 'This place is one of the wonders of the world.'

'Shucks, this isn't as wonderful as some of the things you can see in New York, my friend. You ain't seen nuthin' yet.'

Goldman led Nimmo outside, on to 42nd Street, where immediately the sight of so many yellow cabs and so much human hustle and bustle struck Nimmo as inherently laughable. It all looked like something from a cartoon: exaggerated, overdrawn, polychromatic, ridiculous – ridiculous to the point of almost being terrifying. And for a brief second, Nimmo had an idea of what it would be like to be crazy – as Bugs as Bugs Bunny himself. Confronted with so much unremitting strangeness – so much intense meaning that, he thought, you would have to have been the prophet Elijah or Daniel to have dealt with it all – he found himself on the brink of panic. He could see that there was great beauty and burning significance to be seen almost everywhere he looked, but such was reality's imperative – at once spiritual and material – that he felt he might actually be over-whelmed.

Nimmo grabbed Goldman's arm and let himself be guided gently down 5th Avenue. Things had been looking good, but already it was abundantly clear to him that things could look too good, that there could be too much feeling, and that understanding could overwhelm the human mind as a tidal wave might swamp a tiny boat. Maybe a saint or some kind of Indian holy man might have put all this revelation to profitable use, but Nimmo felt dwarfed by it, as a mail box might feel small beside a skyscraper.

By now, Nimmo had sensed that things were not quite right with him, and he was afraid. 'What's happening to me?' he repeated. And then, 'I think I must be losing my mind.'

'You look okay,' Goldman observed with cool detachment.

'And you look just as you should be. Except that you're more than just yourself. It's like I can see inside you, to what makes you real. Who on earth do you think you are?'

'You're right,' answered Goldman. 'I am different on the inside. Inside, I'm real. But I know who I am. Can you honestly say the same?'

'I don't want to know who I am.' Nimmo was shaking his head. 'Where are we?'

'Thirty-fourth Street on Fifth. That's the Empire State Building. At one hundred and two storeys high, it's the tallest building in the world. For my money you can keep the Great Pyramid of Cheops, or the Colossus at Rhodes. You can even keep Grand Central Station. This is it, Jimmy. This is where eternal life begins. Just look up there.'

Nimmo followed the line of Goldman's enormous arm, to the silver

321

edge of his hand, and then the diamond point of his forefinger where it ascended into heaven.

'This is the way to the stars,' Goldman explained carefully. 'Doesn't it shine? Doesn't it give you hope? Doesn't it beckon you to ascend? Look around you, Jimmy. It's time to say goodbye. I'm here to help you do that. I'm here to help you. And do you know why, Jimmy?'

'Why do you want to help me?'

'Because I'm your guardian angel, that's why. I'm here to help you come to Jesus, Jimmy. You're not losing your mind. Not at all. You're expanding it. You're bursting out of your old body and getting ready for a new one. A heavenly body. You're not like these other people any more. You're changing. It's like the moment when a caterpillar becomes a butterfly. And if you see things differently, it's because there's already a little piece of heaven burning inside you. Can you feel it? It's calling you, like a little beacon. That's what told me that it was time to come and find you. You see, I'm a kind of conductor, Jimmy. I'm here to conduct you safely up to heaven. You can see that now, can't you? And if you ask me what you must do to get there, I'll show you. But you have to want it, Jimmy. You have to want it real bad. And you have to trust me. You have to give yourself up to it. Jesus doesn't want people who are reluctant to come unto him. He only wants those who want him.'

Goldman shook his head and smiled. It was just like talking to Jimmy Stewart, he thought. He had never quite seen himself in the role of George Bailey's guardian angel, Clarence, but on the whole he thought he was turning in a pretty good performance. Of course the intent was very different. The whole point was to persuade Nimmo that his wonderful life was over, and that another even more wonderful life – the life in the hereafter – was about to begin. That seemed feasible. But it was another movie that came to mind as he persuaded Nimmo to go into the Empire State Building with him, and ride the elevator up to the eighty-sixth-floor observatory: *King Kong*. Not that he considered planting that image in Nimmo's strongly medicined mind, for a moment. Besides, there was no way to get out on the roof of the enclosed 102nd-floor observatory.

There were only a few people around on the eighty-sixth floor and, surrounded by some of the most remarkable views of the city, none of them paid Goldman and Nimmo any attention. Stretching south toward the Financial Center, Manhattan looked like a giant cemetery. The Flatiron Building on 23rd Street, where Broadway and 5th Avenue crossed, seemed no bigger than a throat lozenge. On the north-eastern side, the Chrysler Building appeared close enough to touch. Bryant Park, in front of the New York Public Library, was as green as an emerald. Goldman drew Nimmo over to the deserted western side of the cold and gusty observatory. No one was much interested in a poor view of the Hudson River, the Long Island Rail Yard, and the rooftop of Macy's at Herald Square.

At the coffee shop in Grand Central Station he had poured a water solution containing eighty micrograms of lysergic acid diethylamide into Nimmo's cup, this being precisely double the dose the CIA chemist at the whorehouse on Horatio Street had recommended as a maximum safe dose. The chemist had seemed more like a beatnik and a pimp than a scientist, with longish hair, a rollneck sweater, suede shoes, and corduroy pants, but then he wasn't supposed to look like Bela Lugosi or Boris Karloff.

'We're not exactly sure how it works,' the young chemist had explained, handing over the medical samples bag containing the supply of LSD Washington had ordered him to give to Goldman. 'We think it may deprive the brain of glucose, which might serve to explain why mystics who undertake long fasts are more likely to have hallucinatory experiences. The more LSD you take, the less sugar your head gets, and the more powerful and durable your hallucinations. But whatever the reason for why it works, it is a very powerful drug and needs to be used only very sparingly. A few years back, one of our own physicians, a guy named Frank Olsen, took seventy micrograms of the stuff in a glass of Cointreau – that's almost twice as much as might be considered safe today – and, after eight days of hallucination, threw himself out of a tenth-floor hotel window right here in New York City.'

'Really?' Goldman had been impressed. 'Which hotel?'

'The Statler.'

'No wonder. The Statler's a lousy hotel. I'd throw myself out of a fucking window if I had to spend eight days there.'

'Don't joke about it, man. This stuff is dynamite.'

'So it doesn't mix with Cointreau. What else? Does it do what it's supposed to? Control minds?'

'It'd make you much more suggestible, in the sense that whoever is there to affect your interpretation of your perceptions, and what you're hallucinating, can make the difference between a good experience and a really bad one. In larger doses, there's a tendency for subjects to become paranoid. That's where LSD becomes really dangerous – not just to the subject, but to the people around the subject. One of the johns here killed a hooker – stuffed a fucking sheet down her throat – because he thought she was a giant snake trying to swallow him. But, to answer your question more precisely, no, it's not mind control. We had hoped it would turn people into human robots, but it doesn't do that. It fucks you up, is what it does, man. Take enough LSD, it fucks you up for ever.'

Nimmo stared into the unfathomable azure that was the living, breathing sky, into the burning purgatorial fire that was the sun, and saw divine light at its full blaze. Beside heaven, the world seemed a poor thing of grey concrete, precarious to stand on, like a rotten tooth in a whole mouth of dead teeth. And the only way to escape the horrors of hell that lay in the pit far below his enlarged feet – from the fear, and the bewilderment, and the earthbound chaos of the streets – seemed to be to reach out, through the protective fence of heaven, and to embrace it, as Goldman suggested.

'I have to go now,' Goldman was saying. 'Because I have to be out there, on the other side of the fence, to catch you. To bear you up in my hands in case you so much as strike your foot on the stone ledge when you jump. You won't see me. But you'll know I'm there. All you have to do is climb on to the other side of the gates of heaven that you see in front of you now, and then fly to me, like the angel you are about to become. Think of that, Jimmy. Isn't it a wonderful thought? Just think how wonderful it will be to be an angel. Not everyone gets this chance, Jimmy. But you have been chosen.'

'Like a caterpillar becoming a butterfly,' Nimmo repeated dumbly.

'That's right. Don't let me down, Jimmy. You can do it. You can fly to God, Jimmy. You can fly like a bloody angel.'

Goldman walked away and rode the elevator down to the ground floor. It hardly mattered to him if Jimmy Nimmo threw himself off the

324

Empire State Building, or not. Even if he did manage to come down from the eighty-sixth-floor observatory alive, the chances were that with so much acid affecting his brain, Nimmo would simply get hit by a truck, or walk in front of a train, or drown himself in the park. Frank Olsen's experience after seventy micrograms had lasted eight days. Well, Nimmo had swallowed eighty micrograms. Of course, anything was possible. Nimmo could be the luckiest guy in the world and end up in hospital with nothing more than a broken leg. But by then it would be too late for him to kill anyone on behalf of Johnny Rosselli, or Sam Giancana. Tom Jefferson was safe now. Nothing could interfere with that.

On 5th, Goldman jumped into a cab and told the driver to take him to 200 Riverside Drive. They drove west along 42nd Street. By the time they reached Times Square, Goldman had started humming 'Auld Lang Syne'.

25

Hollis Fifteen

By the twentieth time Chub made love to Edith, he figured that he was getting the hang of it, at last. Not rushing it, but not taking too long about it either, which made her sore. Practice makes perfect, Edith said. The night before New Year's Eve was to be their last together – at least that was what Chub believed – so he told his parents he was going to stay over with an old friend from Choate, and not to expect him back until sometime on Saturday morning.

More or less as soon as Chub got to the apartment Edith gave him a blow job, the first one he had ever had. Just to make sure of his complete attention. Then she told him her great idea. She told him she owned a beautiful skiing lodge in Franconia, New Hampshire, which is about one hundred miles north of Boston. She and her friend Anne, in Boston – the one she had been visiting before she had met Chub on the express – were planning to drive up there on the night of Friday the sixth, and spend the whole weekend skiing. Wouldn't it be nice if Chub could come along? And not just Chub, but his roommate, Torbert, about whom she had heard so much, and whom she was quite sure her friend Anne would like, maybe as much as Edith liked Chub.

Chub wanted to come very much, but also pointed out that he and Torbert had ten days of examinations starting on 16 January. In reply to this, Edith pointed out that Chub's French was much improved, and that she could probably do the same for Torbert. Moreover, she suggested that the two boys could study in the mornings, and then ski with Edith and Anne in the afternoon. All work and no play.

This seemed such a good idea to Chub that he called Torbert immediately and told him about Edith's invitation, and Anne. At first, Torbert was as concerned about his mid-year examinations as Chub had been. But then Edith insisted on speaking to Torbert, and pretty soon she had him eating out of her hand, too, telling him how beautiful Anne was, and how she had just broken up with a guy, and that she had had a lousy Christmas and was just after some fun, but that at the same time she was quite a scholar, having studied Economics at Yale. So Torbert agreed to come, on the understanding that neither he nor Chub told their parents about it.

After all the arrangements were made, Edith and Chub went to bed, where she fellated him once again for good measure.

The next morning they were up early. Over breakfast, Edith said, 'So when exactly are you returning to Harvard, darling?'

'The Winter Reading Period begins on Monday, January second. I'm planning to catch an early-afternoon train back to Boston, so I should be back in Harvard by around seven o'clock that evening.'

'You promise to call me when you get there?'

'Of course I'll call you. I'll call you every night, if you want.'

'I do want.' Edith lit a Newport, and said, 'I suppose living in Boston means Torbert will be back before you.'

'No, actually, he's planning to get back at around nine. He's got some relations from Europe visiting that day.' Chub kissed her hand. 'Are you sure you're busy tonight, Edith?'

'I told you, I have to go to a New Year's Eve party that's being given by a friend of my husband's. I can hardly take you to that, now can I? And if I don't go, my husband, when he calls from England, will want to know where I was. But I tell you what. Let's spend the day together. We'll go shopping downtown and I'll buy you something nice to go back to Harvard with. Something that will remind you of me.'

'I'm not about to forget you, Edith,' grinned Chub.

'All the same, I should like to buy you something.'

They put on coats and rode the elevator downstairs to the lobby where a strangely accented man was speaking to Gil, the doorman.

'Strange,' said the man. 'Well then, what about Mister Van Buren?'

'There's no one of that name either, sir. I'm sorry.'

'Are you quite sure of that?'

'I've been the doorman here for eleven years, sir. I know everyone in this building.'

'How very odd.'

Chub paid no attention to this exchange of dialogue. But Edith was a trained agent and looked carefully at the stranger. For a second or two she even tuned in to what he was saying. Had she arrived in the lobby a second or two earlier, or left a second or two later, she might have heard the man utter the name of Tom Jefferson, and acted differently. Instead, she heard only the name of Van Buren, and, making no obvious connection between the eighth President of the United States and the fourteenth, under whose name Tom lived in the Riverside Drive apartment, she walked on. There were too many weirdos in New York to be suspicious of everyone.

It was only later on that evening, when she came into the living room and found Goldman watching the RCA *Seven o'Clock News* that Edith saw the stranger's face again, and remembered the first and only other time she had seen it before. The reporter described how the man in the photograph, now identified as James Bywater Nimmo, an assistant police superintendent from Miami, and a former FBI Special Agent, had been rushed to St Lukes Roosevelt Hospital in Manhattan after apparently setting himself on fire in Central Park. Several witnesses described how the man had poured gasoline on to himself before lighting a match and applying it to his soaked clothes. Despite the best efforts of doctors to save him, Nimmo had passed away at four o'clock that afternoon.

'That's the man,' whispered Edith.

Goldman, who was impressed that somehow Nimmo should have got down from the ESB and travelled as far as Central Park, muttered, 'Ognennyi Angel,' the Russian for Fiery Angel, which was one of Goldman's favourite operas, by Prokofiev, and then said, 'Well, I'll be damned.'

'I know him,' Edith now exclaimed. 'That's the man who was in the

328

lobby this morning. He was trying to deliver mail to someone who doesn't live here. My God, Alex, they said he was from the FBI. You don't suppose they know about us, do you?'

Goldman got up from the sofa and turned the sound down on the TV. He did not want to turn the set off. *Perry Mason* was starting in a few minutes, which was one of his favourite shows. And later on, there was Richard Boone, in *Have Gun, Will Travel*, which he also enjoyed. Goldman was not one for celebrating New Year's Eve. It was a time that always filled him with melancholy.

Carefully, he said, 'No, that's not what they said, Edith. They said he was ex-FBI. Something quite different. And no, I don't suppose they know about us at all.'

'But he was here, Alex,' insisted Edith, who was beginning to sound alarmed. 'I swear it was him.'

'Oh, I believe you. I'm quite sure that you saw him here. But it wasn't you he was looking for. I know just what he knew, and believe me, it wasn't much.'

'How could you know that?'

'Because it was me who killed him. Maybe I didn't actually apply the match, but indirectly, I am responsible.' Goldman glanced at his watch and then briefly explained as much as he thought she now needed to know.

Edith got up and went over to the window, and stared out at the New Jersey shoreline. The few electric lights she could see looked like heavenly writing on the blackened wall of the universe. As if God was trying to tell her something.

Goldman stood up and put his hands on her slim shoulders. 'Take it easy. If we all do like we're supposed to, then everything will be all right. We can have no doubts about the legitimacy of what we're doing. If you'd been watching the television news earlier, you would have seen that Raul Roa, the Cuban Foreign Minister, has called for an immediate meeting of the UN Security Council. He has come out and said what KGB and G2 have been saying for a long while: that an invasion of Cuba is less than three weeks away. Edith. Listen to me. We are the only ones who can stop this thing from happening. You, me, Tom, and Anne.'

'But will it? Stop the invasion? I'm not so sure, Alex.'

Goldman shrugged. 'To be honest, I have no idea. But orders are orders. Besides, we can't just sit back and do nothing. Already there have been several attempts on Fidel's life. And they're not going to stop. Just because we've been able to arrest a few of the ringleaders in Havana doesn't change anything. They will keep trying.'

Edith nodded. 'I suppose so.'

'Damn right, they will,' frowned Goldman. 'It makes me so angry. Do you know what the White House press secretary, James Haggerty, said in response to Raul Roa's charges? He said "nuts". Nuts. That's what he would say to you now, if he were standing here, and you tried to tell him about the justice of the Cuban revolution. About how people are happier than when it was Batista and the mob who ruled Cuba. He'd say "nuts". And Edith, if you tried to tell him how evil the Somoza family were, and how the people of Nicaragua want to be free of these bastards, he'd look you in the eye and say the same thing. Remember what Roosevelt said about Anastasio Somoza? He said, "He may be a son of a bitch, but he's our son of a bitch." Haggerty, Roosevelt, Kennedy, they are all the same, Edith. They look at the people of Central America and say "nuts".' Goldman sighed. 'Nuts? I tell you, this country's full of them.'

On New Year's Day, a nor'easter poured more than two inches of rain on southern New England, causing minor flooding, and belting the northern states with two inches of snow. Not that Tom was bothered much by the weather. He spent the afternoon at the Astor Movie Theater on Boylston Street, watching *Spartacus*. This followed a New Year's Eve when he had watched *The Alamo* at the Gary Theater. It seemed that revolution was becoming quite the fashion in Hollywood, even if it was the sword and sandals variety, or John Wayne battling to win freedom for Texans against the tyranny of the Mexican empire. The curious thing, however, was how none of this seemed to have any influence upon the popular American consciousness, vis à vis the popular revolution that had taken place in Cuba.

Tom did not think you could have had a more obvious example of a communist revolution, in all but name, than the story of a slave's revolt. Dalton Trumbo, the screenwriter, had even been one of the 'Hollywood Ten' blacklisted in the forties on suspicion of being a communist. In Tom's eyes, it seemed very obvious that Spartacus had been nothing less than the Leninist archetype. It was no accident that after the Great War German communists had actually called themselves Spartakists. And there were times during the movie when he would not have been surprised to see Kirk Douglas waving a red flag, and Tony Curtis reading Marx and Engels. It was all very strange, this fear and loathing of communism. People in America seemed to have forgotten that but for the sacrifices of the Soviet Union – ten Red Army soldiers killed for every one of the Allies – the whole of Europe and Asia and maybe even America too would have been dominated by the Axis forces of fascism. Tom accepted that there was a lot wrong with communism, as practised in the Soviet Union. But it did not have to be that way in Cuba. Or, for that matter, in the United States.

Reading the newspapers, Tom had the sense that America was girding its loins to do battle with Cuba. Even the *Boston Globe* was full of anti-Cuban propaganda. On Monday, 2 January, the front page carried the headline 'Police State Terror is Stamped on Cuba'. And for the rest of that week the *Globe* featured a series of articles by Anne Davies entitled 'Inside Fidel Castro's Cuba', which, in Tom's eyes, was not much more than a catalogue of all that was worst in the country. It did not seem to matter that there were many good things that had come out of the revolution. And many bad things that had existed before. If it was Cuban, it followed that it was also bad.

That same Monday, around lunchtime, he loaded the station wagon with a Blizzard ski-bag and two large green cloth bags of the type that every Harvard student seemed to carry. The weather was better. Fair, but colder, with temperatures struggling to get much above the high twenties. The Cambridge air was damp and filled with the smell of burning Christmas trees.

Tom drove west along Massachusetts Avenue and parked close to the imposing Johnson Gate. Already there were a few parents bent on the same task as Tom: carrying boxes and luggage into dorms for sons returning to Harvard after the Christmas holidays. Respectably attired in a coat and hat, wearing a Yale tie, and with a pipe fixed firmly between his teeth, Tom fancied he looked as much like someone's dad helping his son move back into the dorm as it was possible to look, short of wearing a cardigan, and trying to pass himself off as Spencer

Tracy. Even so, this was one of the trickiest aspects of the plan. If he was challenged he would have to talk his way out of a spot, which, without flashing his fake FBI ID, might prove to be awkward. As things turned out, being challenged would almost have been easier than being assisted.

Struggling through the open door of Hollis South, Tom found himself facing a man of about the same age as himself and, but for the Yale tie, similarly dressed, too.

'Hi there,' said the man. 'Can I help you carry any of that?'

'It's okay,' said Tom. 'My son must be somewhere around, so please don't trouble yourself.'

'It's no trouble at all.' The man looked about as clean-cut as a dentist from Salt Lake City. 'Here,' he said, grabbing hold of one of Tom's green bags. 'You'd better let me take one of these.' Having taken the bag, he now held out his hand. 'By the way, the name's Wallingford. Buckner Wallingford. My son, Buck junior, is in room one.'

Tom stretched his cold face into a rictus of a grin and took Wallingford's outstretched hand. 'Farrell,' he said, hoping that the two men had never met. 'Chub Farrell. My son, Chub, is in room fifteen. I'm afraid that's right at the top. But really, I can manage.'

But Buck Wallingford was already headed up the stairs, complaining good-naturedly about young men, and how much stuff they seemed to bring with them back to the dorm, and how he thought they were probably in for some more snow. At the top of the stairs, Wallingford put the green bag down and nodded at the ski-bag over Tom's shoulder.

'Where does your boy ski?'

'Franconia,' said Tom. 'I'd introduce you to him, if I knew where the hell he was. Chub? You there?' They waited in silence for a second, and then Tom shrugged awkwardly.

'Probably in someone else's room,' said Wallingford, and started down the stairs. 'Well, I'd better go and find Buck junior. I imagine he'll want some money.'

'Yes, don't they all?'

'Nice meeting you, Chub.'

'You too, Buck. Thanks a lot for your help. Saved me a heart attack.'

332

'Don't mention it.'

Tom watched with relief as Buckner Wallingford disappeared from view. Seconds later, he was fitting one of his keys into the lock on the door of Hollis Fifteen. The key went in easily enough, but to Tom's momentary horror, it did not turn. Quickly he pulled the key out and dripped some oil on to the blade from a small can he had brought along in his coat pocket, along with a small locksmith's file, for this very possibility. Then he tried again, only this time he pulled the ancient door toward him experimentally, and this time the lock clicked loudly open. In a matter of seconds, he transferred the bags from the floor of the hall into the room, and, closing the door behind him, locked it again.

Tom breathed another sigh of relief. The room was cold. Almost as cold as it was outside Hollis, but Tom was already covered in sweat. He sat down in one of the library chairs to collect himself and to remind himself of the room's topography. Since arriving in Cambridge, Tom had read several books about Harvard and was aware that most of the freshmen dormitories in the Yard were pre-revolutionary. Hollis Hall had been built in 1763, at around the time when most Americans who called themselves Americans were chafing under the Stamp Act, and Tom could not help wondering what people like George Washington and Benjamin Franklin, not to mention his own name-sake, would have thought of Cuba's struggle for freedom.

Leaning forward in the chair, Tom unzipped the ski-bag, the length of which had been kept straight by two six-foot pieces of dowel to help disguise the fact that the bag contained not a pair of skis but a .30-calibre Winchester rifle, matt black, and fitted with a Unertl scope. Tom snapped the dowel into smaller lengths and tossed the pieces into the empty ski-bag. Then, wearing gloves, he picked up the rifle and went over to one of the closets. These were large, heavy pieces of mahogany furniture that looked as if they had been in Hollis since the time of Thoreau. At the top of the closet there was a gap of at least two inches between wood and wall, which narrowed to less than half an inch at the level of the skirting board. Tom poked the rifle into the gap, barrel first, and let it slide comfortably into the space.

Pressing his head against the wall, he looked into the crack, but the black rifle was all but invisible.

Next, Tom drew open the string at the neck of one green cloth bag, and slipped away the material to reveal the Hallicrafter short-wave receiver he had purchased in New York. By tuning the radio to whatever frequency the Secret Service might use on their DCN handsets, he and Alex Goldman, who was familiar with presidential detail codes, might easily follow the Senator's progress during his entry and exit from Harvard Yard. But hiding the radio, an object the size of a shoe box, was not so easy. Which was why he had brought the second green cloth bag, containing a hand-drill, a jimmy, a screwdriver, a hacksaw, and a tin of antique floor polish.

During the reconnaissance visit he and Goldman had made to Hollis Fifteen, Tom had noticed that there were some loose boards on the old and uneven floor and, pulling back the rug, he inspected these more closely. It took very little effort to jimmy two of the loose boards up, revealing a space between the joists that was big enough for the radio, the ski-bag, the pieces of dowel, the tools, and, for that matter, the rifle too. It was almost a cause of regret to Tom that he had not thought to inspect the space underneath the floorboards before hiding the rifle behind the closet. Finally, Tom put back the floorboards using screws instead of nails, so as to facilitate their silent replacement and removal. But he was careful not to screw the boards down too tight, in case Chub or Torbert noticed anything different when they walked across the room. Then he covered the screw heads and the edges of the boards with polish, so as to disguise the fact that they had ever been removed. Last of all, he drew back the rug. Only when he was quite sure that everything looked and felt the same did he leave the room, lock the door, and exit Hollis Fifteen.

The next four days passed slowly for Tom. Each day Edith called the Cambridge apartment to report on her own daily conversations with Chub Farrell. Tom figured that if Chub, or Torbert, found out what was hidden behind the closet in Hollis Fifteen, Chub would certainly inform the woman he loved.

He went to the movies again, to see *Tunes of Glory*, which he liked a lot, and *Exodus*, which he didn't. He watched a lot of television, too.

News mostly, but also junk like *Maverick, Mister Ed, Rawhide,* and *Route 66.* Only *Eyewitness to History* seemed worthwhile. Often, he went out to dinner in Cambridge, usually to the Coach Grille on Harvard Square, which was his favourite. He finished reading *To Kill a Mockingbird,* by Harper Lee, and started *Advise and Consent,* by Allen Drury. But more frequently he read the newspapers and watched the television news. On Monday, 2 January, the start of the Harvard term, President Eisenhower ordered a military alert because of the situation in Laos. But Tom just wondered if that was merely a smokescreen for an invasion of Cuba – an idea that became more persuasive in his mind when, on the afternoon of the following day, Ike announced that he was breaking off diplomatic relations with Cuba.

'There is a limit,' Ike declared, ending the sixty-year tie between the countries, 'to what the US in self-respect can endure. That limit has now been reached.'

Tom was stunned. A Cuban war now seemed imminent. By Thursday, US officials were warning Cuba not only that they intended to keep the naval base at Guantanamo, but also that Fidel Castro would have to be removed from office if Cuba ever hoped to heal the rift in Cuban–American relations – this a response to the diplomatic peace feelers Cuba was apparently extending to President-elect John Kennedy.

That same Thursday evening, Alex Goldman flew in from New York and, after a late dinner, they went straight to bed.

The following morning, just about the first thing he and Tom did was to check the classified section of the *Globe,* in search of the coded message that would tell them whether or not their mission was finally on, or off. Goldman scanned the pages carefully until he found an advertisement containing the operational G2 code for Jack Kennedy, which was 'Submarine Shop'. Finally he found what he was looking for: 'Due to illness sacrifice Submarine Shop within seven days. MI 3-5042.' The Boston telephone number was fake, just to make the ad look slightly less suspicious.

'That's it,' said Goldman. 'We've got the go.'

Tom nodded. 'I didn't figure it any other way. Not after what happened on Tuesday.'

'It sure doesn't look good, does it?' agreed Goldman. 'Still, the weather's improving. I think those boys are going to have some very good skiing this weekend.'

'They'd better enjoy themselves,' remarked Tom. 'In a couple of months, those two boys could be drafted into the army, and at war.'

At lunchtime Edith and her friend, Anne, arrived from New York. Anne was younger than Edith, and even more beautiful. She was also a member of G2, the Cuban Intelligence Service. Tom went through their instructions with them, while Goldman listened.

'Are the boys ready to go?'

'Chub called me last night,' said Edith. 'To say that they are both looking forward to it would be the understatement of the year.'

'When you get to Franconia, call us,' said Tom. 'We don't plan on entering their room until the early hours of Sunday morning. After that, I'm afraid you won't be able to contact us short of coming into Harvard Yard and staring up at our window.'

'They're not telling their parents, so there won't be any messages that might take them away from us,' said Edith. 'Officially, the plan is that we will be leaving Franconia at around eight o'clock Monday morning. Except that the car won't start.'

'How are you planning to disable the car?'

'I'll leave the lights on all night. The car is garaged, so I don't expect anyone will notice. But I'll also remove the rotor arm, just in case.'

'Either of them know anything about cars?'

'Chub can't drive. Torbert has a car. But Chub says he doesn't even know how to change a spark plug.'

'Good girl. Whatever you do, it's imperative that they are not back in Cambridge before one o'clock on Monday afternoon. Have you got that?'

Edith nodded.

'So make sure you give them both a good time. Anne? Are you comfortable with that? You'll have to sleep with Torbert.'

'Yes sir,' said Anne. 'Edith has told me what has to be done.'

'I don't want any arguments, lovers' tiffs and such like. One of these kids gets on a bus back to Boston, and we're in deep shit. I want all your feminine charms brought into play. And if necessary, slip them a mickey.'

336

Edith nodded again.

'When you get back to Cambridge,' said Tom, 'you can rest a while and then Alex'll drive all three of you to Logan. You'll all fly down to Miami and then go your separate ways from there.'

'Be my pleasure,' said Goldman.

'What about you?' asked Edith.

'I'll get the train back to New York, and then on to Mexico City. It's best we don't travel together. Good luck to you both.'

'And to you,' said the two women.

Tom escorted them out to their car, and kissed Edith goodbye. It was not much of a parting, but then it had not been much of a relationship. Just an arrangement occasionally involving sex. In that respect it was probably no different to a lot of marriages.

'If you get a chance,' said Edith, 'come and see me in Nicaragua.'

'I'd like that,' said Tom.

'And Tom? Please be careful.'

'You too, Edith.'

'Lucky boys,' said Goldman, after Edith and Anne had driven away to collect the boys from Hollis. 'I kind of wish I was going along myself.'

'Me too,' admitted Tom. 'I like skiing.'

It was seven o'clock when the telephone rang in the Cambridge apartment, around the same time that Kennedy was boarding the *Caroline* in Palm Beach, to fly up to Washington. It was Edith, to say that they had all arrived safely in Franconia.

'Any problems?' asked Goldman. 'How's Torbert getting along with Anne?'

'No problems at all. I don't think I ever saw a boy fall in love so quickly.'

'That's how it is when you're eighteen,' chuckled Goldman. 'You fall in love just as fast as you can drink a Coke, or blow up bubblegum. Don't last a hell of a lot more than that, either. You call me if there are any teenage dilemma situations you need advice on. Otherwise I'll speak to you the same time tomorrow night. Oh, and enjoy the skiing.'

'I will if I get half a chance. I think Chub has other activities in mind.'

Saturday morning came and it was warmer, with the temperatures in the low fifties – more like a spring day than mid-winter. The snow in Cambridge began to melt, and by the end of the morning you could see the grass again. It was, observed Tom, perfect weather for a presidential walkabout.

'Let's hope it's like this on Monday,' agreed Goldman.

The *Boston Globe* published the details of Jack Kennedy's visit to Boston. Tom and Goldman studied the article closely in case there was anything they had overlooked. The *Globe* reported that Secret Service agents had inspected the State House for security purposes the previous night: 'Every step Kennedy will take, from the time he enters the State House until he leaves, has been carefully charted by the Secret Service agents.' But, almost as if Harvard was considered a safer place than Beacon Hill, the paper reported only a modest level of security precautions being taken on campus: 'His safety will be left to the Secret Service. But university police have already begun planning for the protection of students who, among other restrictions, will not be allowed to stand on the statue of John Harvard outside the entrance to University Hall.'

'For the protection of students?' Alex Goldman was scornful. 'What the hell are they thinking about? Do they really think that stopping a few kids from climbing on a lousy statue is going to stop Kennedy from getting shot? Jesus, those guys must be crazy. I would have thought he would be safer in the State House than anywhere else. I mean, the guy is going to walk around in the open air, for Christ's sake.'

Meanwhile, neither man failed to notice, in the same edition, a report from Havana describing how Cuban troops, anti-tank guns, and four-barrelled Czech anti-aircraft guns were being deployed all along the capital's seafront, on Maleçon Drive.

'What do you think of that?' Goldman asked Tom.

'I think that Monday can't come quick enough.'

During Saturday afternoon Tom and Goldman took their cameras and, posing as tourists, took a stroll around Harvard Yard, keeping a

338

careful eye on Massachusetts Hall where, a late edition of the paper reported, federal agents would meet with the Cambridge police chief and the head of the Harvard University police to co-ordinate the security measures for this part of the President-elect's visit – Kennedy's first to his home city since winning the presidency back in November. But of uniformed police or anyone who looked like a Secret Service agent, there was no sign.

'I'm glad they're not protecting me,' said Tom. 'Dumb bastards.'

Neither man ate much that day. Since they planned to spend almost thirty-six hours holed up in Hollis Fifteen without the facility of a lavatory, they wanted to empty their stomachs as much as possible. For most of the evening they watched television, aware of Jack Kennedy coming nearer to them now, flying from Washington to New York aboard his private plane. In less than twenty-four hours the same plane would land at Logan airport, in Boston, and a motorcade would drive the President-elect to his Beacon Hill apartment at 122 Bowdoin Street.

At around one a.m. the two men dressed in suits and ties and put on warm coats. Then they collected a couple of small bags and went out into the cold night air. A gentle southwest wind tossed a small flurry of snow in their faces as they began the three-quarter-mile walk along Harvard Street and Massachusetts Avenue. The streets were quite deserted, almost surreally so. As if everyone in Cambridge had gone to some underground A-bomb shelter. Goldman remarked upon it.

'Maybe they'll go there soon enough,' said Tom. 'I was reading in the paper how the state of Massachusetts is building a shelter, at a cost of two million dollars. Not that you would ever get me in one of those mausoleums. When the bomb goes off I want to be in the fresh air, for as long as fresh air lasts. As near to the centre of the blast as possible. It'd be quicker that way. Like a single shot through the head.'

On Massachusetts Avenue they passed by the Widener main gate that led to the back of the eponymous library. The gate was closed now, but it would be through the Widener that Kennedy's car would enter the campus on Monday morning. Goldman and Tom passed through the smaller gate, near Boylston Hall, that, like the Johnson

Gate, was nearly always open. Entering the east quad of Harvard Yard, they paused in front of the rear entrance of University Hall, where Jack Kennedy would be greeted by the president of the Harvard Board of Overseers. Then they passed into the western quad, with Weld – the freshman dormitory where Kennedy himself had roomed in his first year at Harvard – on their left. They walked quickly across the quad in the direction of Hollis and, still seeing no one about, unlocked the door to Hollis South and went inside.

For several breathless seconds they waited, hearts thumping, in the darkness. All was quiet. The only curfew in a freshman dormitory was one on noise after one a.m. After a minute, they started up the stairs, but almost as soon as they arrived on the second-floor landing they heard a door above them open, and someone, smoking a cigarette, came out to use the bathroom. Tom and Alex Goldman stayed motionless on the creaking staircase as the young man, humming Floyd Cramer's hit 'Last Date', began a loud pee that echoed up and down the staircase. After a good minute and a half, they heard the sound of the toilet flushing and the student returning to his room. Goldman began to climb again, and Tom, with his heart in his mouth, followed. A short while later, having negotiated the stiff doorlock, the two men were inside Hollis Fifteen.

'So far, so good,' whispered Tom, locking the door carefully behind him.

Goldman slipped off his shoes, padded across to Chub's bed, and then sat down. 'As stakeouts go, I guess this is not so bad.'

Tom lay down on Torbert's bed and closed his eyes.

'What are you doing?' whispered Goldman.

'I'm going to get some sleep, that's what I'm doing. The gear can wait until morning.'

'What happened to the usual insomnia?'

'I reckon I'll sleep all right tonight. Don't ask me why.'

'You're a cool one, Paladin, I'll say that for you.'

'Nope, just a tired one.'

On Sunday, it turned a lot colder, but they did not light a fire. They watched TV with the sound turned low, and urinated into empty beer bottles, planning to empty these out of a window after it got dark.

There were few words between them now and they moved around the room without shoes, lest anyone hear them and think Chub, or Torbert, were at home. Once, there was a knock at the door, but after a moment or two they heard a voice shout from down the hall, 'They're away skiing this weekend, with a couple of broads,' which drew the response, 'Lucky bastards.'

In the early part of Sunday afternoon, Tom retrieved his rifle from behind the closet and, out of habit, cleaned it carefully, wearing gloves so as not to leave any prints. The Winchester was as cold a gun as it was possible to find outside of a forgotten foxhole in North Korea, and Tom wanted it to stay that way. Even the serial number had been filed off.

They kept the lower shutters closed, just in case a resident of Hollis South should glance up from the Yard and see someone moving around. But mostly they lay on their beds and waited for the time to pass. Throughout the day, each felt a lump growing inside his stomach that was as much tension as it was hunger. Only Tom was used to this kind of waiting. Patience was an essential quality in a sniper. One time, in the South Pacific, he had stalked a Japanese sniper for a full four days, before finally killing him. But even he had never felt a palpable tension like this. It was almost unbearable.

By six o'clock it was dark, and Goldman opened the shutters to admit whatever light was in the Yard outside. The moon was in its last quarter so there was not much to be had, just the dull sodium glow of a few streetlights in the east quad, and some windows in Massachusetts Hall, opposite. Sometimes they would drink coffee from a thermos flask, or eat a little chocolate, but by nine o'clock the coffee was cold and the chocolate was nearly all gone.

At ten o'clock Goldman put on some headphones, plugged them into the Hallicrafter short-wave radio, and began to hunt for the Secret Service wavelength. Meanwhile, Tom changed channels on the black and white TV in search of a news bulletin. If Jack Kennedy was on time, his plane would be coming in to land at Logan. Finding nothing on TV, Tom tried to picture the scene in his mind's eye. Massachusetts' top political figures there to greet the young Senator: Governor John Volpe, Lieutenant Governor Edward McLaughlin junior, Mayor Collins, the Commissioner of Public Safety Henry

Goguen, Sheriff Howard Fitzpatrick, and the Democratic State Chairman John Lynch. Maybe, if they could stand the freezing cold, there would be some well-wishers. Boston Irish, too thick to feel the cold. And more fool them, thought Tom, shivering inside his coat. It was not a night for a snowman to be standing around outside.

At ten thirty Goldman said, 'He's landed. Kennedy's plane just touched down at Logan. He's here, Tom. The President-elect's in Boston.'

26

The Shot

At precisely eight o'clock on the morning of Monday, 9 January 1961, Jack Kennedy's portly Negro butler, George Thomas, knocked softly on the bedroom door of suite thirty-six, 122 Bowdoin Street. He had served Kennedy for fourteen years, ever since Arthur Krock, an old friend of Joe's, had 'sent him over' to take care of Congressman Kennedy, as he then was.

'It's okay, George, I'm awake.'

George turned to face John McNally, and Ken O'Donnell, who were two of Kennedy's special presidential aides. Behind them stood a tall bald man, holding a breakfast tray. George nodded, and all four entered the Senator's bedroom.

O'Donnell, another Boston Irishman, said, 'You remember Joe Murphy, Senator, the building supervisor? Mrs Murphy usually prepares your breakfast.'

Kennedy sat up groggily as George pulled the drapes. The crowd in the street buzzed a little as it saw movement in the window. 'Sure, Joe,' said Kennedy. 'How are ya? Come on in? How's Mrs Murphy?'

'Not so good, sir.'

'I'm sorry to hear that, Joe.'

'I'm afraid she couldn't do your breakfast, this morning. So I did it myself. Two four-minute eggs, toast and coffee, just like you always have.'

'That's really kind of you, George. And I appreciate it very much.'

Murphy laid the tray carefully on the bed. 'It's my pleasure, sir. And may I say on behalf of everyone in the building how proud we all are of you, sir. And how pleased to have you back in Boston.'

'It's good to be back, Joe. It's been too long.'

'Well, I'll be on my way now, sir. Enjoy your breakfast.'

As Murphy went out of the bedroom, George looked down into the street. Kennedy's apartment was on the third floor, immediately above a barber's shop. The Senator had kept the apartment for about the same length of time he had retained George.

'Cold day outside, Senator,' said George. 'But there's quite a crowd out there already. Must be almost five hundred people.'

Kennedy sipped his coffee, and grimaced. 'Don't I know it. They kept me awake for most of the damn night. And I'd forgotten how soft this bed is. My back aches like the devil's blue balls. Thank Christ we're back at the Carlyle tonight and I can get some fucking sleep.'

O'Donnell, who had a little bit of a headache after several drinks with six Secret Service agents at the Old Brattle Tavern the night before, read the headline in that morning's *Globe*, and then handed his boss the newspaper. 'President-elect Comes Back Home for a Day. Shivering Crowd Cheers Kennedy.'

'Shivering is right,' said McNally. 'It's freezing out there this morning. Real Boston weather.'

Kennedy glanced over the front page and picked out another story. With a wry smile, he said, 'President-elect urged to tell public about Soviet danger.' Now he laughed. 'What the hell do they think I've been doing, for Christ's sake? Whistling Dixie? Jesus.' He tossed aside the newspaper, ate one of the eggs, some toast, and then drained his coffee cup with little evident pleasure. 'I hope Mrs Murphy's going to get better,' he said, and got out of bed wearing just his undershorts. 'I wouldn't like too many breakfasts like that one.'

While Kennedy showered and shaved, George opened a black, brassbound navy foot locker and removed the light-blue shirt his employer would be wearing. Beside it he placed a dark two-button blue suit – as opposed to the three buttons most American males

344

favoured – a navy-blue woollen tie, black socks, and black lace-up shoes.

'How did it go with the judge last night?' asked O'Donnell.

'Frank Morrissey? I thought he'd never fucking leave. Boy, can that guy drink. About tonight's speech, Kenny. How does this sound? For those to whom much is given, much is required. It doesn't sound too much as if it's out of Poor Richard's Almanac, does it?'

'What happened to the city on a hill?' asked O'Donnell. 'I liked that.' Among the staff O'Donnell's word was law. If he didn't like something, even Kennedy was inclined to think twice about it.

'Still in there, but that's John Winthrop, not me. I thought I'd try to work it in somewhere. For those to whom much is given, much is required,' Kennedy repeated, performing now. 'And when at some future date the high court of history sits in judgement on each one of us – recording whether in our brief span of service we fulfilled our responsibilities to the state – and all that jazz. What do you think?'

McNally nodded. 'Sounds good, sir.'

'Thank God, I only have to speak for fifteen minutes. I think I'm getting a cold.'

When Kennedy had finished dressing, he sat down to discuss his day's timetable with O'Donnell, McNally, and Dave Powers – another presidential aide, who was also Boston Irish. There were some who thought Powers and O'Donnell looked not unalike, the two ugly mick sisters to Jack's Cinderella.

'The cars come at ten,' explained O'Donnell. 'There are four. You'll be in the third. We'll get to Harvard at around ten thirty. I've spoken with Devereaux Josephs, president of the Board of Overseers, and he doesn't think that part of the meeting will last longer than about an hour and a quarter.'

'Is he an academic? I've forgotten.'

'No sir, he's an insurance executive, I believe.'

'A Harvard man who sells insurance,' mused Kennedy. 'I could use some myself after that flight last night. Did you see the wingtips when we landed? They were covered in ice.'

'At around noon, you'll leave University Hall and walk across Harvard Yard to have lunch at the new Loeb Drama Center.'

'Place looks like a goddamned aquarium,' complained Kennedy. 'And I hate drama almost as much as I hate baseball.'

'At about two o'clock the cars will take us to Arthur Schlesinger's home on Irving Street. By the way, all these times are contingent on how much traffic you generate. At approximately three o'clock, we'll go to MIT.'

'This is to hear the report from my task force on taxation, right?'

'That's correct, sir. After which, you have a meeting with the president of MIT, Doctor Julius Stratton, at four forty-five. Five twenty-five we get back to Beacon Hill and the State House, where you'll be met under the archway by Ed McLaughlin. From there, we'll proceed to the governor's office where Volpe and an assortment of representatives and senators will greet you.'

Kennedy sighed wearily. 'That's it?' He grinned.

'Yes sir. Incidentally, according to the *Globe* you'll be the first President or President-elect to address the Massachusetts Legislature since Taft, in nineteen twelve.'

'Taft?' Kennedy looked displeased. 'Worst president of the century.'

'Yes sir,' grinned O'Donnell. 'Seven o'clock, we fly back to New York.'

'And not a moment too soon, by the sound of it. We'll need some fun after a day like today, eh Dave?'

'Yes sir. You've got your work cut out today. Just like being back on the campaign trail.'

'We survived that, didn't we? We'll survive this, I guess.'

At nine fifty the Secret Service rang up from the vestibule to say that the cars from Boston Ford were outside.

George Thomas looked at his boss and asked him if he'd like a topcoat and a hat. 'The crowd's the only warm thing out there this morning,' he said. 'And don't forget you'll be walking some, too.'

'George,' said Kennedy. 'When have you ever seen me wearing a hat? Besides, who needs a coat when you have the Secret Service to keep the chill off?'

In the tiny elevator on the way down to the only slightly larger vestibule, Kennedy said to O'Donnell, 'Remind me once again, Kenny.

That old bat who's my neighbour. The one who shook my hand last night. I've been trying to remember her name.'

O'Donnell flicked through some pages that were attached to his clipboard. 'Mary Jenkins,' he said, at last. 'She's a schoolteacher.'

'And the guy who cooked my breakfast again?'

'Joe Murphy.'

Both Murphy and Mary Jenkins were in the vestibule, waiting to see him off, as Kennedy had known they would be, along with Police Commissioner Leo Sullivan, his secretary Charlie Hoare, the Middlesex County Sheriff Howard Fitzpatrick, and a phalanx of Secret Service agents. Kennedy shook a few hands and, flanked by agents, walked out of the front door to greet the cheering crowd. He waved and smiled, before being hustled into the waiting car.

'Jesus Christ,' he said, as the door closed. 'George was right. It's fucking cold today. I think I've been too long in Palm Beach, Dave. That's what it is. I'm not properly acclimatised.'

The four-car motorcade headed down Joy Street along Cambridge Street to Storrow Drive – a route that was heavily guarded by Boston MDC and, after they crossed Longfellow Bridge, by Cambridge police too. At Harvard, the motorcade entered the campus through the Widener main gate on Massachusetts Avenue, and travelled through the Yard's east quadrangle, which was already full of students eager to get a look at the university's most famous alumnus.

'This is almost embarrassing,' Kennedy said with a chuckle. 'I was not a very good student at Harvard. Swimming was my best subject.'

As Kennedy got out of the car, an enormous cheer went up, and to his momentary alarm a man caught him by the elbow and then shook him by the hand, saying he was an Irishman, and that his name was Patrick Shea, and that he was a retired Cambridge policeman. 'And this,' he said proudly, 'is my daughter, sir.'

'Delighted to meet you,' grinned Kennedy, and mounted the steps to the rear of University Hall to greet the Harvard president, Nathan Pusey, and Devereaux Josephs. Meanwhile, the sizeable crowd had started to chant, 'Speech! Speech! We want a speech!'

Kennedy turned and raised his hands for quiet. Then he said, 'I am here to go over your grades with Doctor Pusey, and I'll protect your interests.' But his words were whipped away in the bitterly cold wind and only those who were standing nearest the steps caught his words, and laughed. Still smiling, Kennedy turned his back on the crowd, shook hands with Pusey and Josephs, waved again, and then went into University Hall.

In Hollis Fifteen, Tom Jefferson and Alex Goldman heard the cheers through the open window and saw the crowds of students streaming out of the west quad, and pressing around the corner of University Hall, where Kennedy was making his entrance. There were hundreds, perhaps even as many as a thousand students, and their numbers were growing all the time. As soon as Kennedy was inside University Hall, they began to congregate in the west quad in front of the building. They were not just from Harvard. There were quite a few Radcliffe girls, easily identified by their striking red and yellow sweaters, and many others who carried Welcome Jack signs from Boston University and MIT. Next to University Hall, at Weld, the rather Gothic-looking hall where the President-elect had once roomed, a banner was hung from a third-floor window. It read: 'Jack – Weld is a Depressed Area'.

'What have they got to be depressed about?' demanded Tom. 'Poor little rich kids.'

'Shit, I'd be depressed myself if I had to room in there,' declared Goldman. 'Place looks more like a penitentiary than a freshman dormitory.'

'This isn't exactly the Plaza in here,' remarked Tom.

With the window wide open now, the room was freezing, and Goldman blew on his hands in a vain attempt to keep them warm. Unlike Tom, he had not thought to wear gloves. Since he was not handling the actual rifle, there had seemed little need for them, but he was regretting it now. Swathed in a blanket off Chub's bed, he sat beside the short-wave radio listening in to the Secret Service signals traffic. There were two presidential wavelengths: Baker Channel, emanating from a signals control car in the motorcade, which kept Kennedy in touch with Washington; and Charlie Channel, the radio link between the presidential car and the Secret Service agents who were inside University Hall. It was with the Charlie frequency that Goldman concerned himself.

Tom rolled off the desk he had placed by the window, on which he had been lying in the prone firing position, but without the rifle, and sat down on the floor beside Alex Goldman. Collecting the rifle off the floor, and nervously inspecting the blue sky through the telescopic sights, he said, 'So, are we gonna do this?'

'Sure we're going to do it,' said Goldman.

'I just wanted to hear you say it. Because now that we're here. Well, you know.' Tom shrugged.

'I know what you're driving at, Paladin.'

'I figured you would.'

'And you're crazy. Orders are orders. You know that.'

Tom worked the rifle bolt and sighted a pigeon high in the branches of an elm tree. He pulled the trigger on an empty chamber and nodded. 'Whatever you say, Alex. I'm just the guy who pulls the trigger, you know?'

'That's not what you sound like.'

Tom shrugged innocently. 'Now that we're here. That's all I said.'

'You want to know what your trouble is, Tom?'

'What's that?'

'You think too much.' Goldman shook his head.

Tom worked the bolt and fired the empty chamber again. Even unloaded, it still added a slight smell of gun oil and cordite to the room's cold fresh air, as if an invisible bullet had been fired.

'And stop playing with that fucking rifle. You make me nervous.'

'Take it easy,' said Tom, and lit a cigarette. With the window wide open he was no longer worried that any other students on the top floor of Hollis South would smell his tobacco. Besides, all was silent down the hall. Everyone was now out in the Yard.

'Take it easy?' Goldman repeated scornfully. 'Maybe you didn't see all those fucking cops down there?'

'I saw them. Not so many as I thought. Not so many as they need, if you ask me. I know crowds. I study them. I work with them. I use them. Crowds are my cover. When you've done as many jobs as me, you get to know what a crowd will do when they see someone famous, or hear a shot. And I'm telling you, there aren't nearly enough cops for all the kids there are out there. Must be getting on for two thousand. So forget about them. When the time comes they'll have their work cut out just looking out for Kennedy's ass to pay any attention to us.'

Goldman grinned. 'Okay. You're right.'

'Sure I'm right. You just keep your ear on that Charlie Channel,' said Tom. 'As soon as he comes out of that front door, I want to be ready for him. Okay?'

'Don't you worry about me,' insisted Goldman. He listened carefully to the voices in his ear for a moment, and then said, 'I wonder what's going on in that room, right now.'

'It's a closed meeting. Proceedings are in secret. No press.'

'I know, I was just wondering what they would be talking about.'

'If you ask me, they're pissed at him, that's what's going on. He's been stealing Harvard's best brains to fill his lousy cabinet. Dave Bell, McGeorge Bundy, and Archibald Cox. They'll probably have to resign from the university.'

'I thought these guys could take a year off. A sabbatical?'

'Uh-uh. Kennedy's asked them all to stay on for four years. Harvard only grants its faculty members a one-year leave of absence. I've been reading about it. I'm telling you, Alex. They'll be chewing his balls.'

The January meeting of the Harvard Board of Overseers was held in the faculty room on the second floor of University Hall. There were thirty overseers in all, with five men elected each year to serve a six-year term. John Kennedy, a member of the Harvard class of 1940, was the youngest member of a board that included alumni from all walks of life – everyone from a mountaineer to a bishop. On a raised dais, six inches above the main body of the overseers, which included Kennedy, at a massive round table cut from a huge slab of Philippine nara wood, and scrutinised by the portraits of previous Harvard alumni such as Charles Eliot and Henry Longfellow, five *ex officio* members of the board sat facing the rest. These five included Nathan Pusey, Paul Cabot, David Bailey, James Reynolds, and Devereaux Josephs who, as president of the board, brought the meeting to order with a simple, 'Shall we begin?'

The Harvard University president, Nathan Pusey, then rose to deliver his annual report on the condition of the university. Pusey told the board that the time had come in the nation's history when government and universities should work more closely together.

'We must take thought together how the relationship is to be made as fruitful as possible, and be careful at every stage of the way to provide adequate safeguards for autonomous interests which rightfully exist within the relationship, and must be maintained.'

In his prepared text, Pusey made only one reference to the President-elect when he referred to the constant turnover in Harvard's officers of instruction. 'This natural process,' he said, 'has perhaps recently had a bit more assistance from Washington than we might selfishly like.'

Jack Kennedy grinned sheepishly as, for a brief moment, everyone looked at him. Not that he felt in any way embarrassed about any of his cabinet appointments. The country needed men of the calibre of Bundy, Bell, and Cox more than Harvard. Damn it all, he needed them himself. What better way was there to look like a great President of the United States than by having great men – the best brains there were – working for you?

Pusey, who Kennedy thought looked like the building supervisor at Bowdoin Street, except with more hair, spoke for almost half an hour, after which there were votes taken on appointments, honorary degrees, and the policy decisions of the seven-man Harvard Corporation. Kennedy enjoyed his membership of the board. But at the same time he was glad to have been excused two earlier committee reports from the departments of military science and astronomy. And he was also glad to be leaving the meeting before a report from the chemistry department. Chemistry bored him even more than astronomy. Even routine meetings of the board could sometimes last all day, and if there was one thing Jack Kennedy hated, it was a meeting that went on too long. When he was finally in the White House he was going to try and make sure that no meeting ever lasted longer than an hour. Life was just too short to listen to a lot of hot air.

Surreptitiously, he glanced at his wristwatch and saw that it was nearing midday. Only a little while longer, he told himself, and wondered just how many students there were now in the west quad of Harvard Yard. It sure sounded like a lot of people out there. He hoped everything would be okay.

Even at the best of times Jack Kennedy did not like crowds. Most of all he hated to be pawed, like that jerk from the Cambridge police, with his daughter. Privacy and personal space were very important to him. He could smile and shake hands and make a few jokes, but that was it. Ever since Lyndon's experience in Dallas, when people had spat on him and Lady Bird, he had been wary of large groups of people, preferring to ride in a car instead of walking about. And students. There was no telling what any of them were capable of. His time as a young freshman at Weld now seemed like a lifetime away, but he could still recall that, as a member of the Spee Club and Hasty Pudding, he had displayed some fairly wild behaviour of his own.

At last the meeting was over, and Kennedy caught the eye of John McNally, and then his Secret Service agents. The Ivy League was what he jokingly called them because they were most of them anything but that. Tough sons of bitches was what they were. Sometimes they were a little too cautious of his safety. Like the way they had tried to stop that poor sonofabitch Joe Murphy from coming inside the flat to cook his fucking breakfast. How much of a threat could you pose to the future President of the United States with two hard-boiled eggs?

He stood up from his chair, went on to automatic handshake, and allowed two agents to gently steer him towards the faculty room door. Glancing around, smiling, always smiling, he caught sight of the portrait of Longfellow, and for no reason he could think of, except that he had considered stealing something from *The Psalm of Life* for his speech to the State Legislature, he found himself remembering one particular verse: 'Lives of great men all remind us / We can make our lives sublime, / And, departing, leave behind us / Footprints on the sands of time.' He liked that verse a lot.

They were going down the stairs now. Pusey was saying something about training more Harvard men for policy-making responsibility, and he himself was replying that it had certainly done him no harm. Then the front door of University Hall opened and Kennedy stepped outside into the icy blast. Momentarily dazzled by the midday sun above the rooftops of Hollis and Stoughton, and the enthusiastic roar of the crowd now assembled, he blinked furiously and moved uncertainly down the steps.

Using the window shutter as cover, Tom Jefferson lay stretched out on the desk of Hollis Fifteen and, with the barrel of his rifle supported by one of Chub Farrell's pillows, took aim at the figure emerging from the front door of University Hall. In the space of a few seconds he pressed the butt of the rifle firmly against his shoulder and, tensing the muscles in his upper arm, curled his forefinger lightly on the trigger.

The scope picture was clear, with Kennedy's handsome, smiling, tanned face almost filling the eyepiece. Tom made a deeper inhalation and exhalation, the way he always did, and saw the reticle moving slightly on the bridge of Kennedy's nose. Taking the slack out of the trigger now. Pulling back just to the edge of release. Keeping his whole body absolutely still. The cross-hairs exactly on target. Holding his inhalation as, straight and clean, he pulled the trigger, all the time trying to ignore the curious whirring noise that tickled the air in the room, like the sound of a large mechanical cricket.

The firing pin of the Winchester rifle clicked harmlessly. Tom was only momentarily surprised not to feel the usual recoil that presaged his victim's death. Calmly, he worked the bolt again for a second shot, and said, 'One of us had better be loaded. I'd hate to be wasting my time here.'

'I'll tell you when to stop,' said Alex Goldman. He held the Bolex Rex sixteen-mill cine camera steady on Tom's body for a second longer as once again the marksman squeezed his trigger on an empty rifle.

'Whatever you say, Mister De Mille,' murmured Tom, working the bolt again. 'Just try not to get me in close-up. You're not on my best side, there.'

Goldman thumbed the switch to work the Bolex's powerful zoom, smoothly catapulting his camera view across Tom's head, the barrel of the rifle, and the heads of almost three thousand students as, yelling, shouting, and pushing, they broke through the police line and shoved their enthusiastic way to the future President.

'Beautiful,' murmured Goldman. 'What a great shot. This is real cinema.'

He had an excellent shot of the bemused look on the young Senator's face. And the look of real alarm on the faces of the Secret

Service agents who were trying to elbow a path through the crowd for Kennedy. Such was the scene of near pandemonium that Goldman could see through his viewfinder that it was almost as if Tom had fired a real shot into Kennedy's head.

The rifle clicked harmlessly a third time.

'That's three times, plumb centre of his forehead,' reported Tom. 'If this rifle was loaded, Jack Kennedy would now be as dead as swing, for sure. Pity it isn't.'

Goldman zoomed back off Kennedy and through the window of Hollis Fifteen, coming around Tom's side to take account of Kennedy's progress through the Yard. He stopped filming, and turned the clockwork mechanism of the Bolex quickly. Fully wound, it allowed a shot of between twenty and thirty seconds' duration.

'Move your head out of the way of the scope a second,' he directed. Tom did as he was told, and let Goldman take a shot of the view through the Unertl scope. 'Okay, now work the bolt.' Tom worked the bolt. Goldman shot a close-up of the trigger as Tom squeezed it again. 'You'd have done it too, wouldn't you?' he chuckled. 'You really would have shot him, wouldn't you? Crazy sonofabitch.'

'Well, you know what they say. In for a penny. 'Sides, he fucked my wife, didn't he? If that's not a good reason to kill a man, I don't know what is. How long do I have to keep doing this? I'm beginning to feel stupid.'

'Who's directing this picture? Me or you? One more shot, okay?' Goldman wound the camera again.

Tom worked the rifle bolt a fourth time, and aimed at the tip of Kennedy's ear for a second, then at the knot of his blue woollen tie. 'He doesn't know how lucky he is,' said Tom, squeezing the trigger again. 'Yes, Mister Kennedy, today you were one lucky sonofabitch.'

'Okay, that's enough,' said Goldman. 'I think I must have two or three minutes' worth of film by now.'

Tom placed the rifle on the floor, and rolled off the desk, letting out an exhausted groan. 'Jesus,' he exclaimed. 'I think that's actually worse than doing it for real. I feel kind of vulnerable doing this job without ammunition. Naked almost.'

'Not having any bullets is our only guarantee that we won't get the chair if we're caught,' said Goldman, leaning across the desk now to get a last shot of the back of Jack Kennedy's head, as the Secret Service escorted him through a side entrance of Massachusetts Hall opposite, to escape the students in a dramatic change of plan. 'Look at that mess,' he said contemptuously. 'Another Secret Service foul-up.'

Tom was already replacing the rifle behind the closet, and, once again, he checked that it could not be seen.

'First time I got paid not to blow someone's head off,' he remarked.

'You're forgetting Castro,' said Goldman. 'You took Giancana's money to do that job. Anyway, I think you should be proud of yourself.'

'How do you make that out? This might be bad for my reputation.'

'If this plan works, we could stop a war.' Goldman finished shooting and put the big Bolex back in its leather carrying case. 'Come on, let's tidy up as quickly as possible and get out of here while there's still a crowd outside.'

He lifted up the floorboards to put away the radio, while Tom dragged the desk away from the window, and replaced the books and papers that had been lying on it. Goldman screwed down the floorboards and replaced the rug. Then they made the beds they had slept on. Finally the two men stood in the doorway and inspected Hollis Fifteen.

'The shutters,' said Goldman, and went to close them. Outside, the student body was grouped in front of Massachusetts, chanting, 'We want Jack. We want Jack.'

'Looks the same as it did when we came in,' pronounced Tom. 'Spartan.'

'I think so, too,' said Goldman, and opened the door.

Outside, in Harvard Yard, chaos still reigned. While the students chanted over and over again for Kennedy to come out and make a speech, Secret Service agents were driving three cars up on the grass in front of Massachusetts Hall, and across the cement walk to the front door.

Goldman took out the Bolex once again, wound it up, checked his exposure and speed, and pushed his way through the crowd to try and get a final shot of Kennedy's exit. Tom followed, yelling, 'What are you doing? Come on, let's get the hell out of here.'

Now, two vehicles took flanking positions on either side of

Kennedy's limousine, which was parked immediately beside the door to the hall. A triple line of police began to surround the cars.

'What am I doing?' said Alex, finding a good shot of the crowd and the cars and the police in his viewfinder. 'I'm making a movie, for Christ's sake. To do that well, you have to build your movie around a storyline. You've gotta maintain interest in your picture by mixing long and short scenes. To get that Lubitsch touch, you gotta lead people up to your central idea. You gotta use a whole variety of shots to build suspense. To bring along your audience.'

There was a huge cheer and Goldman zoomed in on the front door as Kennedy and his agents dashed from the building, and into the waiting cars. 'That's my boy,' grinned Goldman. He held the shot and then followed with the zoom as, a moment or two later, all four cars drove out of Johnson Gate, on to Massachusetts Avenue. Finally, the Kennedy party was on its way to the Loeb Drama Center on Brattle Street. Goldman glanced at his watch. It was one o'clock.

'Yes sir,' he said. 'Everything you shoot has got to be tied into your plot. The trouble with most home movies is that people forget to tell a story. But nothing's more important than that. Story is everything.'

When they were safely back in the Center Street apartment, Tom made them both some hot coffee and sandwiches and, while Alex developed the cine film, he watched *The Guiding Light* on TV. For a while he even closed his eyes and dozed a little. He was exhausted. The dummy assassination had been every bit as tiring as the real thing. More so. The sense of anti-climax was almost too much to bear. But it wasn't over yet. Not by a long way.

An hour or so later, at around two thirty, Alex emerged from the darkroom holding a small spool of developed film in his hand.

'Here it is,' he announced triumphantly. 'Today's rushes.'

Tom got to his feet and, holding it up to the light, inspected some of the forty or fifty feet of sixteen-millimetre film Alex had shot on the Bolex Rex, and for which they had risked so much.

'When can we view it?' he asked.

But Goldman was already unrolling a forty-inch screen.

'No time like the present,' he said. 'Of course, you understand this little film classic is unedited. The lab'll need to make a copy before they slice this up.'

Tom turned the TV off. Goldman threaded the film on to a Bell and Howell projector, pulled the drapes, and then sat down on the sofa to watch. The two viewed the short film through several times with Goldman continuing to comment favourably on his own camerawork.

'I reckon it's come out real fine,' he declared. 'Like I was Alfred fucking Hitchcock. Nicely lit, and nicely framed. Even though I say so myself. Damn good camera, that Bolex. I just wish we'd had sound.'

'We agreed,' said Tom. 'The Fairchild was too complicated.'

'Colour's good, though. You and Kennedy make quite a pair,' said Goldman. 'I always knew he was photogenic, but you look good, too. Maybe you should have been a movie actor, Tom. You've got presence, I'll say that much for you.'

'A rifle can do that for you. It lends you a certain something.' Tom lit a cigarette. 'And what about you? Looks like you've missed your vocation, too. Maybe when you get back to Miami you can try your hand shooting skin-flicks.'

'I might just do that.' Goldman glanced at his luminous wristwatch. 'Speaking of skin-flicks, where the hell are those two girls? I thought they'd be back here by now. We've got a plane to catch.'

'They'll be here,' said Tom. 'Relax, will you? There's plenty of time yet.'

'Okay. Do you want to look at it again?'

'You look, Alex. I'm going to take a leak.'

Tom went towards the lavatory, and then halfway along the corridor ducked into Alex's bedroom where he quickly searched the other man's coat pockets and briefcase. Instead of the three air tickets to Miami, he found only one air ticket, in Alex Goldman's name. And a Walther automatic with a silencer. Wherever Goldman was planning to take Edith and Anne, it certainly wasn't Miami. Tom thought it looked very much as if Goldman was planning to shoot them both in the car, most likely in the parking lot at Logan.

Tom came back into the lounge and stood at the back of the room, in the shadows, watching the flickering film.

'If you'd actually done it,' said Alex. 'If you'd actually gone ahead and shot him, this would now be the most famous piece of film in the world, I guess.'

'I guess it would at that,' agreed Tom.

'I wonder if we could have got away with it?'

'Sure we could. All those students? We'd have been gone with the wind.' Tom paused. 'When will you take it to Tampa?'

'I told Ameijeiras I'd hand him the film the day after tomorrow.'

'Alex?' Tom spoke carefully. 'You will look after those girls, won't you? Make sure they're all right when they get to Miami.'

'Yeah, sure. I'll take care of them.'

Tom paused.

'That's what I was afraid of,' he muttered.

'Hmm?'

'Well, I guess I'll be taking the film to Tampa myself, Alex.'

'What's that you say, Paladin?'

The film ended and Alex turned to look at Tom in the white light of the Bell and Howell projector. He found himself staring into the silenced barrel of his own automatic.

'Jesus Christ, Tom,' Alex said with a smile. 'What is this?'

Tom said nothing. What was there to say? Was it revenge? Or was it something else? A necessary precaution. Perhaps, in the final analysis, it was a little bit of both.

'For Christ's sake, Tom. What's the idea?'

'Have gun, will travel,' said Tom, and fired twice in quick succession. The first bullet caught Goldman in the throat, just below the Adam's apple, and, as the impact twisted his body around on the sofa, the second shot struck him in the back, high between the shoulder blades. For a moment Alex Goldman looked too surprised to move. His mouth stayed open on the word he had been about to utter, and then, slowly, he slid silently on to the floor and stayed still.

Tom leaned over the body and pressed his fingers close to Goldman's bloody neck, searching for a pulse. And finding a faint throb, he stood up and fired a third shot into the back of Goldman's head at point-blank range.

That made one for Mary, one for Edith, and one for Anne. Tom sighed and tossed the gun on to the blood-spattered sofa.

'Sorry Alex. But you know, I think I'd better drive those two girls to the airport myself. Just in case. I like Edith. Fond of her, even. I wouldn't want anything bad to happen to her. Not like what happened to Mary.'

27

The Cuba Memorandum

Five days later, Raul Roa, the Cuban Foreign Minister, sent a small package to the President-elect of the United States, at the White House, in Washington. The package contained a short memorandum personally written by Roa, and a number of what the memorandum described as 'evidentiary exhibits'. As a matter of routine the Secret Service removed the package for examination, and all its contents, including the memorandum, were subsequently destroyed. A second identical package, sent to the new Secretary of State, Dean Rusk, met the same fate at the hands of the same, acutely embarrassed, people. A third identical package was sent to Allen Dulles, at the Central Intelligence Agency, and was routinely intercepted by the Security Division. The package eventually found its way on to the desk of Colonel Sheffield Edwards who, upon reviewing its contents, immediately dispatched a number of agents, included Jim O'Connell, to Harvard University.

O'Connell reported back to Washington on the evening of 19 January. As soon as Edwards had heard his subordinate's report, he telephoned Richard Bissell at his home in Cleveland Park, near the Washington Cathedral, and was told that Mr and Mrs Bissell were attending the Pre-Inauguration Gala – a variety show at the city's

Armory, hosted by Frank Sinatra. Edwards called the Armory and waited for several minutes while one of Bissell's aides tried to find him, during which time he managed to hear almost all of Ethel Merman singing 'Give Him the Oo-La-La', which was as near to any kind of Washington gala, or Georgetown party, that Edwards had ever been to. But at last Bissell came to the phone and, hearing Edwards out, called a meeting in his office at eight o'clock the following morning.

Eight inches of snow fell in Washington overnight, which made driving all but impossible. At seven o'clock on the morning of 20 January 1961, as Edwards slowly negotiated the treacherous road between his home and Bissell's L Street office, three thousand servicemen were already hard at work with snow ploughs and bulldozers, shovelling tons of snow into seven hundred army trucks in an effort to get the capital city moving. The sky was blue and the sun was shining, but it was unusually cold, even for Washington, with the temperature ten degrees below freezing. This was still not cold enough to deter the thousands of people all along the Mall, from the White House to the Lincoln Memorial, who had come to see John F. Kennedy become the thirty-fifth President of the United States. Many of them had spent the night sleeping out. And so determined were they to see something of the inauguration that some of them had even lit fires. Driving through the snow, past these fires, and the crowd of vagrant-like people huddled around them in blankets, Washington looked almost primitive, as if a sudden nuclear strike had reduced the country to the level of the Stone Age. It all helped to make Edwards feel awkward and unsettled, as if everything around him was coming badly unstuck.

It was seven thirty a.m. when Edwards arrived in Bissell's office. O'Connell was already there, as was Bissell's secretary, Doris Mirage, and together they had set up the cine projector and a rollaway screen. Gradually, the others arrived – Barnes and Bross, bleary from the night before, then Flannery, and finally Bissell himself, who showed no ill effects from having remained at the gala until Kennedy had left, at three a.m.

Straight away, Edwards took charge of the meeting. He explained the circumstances of the package's receipt and that Allen Dulles had not yet been informed of its contents. He also added that it was his information that the Secret Service had intercepted two similar packages which, according to his source on the State Department security detail, had both been destroyed. Edwards then proceeded to read the Cuba Memorandum.

'Since January nineteen fifty-nine, and the defeat of the Batista dictatorship, the democratic peoples of Cuba have suffered the most vile, criminal, and unjust campaign to overthrow their popular republic. In the two years of the Cuban republic's existence, the United States government and its security agencies have countenanced, plotted, encouraged, and executed several attempts on the life of the Prime Minister of Cuba, Doctor Fidel Pino Santos Castro. The Cuban people are not a savage people, or a criminal people, but the most feeling people in the world, and wish only to live in peace with our neighbours, the United States of America. Doctor Castro himself believes that nothing and no one can derail the revolution, and that his death could only strengthen the resolve of all Cubans to live as they, and not the US government, would wish. Nevertheless, Doctor Castro is beloved of the Cuban people who tell you now, in the name of peace, liberty, and international law, that all attempts to assassinate the Maximum Leader must cease forthwith, otherwise President John F. Kennedy will himself be assassinated. Indeed, he would already be dead now but for the goodwill of the Prime Minister and the most noble people of Cuba, as the accompanying evidentiary exhibits will confirm. Should the current campaign of homicidal aggression against our Prime Minister and the government of this island be continued, it is certain that no such goodwill will be forthcoming again. In short, President John F. Kennedy will not be so fortunate a second time. Watch the film, and mark well how close he came to death, and then consider carefully how close he might come once again. This memorandum is not a threat, but rather, in the proper sense of the word, it contains something to be borne in mind, and remembered well. President Kennedy's health and happiness, which is our most earnest desire, is in your hands. Yours sincerely, Raul Roa, Minister of Foreign Affairs, Cuba.'

Edwards put down the Cuba Memorandum, as the document henceforth was known, and nodded to O'Connell, who got to his feet and pulled the drapes against the strong reflected sunlight. When the room was darker, Edwards switched on the Wollensak projector, and the meeting sat back to view Alex Goldman's film in silence.

When it was finished, there was a long pause before Bissell said, 'Can we see it again, please, Jim?'

O'Connell pulled back the drapes, wound the film back and, while he re-spooled the sixteen-millimetre film, Edwards continued speaking.

'The film was accompanied by this – a thirty-calibre bullet, fitted with an accelerator which snipers use to help slugs achieve a much higher velocity. There was also a copy of the *Boston Globe* describing Kennedy's January ninth visit to Harvard University, which is where the film was shot. Since receiving it, we have been able to identify the marksman's vantage point within Harvard, as Hollis Hall. Agent O'Connell visited Hollis Hall yesterday and, during a search of room fifteen, recovered a thirty-calibre Winchester rifle that was hidden behind a closet, and was, we believe, the rifle used in the film. The two students occupying the room were not in Harvard on the weekend prior to Kennedy's visit. Nor were they in Harvard on the morning of Kennedy's walkabout. They have been questioned, and their alibis check out. Although some of the facts affecting them remain to be resolved, we are satisfied that they were not involved in the plot to kill, or rather not to kill, President Kennedy.

'It's our best guess that the man in the film is most probably Tom Jefferson. Alex Goldman, the FBI agent we dispatched to try and bring Jefferson in for us, was found dead in a Cambridge apartment just a few days ago. Most likely he was murdered by Jefferson. The connection seems to speak for itself. However, the identity of the cameraman remains a mystery to us. Ready, Jim?'

O'Connell nodded, and pulled the drapes once more. He switched on the projector.

This time, as he watched the film, Bissell said, 'Could the film be a fake, Sheff? Films like this can be faked, I believe.'

'I had the same thought myself, sir. And I had the film examined by an expert from TSS who informs me that although the film has been edited, there are no anomalous characteristics that would lead him to believe that the film was a fake. There are no tracking errors, no inconsistency in ground shadows, no magnification anomalies, nothing. The film is completely genuine, sir.'

'In which case,' sighed Bissell, 'the Cubans could very easily have done it. Killed the President.'

'Filming it and doing it are two very different things,' objected Tracy Barnes. 'There's the small matter of nerve to be considered.'

'I don't think those two men lacked nerve,' said Bissell. 'They could easily have been shot and killed if the Secret Service had been doing its job properly.'

'Since it so obviously wasn't doing its job,' said Flannery, 'it becomes easy to see why they've suppressed the film and the accompanying memo. You're quite sure the President hasn't seen this, Sheff?'

'Quite sure.'

The film finished a second time. O'Connell pulled the drapes again, and then returned to his seat. He could recall the look of astonishment on the faces of Chub Farrell and Torbert Winthrop when he found the rifle in their room at Hollis Hall, and smiled. They had been terrified. Still were, probably. They had a lot of explaining that remained ahead of them.

'Interesting,' muttered Bissell, and glanced at his watch. 'In less than four hours John F. Kennedy will be inaugurated as President of the United States. But it is quite clear to me that it could just as easily have been Lyndon Johnson we were inaugurating as President, this morning.'

'Now there's a thought,' said someone. 'LBJ in the White House. Be like having John Wayne in charge of policy.'

'Better than Kennedy,' said someone else.

'You might as well know,' said Bissell. 'Last night President Kennedy more or less told me that I would succeed Allen Dulles as DD/I.'

'Congratulations, sir,' said Barnes and Bross.

'Under the circumstances, I think it's a little early for that. Quite obviously I feel a loyalty to the man. But at the same time I now have this agency to think of. So the question is, what do I do with this information? Am I to treat this as In-House Communications, and keep it secret to this agency? Or should I bring it to the attention of the President and his security advisers? What do we think?'

'If we tell the President,' opined Barnes, 'then it might very well impact upon JMARC. Right now, Kennedy's four-square behind plans to invade Cuba and get rid of Castro. But there's no telling what might be the result of a full disclosure. After all, he's only human. If it was me that rifle had been pointed at, I might very well turn around and say, "Okay, live and let live. Communist or not, Castro could have killed me and didn't. It would hardly be the action of a gentleman to reply in any way other than to call off the AMTHUG programme." I think he might very well cancel the whole deal, sir. The invasion, everything. And where would that leave us in DD/P? A Directorate of Plans without a plan is not much of a directorate.'

'I am of the same opinion,' said Bissell. 'Besides, if the Secret Service have already suppressed this information because it shows them with egg on their faces, then it's hardly our responsibility, I'd have thought. Frankly, it was their call, not ours. And they've made it. If we said anything now, it would upset the whole damned apple-cart.'

'But surely we can't just ignore this,' said Bross. 'What about the President's security? If we go ahead with the Cuban invasion plans, and another assassination attempt on Castro's life, then they may well turn out to be as good as their word. And try and kill him again. What then?'

'No, we can't just ignore it,' said Bissell. 'Nor are we going to. I'll speak to Gerald Behn at the White House. See if he can't ginger up his Secret Service detail. Discourage the President from any more walks around Harvard Yard, that kind of thing. Make sure he only rides in the presidential limo from now on. If I know Gerald, he will have done something like it already. But perhaps my mentioning it will encourage him to go the extra mile. Maybe some new blood in the Secret Service is what is needed. New procedures. Some of those guys are as old as I am. But I don't think there's any undue cause for alarm, John. As Tracy has said, doing it for real is a very different proposition to making a movie about it. But I must say, looking at the film, and the way this whole thing has been handled, it gives me a new respect for the Cuban Intelligence Service. This was a very skilful operation. Just goes to show what can be done with a little guts and know-how, eh, Sheff?'

'Yes sir. It just goes to show what can be done.'

Just what could be done was a matter of equal interest to Sam Giancana when, less than three months after Kennedy's inauguration, Johnny Rosselli met with the Chicago gangster to tell him what he had been able to glean about the hit on Kennedy that never was, from conversations he had had in Washington and Las Vegas with O'Connell and Maheu.

'It seems like Jefferson actually had Kennedy in his telescopic sights,' said Rosselli. 'Apparently, on the film, he actually pulls the trigger, three or four times, before the camera zooms right in on Kennedy's head. Almost like it's a bullet. I'm told that it's a very nice bit of camera work.'

'That's one movie I'd like to see,' admitted Giancana. 'Jefferson had balls. I always said so. If he was here now, I'd probably shake him by the hand. Too bad he didn't do it for real, huh?'

'It's true. Things are different now,' admitted Rosselli.

They were seated in a cabana by the pool, at the Fontainebleu Hotel, in Miami. Giancana had been in town to see Phyllis McGuire and her sisters perform at the four-thousand-seater Cavalcade Theater, on 3 April. But plans to fly to New Orleans the next day, for a sit down with local mob boss Carlos Marcello, had been abandoned following Marcello's arrest and subsequent deportation to Guatemala. Giancana was still profoundly shocked by what had happened to the other gangster.

'That fucking Kennedy,' seethed Giancana. 'Instead of slacking off on us, like he was supposed to, Bobby's been beefing up the whole Justice Department and its organised crime section. There are four times as many attorneys working in that department now, compared with last year. And this guy Bobby's got running the show. Silberling. I hear he's gotta list of top hoodlums. So-called. Carlos Marcello was at the top of it.'

Rosselli shook his head. 'Marcello will beat this. You mark my words. It was an illegal deportation. For the Justice Department to organise something like this is a scandal.' He sipped his Smirnoff on the rocks. 'His lawyers will fight it in the courts and win. Same way you beat the rap last time.'

'Yeah, but who'll be next for the out-patient treatment? Me? I was born in Chicago. But you, Johnny Sacco. They find out about that fraudulent birth entry and where you were actually born, they might try and deport your ass back to Italy.'

'Believe me, Sam, it's been on my mind a lot these past few days.'

'I don't know, I really don't. I thought we had a deal with that mick fucker. And now look. What does Frank say about it?'

'Oh, Frank is very embarrassed. He thinks you're mad at him.'

'He must have a guilty conscience. One minute he tells me this, the next minute he tells me that. He's talked to Bobby, then he's talked to Jack. I don't know what to believe.'

'To be honest, Momo, I'm not sure Frank knows himself. But that's people in show business, for you. They're full of shit. Say one thing, do another. Deluded. Most of them live in a fantasy world. Look at Marilyn. They think they walk on water. Frank still thinks he can be a fucking ambassador. But he's the only one who thinks so. Those Ivy League types would never let him do something like that. They'll go to his Pre-Inauguration Gala, and then piss all over it when they get home. That's those people all over. They fuck you like a whore and then they walk. Those people are full of promises that they never deliver.'

'What about you?' said Giancana. 'Look at you. All that work for the CIA, and now the feds are trying to fuck you, Johnny. And all because of that Dan Rowan wiretap.'

Rosselli had been tipped off that the FBI were about to re-open a years-dormant probe into the status of his citizenship.

'Where's the fucking justice in that?' demanded Giancana.

'I love America, Sam. It's been good to me. I was just trying to put something back in, you know?'

'We should have gone for Nixon's deal.'

'We've always been Democrats, you know that, Momo.'

'Yeah, but Nixon is straight. You can trust Nixon. When Nixon makes a deal he sticks to it. Our kind of deal. Next time we should back Nixon.'

'Maybe Jefferson should have shot Kennedy after all. Then we wouldn't be in this spot.'

'I'll buy that. They're still going ahead with this dumb invasion?'

'Very much so. I hear April seventeenth. Somewhere on the south coast. The Bay of Pigs.'

'And, in spite of everything that's gone down with Carlos, they're still expecting us to kill Castro for them? Just like before? Like nothing happened?'

'We're not supposed to know, but the whole fucking invasion rests on it. This doctor I know, Tony Varona, is gonna poison him.'

Giancana paused and lit a cigarette.

'Not any more,' he said. 'That's what I wanted to talk to you about. I want you to tell this croaker to lay off.'

'How's that?'

'I just decided. Not any more. It ends here, Johnny. You understand me? All this shit with Castro. We're out.'

Rosselli knew better than to argue with Sam Giancana.

'Whatever you say, Sam.'

'Listen to me, Johnny. Why should we help them? When they won't help us?'

'Reluctantly, I'm forced to agree with you, Sam. You're probably right.'

'You're damn right I am.' Giancana laughed harshly. 'Just make sure you tell that doctor. All bets are off. Fuck the CIA. And fuck Jack Kennedy.'

'Okay, Sam. I'll tell him. If that's what you want.'

Giancana laughed. 'It's what I want all right. I decided last night. After what happened to Carlos. Boy, are they in for a big surprise, when the hit on Castro doesn't happen.'

'Frankly, it'll be the biggest surprise of his playboy presidency. Probably fuck him for good. Just let him try and get elected again after he screws this up.' Rosselli smiled, coming round to the idea. 'You know? I'm beginning to like this new angle a lot, Sam.'

'Don't you tell them. I don't want to spoil the surprise. You keep stringing them along, Johnny. That's what you're good at.'

'Sure, sure. Whatever you say, Sam. Not that the invasion stood much of a fucking chance anyway. They're only sending a force of about fifteen hundred men.'

'Is that all? Jesus. Those crazy mick fuckers. What do they think they can do with a force that small?'

'They're Cubans mostly. There's not a marine among them. Kennedy figures Castro's assassination and the landing will provoke a widespread revolt among the Cuban population at large.'

'What about air support?'

'Contingent on Castro's assassination. No body, no bombs.'

'Too bad for those guys on the ground. Sounds like it'll be mass murder.'

'What the hell? They're pimps and dealers. Full of shit and machismo. Most of them only know how to fight with a switchblade.'

'Good. That should help to make Kennedy very unpopular with the Cuban community.'

'Oh, his name will be crap, Momo. Take my word for it. He'll probably never dare set foot in Florida again.'

'Even so, those Kennedys must feel they're pretty well tucked up in the White House.'

'How do you mean?'

'I mean them ordering another Castro assassination. They're not bothered by this Cuban Memorandum?'

'Momo. They don't know about it. Didn't I say? The Secret Service didn't tell him. On account of the fact it made them look like a bunch of fucking pricks. Nor have the CIA. Because they figure it's none of their business. And because they didn't want Kennedy to pull the plug on this Bay of Pigs shit.'

Giancana laughed. 'You're kidding me.'

'Not at all.'

'Then maybe there is some justice after all.'

'How's that?'

'Think about it. Who the fuck can they trust? Not the CIA. Not the Secret Service. Who? Hoover?' Giancana shook his head. 'Forget about it. There's no one. Not even their old man. Bootlegger Joe. No one trusts that bastard.'

'You make a point.'

'So did Tom Jefferson. He made a point, too. A very good point.

The guy got close. Close enough, and walked away. Your F-word, Johnny.'

'Feasibility.'

'Right. He made it look like it was feasible. It just goes to show what can be done. If you need to do it, I mean. It just goes to show what's possible.'

Rosselli grinned. 'Momo, this is the United States of America. Anything is possible here. Anything at all. Besides. There's always next time.'